MW01608085

Hope's Ordeal

Being the first part of the Legacy of Mana chronicles ©

Thomas M. Gofton

Hande Barutçuoğlu

ISBN-10: 0987768107
ISBN-13: 978-0987768100

First Edition Print 2012

DEDICATIONS

To Dave McDougall - a man of inspiration when I first wrote this 128-page idea down in grade 8. To Chad Archibald - my brother... this kingdom is yours "Lo Bellore Rae". To Christopher L. Zweerman "369", your name shall forever be rendered immortal within this fiction. Your contribution to helping me grow this epic is insurmountable Chris, you will always be remembered, Heyooo! To Hande - for continuing this quest - long after the Iltherian's verdium burned out...

Ultimately, to Cecil Iounestone - You saved me...

Knights of Baron - mark well these tales as they reflect a lifetime ago and an era of pure imagination and magic. Together we built an empire in our minds and now it is written in fiction for all to know. To my Queen... you are forever my archer, Annika and our children will inherit our earth...

~Thomas M. Gofton

To friends and family of another world - Azuriel, Finnian, Zavienda, Adison, "Lady" Griselda and Keeva... and to Ceycil and Roessa, for their friendship and valor.

~Hande Barutçuoğlu

We, in the ages, lying

in the buried past of the earth

Built Nineveh with our sighing,

and Babel itself with our mirth

And o'erthrew them with prophesying

to the old of the new world's worth

For each age is a dream that is dying,

or one that is coming to birth.

-*Arthur O'Shaughnessy*

ACKNOWLEDGMENTS

Written by Hande Barutçuoğlu

Created by Thomas M. Gofton

Creative Contribution by Christopher L. Zweerman

Illustrations by Sean England

Cover Art by Mike Gauss a.k.a. Helmutt

Edited by John Montgomery of EditorDoc

Additional Edits by Chris Feres and Aron Murch

Font by Nancy Feres

Map by Chris Feres

Legacy of Mana Series

www.legacyofmana.com

Here we go! Heyoooo!

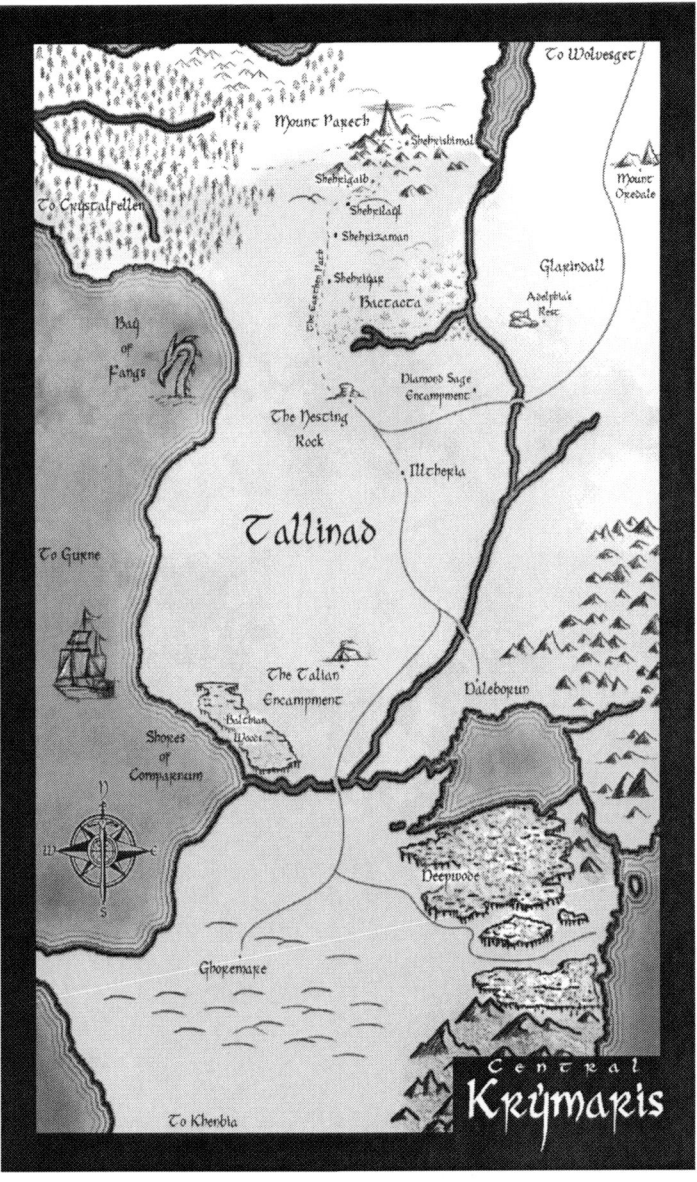

THOMAS M. GOFTON   -   HANDE BARUTÇUOĞLU

Scattered.

The old wizard couldn't think of another word to describe the scene. Scattered like the rocks on the shores of Comparnum where they stood. Scattered like an ants' nest that had just been poked with a stick. Scattered like dandelion seeds in the northern wind...

A red-haired child sat among several armored bodies that still stank of blood and magical smoke, hunched over a lifeless old man that seemed to be made of feathers rather than of flesh and bones. There was no open sadness in his face, but the emptiness of a loss so deep that it went beyond any expression. His fingers ran mindlessly over the bloody feathers that covered the man's body.

"Rooks," Kazan called out to the boy in a gentle voice. "Serje is gone."

The red-haired child nodded solemnly, but offered neither reply of words nor tears.

The wizard was as distraught by the death of his comrade as the boy he was trying to comfort, but he did his best not to show it. The Iltherian army would be on their back any moment, it was no time for an emotional breakdown. His eyes wandered to his daughter and the young man next to her whom he raised like a son. He had given twenty years of his life to keep Roessa and Ceycil away from the Iltherian knights, at the expense of having to move from forest to forest, from cave to cave without ever stopping to settle down. In less than ten minutes, all his efforts had been blown to dust. *They will never be the same*, he thought. *We will never be the same.*

The Khenbish woman emerged from the woods suddenly and quietly, like a specter that came to haunt their camp. Just moments earlier and close on her trail, she brought a group of Iltherian knights on the hunt for runaways. Runaways like Kazan and his motley crew of companions. The knights recognized the wizard immediately, with their swords ever hungry for his mana, ready to devour it as they devoured the mana of the elves, the fey, the arials and the land itself. Still, Kazan was not a wizard to be trifled with, and even Iltherian swords had their limits when it came to handling vast amounts of mana. Against an army of knights, Kazan still would not have stood a chance, but the Iltherians on the woman's trail were only a handful. Between his spells, Roessa's arrows and Ceycil's sword, the knights went down fast. However, Serje, the shaman mutant birdman that raised Rooks, gone down with them.

The wizard turned to the Khenbish woman, *what is she doing in this part of the land?* Khenbia was at least several months' journey away, in the southern sand regions of Krymaris.

"Explain!" he demanded. His voice was no longer gentle, but firm, deep, and full of authority.

The woman perched on a nearby rock and sheathed the dagger she was still holding. "Before an explanation, I owe you an apology," she said, and something in her slanted eyes told Kazan that she really meant it. "If I had known that you were here, I never would have run this way." She shook her head. "It wasn't my intention to share the wrath of the Iltherians with you. Now your friend is dead, because of me. I am truly sorry." She took a deep breath. "I also owe you my gratitude, since you saved my life regardless, though I suppose you didn't have much of a choice but to fight the knights. As for the explanation, I will do my best." She glanced over at Roessa, the wizard's daughter, who was staring at her with apprehension.

"I am Sainaa, the last of my people," the woman continued. "As you might know that the Iltherians are notorious for shamelessly exterminating entire nations. My companions and I have been on the run since our land was invaded by the knights more than a year ago. Today our location was betrayed, and the knights have caught up with us. My companions fell to their swords, and I alone made it this far, only to drag all of you into my own mess. Once again, I am with the deepest of apologies."

Kazan nodded. "I believe you," he sighed. "At least for the moment. If you prove yourself a liar, know that you will be dead before the thought of betrayal even surfaces your mind." Then he continued with a more casual tone. "You are free to stay with us or leave, though I must warn you that the Iltherians will be back sooner or later. What we have seen was only the nose of the wolf. The knights never travel in groups this small. There is probably an entire troop of them somewhere in the forest."

"You are a wizard, a user of mana," the Khenbish woman observed. "I did not think there were any of those left."

"Like you, I am the last of my people as far as I know," the wizard answered with a solemn voice. "And like you, I will be hunted down if the rest of the Iltherian army finds out that I exist."

Mana was the essence of the realms. The link between life and beyond. Some say using mana is like wielding the strongest of magic, the root of all things magical and wondrous. A beauty the Empire of Iltheria seeks to obliterate as an active volcano would smoulder the forests surrounding it, covering it with ash and stripping the realms of color.

The Khenbish woman opened her mouth to make another comment, but seeing Ceycil walking towards them with his bloodied sword in hand, she remained silent.

"Kazan," Ceycil said heatedly. "Those knights. The Iltherians. There will be more of them coming?"

The wizard had been dreading this conversation. Over the years, he explained the nature of the Iltherian knights to Ceycil and Roessa that the knights' swords had the power to absorb mana, and that they were the military force of a tyrant that made it his mission to unite all the tribes and nations in the world under one empire. Along their travels, they had seen the towns and villages destroyed by the knights. They even met the occasional survivor that witnessed the Iltherians' wrath and still managed to avoid being killed or enslaved. But they never encountered the knights themselves, until today. Kazan carefully avoided any discussions of whether anything could be done to oppose the empire. It had not been easy, considering Ceycil's stubborn nature and the pig-headed confidence brought by his youth. But the wizard had managed to keep his bursts of rebellion under control. Except now that the first battle had happened, Kazan had a feeling that Ceycil would be even less likely than before to listen to him.

He closed his eyes and nodded slowly. "Yes, there will be. And we should best be away from here before they come."

"But…" the young man white-knuckled his sword and shook it at nothing in particular, "why have we run from them for this long? We've beaten them once. We can beat them again, can't we? Why are we always running instead of fighting them?"

Kazan sighed. He would have liked to roll his eyes, but he knew it wouldn't help with Ceycil's frustration. "Son, you do not understand," he said patiently. "There are thousands of them. *Thousands.* Can you even picture that in your mind? And how exactly do you propose we fight them all?" He tried to keep a calm tone, but he couldn't help his irritation leaking into his voice.

"There's got to be a way," Ceycil muttered to himself. "There's got to be a way to fight back…" He pointed one hand towards where Serje lay, and shook his head like a bull ready to charge.

Kazan gave him a look with an edge like a razor.

The young man let out an exasperated cry and threw his rusted sword across the beach. The blade landed on the rocks with a loud clang, matching Ceycil's footsteps as he turned his back onto the wizard and stomped away.

Kazan let out a deep sigh. *What am I going to do with you, son?* He pondered. *What am I going to do with us all?*

*   *   *   *

Packing up their meager camp took less than a few minutes. They hadn't even given Serje a proper burial, just a few rocks on his grave and a quick prayer muttered for his soul, and then they were back on the road.

As they marched through a narrow forest path, a tall, skinny figure brought up the rear, still trembling with the shock of the battle, which he mostly hid from. He looked at his shaking hands, and then at the crossbow at his side. *I could have saved him*, he thought. *I could have saved Serje. That knight was close; I could have shot him with my crossbow. But what if I missed?* He didn't want to think about it. If he shot and missed, there was no way he could escape from sharing Serje's fate under the Iltherian's sword. But still, as he was standing so closely in the trees, he could have hit the knight… Thousands of Iltherians, the wizard said. Thousands of slayers waiting for him outside the woods like the ones that drove him from his homeland across the sea. Chalco looked at his light brown hands, still shaky, and wondered how many times they would shake like this before they fell still forever.

Ceycil and Roessa marched ahead of him, keeping up a whispered conversation as they walked, and turning back to check on Chalco every time he squealed in terror, startled either by a fluttering bird or a passing rabbit. In his mind, Chalco couldn't help seeing knights behind every tree and within every shadow. In every rustle of dry leaves the autumn wind blew in their face, he heard the clip-clop of horses' hooves and heavy-armored footsteps.

Kazan led them through the forest quietly and surely. When the night began to fall, he announced that they would be setting up camp again. There was no point in marching through the night in the Balthian woods, the forest was not particularly thick, but it was full of unpleasant surprises in the dark, with or without Iltherians on their trail.

The camp consisted of a few ragged bedrolls thrown around a campfire, which offered warmth and light, while still small enough to avoid being observed from any distance. Chalco volunteered to take first watch. Even staring into the darkness seemed to be better than the nightmares he would have to face if he tried to sleep. Ceycil agreed to keep him company, even though it was common knowledge that Chalco never slept on watch. He would be too terrified of what could befall him if he did sleep. He felt that Ceycil's offer to join him was still more out of distrust than out of companionship, but it comforted him nevertheless. It meant that if they were to face danger at night, he didn't have to confront it alone.

It did not take long before the rustling of the bedrolls gave way to quiet breathing, and the silence of the camp blended into the subtle sounds of the night. Chalco ran his fingers over his crossbow, over and over again, trying to shake off the terrible sense of guilt that boiled and frothed inside him. *I could have saved Serje,* his thoughts kept breaking through again and again, like an unpleasant melody stuck in his head. *If I only knew they would have killed me instead…* The more he thought, the more his guilt overwhelmed his senses. The darkness seemed to close over him like a prison. "Ceycil," he whispered, desperate to break out of his self-inflicted panic.

Ceycil sat with his back turned towards the fire, staring into the trees. He, too, seemed to be lost in thought.

"Ceycil…" Chalco called to him again.

"What?" Ceycil broke out of his dreamy state and gave him a brief glance that looked more annoyed than anything else.

"It was… my fault, you know." Chalco tried not to choke over his own words.

"What was?"

"Serje… he died because of me."

Ceycil shook his head. "Of course it wasn't your fault," he said hastily. "Stop worrying about everything. Look at you, you're a nervous mess. Try to relax for once." Without waiting for a reply, he turned away from Chalco and slipped into his own thoughts again.

Silence reigned in the camp. Chalco could not bring himself to speak out his thoughts any further for fear that Ceycil might snap at him. The hooting of owls blended into the howling of wild dogs in the distance, sending shivers down his spine.

Then he saw it.

He let out a gasp. What he saw was no more than a shadow, like that of a tree branch swaying in the night breeze. Except it moved smoothly, in a way neither a branch nor animal would.

Ceycil sighed audibly. "What is it this time?"

"I… I thought…" Chalco tried hard not to stutter, failing miserably. "There's something dark, moving among the trees. In the shadows." He clutched his crossbow with both hands. They started to shake again.

"You know, Chalco, you need to quit seeing things in the shadows." Ceycil shook his head, and pushed his shaggy hair out of his face. "You also need to stop jittering like a fool. You can't shoot a watermelon from two yards if your hands keep shaking like that."

"But…" Chalco's voice died into a whisper. "It's there… *He's* there!" Chalco was numb with fear. He could not breathe, and he thought his heart was going to burst his chest open. He tried to hold onto his crossbow, but it was impossible. It slipped helplessly through his fingers, which were shaking so violently that he looked like he was having a seizure.

Ceycil turned around sharply, and gave the earthen-skinned man a stern look. "Look here, either stop freaking out over nothing, or have someone take over your watch and spare me the headache."

Then he froze.

It was, *he* was really there.

Ceycil knew immediately that the knight standing in front of them was no Iltherian. For one thing, his armor didn't shine with the visual cacophony of the orange and green of the Iltherians. It was pitch black, so dark that the night seemed a shade lighter in contrast, with intricate figures carved onto it, twining across the metal in serpentine patterns. As the flames of the campfire flickered, hues of purple and gold seemed to appear on the folds of his black cloak. The knight seemed to be made of shadow, and the only true color he bore was the bright green of his eyes that pierced Ceycil's gaze through their tiny slits in the black-horned helmet.

Ceycil managed to remain calm just long enough to do the only sensible thing he could think of. "Kazan!" he yelled.

The wizard awoke instantly, the startled expression on his face momentarily betraying his surprise. The others, too, were awakened by Ceycil's call, and looked equally baffled.

"Who are you?" Kazan asked in a hoarse, but not sleepy voice. "What do you want?"

"What a kind and hospitable gentleman!" The knight laughed. It was a menacing, metallic laugh, like the sound of sword blades clashing. "Do you always treat your guests this way, or is it because I'm late for supper?"

Kazan kept his composure, shrugging off the knight's smart talk. "I said, what do you want? If you are out looking for your death at this hour of night that can be arranged."

The knight crossed his arms casually, and shook his head. "Tsk tsk… No need to get yourself all worked up now, old man." His voice quickly lost its edge of sarcasm. "I want you out of this forest. Now."

Something small and shiny whizzed past the campfire, towards the dark figure. The knight reached out and plucked it out of the air as easily as a child would pick a wildflower. It was a dagger. Tossing it dismissively aside, he scoffed, "And tell the Khenbish woman I have no time for games."

Ceycil stared at the knight, astonished. Not only had he not heard him approach the camp, he also couldn't explain how the knight could possibly have stopped Sainaa's well-aimed dagger in mid-air. It had to be mana manipulation, except this looked nothing like the wizard's use of mana he had seen Kazan do. The knight had shown no signs of casting a spell, not a sound, not a word, not a single motion except the simple reflex of reaching out for the dagger flying through the air. But if it wasn't mana, then what could it be?

Without further thought, Ceycil jumped to his feet, attempting to draw his sword, but Kazan immediately motioned him to stop.

"Do not be foolish, son. We have lost enough companions as it is." Then the wizard turned to the knight. "You win, for now. We will leave this minute, and get out of your accursed woods as fast as we can. In return, stay out of our path. If we meet again, I might be even less hospitable."

Before Kazan finished speaking, the knight had already vanished into the shadows.

Ceycil thought he would have been relieved by the knight's disappearance, but instead he found himself angry. Once again, Kazan had stopped him from fighting for their right to stay and rest. And once again, they were leaving, fleeing like a bunch of cowards.

*   *   *   *

Marching through the forest in the night was not as scary as Roessa thought. The darkness even comforted her, when she got herself to believe that that's all there was to be afraid of. *Darkness is emptiness*, she kept telling herself. *It's just a lack of things. Lack of wolves, lack of monsters, lack of Iltherian knights, and lack of light. That's all.*

Her father led the way, holding up a small torch. He could have easily created enough magical light to get them through the night, but that would attract the Iltherians like flies to a carcass. Their swords, it was said, acted like magnets for mana essence, which was used to elicit magical effects. If there were any knights near where they marched, they could detect an unshielded spell from a mile away.

Roessa sighed deeply. She had marched enough to last her a lifetime. In fact, that's precisely what she had, a lifetime of marching. She had seen few towns as she traveled from one secluded hiding hole to another with Kazan and Ceycil, but they were all deserted, their inhabitants slaughtered or enslaved by the Iltherian army. Only a few escaped, becoming runaways like Roessa and her companions. Sometimes as they marched, she kept her mind busy imagining what life would be like in a real town, with people going about their lives. Secretly she longed to live in one and call it her home.

She sighed again and felt for her bow, wondering how many knights she needed to kill to rid herself of all her anger. She didn't even have to worry about a guilty conscience. The knights were practically inhuman, Kazan told them many times. When the Iltherian troops captured a group of runaways, the captive men were forced into knighthood. And once they received their ugly armor and sickly green swords, they were no longer who they once were. The green metal of the blade was rumored to be alloyed with a human soul, so that it took over its owner from deep inside. It did not control their minds, Kazan repeated. Instead it twisted their entire being, until they were a mangled mob of hopeless rogues, with hearts wrought into cold rusty scraps. They even lost their names to square metallic numbers, which they wore on a green sash over their armor. There were the occasional exceptions, of course. Once in a while travelers told stories of renegade Iltherians that managed to break away from the curse of their swords to reclaim their names again, and turned against their own kind. Roessa wasn't sure if she believed in those stories, though she really wanted to.

When at dawn they reached the edge of the woods, she was slightly surprised that Chalco was still alive. All through the night, he looked like he was going to collapse in a heap any second. He whined, wept, and uttered prayers to strange spirits under his breath. He hyperventilated to the point of choking, and tripped over his own sandals while trying to run away from whatever shadows he saw among the trees. Yet he had survived the night. Roessa briefly wondered what went through this stick figure's mind, but decided that she'd rather not know. Whatever it was, it did not do Chalco any good.

Forcing her mind to think more pleasant thoughts, she concentrated on Ceycil, now a silent figure trudging on in front of her. His hair had grown so long, it was brushing against his shoulders. Strong broad shoulders, she noted. Not hunched like Chalco's, or sagging like Kazan's. *I should trim his hair when we rest,* she thought. She imagined her fingers brushing through the brown wavy locks, and a warm, soothing feeling spread inside her like morning mist over a calm lake. Holding fast onto that feeling, she marched on.

As soon as they were out of the forest, Kazan called for a rest. "In broad daylight?" the Khenbish woman protested. "We'll be too easy prey for the knights if they are around."

Kazan shook his head. "I admire the endurance of your race, Sainaa. We are, however, all exhausted. If we are to face Iltherians, I would rather do so when I am somewhat rested." He proceeded to pull chunks of dried meat and hard bread from his sack. "There is a good hideout on the eastern side of these hills south of the old elven forests of Crystalfellen, called the Nesting Rock. It looks like a giant bird's nest, with a secret entrance that leads right into it."

"Like a cave without a ceiling?" Roessa sat down on the dead yellow grass and reached for the bread.

"Yes, precisely."

Sainaa looked like she was enjoying the dried meat, tearing into it with her teeth as if it was a fresh juicy steak. "So," she smacked her lips, "you think we will be safe there for a while?"

Kazan nodded. "The knights will not bother to go there. It is too barren a place to harbor life, or to harbor mana, for that matter."

"Does that mean we can get a good night's sleep there without having to stand watch?" Roessa asked hopefully. She, too, couldn't help but admire Sainaa's endurance. Years of marching, hunting and hiding had built Roessa into a hardy young woman, but even the toughest traveler needed food and sleep to keep up a steady pace. Sainaa's small, slender body seemed to be fueled by air alone.

Kazan ignored her question, but Roessa didn't mind. She was used to her father treating her like a child, even though lately it started to irritate her. *I'm almost twenty summers old,* she thought. *And for Father, I am more of a child than Rooks.* Then again, Rooks did not exactly act the way children did. Roessa wasn't sure if he even knew how, having spent all his life with Serje, the eccentric Birdman of the sky realms.

Rooks and Serje traveled with them for several seasons now, and as much as the Birdman had been wild and flamboyant, the boy was quiet and reserved. He was more like an old soul than a child, and more a mystery than anything else. And now that he had lost the only person he belonged to, Rooks reminded Roessa of a sealed jar trying to contain a tornado.

As casual chatter took over the breakfast circle, she watched the red-haired boy pull an ornate box out of his pack. It was made of a dark, unpolished wood, with detailed swirling figures carved all over it. Inside, wrapped up in a piece of velvet, lay four glass vials, each as ornate as the box they were in. Rooks took the dark blue vial out, letting it roll between his fingers for a while. It was shaped almost like a spiral, with silver swirls etched into the glass. Inside was a liquid that splashed and dripped on its own, even when the vial sat still in Rooks' palm. The boy closed his eyes tightly, and gently pulled its cork stopper out. As he did, a light blue rush of an ethereal presence filled the air around him. It formed a shape that was almost humanoid, with two points of focus on one end that looked much like eyes. Slowly, almost with a maternal embrace, the blue spirit wrapped itself around the droopy body of Rooks, his eyes closed, a single tear rolling down his cheek.

Kazan sat quietly in his corner, watching Rooks and muttering something under his breath. Roessa was aware that the wizard was using his own power to mask the mana radiated by the spirit. She guessed it was in order to render the spirit undetectable to any Iltherian swords nearby. *He could just ask Rooks to stop the bottle*, she observed. *Instead he chooses to waste his own energy.* That effort made her realize that her father more or less adopted Rooks now that Serje was gone. The Birdman had been an old friend to the wizard, perhaps the only friend of his that Roessa had ever met over the years. *It must be a terrible feeling,* she thought. *Losing the only friend you have.* She, too, was fond of the Birdman. Over the past spring, he had taught Roessa how to use a bow, how to hunt small animals for food, how to tell edible berries from poisonous ones. Still, the more she thought about it, the more Roessa realized that she knew very little about Serje or where he even came from for that matter.

Her eyes wandered back towards Rooks in the embrace of his water spirit. *At least this way he's not alone,* she tried to comfort herself. *At least Serje left someone to stay close to him.*

Chalco set his back to Rooks and the water spirit, which was just as well. He disapproved heartily of the spirits in the vials, not to mention of Rooks himself. They terrified him. *A child who doesn't know how to play,* he thought, *can only be a ghost like those he keeps in bottles.* As he attempted to gulp down some breakfast, he tried to push the horrors he imagined through the night out of his head. He was hugely relieved to be out of the woods. Even though the hills ahead looked rather uninviting in the dull autumn hues and his bare chest and sandaled feet were already getting cold, at least the hills wouldn't cast any ghastly shadows like the trees did. For the first time in days, he felt he could breathe freely, and his hands didn't shake nearly as much anymore.

The breakfast conversation went on for a little longer, mostly over the best course to take towards the Nesting Rock, but Chalco paid little attention to it. He trusted the protecting power that Kazan wielded, and he was ready to follow the wizard wherever he went.

The earthen-skinned man finished his breakfast and started helping the others pack up the camp, not joining in the argument as the younger people tried to figure out the best way to reach the Nesting Rock. There was a river ahead, which flowed down one of the hills and through the woods, all the way to the sea. Ceycil wanted to cross it in the hopes of putting the knights off their trail, while Roessa thought it would be better to go along the river and up the hill. "We'll have to climb the hill eventually, since the Nesting Rock is on the other side. Crossing the river will only lose us time. Besides, it's not like the knights can't go across water. If we are seen, we will be caught regardless of where we are."

"That is a good point," Sainaa joined in heatedly, "except…" Then she stopped abruptly, her words hanging in mid-air. She sat up, alert, and put a finger to her lips.

Silence fell over the camp like fog. Chalco froze with a bedroll in his hand, the beating of his heart echoing in his ears like battle drums.

There was a moment of stillness.

Then in a flash, Sainaa picked up her dagger and jumped to her feet, ready to launch it into the trees at any second. "Reveal yourself!" she yelled with an icy voice. "Or die."

A tall, slender figure stepped out of the woods, hands raised casually but shyly. "Sainaa, it's me." His voice came in a hoarse whisper.

The Khenbish woman lowered her dagger.

*   *   *   *

The surprise was anything but pleasant for Kazan. The unexpected visitor wore the green and orange armor of the Iltherians, complete with the sash number 451 and a sword that he knew could drain a good amount of his mana using.

Sainaa, to his surprise, looked oddly relieved to see the Iltherian. "I thought you were dead when the raiders came." She strode hastily towards the stranger.

"I managed to fight a couple of them off," said the knight. "The rest were, unfortunately, busy hunting down your people. Fortunate for me, I suppose…" he added almost guiltily. "I hid in the forest until they left, then started wandering. I was just heading to the stream for some water, but then I heard the voices coming from your camp."

Kazan let out a deliberate cough.

The knight spared him a brief glance and ignored him. "I didn't expect to see you, of course. I thought you may have…"

Kazan coughed again, louder. He was not used to being treated as background.

The knight turned towards him with open annoyance, but then his expression morphed into one of genuine surprise.

Kazan's eyes met the knight's stare. *Iltherian or not, you do not ignore a wizard, son.* "Who the bloody hell are you?" he demanded coldly, though calmly. "And what the bloody hell are you doing in my camp with that sword?"

The knight took off his sword belt and laid it on the ground. "My name is Versai," he said. "I have been a travel companion to Princess Sainaa before her people were attacked by the Iltherian troops."

"He's a renegade," Sainaa added.

Kazan shifted his heavy stare towards Sainaa. "And you are a princess?" This was unpleasant news altogether. Iltherians were dangerous, renegade or not, and royalty always came with royal trouble.

Beside him, Roessa's bow was already strung tight, as Ceycil's sword was raised. Chalco alone quavered and whined like a wounded animal, his crossbow shaking uselessly in his hands. "Kazan," he moaned. "We can't let him… He's…"

"Calm down, son," said the wizard to Chalco, without taking his eyes off Versai. "Let us hear what else they have to say." There was a note of authority in his voice, making it clear that this was an order, not a suggestion.

"It's true that I'm a princess," Sainaa began. "But that doesn't really matter, now that I no longer have a nation to rule."

"You are of royal bloodline, though," Kazan corrected her. "You are still connected to Khenbia. If you survive, the land can recreate your nation with its mana."

"If I survive." The Khenbish woman frowned. "*And if the Iltherians have left any mana in the land of Khenbia*, she added to herself.

Versai was the next to speak. "If you fall to the knights, though, their swords will desecrate your blood, and there will be nothing left of your people."

"I know…" she whispered. "That is why they gave their lives to protect me, Altun, Sukh, Lanbatour and Batzorig."

"Sukh lives," said the knight casually. "And so does Lanbatour."

Sainaa held her breath. "What did you say?" The image of Lanbatour's dark slanted eyes appeared in her mind. She recalled the way his long black hair always smelled of fresh earth, spice and campfire smoke. She had been so sure that she lost him forever.

"Sukh and Lanbatour," Versai repeated. "The Iltherians took them alive. They are at the Talian encampment as prisoners."

Sainaa took a deep breath. She looked around at her companions almost apologetically. Rooks was still sitting alone in his corner, barely aware of the intruder. The water spirit was back in its vial, though Rooks' freckled face was still dripping. Whether it was water or tears, Sainaa couldn't tell. She couldn't help feeling responsible for the child, since it was her arrival that caused Serje's death. *I have brought them nothing but ruin,* she thought bitterly. *The least I can do is to stay with them, fight beside them, protect them the best I can. Leaving them now would be no less than treachery. If I bear royal blood, then I must live up to it with honor.*

She faced Versai once again. She opened her mouth to speak, but Ceycil's voice interrupted her. "How do we get there?"

Ceycil felt all eyes turn towards him. He felt his knuckles hurt slightly, and realized that he was still holding tight onto his sword.

"How do we get where?" Kazan asked crossly.

"To the Talian encampment." Ceycil said, trying to sound casual. "We're going to help Sainaa rescue her people, won't we?"

Kazan frowned. "Son, do you have any idea what you are talking about? The Talian encampment is swarming with Iltherians, not to mention any other horrors that they might have gathered. Walking into it would be suicide."

Ceycil gritted his teeth. He knew this wasn't going to be easy. "You mean we'll let the last of her nation perish in the hands of those foul knights because we are too scared to do something about it? I don't think so!"

Kazan gave him a stare like a brick wall, heavy and unyielding. "You have witnessed the Iltherians' power, and they are capable of much worse. We held them up only because their numbers were few. If you expect to do the same against an entire platoon, you will not live long enough to prove yourself wrong."

Ceycil felt his face flushing, and something rising up his throat like hornets pouring out of a disturbed hive. He tried to control his voice, but to no avail. "They have killed Serje," he yelled. "What could they do that is worse? I'd rather die by their swords than keep living this coward's life, running from hole to hole like some wretched worm!"

Kazan's grey eyes turned fiery at Ceycil's words. He rose to his feet. "I did not raise you to have you killed by the Iltherians," he whispered.

"Then what have you raised me for, to follow you around like a puppy all my life?" Ceycil was out of breath. He already regretted some of his words, but it was too late now. "I'm going to Talia," he said flatly. "Try to stop me if you like."

2

It was exactly as Chalco had feared. Despite all his anger, Kazan caved to Ceycil's rebellion. He wondered how such a great wizard could make such a foolish decision. They were marching to their deaths, that he was sure of, but he was too scared to break away from the group. By himself, he had no chance. He probably couldn't even get through the hills without being attacked by a bear or devoured by wolves. He had to stay close to the wizard, that way he could at least survive until they got to Talia. And the knight…he gave Chalco the creeps. There was nothing worse than waking up in the night to face his green and orange armor, not to mention his crooked smile. To make things worse, he seemed amused by Chalco's fear. As they marched, the knight made a habit of jumping out of the shadows or grabbing Chalco's arm just to see him blanche with terror. Chalco gritted his teeth and held his crossbow closer. No, he didn't like this at all.

Kazan wasn't exactly happy with the turn of events, either, but he knew there was no stopping Ceycil once he put his stubborn young mind to something. Nothing short of binding him with a spell would keep him from going to Talia, and that would be wasting valuable mana, if not setting up a beacon for the knights to track them down. Besides, he wanted Ceycil to see for himself the extent of the power that the Iltherians possessed. What they were about to attempt was pure madness, the wizard knew. Sneaking into an Iltherian encampment to rescue a couple of Khenbish men was no different from walking into a straw hut on fire, they were bound to get burnt. *And it is not just any hut we are walking into,* he thought. *This one is haunted, too. Even if the fire does not get to us, the ghosts will devour our souls.* Still, Kazan kept on marching, keeping his eyes on the renegade knight as they walked. If they were lucky, the sight of the Talian camp would be enough to bring Ceycil to his senses. If the boy had any to begin with, that is. Despite his hopes, the wizard felt a strange feeling Ceycil would not turn away from his fears and not by his conscious choice.

Behind him, Roessa walked with her arm around Rooks' shoulder. With Sainaa beside them, the wizard could hear her dragging the toes of her soft boots across the ground. "I'm really grateful that you are doing this for me," she said, shaking her head. She took a deep breath. "I would gladly give my own life if it would save Lan… my people, but I have no right to risk yours, you have saved my life once already."

Roessa's responded in a light-hearted voice, but with an undertone of silent worry. "Ceycil is right, we can't keep running forever. And if there is fighting to be done, I'd rather do it and know we tried. If we can save your people from the camp, at least Khenbia might have another chance some day. If we give up, the whole of the realms are doomed to crumble under Iltherian rule." She always spoke a tad faster when she did not really agree with their next step of action but out of respect could not get herself to really object.

The Khenbish woman sighed. "Heroism and miracles," she said, more to herself than to Roessa. "I wish I were young enough to still believe in them."

Kazan nodded to himself, quietly agreeing with Sainaa. Then, to his surprise, he heard Rooks' voice join in. The red-haired child broke his silence for the first time in days.

"Then it's time you were reborn," he said with a solemnity odd for his age. "Because those are the only things that will save us."

Under the hood of his cloak, the wizard smiled in spite of himself.

* * * *

As the sun was setting over the Talian horizon in crimson hues, Versai tried to make sense of the last couple of weeks. The journey from the Balthian woods to Talia had been long, though fairly uneventful. They had only seen Iltherians twice and had managed to hide from them both times. Still, his mind was a jumble of thoughts that couldn't quite link together no matter how hard he tried. When he mentioned Lanbatour's name at their first meeting, he had expected Sainaa to fall to pieces. She was supposed to drop everything and run to rescue her lover, wasn't she? After all, she was female and wasn't that how women worked? Instead, she remained dead silent. If it wasn't for the foolish boy's burst of heroic pride, all his efforts of tracking them through the forest would have been in vain. He smiled at the memory. It was truly a strike of luck. Now not only was Princess Sainaa heading to the Iltherian camp on her own will and depending on him for her rescue plan, but she was also dragging along the last of the known wizards. Versai took a quick glance at Kazan, walking closely behind him. *He won't be easy to deal with*, he told himself, *but with great challenges come great rewards.* He tried to suppress a smile. *Two mice with one trap*, he thought. *Almost perfect.*

Despite everything, there was something in the air the knight couldn't quite put his finger on. He felt restless, oddly uncomfortable, and he knew it had nothing to do with the wizard's intense mistrust in him or the disturbingly steady stare the red-haired child kept shooting his way. Something didn't quite seem right. It didn't quite *feel* right.

He shooed his thoughts away quickly as they approached the lights from the Iltherian campfires. There was work to be done.

*   *   *   *

Sainaa hid in the shadow of a rock, uncomfortably close to the Iltherian torches lighting the boundaries of the camp. Versai walked into the encampment a few minutes prior, making sure that nobody would be around the prisoner tents when she stealthed in. With his helmet on and his infamous sash number replaced with one he had stolen from a fallen comrade long ago, it was impossible to tell him apart from the other knights. His voice, however, was unmistakable as he barked orders at the sentries with the confidence of an officer, sending them off to various nonexistent emergencies on the other end of the camp.

As soon as the path was clear, Sainaa crawled out of her spot. Hopping from shadow to shadow, she made her way through the numerous dirty green tents. The prison tents were right near the western edge of camp, where Kazan and the others were hiding in the rocky terrain. Kazan insisted on coming with her, but she refused. She didn't wish to put them at any more risk than she already had.

Most of the prison tents were packed with poor unfortunate souls from various parts of the continent, all bound up and piled in a corner like bundles of rags. She would have liked to free them all, but she knew it was impossible. She was here to find Lanbatour and Sukh. Gritting her teeth, Sainaa moved on.

Some of the tents reeked so strongly of blood that she passed them by without daring to look in. Nothing living could be at the center of such stench.

She crouched behind one of the tents, and her eyes went in search of Versai. He was still busy ordering the sentry knights about. She knew his act wouldn't last for very long, but there were dozens of tents to look through still, and Lanbatour and Sukh could be in any of them. She closed her eyes and took a deep breath, letting her sight shut down momentarily so that her other senses could take over.

Clanging of armor. Moans. Heavy boots on rocky soil. Crackling of flames. Flapping of tent cloth in the breeze.

Smell of dried blood. Dust. Fresh blood. Campfire smoke. And a faint, very faint tinge of fresh earth, and a familiar spice...

Sainaa's eyes snapped open. She took another deep breath. Faint but unmistakable. She took a quick glance around and dashed into one of the tents closest to her.

* * * *

The tent was small and empty save the thick wooden pole in the center that held it up. Tied to the pole with his wrists above his head was Lanbatour.

Sainaa's heart stuttered at the sight of him. He looked anything but alive. His bare chest looked like it had been slashed with hundreds of blades, with pieces of his ribs sticking through the wounds, and a thin stream of blood trickled down his lips. She thought she could almost see his heart beating through the bloody mess. *Beating,* she told herself. *He's alive. He has to be!*

She didn't even notice the tears rolling down her cheeks as she tried to untie his wrists. He didn't move as she worked her way through the rope, but she could hear him breathing weakly, each breath a horrible rasp.

Lanbatour lay motionless on the blood-soaked earth, his head resting on Sainaa's knees. Sainaa tried to think fast, to figure out a way of getting him out of this tent that had been his hell, but a single thought seemed to run through her mind over and over like an ugly floating banner. *He's dying. He's dying. He's dying…* She was lost in another world where she used to sneak out of her chamber in the dark of the night to meet Lanbatour by the rose bushes of the palace gardens. The rose's bloomed coal black, she recalled. A world where a princess and a simple soldier lived in a midnight dreamland of secrets, black like the roses that witnessed their love, and just as beautiful. A world where even the forbiddances of royal tradition could be denied in rebellion. The forbiddance brought by death, however, was forever. There was no rebelling against it.

Sainaa barely heard the commotion that broke outside. The footfalls of heavy boots got stronger and closer, but she was too entranced to take notice. Only when she

34

heard the tent flap open did she crash back into bitter reality. The armored figure of an Iltherian knight stood staring at her, and she heard the voices of many others approaching. *This is where it ends,* she thought. *This is where we end.* She didn't even bother to draw her dagger. If she fought, maybe she could get out of the tent alive, but she knew she couldn't get very far. With Lanbatour bleeding to his death beside her, so far from her lands, she had very little will left to live. She stared back at the Iltherian and his sword thirsty for the mana-linked essence in her blood.

The Iltherian stood motionless, looking as stunned as she was. To Sainaa's surprise, he didn't draw his sword. Instead he reached to remove his helmet.

"Sukh?" she whispered to her once-companion. His eyes held a tormented look to them, and he seemed much older than when she had last seen him several weeks ago. Still, there was a glint of malice in his stare, one she knew came with the armor he was wearing and the evil weapon at his side.

Sainaa was full of questions, but she knew she had no time to ask them all. "What did they do to him?" she demanded, shifting her gaze to Lanbatour.

A brief sign of annoyance crossed Sukh's face. "They tried to find your whereabouts. It's you who has the bloodline that they seek. He didn't know where you were, of course…" His voice trailed off.

Sainaa felt her grief melting into a rising wave of fury. "Even if he did, do you think he would betray me the way you did?" Her stare was piercing, her voice firm and thorny.

Sukh was taken aback. "That's not what I meant! Sainaa, it wasn't… I didn't… I swear I didn't give away our hideout to the knights." He stuttered, shaking his head. The commotion outside the tent was increasing by the second. "It was…" He started to speak again, but a flash of green metal emerged from his chest and Sukh fell on the ground beside Lanbatour, with Versai's sword stuck between his shoulder blades.

Sainaa only recognized him by his fake sash number. "We have to run," said the renegade, retrieving his sword and grabbing her by the arm. "They have realized that my emergency call to the eastern border was a false alarm, they're coming for us."

The princess tried to yank her arm free from the knight's grasp, but it was useless. "I'm not leaving Lanbatour," she said.

Versai practically dragged her towards the darkness outside the tent, she was unusually weakened. "There's nothing you can do for him. He'll be dead before you can get him out of the tent. At least save yourself, otherwise he'll have died in vain."

As much as it tormented her to leave Lanbatour in this state, Sainaa knew that the Iltherian was right. As she turned to go with the knight, she couldn't help glancing at Lanbatour one last time. Then she gasped and burst into tears. The young Khenbish soldier opened his eyes, and was looking at her with the slightest hint of a smile on his handsome face washed with pain. A single word formed on his bloodstained lips, silent but clear: "Sainaa…"

The princess reached out her hand, and screamed as Versai grabbed her by the waist and dragged her out the tent. She screamed and struggled with all her might, but the knight was considerably bigger than her, and much stronger. Before she knew it, she was being carried away from the encampment at a dizzying pace. She hoped with all her heart that her screaming would attract the Iltherians to take them down, but all they got was an arrow that missed Versai's shoulder by a couple of inches. Sainaa wondered for a brief moment why she had never seen knights with bows before, but the thought flew away fast in her hysterical, sinking grief as her last sight of Lanbatour appeared in her mind again.

*   *   *   *

Kazan watched Versai's officer act from up close, hidden under a spell of invisibility. It took him all his mental power to keep the spell working and mask its magical residue from the Iltherians, but he managed. He knew that by coming to the encampment, they placed themselves in great peril. The sight of the endless stretch of tents and burning fires, all buzzing with Iltherians, had not even made Ceycil wince, and the wizard wasn't sure whether he was disappointed in the young man's folly, or proud of his extraordinary courage. *A little more danger to avoid more danger,* he told himself as he paced around the prisoner tents, staying close to Sainaa and trying not to bump into anything or anybody that might reveal his presence.

He left the others in relatively safe spots, Roessa and Rooks hidden behind a boulder that had a convenient spying hole, and Chalco and Ceycil lying flat on the top of a small rocky hill. He had told them to stay on the lookout, just in case. One could not be too careful with several hundred Iltherians walking around.

The Khenbish woman and the renegade did not need to know that he was following them. Sainaa had already refused his offer to accompany her, and the wizard wanted to make sure she got out of this place alive. If she was the last standing bearer of the Khenbish bloodline, her death under an Iltherian sword would mean the death of the

Khenbish race. If need be, Kazan would kill her himself to avoid that. At least that way she and her race could be reborn out of the Khenbian land one day if the Iltherians ever removed their forces from there. As for Versai, keeping an eye on him wouldn't be a bad idea. The wizard heard his name numerous times through various travelers he ran into. The runaways seemed to revere the renegade knight as an odd yet noble-hearted comrade who had managed to conquer the power his sword and armor had on him. *Perhaps I am just an old man of old habits,* thought Kazan, *but Iltherians are Iltherians. I cannot trust him with our lives.*

He followed the princess around quietly for a while. Versai's act seemed to be working well, as most of the soldiers around the prisoner tents promptly ran off to take care of whatever they were told was happening on the other edge of the encampment. As Sainaa's search grew longer, Kazan grew restless. He was afraid that her companions weren't there, that it was a trap set by the knights, but soon he took a breath of relief as the Khenbish woman found someone she was looking for. The wizard didn't go into the tent with her, but chose to stay on the watch for any mishaps that could happen. There were just too many things that could go wrong.

And sure enough, they did go wrong.

Kazan heard somebody yell, "False alarm! Sentries back to prison area! Repeat: sentries back to prison area! Search the tents, make sure nobody is missing!".

It was a dreadful voice, and it seemed to come from the central tent where the Iltherian officers gathered. The call was followed by the stomping of feet running his way. Kazan clenched his teeth and grimaced. He heard that voice before, many times and long ago, and it almost always signaled oncoming trouble.

Hell broke loose in a matter of seconds, and Kazan found himself trying to dodge the bodies of running knights, coming from all directions. They couldn't see him, of course, but they were obviously looking for somebody. The wizard concentrated hard, trying not to lose his invisibility or his magical shroud that prevented the mana of his spell from being detected by Iltherians. And why was Sainaa still in the tent? Hadn't she heard the commotion?

He tried to stay close to the tent, but it was impossible with all the knights running around. At one point, as he was trying to avoid a particularly tall knight from running into him face on, he saw an Iltherian walk into Sainaa's tent. *I hope you can handle yourself, Princess,* he thought desperately. No screams or clashing of metal followed the encounter, which the wizard found odd, but no news was always good news. Almost immediately after the Iltherian, Kazan saw Versai walk into the tent. After a moment of silence, the renegade ran out of the tent with the screaming princess thrown over his shoulder.

It made no sense.

Kazan ran after Versai on instinct. He seemed to be heading for the mountain range on the other side of the camp. *Works for me,* he thought. He could easily tackle the renegade as soon as they got out of the encampment.

Then came the arrow.

It missed Versai by barely an inch or two, but it was enough to get the attention of several Iltherians. As they turned around to charge at the source of the arrow, Kazan, too turned around.

As soon as he did, he threw caution to the wind. He dropped his shrouding spell, and with a magical ball of flames, set the central tent on fire.

*   *   *   *

Roessa knew that shooting was a foolish idea, but she couldn't get herself to just watch as Sainaa was carried off by an Iltherian knight. She practically grew up with the stories of the royal bloodlines, and how they were bound to the land by an ancient mana that was only breakable by Iltherian swords. As long as the bloodlines remained, the land would give rebirth to the nations sooner or later. Along years of traveling, those stories were her only foothold of hope that the royal families would indeed return some day, and restore the contented life of olden days into the kingdoms. She longed for those days she never got to live, and the peaceful, ordinary life that was stolen from her. Seeing Sainaa taken down by an Iltherian meant that for one part of the world, those days would never return. Roessa couldn't bear the thought of it.

When she strung her bow, her intention was to shoot. If she shot the knight, great. If she shot Sainaa, still better than having her murdered by the Iltherian and her bloodline destroyed forever. From that distance, Roessa couldn't see Versai's sash number, and it never occurred to her that it might be the renegade who was carrying the struggling princess over his shoulder. She let her arrow loose…

…and missed.

She cursed her aim so heartily that Rooks, behind her, squealed at her words. Everything after that turned into a hurricane of a nightmare.

She saw a handful of Iltherians follow the path of the arrow back to her. One of them pointed in her direction, and yelled hoarse orders at the knights around him. Next thing she knew, there were dozens of green and orange figures charging into the rocky terrain, towards where she and Rooks were hiding.

Her first instinct was to pull Rooks closer to her, and take a step back to better cover behind the boulder. Then she started shooting madly, like a wild animal that was cornered, her arrows flying until she could no longer feel the muscles in her arms.

At first her shots were random, aimed at whoever was easiest to hit or nearest to their hideout. There were too many of them, she realized. Too many for one person to take down. They were closing in fast, and she knew it was a matter of minutes before their swords met her skin. When she first saw the Iltherians, she found their colors weird, almost comical for their murderous nature. Now the green reminded her of mold and disease, and the orange of rotting leaves. The knights' battle cries were the screeching of vultures over a carcass. They even smelled of death.

Roessa could feel loathing fill her veins like a poison. Out of the corner of her eye, she saw the big central tent burst ablaze with fire. It distracted some of the knights charging at her, and sent them running back to the camp. She was still left with more than she could manage, though. As she kept shooting, she wondered how much longer she could hold on until she ran out of arrows or was overcome. It was only then she realized that there was something else moving towards her among the knights, not green and orange, but a familiar shade of brown, like the earth. Ceycil was trying to fight off the Iltherians with his sword, doing his best to keep them from reaching Roessa. Immediately she adopted a new strategy, and started sending her arrows towards the knights that surrounded Ceycil. Rooks was still beside her, his hands clenched onto her tunic, shaking like a fledgling sparrow.

Ceycil made his way towards Roessa, slowly and painfully. The knights, up close, seemed like huge monsters. His old sword was no match for their heavy green blades, but at least without a heavy armor to carry around, Ceycil was much faster than them, and it was more his speed than his swordsmanship that saved him. By the time an Iltherian wielded his sword high enough to strike, he could stab them once or twice through the weak spots of their armor, the armpits and the groins. Considering the sturdiness of Iltherian armor and the rustiness of Ceycil's sword, his blows probably didn't kill the knights, but it was enough to make them miserable enough to stay out of Ceycil's way.

As he fought his way down the hill and towards the boulder, he took a moment to glance at Roessa between the blows, making sure she was standing. Something inside him told him that if she fell, in his fury he could probably smash all the metal-clad knights into ground meat and razorblades.

The thought suddenly gave him courage. *Why not smash them to bits now? If I have that power in me, Roessa shouldn't have to die for it to come out.* He swung his sword harder and faster, hacking and slashing his way through the green-and-orange plague. As he approached the boulder, he spared another glance at Roessa, still shooting her arrows to keep him relatively safe. An Iltherian he had juststabbed chose that moment to pull himself up and swing a blind blow at him, catching him on his left shoulder.

Ceycil felt a warm wave run down his left side, followed by an intense rush of pain that burst like fireworks exploding over his collarbone. A flash of dizziness followed by a momentary darkness blurred his vision for a second, and if it wasn't for Roessa's arrow taking down the Iltherian, he probably would have been killed under the next blow.

Even afterwards Ceycil could not remember how he fought the last few knights in his way to reach Roessa and Rooks, with his shoulder bleeding a river. *It must have been my destiny to survive,* he told himself later, for no other force he could think of could have gotten him out of that battle alive.

He blinked a vague memory of seeing an expression of utter horror on Roessa's face. It was followed by a single scene frozen like a picture in his mind, of Kazan lying on the ground in the distance, looking tiny and helpless with dozens of knights swarmed around him, one of them obviously an officer.

His next conscious thought was that his lungs, along with his shoulder, were about to burst into flames. Only then he realized that he had been running, tugged along by Roessa and Rooks holding her by the hand.

Where had all the knights gone?

Where were they running to?

Why were they running?

"Kazan," he gasped. "He's… we can't!.."

Roessa practically yelled back at him, her voice surprisingly cold and calm. "Shut up and keep running!"

Rooks later claimed that he kept running for almost an hour before passing out, and that he seemed perfectly coherent at the time. All Ceycil could remember for himself from that night was a blackout stretching like a shroud over his mind, overwhelmed by a feeling of doom.

THOMAS M. GOFTON   -   HANDE BARUTÇUOĞLU

3

I have a shoulder, thought Ceycil as his consciousness returned. *I know I have a shoulder, because it's screaming very loudly.* He blinked into the sunrise from what seemed to be the mouth of a very shallow cave.

"He's awake!" he heard Rooks whisper. Then came a deep sigh of relief from Roessa. "About damn time, too. How are you feeling?" Despite the casual tone in her voice and her attempt at a smile, she looked sullen. She was busy feathering some new arrows, her shoulders sagging, with black circles under her eyes. Ceycil had never seen her like this before.

Rooks, too, looked like he hadn't seen daylight in years. He was pale as cotton wool, and his green-blue eyes seemed much bigger than before on his small face. His gaze was dull like shattered glass.

Ceycil attempted to sit up with an instinctive desire to comfort them, but was immediately reminded of why he was awake in the first place. He almost blacked out again.

His shoulder was bandaged tightly with what appeared to be a piece of Roessa's old tunic and a bunch of grizzly feathers identical to the ones on her arrows. It was no longer bleeding, but it still burned with an ungodly pain if he tried to move. "I feel all right," he grunted.

"Rotten liar." Roessa tried to smile again.

Her sadness touched Ceycil. He searched his memory for what happened, for what could have grieved her such. His heart sank as it all came back to him.

The knights.

The terror.

The image of Kazan surrounded by the Iltherians. No, he couldn't be…

"I'm sorry," he whispered, half to Roessa and half to himself. "Kazan, your father…"

Roessa shook her head, her eyes fixed on the crimson horizon. "It was my fault," she said. "If I hadn't shot that arrow, none of this would have happened. I'm pretty sure it was him who set that tent on fire to lure the knights away from us. That must have revealed his place to the Iltherians. He always said their swords could practically pinpoint the presence of mana use." She frowned and bit her lip. "We had to run, though," she shook her head again. "We had to run, otherwise we'd all be dead, and he wouldn't have that. It would be throwing his whole life away, all his efforts trying to keep us safe."

Rooks was fingering his strange box of vials again. His voice seemed to come from another world that he was walking somewhere. "Do you think he's…?"

The blonde girl snapped the feather in her hand and threw it over her shoulder. "I don't believe so," she muttered as she picked up another one. "If those damn knights had not suffocated any brains they might have underneath those helmets, they would know better than to kill a wizard like him. Then again, they seem to be all about the killing, you never know." Her voice trailed off.

Rooks was playing with the brown vial, which was domed like an egg and contained some gold-colored dust that seemed to form little rolling dunes on its own. He popped the stopper open and sprinkled some of the dust on the rocky soil, which grew into a pile and started building itself up like a tall mound of earth with two dimples at the top like eyes.

Roessa immediately reached over and put the stopper back onto the bottle, making the spirit disappear back into it.

Rooks looked a bit startled.

"Sorry Rooks," she said softly. "You have to keep your spirits contained for now. Father is not here to mask their mana, and the Iltherians are already close on our trail. We can't risk being spotted now."

Rooks sighed and nodded quietly. "What do we do now?" He whispered.

It was a very good question.

Ceycil never thought that there would come a time when they would have to make a decision without Kazan's opinion. All of his life he was so used to following advice that not having it filled him with an indescribable emptiness. He thought of the last time Kazan tried to give him advice. The memory of their fight and the words he yelled at the old wizard came flooding back to him in a wave of remorse. "It was my fault, not yours," he said to Roessa. "We shouldn't have gone to that accursed camp in the first place."

Roessa was about to say something, but Rooks cut her off. "That doesn't matter now," he said. "The past is past. What do we do now?"

"You're right," said Roessa. "The past is past. I just wish we knew what happened to Sainaa. I hope she got away from that knight, otherwise all our trouble has been for nothing."

"Speaking of trouble, I wonder what became of the renegade." Ceycil mused. "I almost wish we'd never met him. Did he get taken down, too, or did he run away like a coward?"

"Don't say that," said Roessa. "I'm glad we met him, regardless of all the trouble he brought. It's good to know that it's possible to break away from the curse of those swords, it gives me hope. And speaking of cowards, where is Chalco?"

Ceycil gave her half a shrug with his good shoulder. "I left him on top of the hill where we were hiding. I think he actually shot a few bolts at the knights, but he must have run away afterwards. I didn't really expect him to stick around to cover my back."

Roessa sat very still for a few seconds. "You know," she said, absent-mindedly. "There might just be a way to find out whether the others are... you know, alive."

Ceycil cocked his head, and scowled in pain. "How, exactly?"

"The Nesting Rock." She turned to look him in the eyes. "That's where we were planning to go, right? Once Sainaa rescued her companions, that's probably where we were going to head to."

"Do you think they'll be going there? The others, I mean."

Roessa nodded. "If they're still alive, I should think so. Sainaa doesn't have anyone else left to turn to, and Chalco isn't exactly cut out for the solitary life, if you know what I mean. They'll be looking for us."

"I think you're right." Ceycil sighed deeply. "God, I hope you're right."

*   *   *   *

It took Sainaa a while to quit her hysterical screaming and calm down enough to be able to think straight. Her soul was ripping itself to shreds at the thought of having left Lanbatour to die, but her mind gave her a quick kick in the shins. *He died for your sake,* it said. *So pull yourself together and do what you need to do. You need to save yourself first if you ever want to save your nation.*

Versai seemed to be heading towards the mountains. Once they were out of the camp, she got him to put her down, and they started running together. Nobody seemed to be following them, the knights were busy fighting the fire and the intruders on the other edge of camp. *The intruders,* she thought as she ran. Over Versai's shoulder she saw the knights running towards where the others were hiding. A feeling of guilt covered her like a heavy cloak. *A fine way of thanking them for helping me.*

Only when they reached the worn path at the foot of the mountain range did they stop running. It was still dark, and Sainaa and the renegade were both gasping for breath. The cold night air burned Sainaa's lungs. She threw herself on the ground. "What's this all about?" she demanded wearily.

Versai threw himself beside her. "I saved your life," he said as casually as he could with his chest heaving and his face red with exertion.

"I saved your life." Sainaa stoically suppressed the urge to turn around and strangle him. She gritted her teeth instead. "You killed Sukh, practically kidnapped me and brought me to this desolate place instead of going back to

49

the wizard and the others. What *is* this all about?" There was a hint of menace in her voice.

The renegade remained silent for a minute, then sat up. "Sukh became one of them, you saw it yourself. He would have murdered you if I hadn't taken him out. Besides, I couldn't let the traitor live, not after I saw what the Iltherians did to your people when we got ambushed."

Nice try, scumbag, thought the princess. *Sukh has never been a valiant man, but he wouldn't lie to his monarch. You killed him because he was about to tell me who it was precisely that betrayed us.* Her expression, however, didn't give away a single thread of her thoughts. There was acting to be done. "Why bring me here then? The wizard could have protected us."

"You keep forgetting that with my helmet on I look like just another Iltherian. If one of those two kids saw me running towards them, they wouldn't hesitate to shoot me down. In fact, I think one of them shot at me anyway."

Sainaa slapped her forehead. "The arrow! So the knights really were going after them. Great!"

The renegade put his hand on her arm. "Look Sainaa, you are the last of your people. I need to keep you away from the Iltherians. That's all that matters."

YOU need to keep me away from the Iltherians? The Khenbish woman took a deep breath. "And how do you propose we do that when they are all over the land?"

"We can disappear. I know all the places the knights would not go near. As long as it's just you and I, we can stay in hiding for as long as necessary." Versai smiled affectionately, showing his teeth that were almost too straight for a soldier.

As long as it's just you and I? Sainaa felt fury bubbling up inside her as the tortured image of Lanbatour once again appeared before her eyes. This was just too much.

She stared into Versai's eyes for a while. Then her lips, too, stretched into a smile. "You know, that could actually work," she said softly, reaching her hand out towards his face. "Running far and away…"

Versai smiled at Sainaa's words, as broadly as his wind-chapped lips allowed him. He loved his charms, and he loved the way they worked on women. He closed his eyes, expecting to feel the soft palm of the princess against his unshaven face.

Instead, he felt cold metal against his throat.

He snapped his eyes back open, and out of the corner of his eye, saw Sainaa holding a sharp, jagged dagger. He felt beads of sweat form over his brows.

The Khenbish woman's thin lips curled from a smile into a ferocious snarl. "Over *your* dead body," she hissed. "I'm heading to the Nesting Rock. And pray to your gods that Kazan and the others are there, otherwise I'll make sure that your end is even worse than Lanbatour's."

*　　*　　*　　*

Kazan stared at the tall, green and orange figure standing in front of him. The sash number read 1001. It was extremely familiar. He wished his wrists weren't chained to the pole he was backed against. He didn't need a mana source to take his anger out of this particular knight, his fists would suffice.

"Merry meet, wizard," said the knight in a mocking, husky voice with an edge like a battle-axe. It was the same voice that made the alarm call, a voice that Kazan only knew too well.

"Quit your silly games, Yakutska," said the wizard. "I know it is you behind that helmet."

The knight removed the helmet, revealing a woman's face and a thick blonde braid. She displayed a cold beauty, with an angled face like a finely chiseled ice statue. In her crystalline blue eyes there was a glint of twisted amusement. "You've always been smart, brother of mine," she said with the same husky voice, which did not sound at all feminine. "But I'm afraid your brains won't save you this time." She took a step towards Kazan and hit him across the face with the back of her hand. The spikes on her gauntlets made a deep gash over his cheekbone, dripping specks of blood on his grey tunic. "So tell me, which wind was it that blew you this way? Sneaking into my encampment, setting my tents on fire… and bringing your brats along, too. A shame my idiots couldn't catch them this time, looks like you've taught them a trick or two. We'll get them sooner or later, though, don't you worry." She smiled, revealing a golden canine tooth, shiny and pointy. "What are you after? Tell me!" She hit him again, opening the wound even deeper.

Kazan didn't even flinch. "None of your business, you two-coin whore," he said with his usual calm tone. "Are you not supposed to be in an officer's bedchamber instead of wasting your time here? How are you going to rise in your ranks if you keep your patrons waiting like this?"

Another slash of the spiky gauntlet across his face.

Kazan thought he could almost see smoke coming out of Yakutska's ears. Her eyes were flashing with fury. *Oh you silly girl,* he thought. *Even as a child you could not bear being teased.* And even as a child, he enjoyed tormenting his sister with insults. He was so entertained by the knight's fuming anger that he burst out in genuine laughter. If he was about to die, at least he could thoroughly enjoy annoying Yakutska one last time.

The laughter did the trick. The woman roared like a wounded bear in her frustration, punched the wizard on the chin and stormed out of the tent. Kazan watched her stomp off out of the corner of his right eye, which was almost swollen shut by this point. He spat out a mouthful of blood and chuckled to himself. Some things never changed.

He heard the woman address another soldier. "Get him to talk, I don't care how," she barked. "If he tries anything funny, you have a sword and you know how to use it."

*   *   *   *

"I'm coming with you," said Versai. Regardless of the dagger being held against his throat, having Sainaa so close made something inside him overflow. He could feel her scent fill him up, it made him dizzy with desire.

"Oh no, you're not!" the Khenbish woman spat. "You're either not moving until I get out of your sight, or I'm slaughtering you like a goat right here and right now."

"Sainaa, listen… I'm sorry for what happened at the camp. To Lanbatour, I mean. Please, let me come with you. I told you, I know all the places you could hide from the Iltherians. If you leave on your own, you'll run across them before you get to the Nesting Rock. I can't have that happen." *Not before I make you mine.*

The princess lowered her dagger by an inch or so. "Perhaps you're right," she said, more to herself. "Perhaps I can use you. You owe me that much anyway." She took a deep breath, and spat through her teeth. "One false move, Sir Renegade," she hissed. "One false move, and I swear by Lanbatour's blood that I will shove this blade up your nose." She sheathed her dagger and motioned at the mountain path with her head. "Get going," she said. "You got me into this mess, you better get me out of it. I'll be right behind you."

*   *   *   *

Kazan stared into the eyes of yet another Iltherian. He expected to face another rough-hewn officer coming in to torture him. Instead, number 369 was a young, plain soldier. His eyes belayed a look of having seen far more than he should have at his age.

The shouting and the beating that Kazan was awaiting never came. The knight sat in front of him on the dry ground, and removed his green helmet. Even with his youth, his light brown hair had streaks of white. "So you're the wizard," he said wearily.

Kazan nodded. There was something odd about number 369. Whenever the wizard approached an Iltherian knight, he felt his mana rattle him like an internal earthquake. With this one, there was nothing. Not even a flutter. He glanced at the mana-trapping weapon at the knight's side. It was an Iltherian sword all right, but this wasn't an ordinary Iltherian he was facing. "You are not one of them," Kazan stated. It wasn't a question.

"Am I not?" said the knight with a thoughtful frown. "I've lived with them and I've killed with them. I never wanted this sword and this number, but I'm afraid I've become one of them now." He took off his gauntlets and stared at the palms of his hands. "I've taken lives in the name of the empire," he said. "I've even captured people like myself to shove them into knighthood against their will. Tell me, mana-user, how am I any different from those outside this tent?"

"You question," said Kazan. "And you regret."

"I'm sick of regretting," the knight sighed. "And I'm sick of fighting for nothing. They told me that you're fighting for the land, to free it from the empire's forces. That's why I took your watch."

Kazan blinked his one good eye. "They told you wrong, son. I am only fighting to stay alive."

"You have magical power," said the young knight. "Magical power from the mana that my land had before they... before we sucked it right out with these swords." He glanced at his blade quickly, as if it hurt his eyes to do so. "Do you think... do you think it would be possible to put it back? To give the mana back to the land, I mean?"

The wizard thought about it for a moment, then shook his head. "No. I am afraid the damage is irreversible. Besides, no wizard could have enough magic ability to replace the mana that the Iltherians have taken out." He paused. "However, there is still hope for some places, the countries where the royal bloodline has not yet been destroyed. Those nations can still be revived if the empire ever withdraws its forces."

The knight blinked, with a puzzled expression on his face. "How is that possible?"

Kazan sighed. *Young people these days,* he thought. *They never seem to know anything.* "Every royal bloodline is connected to its homeland," explained the wizard. "This is an ancient mana connection, even beyond what the empire can destroy. Even if the entire nation dies out, the land recreates the people. Nobody knows quite how. However, the mana that is in the royal blood itself can be taken by an Iltherian sword. So if an entire blooded family is killed by the knights, there is no way the nation can be recreated. The link between the land and the people is broken."

Number 369 took a few minutes to digest what he just heard. "And you are telling me that some of the bloodlines are still alive?"

Kazan nodded. "More of them than you think." He realized that he was giving too much information to this unnamed soldier. A knight was a knight, after all. The stillness in his mana flow, however, was unmistakable. *This is no ordinary Iltherian,* he reassured himself. *Besides, I have nothing to lose at this point.*

The knight fell silent again. Then he got up, pulled a small dagger out of his boot and started cutting the cords that bound Kazan's wrists to the pole.

It took even less convincing than Kazan thought. In fact, it had taken no convincing at all... "What are you doing?" he asked, genuinely surprised.

"Letting you go," said the young Iltherian casually. "Just make sure you strike me with a spell before you leave, so that they'll think you made your own escape."

Kazan shook his head in disbelief as he rubbed blood back into his wrists. "That can be arranged," he said gruffly.

"If they don't kill me for letting you escape, we may just meet again. Hopefully some place away from this mob of murderers. I have a lot of blood and dirt to wash off my hands." He threw another disgusted look at his hands, and put his gauntlets and helmet back on.

Kazan quickly cast his shrouding spell to make sure his mana use would go unnoticed for a little while. "What is your name, son?" he said, as he raised his hands to cast his next spell.

"Kristoff," said the knight, bracing himself for what was about to come.

"Well Kristoff," said Kazan. "Yakutska made a point when she called you lot idiots, but I must say I admire your courage."

Before Kristoff could answer, a ball of magical energy caught him straight in the chest, and he toppled over unconscious.

*   *   *   *

Chalco looked over the crest of a reddish jagged rock towards the hills ahead, and shivered with cold and fear. He slinked around the Nesting Rock for almost a whole day now, and the place gave him no comfort.

He didn't know how he managed to make it all by himself, walking for days if not weeks, over hills and rocky plains during the days and sleeping behind rocks and bushes at night. He hadn't even come across any trees to climb for safety, and what little sleep he managed was restless, interrupted by every hooting night bird and scurrying rodent. All along his march, one thought tormented his mind, biting into it like vermin. *I could have saved him, too.* He witnessed the wizard go down, tackled by an Iltherian, his invisibility spell broken with the impact. They were well within the range of his crossbow. It would only fell upon Kazan, and maybe he would have had a chance to make a run for it. Chalco remembered lying on top of the cold hill with his crossbow shaking madly with his hands, unable to fire a single shot. *If I miss, I'll be the next one dead.*

He cursed his cowardice. Without Kazan, he felt completely defenceless. Helpless, small and alone in this foreign land that seemed to be full of nasty surprises. And the others, where were they now? When Kazan had fallen, Chalco ran away as fast as his legs would carry him, driven by panic and instinct alone. Once he found himself in relative safety, it occurred to him that the best thing to do would be to head for the Nesting Rock. It was the only place that was mentioned by the party as a possible destination. It was beyond the hills; that was all the wizard had said. Further than that, Chalco had no idea how to find it.

Getting back to the hills took him considerable time, but he was glad to see that once he crossed them, the Nesting Rock was fairly easy to spot. Finding the secret entrance into the Nest itself, however, had taken him the entire day. And now that he was in, he felt his panic rising again. *Why aren't they here?* He had lost enough time on the way trying to find food and losing his way every now and then, he thought they would make it to the Nesting Rock well before him. The thought of somebody waiting for him was the only thing that pushed him through the long days of loneliness. And now he realized that the light at the end of the tunnel was nothing but a firefly. The Nest was empty and bitter.

Chalco shivered again. It had rained for the past couple of days, making his trip even more dreary. The breezy autumn air was molding into a sharp, harsh winter, and all he possessed to cover his bare chest were the hides of the three rabbits he managed to hunt along the way. The hides smelled bad and weren't exactly warm, especially when soaked. He tried to calm himself down, but it wasn't working very well. *Why aren't they here?* The wind made his black hair stick to his face in stringy bundles. He briefly considered going under one of the shelf-like rocks to stay out of the rain, but immediately changed his mind. From there, he couldn't see the hills or any approaching dangers.

He wiped the heavy raindrops from his eyes and stared into the scenery that was hazy with the falling rain. He tried to focus on the path that came down through the hills, and his heart gave a jump. There was a dark shape there, moving very slowly. *I am saved,* he thought, *or I am dead.*

*   *   *   *

"We need to stop," said Ceycil, gasping for breath. They had been walking the hills for over half a day now, and he looked fatigued. It had been slow going, and marching for hours at a time wasn't exactly ideal for a speedy recovery. His wound was mostly closed now, but he was still weak and pale as the grey sky. Roessa had suggested several times that they stop somewhere for a week or so to let his shoulder heal, but Ceycil wouldn't hear of it. "We need to keep going," he said. "If people reach the Nesting Rock they'll think we're dead if we don't show up for days. We've lost enough time already, we have to press on."

Roessa didn't insist. It wasn't often that Ceycil talked sense, and this was no time to discourage him. Besides, it was getting wetter and colder by the day. Getting hit by the first flare of winter on the road was enough of a nuisance already. Ceycil was getting his fair share of feverish nights thanks to his wound, what would happen to him if frost was to add to the deal? He'd catch his death in no time. They needed a shelter, Roessa knew, and they needed it fast.

Rooks pointed at a large, bowl-like rock formation in the distance, over the narrow plains that surrounded the eastern side of the hills. "I think that's it," he said. Roessa turned to look where the red-haired child was pointing. It really did look like a giant bird's nest. "I think you're right," she murmured. The rain broke a short while earlier, but the sky was still a mean shade of solid grey, signaling wetness to come. Ceycil, slumped on a rock, made a wheezy attempt to get up, but Roessa put a hand on his shoulder and sat him back down. "Take your time," she said, sitting down next to him. "We can spare a few more minutes. You're no good to me if you're dead." She smiled for the first time in days. They were almost there. The seemingly endless marching was almost over, at least for a while.

She didn't dare think about who might be waiting for them at the Nesting Rock, or rather, who might not be waiting for them. She closed her eyes, leaned gently against Ceycil and took a deep breath. *Anything is better than an empty nest,* she thought.

*   *   *   *

Ceycil threw himself against the colossal structure of the Nesting Rock. The night was sinking onto the land like a heavy velvet curtain, with the rain falling so hard that it was hard to keep his eyes open. "We made it," he sighed.

Roessa laughed. "We made it!" She ruffled Rooks' hair affectionately, and the boy awarded her with a rare smile. They were all drenched to the bones, but it didn't matter. Roessa wiped the water out of her eyes with her sleeve. "The question is, how do we get into this thing?"

A familiar voice came out of the darkness. "This way!" It was little more than a sigh of relief, unmistakably belonging to Chalco.

Ceycil felt a twisting feeling in his stomach. "Of all the realms…" He almost sobbed in frustration. "Of all the people to find here, did it have to be him?"

Roessa kicked his leg gently, motioning him to get up. "Stop complaining and follow me," she said. "It'll be drier inside."

Chalco's voice led them to a tunnel hidden in the shade of a small rock, going directly underground and emerging inside the Nest. It was indeed drier inside. Even with the top of the Nest being open to the sky with the rain pouring in, the rocks on the sides provided enough shelter to create several dry spots. As they huddled into one of them, Chalco spoke again. "It's good to see you."

Ceycil's initial instinct was to scream his head off at Chalco for running away from the camp, but the simple sincerity he felt in those words caught him off his guard. As he took a better look at the scrawny man wrapped up in stinky rabbit hides, he felt his anger dwindling away. Chalco looked awful, much worse than Ceycil with his pale face and weak, wounded body. He was even skinnier than before, his dark eyes sunken and his bare arms chapped and chafed with the wind. His bony shoulders drooped almost with a look of defeat. *The poor bastard,* thought Ceycil. *He looks too dead to be still alive.* As Chalco stared at them timidly, Ceycil could almost see the unspoken questions in the earthen-skinned man's mind. *Where is the wizard? What became of Kazan?*

He took a deep breath and crouched down onto a dry spot, motioning the others to do the same. There was a brief exchange of stories. Chalco threw anxious glances at his companions as Ceycil recounted their escape from the Iltherian encampment. Ceycil, in turn, gritted his teeth as Chalco's stuttered words tried to rationalize his flight from the battle. When silence finally settled in, it was Rooks that broke it. "What do we do now?"

Ceycil opened his mouth to speak, but Roessa interrupted him. "We are staying here, Rooks," she said. "No point in leaving in this weather, especially since we don't know where to go from here. Besides, Ceycil needs to rest, and we need to wait for the others." *If they're in any shape to be coming,* Ceycil added mentally.

Rooks nodded in approval. "I like this place," he said as he fumbled with his carved wooden box. "We should stay."

Ceycil shrugged one shoulder. "Fine with me. I wouldn't mind getting some sleep." He started laying out his bedroll.

As the others prepared to sleep, Chalco offered to take the first watch. To his surprise, nobody objected, which he took as a sign of exhaustion rather than trust. He looked around himself, taking in every detail that his tired eyes could perceive. The Nest didn't feel nearly as threatening, now that others were with him. It certainly seemed a lot more inviting than the stormy plains around them. *Stop fooling yourself,* said a voice inside him. *Waiting will do you no good. The wizard is dead. He won't come.* Still, waiting was all Chalco had the energy for. Wait and hope, and pray.

The earthen-skinned man remembered the first time he ever prayed. It was the day when his village was raided by Iltherians, when the empire had invaded Thalagrant, the continent across the sea. He had run away from that battle, too, though for different reasons…

He boarded a small boat along with a handful of others, the only survivors of his tribe, and they sailed out into the wild open ocean. When the storm hit and their little vessel started rocking on the huge waves like a leaf in the wind, Chalco prayed to spirits he never believed in until then. *The spirits did not listen,* he thought bitterly. *Perhaps they were angry with me for not believing before.* The ship sunk, and for all Chalco knew he would have been dead if Kazan and Serje not found him washed up on the rocky shore of this foreign land. *How well I repay them for their kindness,* Chalco thought. *I left them both to die.* A sour feeling of fear and regret stirred inside him. He felt nauseous, disgusted with himself. Feeling utterly helpless, he started praying again, hoping that this time the gods were kind enough to listen. If they existed at all.

THOMAS M. GOFTON   -   HANDE BARUTÇUOĞLU

4

Ceycil walked slowly, taking in the landscape. He was ankle-deep in mud, but his footsteps felt oddly light. The scene around him was desolate, a sickly-looking swamp with the roots of long-dead trees sticking out of the muddy soil. There was a fast-flowing river in the distance. Ceycil found himself to be strangely calm.

He walked around aimlessly, stopping occasionally to examine a rotting stump or a rock embedded in the mud. His gaze wandered over his surroundings, all brown and lifeless. Then out of the corner of his eye, he thought he saw color. A tiny green spot appeared on a shriveled, dead tree.

It was a leaf the size of a pea.

Ceycil's amazement grew as the tiny green shoot grew into a green branch, covered with dozens of leaves as big as his hands. He watched as more shoots appeared on the tree, growing and reaching out high into the sky. The rotting bark covering its trunk smoothed itself into fresh wood.

A magnificent maple tree stood where the shriveled stump had been before.

Ceycil heard a clattering noise behind him, and turned around. He found himself facing an odd sight;: an empty castle courtyard, a throne and a most unusual monarch.

The man sitting on the throne was fairly young, and he absent-mindedly tapped the silver crown in his hand against the armrest of the throne. Something about him looked inherently familiar, but Ceycil couldn't put his finger on it.

"Maybe I shouldn't have it made after all… what do you think?"

"Umm…" Ceycil stuttered. "Made what, exactly?"

The man didn't seem to hear him or acknowledge his presence. He froze in his thoughts like a picture, staring into open space, his eyes the same shade of green as the fresh shoots of the maple tree.

"Who are you?" Ceycil asked.

No answer.

"Do I know you?"

Still no answer.

Ceycil shook his head in mild frustration. He was almost certain that he seen the man before, but he had no idea where or when.

The castle courtyard dissolved into a royal court bustling with activity, but the throne stayed in the same spot, looking no more out of place than before. Aquamarine velvet curtains decorated the amber stained-glass windows over the throne, depicting the acts of heroes. Noblemen in rich clothes sat at a table with several sleepy hounds at their feet, discussing politics and the latest hunting party. A house cleaner scurried around with a dusting brush in her hand.

"My Lord," Ceycil jumped as he heard the familiar voice, and the feather-covered figure of Serje appeared by the throne like a ghost, materializing out of nowhere. "The sword… wouldn't it be wisest to hide it? It is too powerful."

"I already have, Birdman," said the monarch. "The Time Tree in the north near Bactacta will watch over it until it finds the hands it belongs in."

"*Well thought, my Lord,*" *said Serje,* "*but I still see you worried.*"

"*It can't be helped, Birdman. Fate always has its way, and it's seldom a way I like.*"

For the first time, Ceycil found himself agitated. "*Serje!*" *he yelled.* "*What's going on? Where am I? What is all this about?*"

The Birdman, too, seemed to be oblivious of his presence.

The scene froze once again. All movement stopped in the courtroom. The noblemen fell silent in mid-discussion. The house cleaner froze with her brush in the air. Even the hounds' snoring stopped.

Ceycil caught sight of his feet.

They were still buried in mud.

The mud around his feet started to spread, washing over the court room, and the vision of Serje and the young king melted into the dreadful swamp again. Startled, Ceycil turned around. The tree was still there, but its leaves now autumn hues of red, orange, and gold. Among the Time Tree's roots was a sword, its shiny blade planted in a small, crystal-clear puddle that appeared by the tree.

The sword was plain in appearance. No gems, no decorations, no crest indicating who its bearer might be. When Ceycil looked closer, he realized that the hilt had an hourglass embedded in it, filled with silver sand that trickled down from one slender chamber into the other. He saw that the top chamber was almost empty.

Somebody's time was running out.

Instinctively he stepped closer to the sword. Reaching out, he pulled it out of the puddle. It was surprisingly light. The tree, almost in response, shed a golden leaf off its branches into the swamp. Then another, and another.

As Ceycil gazed at the falling leaves, he saw something move in the distance. A tall, dark figure was approaching the tree from the other direction. He felt calm, with no trace of fear in his mind. The sword felt solid in his hands, cool and deadly.

Yes, he was ready to face anyone and anything.

He was startled momentarily, as the black-clad knight that appeared before him was no stranger. *"All right boy, let's see the back of your head."* The knight made no attempt to hide his malice. *"This is my swamp. Hand me the sword and piss off."* He held out his hand expectantly, as if beckoning to a dog to drop the bone in its mouth.

Ceycil stared into the knight's bright green eyes, and shrugged. *"Try and take it,"* he said casually.

The knight sighed in obvious annoyance. Reaching into the purple-and-gold shimmering folds of his cloak, he pulled out his own sword and without any warning, swung it at Ceycil.

Ceycil parried the blow, surprised at his own agility. He wielded the sword as if it was no more than a large feather, blocking and dodging every strike with ease. He swung, jumped and danced around the knight with the skill of a master swordsman, a feeling of delight rising inside him like a fluffy cloud. As the knight was sweating and cursing to keep up, Ceycil was laughing like a child playing his favorite game.

He swung and slashed until the knight was backed against the Time Tree itself.

Then something very odd happened.

Ceycil lifted his sword and as he swung, he felt a vibrant force travel down his fingers, towards the tip of the sword, followed by a wave of intense cold.

The knight was lifted off his feet, almost by an invisible hand, and thrown into the puddle that the sword was planted in. Then a ray of subtle blue light emerged from the tip of the sword and hit the water, freezing it solid with the knight still lying on his back. The horns on his helmet were the only things sticking out of the glassy ice.

Completely bewildered by what he had just done, Ceycil felt his heart thumping against his chest. As the tree and the swamp disappeared from his sight, he heard a strange, sandy voice in his head:

"Awake, son of Lynnvander, for it's time to meander."

68

*   *   *   *

Ceycil woke up out of breath, his heartbeat bounding in his temples.

Roessa stirred beside him. "Nightmare?" she murmured sleepily.

"Something like that."

"Go back to sleep," she said. "It was just a dream." She rolled over.

"Right," said Ceycil, more to himself. "It was just a dream."

*   *   *   *

Somewhere else, someone else woke up to his own heartbeat. Valharess brushed the shards of ice off his scarred face and cursed heartily. "Damn you, Lynnvander." He sat up in his bed and looked around. He was still in the guild's underground den. The fire crackled in a fireplace carved into a rough stone wall, casting shadows into the cavern that was his quarters. "Renzo!" he yelled.

A slender, elegant figure appeared at the door, adjusting his monocle carefully. "Is everything all right, my Lord?"

"All right is not the phrase I would use," Valharess huffed, trying to contain his anger, which was leaking out like soup out of a pot boiling over. He took a deep breath. "That brat the wizard was dragging around... how dare he?!" He pounded his fist against the wall.

"Relax, my Lord. There is no problem without solution." Renzo smiled sardonically. "What about the brat, what did he do?"

"That miserable worm has my sword!" Valharess snarled. "I want that sword, Renzo. It's mine. It's my right to have it, do you hear me?"

Renzo covered his ear with a gloved hand. "Yes, my Lord. I hear you just fine," he said patiently. "If the sword is to be yours, then we shall make sure it will be yours indeed. In the meantime, I pray you refrain from bringing the ceilings crashing down."

Valharess managed to calm himself down. Renzo was right, there was no benefit in letting himself blow up, it was best to save his energy for planning. "Get that dagger-slinging twit Gabriel to help me get into my armor," he said, motioning at the pile of ornately carved black metal lying in a corner. "Then tell Gruff to get ready, and get the men together. We have business to do."

*   *   *   *

The morning was full of surprises.

Ceycil, having fallen asleep again after his dream, woke up to more wetness and the ringing sound of laughter. His bedroll, though not soaked, was too humid to be comfortable, and his shoulder still throbbed. He sat up and squinted in the direction of the laughter. A beaming Sainaa and a rather harassed-looking Versai were sitting around a small fire with Roessa, Chalco, Rooks and a grey-cloaked figure that had his back towards Ceycil.

Still groggy and shaken by the dream he experienced, Ceycil's mind tried to put the pieces together.

Grey cloak. Fire. In the rain.

"Kazan!" He jumped to his feet, suddenly wide awake.

The wizard turned around and made a bad attempt at a smile. He looked like he had been trampled by a herd of oxen. Half his face was bruised and swollen, with a deep gash across his cheekbone. His cloak and breeches were tattered and torn, his tunic blood-stained, his grizzled beard caked with dirt. He looked visibly older and thinner. "Merry meet, son," he said in a tired voice. "I hope you have behaved yourself when I was gone."

A tiny spark of irritation shot through Ceycil's spine, but was instantly quenched by a wave of immense relief. Kazan was alive. Sainaa and the renegade were back. Not all was lost, and now they could pick up where they left off.

The question is, where have we left off? He hoped that the wizard possessed an answer for that. "Where have you been?" he asked. "What happened to your face?"

Kazan shrugged. "The Iltherians may be very powerful of body, but not so much of mind. I left the camp a few hours after you. I heard that you got away, so I figured I might find you here. I was right."

Ceycil nodded. "How come you didn't catch up with us on the road if you only left a few hours later? We've been going very slowly."

"I took a detour. The knights were after me like a pack of hounds, so I made sure they tracked me in the exact opposite direction for a few days. Then I conveniently disappeared." The wizard chuckled to himself. "I am sure their captain will be delighted to hear that."

Knowing that this would be all the explanation he would get from Kazan, Ceycil turned to Sainaa. "It's good to see that you're in one piece. Did you find your people after all?"

Sainaa's smile melted away instantly. "No… they're dead." She shot a sharp glance at Versai. "Murdered by the Iltherians."

The renegade's expression remained solid.

"I'm sorry…" Ceycil whispered, embarrassed.

The Khenbish woman sighed. "It's all right, there's nothing we can do about it now. I appreciate your help and your courage. We tried, and we failed… At least we are together again."

The breakfast exchange of stories went on for another hour or so, with everyone munching on soggy weeds and bitter roots that Chalco dug up around the Nesting Rock. Roessa fussed over Kazan's swollen face and Ceycil's still-healing shoulder as Sainaa boiled putrid herbs to put on the wounds. Rooks let loose the air and fire spirits from his vials, and watched them play-fight while Chalco eyed them nervously from his corner. Now that Kazan was back with them, the spirits were safe from Iltherian swords that may be wandering nearby.

Versai remained silent despite the festive air. He was not at all happy to see the wizard. True, it meant that if he could lead them into an Iltherian ambush, he would be rewarded ten times as much for helping capture the wizard. However, it also meant that if the wizard suspected anything, he would be the first one to go up in smoke. Only silence could buy him time at this point. He knew that if he said anything that the Khenbish woman could snap back at, he would be the prime suspect for anything that could befall them. Words, he knew, were like cards that had to be played at the perfect time. Until that time came, Versai would hold his tongue and watch for the aces that might come his way.

Ceycil winced as Sainaa handed him a cup full of some rather foul-smelling healing tincture. He took a sip and almost coughed it back up his nose. Sainaa grinned. "It's medicine," she said. "It's not supposed to taste good."

Kazan seemed to have no problems gulping the liquid down. Ceycil was always amazed by his incredible willpower. The wizard was always sturdy as a castle.

A castle. A courtyard. A king. A sword.

His mind worked quickly, linking one image to another, until the dream he had the night before was once again clear in his head. It still made no sense.

"Kazan," he said. "Who is Lynnvander?"

The wizard looked up from his cup and raised his eyebrows. "Why do you ask?"

Ceycil smirked an irresistible urge to give Kazan a taste of his own poison. "That is of no consequence," he said, imitating the wizard's mannerism perfectly.

That is of no consequence. It was the one and only reply he always received when he asked Kazan a question he didn't want to answer. Why were they always running? Who were his parents? Why had they given him to Kazan's care? Had Kazan ever been married? Were there any other wizards left? Those were all "of no consequence", and for years the lack of answers drove Ceycil mad with exasperation. He finally gave up asking, but he wasn't going to miss an opportunity to take revenge on the wizard.

Kazan sighed. "Nobody you would know," he said.

Ceycil tried to sound casual, but his voice gave away his excitement. "Maybe, but I heard someone call for his son."

"You heard what?!"

"Someone calling for his son. Last night, in my dream. Someone was calling for Lynnvander's son to wake up and wander, or something like that. Then there was this sword that I was holding." Ceycil paused for a moment, recalling the wonderful feeling he felt when he yielded the sword and fought the black knight with it. "That sword seemed important to me in the dream, I don't know why. It was in a swamp near a river, next to an odd-looking tree." He slowed down to take a breath. "There's a swamp up north of here, isn't it? Do you think we could go there and take a look?"

Roessa shook her head. "Don't be silly. You've had a dream, that's all. It doesn't mean that sword really exists, and it certainly doesn't mean the swamp you saw in your dream is the swamp you're talking about."

Ceycil blinked. "You don't understand," he said. "It was very real. I saw the swamp and the sword, and a king on his throne. I also saw that black knight we ran into in the woods... and Serje."

At the mention of the name, Rooks looked up from his corner. He led the spirits back into their vials and started listening, his head resting between his palms.

"I still think you're being ridiculous," said Roessa, sounding more amused than angry. "How seriously can you take a dream?"

Ceycil was about to protest again, but Kazan cut him off with a motion of his hand. "As seriously as we need to. We will go to the swamp. I was planning to take you through it anyway. There is a good hiding spot across the river."

Ceycil opened his mouth, ready to fight back. Then he realized that there was no need. *We are going to the swamp? Really? Since when does Kazan agree with me?* He was full of questions once again, but did not dare voice any of them for fear that the wizard might change his mind. There was something going on beyond his own understanding; that much he knew.

Sainaa was listening to the conversation from her spot on a rock. "Are you saying that Ceycil's dream was real? I have heard the Khenbish shamans talk about dream walking, but I have never met anyone who has experienced it. So you believe it is possible?"

"I'm not saying anything." The wizard frowned. "Regardless, we are going to the swamps of Bactacta tomorrow."

Sainaa shrugged. "You followed me to the Iltherian camp, I will follow you anywhere."

Chalco shivered. "Kazan," he squeaked. "Please, reconsider. It's a swamp. It's… dangerous. And if the dream is real, what about the black knight? What about ghosts, like those… *men* that Ceycil saw?" He was ecstatic when the wizard had showed up again, but now he looked like his usual mouse-like self, timid and frightened.

Versai, too, didn't look too pleased with the idea. "I agree with Chalco, it's foolish to…" he began.

"You don't have to come if you don't want to." Sainaa's voice was as sharp and jagged as the Khenbish knife hanging on her belt.

"Of course… not what I meant, of course I'll come," the knight muttered, and sank back into his silence.

Ceycil cleared his throat, trying to sound as casual as possible. "So, this Lynnvander… is he a friend of yours then?"

The wizard shot him a deadly look. "Yes, and he was every bit as much trouble as you are," he snapped. "Enough of your questions now. We will leave tomorrow. Those who wish to stay will find the Nest a safe haven." Kazan's voice commanded an unmistakable edge of finality.

Nobody dared to protest.

THOMAS M. GOFTON   -   HANDE BARUTÇUOĞLU

5

The swamp was less than a week's walk away, but it seemed much longer to Ceycil. As they marched in the still-falling rain that came with the dawn of the final day, he was unusually quiet, thinking about the sword and trying to recall all the little details of his dream. Which hand was the king holding his crown with? What color was the court house cleaner's dusting brush? Did the sword feel cold or warm in his hands? Some answers came easily, while others were lost in the hazy corners of the dreamscape.

Hours after their boots finally touched mud, Ceycil was still lost in his thoughts. Kazan had called for a stop, and Ceycil found that everybody was staring at him expectantly, blinking constantly from the droplets of rain. He looked around at the familiar landscape. "This is it." He nodded confidently. "This is the swamp from my dream."

The stink of sulfur and decomposing vegetation was overwhelming. Rooks held his nose. "It smells here... Was it this stinky in your dream?"

"How do you know it's the same swamp?" Sainaa asked, genuinely curious.

Ceycil kept his eyes on the lifeless field of mud stretching before them, ripples from the rain competing to be the largest ripple in the otherwise still pools of grey water. "Look, I just know. There's the river that I saw, and that's where the king sat on his throne." He pointed towards a handful of rotting trees in the distance. "So the tree should be..." He scanned the swamp for any traces of green, but there was none to be found. He could tell roughly where he stood in the dream, and where the castle and the royal court appeared and disappeared before his eyes. The tree and the sword would have to be right across from that place, towards the river, but there was no sign of either.

"Should be where?" Roessa cocked her head.

Ceycil sighed. "Somewhere around there. I don't know."

Roessa shrugged. "Oh fine. Let's go take a look."

Chalco shivered. He looked even skinnier and weaker with his black hair wet and stuck against his face. "Do we *have* to go *deeper* into the swamp?" He asked meekly.

"Yes." Kazan's answer was definite. "You can stay here if you like, but we must go further in." He walked through the mud, which got deeper with every step, followed by the others. Chalco followed doggedly. "If there is one thing worse than being deeper in a swamp, it is being alone in a swamp," he muttered.

It was slow going. Every step taken carefully, to make sure that the mud wasn't too deep, and they had to stop once every few minutes to let Versai catch up with them. Heavy armor and swamps did not go together very well, making the brief walk a test of endurance.

Ceycil led the way, and didn't bother to wait for the renegade. He reached the dead trees before everybody else and stood there, looking for any detail that could be a clue to lead him to the sword. He examined every rotting stump, hoping to see the little green shoot that would transform it into the Time Tree, but in vain. When the rest of the group reached him, he was almost in tears.

The wizard took a look around and frowned. "There is nothing here, son."

Thanks Kazan, Ceycil thought. *Rub it in, will you?* "There's got to be…" he muttered to himself. "The sword's got to be here. I saw it." *And I held it, and it felt so perfect.*

Kazan opened his mouth to make another comment, but Sainaa grabbed his arm suddenly. "Look!" she whispered, pointing at the river in the distance. A black swarm formed on the riverbank, and it was moving towards them at an astonishing speed.

"What's that?" Roessa squinted at the horizon, sounding more confused than anything else.

It took Ceycil less than a second to spot a pair of horns in the approaching blackness. "It's the black knight!" he exclaimed. "He's come for the sword as well!"

The blonde girl shook her head. "No, not that. What's *that?*" She pointed further away at something solitary and rather massive.

Ceycil turned slightly pale at the sight of it. "Probably trouble, is what that is. It's big, it's fast… "

"And it's coming straight for us!" cried Chalco.

"So it wasn't part of your dream?" Roessa added.

"Definitely not!" Ceycil felt a surge of intense fear run down his spine. *Being scared out of my wits was not part of my dream, either,* he thought bitterly. *If I could only find that sword…*

Sainaa spat through her teeth as she drew her own sword, long and slender like a rapier, but curved. "Maybe it's a good thing the sword's not here then. At least if we can't have it, they won't, either."

Kazan's first reaction was to literally toss Rooks up the tallest dead tree he could find. "Stay there," he said. "And be safe." Rooks nodded gravely and climbed higher on the tree, never showing the slightest sign of fear.

Chalco, on the other hand, was in full blown panic. He tried to run away, but before he could take more than a few steps, he began to sink into the soft rancid mud. He struggled to free himself, which only caused him to sink further, until he was up to his chest in the stinking goo.

Versai was not doing much better than Chalco in terms of mobility. He was practically stuck in one spot, though he was not nearly as deep and had plenty of space to swing his sword. "So what's our strategy?" Ceycil heard him ask, with the voice of a soldier that's used to taking orders.

"Stay alive," was Kazan's answer. He hung his sack on a dead branch and started fumbling with his belt pouches that contained his spell-casting materials. "And keep away from our friend the black knight. I know how to take a bull by the horns."

*   *   *   *

There were several dozen of the black-clad people, most of them wearing plain black clothes instead of proper armor. Even though Roessa and Kazan managed to take out a few of them from a distance with arrows and balls of fire, there was still quite a clash when the two parties met.

Then there was the third side: the solitary figure that was approaching from the other direction turned out to be a giant of a man, over eight feet tall and made up of more scars than skin. In his gargantuan hands that were cuffed together with a rusty chain, he held an equally oversized sword with a blade that was molded into an axe towards the tip. The obvious impression he gave was that he was not someone to be taken lightly, which he set out to prove immediately by attacking anyone within his reach regardless of which side they happened to be on.

It was pandemonium.

The people in black were agile beyond human skill. Ceycil felt like a complete klutz in their presence, especially with his rusty old sword. He noted with regret that he was neither as fast nor as strong as he was with the sword in his dream. Again and again he swung and parried, knowing all the time that if it wasn't for Kazan shooting a spell in his direction once in a while or Sainaa throwing a well-aimed dagger, he would have been dead several times over.

Everyone else had their hands full, too. Sainaa was engaged in an intricate dance of blades with a tall, lanky swordsman that wore a single odd eyeglass. The man handled his thin, delicate rapier with unbelievable finesse despite the wind blowing the rain directly in his face. Even though Sainaa possessed reflexes to match his, he barely seemed to be straining.

Roessa was standing further away, busily sending her arrows in all directions and taking down the occasional nuisance that tried to attack someone from behind. There was only one shadow-fighter that annoyed her immensely, by aiming his daggers so well that half the time Roessa's arrows were cut in two in the air before they ever reached their target. It was a young man with tanned skin and slight points coming from the hood of his cloak, and he seemed to be enjoying himself as he inched his way towards Roessa. She tried shooting him down, but it was useless. He was too fast, and his daggers too sharp. *Where the hell does he get all those daggers?* Roessa couldn't help thinking. *I'm almost out of arrows here, and he seems to have an infinite supply under that cloak of his.* She tried to concentrate on her aim, trying not to waste a single arrow, and cursed as another one fell to the ground in two pieces.

Versai sensed a greasy-haired wizard among the shadow-fighters, and seemed to be enjoying himself thoroughly. Mad laughter and hearty curses erupted from the battlefield periodically, as every time the wizard let loose a spell, the Iltherian sucked it up into his green sword blade and threw it back at one of the shadow-fighters. Every now and then, he would get carried away and steal the mana from one of Kazan's spells, receiving an even more colorful curse in return. His principal targets were those that surrounded Sainaa, since she had enough on her plate with the sleek swordsman, who managed to dodge the spells thrown in his direction with cat-like agility. At one point, he waited for the black-cloaked wizard to conjure up an especially large sphere of magical energy, then promptly sucked it into his sword and blasted into oblivion two shadow-fighters that were approaching Sainaa.

"You seem to be enjoying this a tad too much," the Khenbish woman commented in mid-combat.

The renegade shrugged and let out another hysterical laugh. "Allow me the pleasure," he said. "This is the only thing I know how to do well!" He spotted another shadow-fighter running towards him. The greasy-haired wizard had not prepared another spell yet, so Versai just borrowed one from the other side of the battlefield.

"WILL YOU STOP THAT?!" Kazan roared in rage.

"Habit." Versai shook his head. "Orc-bones, what a temper!"

Kazan had good reason to be mad. He was engaged in an intense battle with the black knight, which involved complex spell work, quick reflexes and lots of frustration.

His first impression was that the knight was far more solid than he looked. He soon realized he was wrong. The knight was far *less* solid than he looked. The wizard had never seen anything like it. The knight was almost impossible to hit. Instead of dodging Kazan's spells by getting out of the way, he seemed to merely shift his existence to a spot nearby. It happened so fast that it gave the impression that he was everywhere and nowhere at the same time. When he was attacking, bolts of lightning materialized at the knight's metal-clad fingertips, drawn through a thread-like line from the clouds. With every bolt of lightning, the rain slowed down and the clouds began to dissipate. It was almost as if the knight was speeding up the rainstorm and channeling it through himself. *This is not normal mana manipulation,* Kazan thought. *It does not feel like mana. It does not smell like mana. It is not something from the land, it is something from within.*

As soon as the thought crossed his mind, an irrational fear washed through his spine. It was highly unusual for Kazan to feel such fear, and extremely unnatural. *Where is this coming from?* He thought as he tried to shield himself from a lightning bolt with a mirroring spell. *This is not my fear.* His spell deflected the bolt, which missed the black knight's shoulder by a few inches.

Valharess let out a hollow, metallic laughter. "You're right, old man!" he yelled. "It's not. But it will be, I assure you!"

A psion? Kazan heard of people training in the powers of the mind. Many of them went insane before they ever mastered it. Psions did not work with magical energy. Instead, they manipulated the world around them, making the rules of nature obey the commands of their mind. They could neither create nor destroy, but they could use whatever was available in their surroundings. *Like a convenient storm,* the wizard thought, gritting his teeth. "I do not think so, sir black buffalo or whatever your name is," he snapped. "*I* assure *you* that before I have that kind of fear, I will make hell freeze over, and you with it!"

The black knight paused momentarily. The rain stopped, and the clouds were beginning to part, letting sparse beams of sunlight shine over the swamp. "Valharess," he said. "They call me Valharess. Now, where is the sword?" he asked calmly, his voice as dark as his ornate armor.

"Not here, if it exists at all." Kazan took the opportunity to catch his breath.

"We're both too old for games, wizard." said Valharess. "Now tell me like an honest man. I know your little sidekick there got the sword from the Time Tree. Where did you hide it?"

"I told you, the sword is not here." The wizard wiped his face with his sleeve. "What part of that do you fail to understand?"

The knight scraped the muddy ground with the sole of his boot, like a raged bull ready to charge, and raised a hand towards the sky again. "I know the sword was here, and I know that brat beat me to it," he said in a bored tone of voice. "Now tell me!"

Kazan rubbed his hands together. "Looks like your skull is as thick as your helmet," he said as he prepared to cast another spell. "Let me see if we can soften it up a bit."

*   *   *   *

Roessa watched Kazan and Valharess from a distance. Her knuckles were white as she drew the string of her bow. *This is my last arrow,* she thought. *It had better be useful.* She glanced at the tan-skinned shadow-fighter, who was dangerously close to her now. *The black knight or the dagger man?* Shooting at the black knight made more sense. The shadow-fighter would probably just cut her arrow into two again anyway.

Her arrow went off with a loud twang. Traveling with mind-boggling speed, it hit the black knight square on his horned helmet. The arrow made no more than a scratch in the black metal, but it did catch Valharess by surprise. The knight's moment of distraction was enough for Kazan to unleash a spell. A rather dense wave of hot air spiraled out of his hands and engulfed Valharess like a burning tornado. It swept him off his feet and hurled him several dozen yards across the swamp, leaving him washed down like driftwood on the shore.

It all happened within seconds. The tan-skinned shadow-fighter stopped in his tracks, several feet away from Roessa. Seeing his master thrown about by Kazan's spell, he produced yet another dagger at his fingertips. Perhaps it wouldn't be deadly from this distance, but it would definitely hurt.

At the sight of the dagger aimed at her father, Roessa flared up like a maddened tigress. By pure feminine instinct, she lanced herself at the shadow-fighter and slapped him across his angular chin.

Being a rather unorthodox act in a full-blown battle, it did the trick. The dagger left the shadow-fighter's hand at an odd angle. Roessa saw it hit the back of Kazan's head with the blunt hilt. The wizard staggered for a moment, then fell backwards into the mud.

The shadow-fighter seemed more baffled than anything else. "Did you just slap me?!"

He never got the answer to his question, as Roessa in her fury let out a fierce growl and broke her bow over his head, knocking out the shadow-fighter. Not even bothering to pick up the pieces of her weapon, she ran for the tree that Rooks was sitting in.

*   *   *   *

On his side of the battlefield, Ceycil was trying to catch his breath. His last opponent, a rat-faced shadow-fighter, was blasted into a smoking heap by a conveniently deflected spell from Versai's sword, and nobody else seemed to be coming for him for the moment. He stared at the sunbeams breaking through the clouds for a few seconds, and blinked in disbelief. Not far from him, a beam of sunlight shone onto a crystal-clear pool in the middle of the swamp. Deep in the water, he thought he could see the branches of a great maple tree, and he knew precisely what lay at its roots.

In the distance, Valharess sat up in the stinking mud, shaken by the spell that torched him only seconds ago, sweat trickling down his face inside his helmet. He knew that if he hadn't landed in the cooling mud, the spell would have baked him in his armor. Staring ahead, two things caught his sight: the wizard flat out on his back, and Ceycil running away, no, towards... water? "GRUFF!" He shouted with all the strength he could muster, his voice carrying across all the fight and commotion, deep and clear like the tolling of a temple bell. "GET THE BOY! HE'S GOING FOR THE SWORD!"

Gruff grunted in mid-battle. He wasn't quite as tall as the giant that he was fighting, but he was almost twice as wide, and certainly looked just as intimidating. As the giant brought his sword-axe down again, the massive shadow-fighter jumped out of the way and made a run for the pool. Quickly dropping his helmet and stripping off his heavy breastplate, Gruff dove into the water after Ceycil.

Ceycil swam for the tree, wondering if his breath would last that long as he got deeper and deeper. The water in the puddle was more like liquid air, it was too dense to breathe, but he could see through it clearly. He heard something else splash in after him, but he was too concentrated on the sword standing at the bottom to care. Only when he felt a tug at his ankle did he realize that he was in trouble. There was a beast of a man behind him, holding onto his ankle with a grip of steel and looking anything but friendly.

The man pulled Ceycil towards himself, and wrapping his huge arms around him, squeezed the air out of his lungs. Ceycil barely had the chance to struggle before his vision blurred and everything went dark.

*   *   *   *

Gruff reached for the sword, and found it stuck at the bottom of the pool, jammed between the thick roots of the underwater tree. He tugged at it with all his might, his muscles twitching from exertion, but to no avail. The sword wouldn't even budge. He decided to swim to the surface for a breath before giving it another try. Now that the boy wasn't in his way, he would have more time for the sword before he ran out of air.

As he made an upward stroke, he realized that the branches of the tree were closer together than he thought, almost forming a ceiling of wood and leaves above him. He tried to swim his way around them, but the branches were everywhere, thin and spiky. A surge of panic spread through the huge man as he realized that the branches were moving, growing to be more precise. He tried to swim away from the tree, but it was impossible. He was trapped, and the cage of living wood around him was getting tighter and tighter.

Ceycil opened his eyes, surprised to find out that his lungs weren't filled with water, but with air. He was lying by the roots of the Time Tree, with a faintly-glowing bubble wrapped around him tightly like a suit. There was something vaguely familiar about it, but he wasn't quite sure what. He was even more surprised to see that the sword was still in its place, planted with its hourglass hilt pointing towards the surface. Looking up, he thought he could see pieces of black cloth sticking out of a mangled mess of branches and leaves up on the Time Tree. The sight made Ceycil wince. Even for a brute, it was a nasty way to go.

He stood up and swam his way towards the sword, the bubble moving with him. When his fingers touched the hilt, a little tingle like electricity ran up his arm. It was an oddly pleasant feeling. It took a couple of sharp tugs to free the sword from its place, and once he shrugged it loose, Ceycil swam for the surface.

As soon as his head rose above water, the glowing bubble surrounding him steamed out of the pool into a familiar humanoid figure. It was Rooks' air spirit, one of the four he kept in his vials. Ceycil glanced at the child sitting in the tree not far from the pool. Rooks smiled as the air spirit quietly floated back into her crystal vial.

Ceycil pulled himself out of the pool back into the knee-deep mud, unable to keep his eyes off the sword in his hands. It wasn't nearly as light as he remembered from the dream, but still just as captivating. He didn't have much time to admire it, though, for he soon found himself staring at an oversized belt buckle. What was really disconcerting about it wasn't its size, but the fact that it was almost at Ceycil's eye level.

It was pure instinct that made him jump out of the way of the massive sword-axe that swung to the ground just inches from him. Ceycil looked up into the giant's face, crowned with a tuft of black hair on his scalp that was as leathery as the rest of his skin. His looks reminded Ceycil of an aged elephant, an image complemented by a pair of overgrown lower canine teeth resembling tusks, one of them broken in half. Before the giant could lift the heavy sword-axe for another strike, Ceycil already flicked his new sword in the air. Without another thought, he brought it down as hard as he could.

There was a loud clang as the sword cut through the rusty chain that held the giant's wrists together. The giant looked into Ceycil's eyes for a moment. Then he nodded and lifted his sword-axe again, and without a word, turned around and swung it at the nearest shadow-fighter.

Ceycil stood frozen in his spot. He had no idea why he did what he did. It was a momentary instinct, a voice from deep within him that spoke to him, a feeling that suddenly soaked through him the same way water soaks up the roots of a tree. He knew immediately that he was not meant to fight against the giant, but beside him.

In the distance, he heard Valharess barking orders at his men. He saw Roessa grab Rooks out of his tree, and a group of shadow-fighters running towards him like a swarm of locusts. It all seemed unreal for a second, as if he was watching everything behind a glass window. It was Roessa's yell that brought him to his senses. "Run, you idiot! They're coming for you!" He saw her pointing towards a few wooden rafts on the riverbank, undoubtedly used by the shadow-fighters to get there. Leaving his old sword lying by the pool, he broke into a frantic run towards the river.

*   *   *   *

Versai stood in the middle of the battlefield with his sword pointing towards the sky, sniffing the air like a wild animal tracking the scent of its prey. When the black knight and Kazan were fighting, he sensed an odd sensation. His sword had picked up the usual sparking vibrations of the wizard's mana, but also something else. The black knight's lightning bolts were not made from normal mana, but drawn down from the clouds like natural lightning. Still, the force that was drawing them down was nothing of nature. It was an energy unlike anything the Iltherian felt before. Wizard magic tended to flow like thick custard, warm, sticky and interconnected. It was enough for Versai to reach out with the power of his sword and touch a blob of mana, and the whole spell would follow, streaming into the sword effortlessly. What the black knight used was more like little silver threads, wiry and metallic, perhaps mana still but in a different form. Versai tried tapping it into the sword, but all it did was to scatter itself around where the Iltherian tried to touch it, and gather again in the same spot as soon as the power of the sword receded.

The Iltherian licked his lips. The black knight's energy, whatever it was, astonished him. If he could only get a hold of it with his sword… but no matter how hard he tried, the threads slipped away like cold slimy noodles around the mana-draining power of his blade.

He kept fighting, using the black-clad wizard's spells to attack the shadow-fighters around Sainaa, but always keeping an eye out for the horned helmet. When he saw Kazan hurl the black knight across the swamp with his spell, Versai decided to give it one more try. As the horned figure shook himself out of the mud, the Iltherian closed his eyes and reached out for the little silvery threads once again. The slippery strands of psionic energy danced around Versai's fishing line of anti-magic, but without a single bite. *There's got to be something I can grasp onto,* he thought. *Where's the needle in this haystack?*

Then almost immediately, the image brought him a different idea. It wasn't a haystack at all, he realized. It was a whole pile of needles. *And how do you pick up a pile of needles without pricking your fingers? With a magnet, of course.*

A smirk of mischief appeared on Versai's lips. He opened his eyes to see the black knight getting ready to call down another bolt of lightning. He was so thrilled by the thought of what he was about to try that he didn't even notice that the lightning was aimed right at Ceycil running towards the river with a strange sword in his hand. As the silvery threads of psionic energy molded the electricity in the remaining storm clouds into a deadly stream, the Iltherian's consciousness was already connected with that of his sword.

Now that Versai knew what he needed to do, the sword knew precisely how to do it. Its anti-magic presence beckoned to the threads like a snake-charmer. First, a single thread gave in to the attraction, overwhelmed by the power of the sword. Then another followed, and another. Within a couple of seconds the Iltherian was grinning like a maniac, with a mat of tangled psionic energy wrapped around his sword, not tingling like wizard magic but buzzing like a swarm of angry hornets. As the black knight let out a ground-shaking roar of frustration, Versai swung his sword and discharged the captured lightning bolt onto a hapless shadow fighter behind Sainaa, crumpling the man into a smoldering heap. Number 451 nodded, pleased with his work.

*   *   *   *

Roessa, with Rooks at her side, met Ceycil halfway to the river. As they ran, she couldn't help glancing back, her eyes in search of her companions among the mess of the battle she just left behind. Versai dropped his heavy breastplate and helmet, and was running close behind them. Sainaa was near him, somehow managing to fight off the shadow-fighters that followed them as they ran.

"Where's Kazan?" Ceycil was panting like a wolf cub. "I can't see him fighting."

With a sinking feeling in her chest, Roessa looked around for the spot where his father lay unconscious. "No, he just got knocked out," she answered, trying not to slow down her steps. She felt guilty leaving him to his fate for the second time, but she knew that Kazan would never forgive her if she risked her life in a foolish attempt to save him. Apart from the dark-skinned shadow-fighter, she was the only one who witnessed the wizard get hit with the blunt end of the dagger, so at least everyone else assumed him for dead and left him alone. Except now, Roessa realized that the wizard was no longer lying where he had fallen. Taking

LEGACY OF MANA : HOPE`S ORDEAL

another look around the battlefield, she let out a shriek. "Ceycil, that monster has him!" The giant, too, was running towards the river with a mud-covered Kazan tucked under one gigantic arm like a parcel.

Ceycil shook his head. "Don't worry," he said. "He's on our side."

"What?!"

"I said don't worry! Just keep running, we're almost there."

Chalco watched them from a distance and cursed everything he could think of, including the damn mud, his cowardice, and the blasted spirits themselves. He was seized by such a terror that he couldn't tell one end of his crossbow from another, let alone being able to shoot. The shadow-fighters hadn't even spared him a second glance as he stood worthlessly stuck in the swamp, which left him alive, but what did that matter now? He was sure he was about to die within a few seconds, and all his lonely journey and his efforts to stay alive were in vain.

The hideous giant was coming directly towards Chalco with great swinging steps, brushing off shadow-fighters as if they were black flies pestering him. Only another dozen yards or so, and Chalco was sure his life would end, crushed like an insect by the massive sword-axe. His hands shook madly as he fumbled with his crossbow. Normally it was designed to hold and shoot several bolts at once, an intricate weapon unique to Chalco's tribe across the sea, now on the verge of extinction like the race that made it. With trembling fingers, he managed to load one bolt onto the crossbow. Gathering what little nerve remained, he raised his weapon. *This is not how I die,* he thought. *This can't be how I die. Please give me my one chance to do something right, just once.*

He didn't need to take aim. The man coming towards him was so huge that even with his hands shaking like leaves in the storm, it was impossible to miss. As the monster stepped closer, Chalco drew a deep breath, and fired his crossbow.

The bolt hit the giant right below the collarbone. He paused, but only to let out a huff of annoyance. Slipping the sword-axe into a leather scabbard on his back, the huge man plucked the crossbow bolt out of his thick skin and threw it over his shoulder. Then he grabbed the screaming Chalco by the back of his makeshift rabbit skin shirt and ran for the river.

*   *   *   *

It took Ceycil several strokes to cut the ropes that held the raft on the riverbank. The sword was definitely sharper than his previous one, which was little more than scrap metal, though it was neither as sharp nor as light as it seemed to him in his dream. It was mildly frustrating. As Roessa and Sainaa tried to hold the raft steady, Versai was busy stealing the black wizard's mana and trying to slow down the shadow-fighters that were approaching the river like a plague of vermin. The wizard had to be a rather powerful one to keep going; otherwise, the Iltherian would have drained all his mana by now. *Powerful, but not terribly smart,* thought Ceycil. *Versai has sucked up every single spell he has cast and used them against the shadow-fighters, and yet the wizard still keeps trying.* "All right," Ceycil yelled when he was finally done. "We're loose, all aboard!"

Everyone scrambled onto the raft, which was no more than a shallow box made of thin logs tied together. As Ceycil gave the riverbank a push, he saw the giant approaching with Kazan under one arm and Chalco dangling from his fist like a scruffed puppy, and the raft slid into motion with the flowing water.

The shadow-fighters, led by Valharess and the black wizard, were at the giant's heels like hounds chasing an oversized rabbit. The wizard finally stopped casting spells, and Valharess seemed reluctant to use his lightning. A few arrows and daggers protruded from the giant's back as he ran, but they caused him no inconvenience. When he caught up with Ceycil and the others, the raft was already running at full speed down the river. As the shadow-fighters were busy getting on a raft themselves, the giant took a few strides and leapt off the riverbank with a shout. "HOLD TIGHT!!"

All Ceycil saw was a massive figure hurling itself towards them and before he could do anything, the giant landed face-down on the edge of the raft, almost sending Roessa and Rooks flying off into the water. Chalco was thrown across with the force of the landing, knocking Versai onto his back into the raft. "What the…" the Iltherian swore aloud. Sainaa coughed up a mouthful of water, drenched by the splash of water that propelled them further away from the shadow-fighters' raft, and Ceycil was barely saved from being crushed by Kazan's unconscious body.

When the giant finally managed to pull himself up and the raft stopped rocking madly, Ceycil let out a sigh of relief.

His sigh reversed into a gasp as an arrow whizzed by his ear, and he turned around to see another raft full of shadow-fighters following them. In the face of the constant flow of the river, they seemed to be getting closer. "Rogues!" he yelled, as a shower of daggers and arrows followed the first one.

Everyone ducked, except for the giant. "Ah," he said, plucking an arrow out of his forearm and watching a tiny drop of blood trickle down. "These things again… What a nuisance." Though his words came out slowly like a child just learning to speak, his voice was surprisingly smooth and musical. He spread his arms, practically forming a wall between the flying arrows and his newly-acquired companions. "Just stay down," he said calmly. "They'll give up eventually."

"What's going on?" Sainaa whispered towards Roessa, though a bit too loudly. "What's this *thing* doing here?"

The answer came from the giant himself, with no hint of anger in his voice. "Trying to save your fair skin, miss." He plucked another arrow out of his thigh and threw it into the foaming water, as a dagger hit his chest and bounced off onto the riverbank.

The arrows seemed to cease for a moment. "See?" said the giant. "They gave up. They always do in the end."

Ceycil looked up from his spot. "No," he shook his head. "They didn't. Look at the wizard and the black knight!" He pointed at the bow of the shadow-fighters' raft. Valharess and the greasy-haired wizard both waved their arms flailing in fancy gestures. The clouds were already sparking with electricity condensing somewhere above Valharess, and the wizard was rounding up a massive sphere of mana around himself.

Versai was lying motionless across the bottom of the raft until then, well hidden from sight. When he heard Ceycil, he lifted his head momentarily to glance at their followers. "Leave it to me," he said calmly.

"What are you going to…"

"Just duck when I tell you." A smirk appeared on the Iltherian's face.

Out of the corner of his eye, Versai saw the wizard's spell come whirling across the moving water as Valharess unleashed his lightning bolt. The Iltherian, without getting up, lifted the tip of his sword slightly, pointing it towards the sky.

"Now!" the Iltherian yelled. Everyone, including the giant, threw themselves flat onto the raft.

First, the sticky sphere of magical energy caught itself on the green metal of Versai's sword, gooey like a blob of glue. Versai grinned. Then his consciousness reached out for the little silver threads that were steering the bolt of lightning down from the clouds. The threads of psionic energy wrapped around the sword immediately, covering the sticky wizard spell like cotton candy. The Iltherian grinned wider.

As Versai got ready to return his new toys back to their respective senders, he realized that something wasn't quite right. The sword was now glowing like white-hot iron, with an internal growl like a volcano right before it erupted. The Iltherian's eyes widened as panic hit him. *Fate help us all,* he thought, with fireworks exploding inside his head. *It's overloaded!* He jumped to his feet, pushing Sainaa out of his way with his shoulder. At the risk of falling overboard, he swung the sword with all his might and with a wild un-knightly shriek, hurled it away from the raft.

The sword hit the river right in front of the raft full of shadow-fighters, causing an explosion of blinding light and ice crystals sharp as shards of glass. The part of the river where it fell was frozen solid, with numerous black patches of shadow-fighters trapped inside. Ceycil thought he could see a pair of black bull's horns sticking through the ice.

Their raft was pushed forward by the explosion, heading downstream at a neck-breaking speed. Ceycil braced himself against the side of the raft and brushed the needles of ice off his shirt. His arms were bleeding where some of them penetrated his skin. He looked around at his companions, all blanched with terror and cold.

"What the hell was that?" Roessa asked, her arms wrapped around Rooks who was shivering, with tears running down his face.

"Even an Iltherian sword has its limits," said Versai, shaking his head. "I had to get rid of it; it would have killed us all." He looked extremely disappointed even with their narrow escape. Along with his sword, Ceycil knew that the knight gave up his anti-magic ability. He was no more than a well-trained fighter now.

From his corner, Rooks made a sobbing sound.

"It's okay," said Roessa, running her fingers through the child's red hair. "We're safe now."

Rooks made the same sound again, his eyes fixed ahead of the raft, except it wasn't a sob at all. In a hoarse whisper, his lips formed the word "Waterfall".

Ceycil slapped his forehead. "Oh no..."

Unfortunately, Rooks was very much right. The raft was speeding towards what appeared to be the edge of the world. Up ahead, the flat riverbed ceased to exist, cut like a neatly snipped ribbon.

Chalco was frozen with fear since he was picked up by the giant. Even seeing his comrades hadn't broken his state of paralysis. Rooks' quiet warning brought him to life like a wizard's magic word. "Waterfall!" he screamed in total panic, flailing around madly. "Waterfall! We're all going to die! I want to get off, get me off this raft!!"

The giant gave him a look of genuine concern, not looking the least bit startled by the thought of impending doom. "Okay," he said with a shrug. Before Chalco could protest, the giant picked him up by the back of his rabbit skin shirt again and hurled him off the raft.

Ceycil didn't see whether Chalco ever made it to the riverbank. The last scene before his eyes was the frightened, helpless faces of his companions, and he had a split second to wonder whether he would ever see Roessa again. Then he was engulfed by the deafening noise of falling water, and he felt himself get sucked into a dark, crushing oblivion.

6

Chalco struggled onto his feet, dizzy with fear and the force of impact. The giant had thrown him onto a relatively solid part of the riverbank, where the mud wasn't soft enough to suck him in. *The giant,* he thought. *The others. The raft. The waterfall.* "The waterfall!" he squeaked, with no one to hear. He half ran, half crawled his way toward the ridge that formed the waterfall. Looking down made him even dizzier. It was so high that the river, at the bottom, was tiny as a trickle of water. With the burst of white foam where the waterfall ended, it looked like a kite string attached to a star, infinitely far and equally impossible. Chalco's eyes searched for little dots among the foam, but found none. No sign of the raft, nor any of his companions. He bit his lip. *This time they are gone for good,* he thought. *Now I'm really alone.*

The realization hit him hard. Almost as an instinct, his hands searched for his crossbow. It, too, had disappeared. He clearly remembered the feeling of the weapon grasped in his hands when he was flung across the water. It had to be somewhere near. Being alone in a dreary swamp after losing his companions to a terrible end was one thing. Being alone *and* unarmed was quite another. Stretching up like a prairie dog, Chalco looked around apprehensively to see whether there were any shadow-fighters around. In the distance, he could see the frozen surface of the river breaking apart as a few black-clad figures slowly recovered themselves. He definitely needed his crossbow.

He fumbled back to the spot where the giant threw him. Looking around, his eyes caught a glimpse of an unusual piece of driftwood caught between two rocks, not far from the riverbank. "There it is!" he breathed, thanking all the gods he could think of. *Please, don't be broken. Please please please don't be broken.* He took a careful step onto a moss-covered rock, then onto another. It was almost within his reach now. With nothing to brace himself against, he stretched out his tanned arm slowly. He let out a sigh of profound relief as his fingers wrapped around the crossbow. His sandals, made more for treading on sandy soil than on mossy rocks, chose that moment to slip, and he fell face-first into the running water.

The splash of icy chill that Chalco expected never came. He felt something like a tendril of force fold around him and suck him down like a pea through a straw. He didn't know how long it lasted, nor what it was that was pulling on him. He couldn't see anything beyond a greenish blur, and all he could hear was the bubbling, gurgling sound of the water, which surrounded him but somehow did not touch him. The feeling of having his stomach somewhere in his throat made it clear that he was falling, but that was all he could tell.

*   *   *   *

When his vision finally cleared and the rumbling in his ears ceased, Chalco found himself lying on dry sand, staring at a ceiling with strange moving lights. His heart was beating so fast, he could feel his ribs pulsing. It took him a few seconds to realize that the ceiling, if it could be called that, was made of water, and the strange lights were the burst of foam he saw from far above.

He was underneath the waterfall.

"Ah, it's him," he heard a familiar voice say. Sitting up immediately, he found himself surrounded by his companions, all looking as baffled as he was. The giant was staring at him with an apologetic look in his black eyes. "I'm sorry," he said to Chalco. "Did I not throw you far enough?"

Chalco gulped. "Um. No. I mean, yes, you did. I just…" His eyes wandered towards his crossbow lying on the sand beside him. It was a bit scratched, but otherwise looked intact. Laying a hand on his beloved weapon, he shifted his attention back to his surroundings. It was a dim cave, lit only by what little light came through the water-ceiling. The only wall he could see was bumpy and irregular; made of a deep crimson earth with small dull rock crystals sticking through it like the teeth on a comb. If it weren't for his companions, Chalco would have been terrified to be in such an odd place, but their presence comforted him. What delighted him most was seeing Kazan conscious again, who was observing the cave with keen eyes like an owl scanning a field for mice. "Where are we?" Chalco asked in a curious whisper.

"I wish I could tell you, son," came the wizard's reply.

Rooks was already on his feet, running his fingers up and down the crystals in the wall of the cave. "Pretty," he muttered.

"Pretty is the earth to the eyes of fire," said a voice from the depths of the cave. "When air is within you and water is higher."

The red-haired child turned around sharply.

Ceycil and Versai already jumped to their feet. "Who's there?" demanded Versai, reaching for his sword instinctively and finding his scabbard empty. "Show us yourself," spat the Iltherian.

A small sphere of light appeared further down the cave, shining on a scrawny figure sitting in a black, oddly-shaped chair. He was holding an open book, and something about him looked unusual, even from such a distance. Upon Versai's question, the stranger shut the book in his hands and slowly stood up and walked towards the Iltherian, the little sphere of light following him as he moved. "False mask, disguise. Step back, be wise," he said calmly.

Versai backed away reluctantly, and sat back down, keeping his eyes fixed on the odd figure.

"I know you!" Ceycil breathed. His face was flushed with excitement.

"You know me not, in person or in sight," said the stranger. From up close, Ceycil could see precisely what it was about him that seemed unusual. The tips of his ears showing through his long brown hair were not rounded but pointy like a bat's, and his eyes resembled Sainaa's slanted eyes, except they were a sharp dark green like pine needles.

"An elf?" Kazan whispered to himself in obvious surprise. "Now, that is news indeed!"

"I know your voice," said Ceycil defiantly, ignoring the wizard's comment. "You were the one I heard in my dream. You were calling for the son of some Lynnvander person, whoever that is…"

"He is who he is," said the elf. "No one you have learned to miss."

Ceycil frowned. "Do you always speak in riddles?"

The elf smiled in return. "Riddles and rhyme I have learned with time." Then he added more solemnly. "In rhyme my words are bound to my fate and my wisdom, like this timeless cave binds away my freedom." To Ceycil, he looked neither young nor old, with a boyish sparkle in his eyes when he smiled. Still, there was the graveness of an ancient man in his smooth voice.

"I thought your race perished long ago," said Kazan. "But I suppose some always remain." He stepped up to introduce himself. "My name is…"

"You are Kazan," said the elf with a nod. "A true mana wielding man."

Ceycil was taken aback, more so than Kazan appeared to be. "How did you know that?" He frowned. "Who are you?"

The elf shrugged. "Whatever you call me, to me it's the same. But if you must know, Korinth is my name."

Ceycil shook his head. "I don't understand. First the dream, then all your riddles and this place." He was more confused than frustrated. He felt like he was holding the pieces of a child's puzzle, but whichever end he grabbed, the pieces did not quite fit. "You brought us here, didn't you? That thing pulling us through the water… that was you." That he was almost certain of, but no matter how hard he thought, he could not come up with any reason the elf could have for saving them.

The elf nodded again and sat down on the sand, motioning Ceycil to do the same. He rested his book, which was bound in something like tree bark, on his knees, and slowly started to speak. "Here my words shall tell a tale for you," he said calmly. "Those who surpass it in greatness are few. So mind your past and think you through, for every memory is a clue to who you are and what you'll be as time itself will come and flee." Korinth paused to take a breath. Focusing his eyes on Kazan, he went on with his story.

"In this cave I was entrapped, by a man of mana skills unmatched. I knew of a sword made of time in essence, that if brought here, the cave`s hold on me lessens. So I called on a noble mind, for him to bring… to me the sword of Lynnvander, the king." He turned around to face Ceycil. "Young Ceycil here wisely answered my call to claim his father's sword, and free us all."

There was silence in the cave.

Ceycil stared at the elf, his mind whirring. "Wait…" One piece of the puzzle just clicked into its place, and he wasn't sure if he liked it. "I'm the son of Lynnvander?"

Korinth nodded slowly.

"And he was the king?"

Another nod.

"Oh." Ceycil tried to process everything in his mind at once, and failed miserably. Then things started to add together, little by little. "Hold on," he said slowly. "If Lynnvander was my father and he's dead, then that makes *me* the king!" He tried to suppress the grin that was starting to spread on his face. *I'm royalty? Seriously??*

Before anyone else could say anything, Sainaa broke in. "The king of where, may I ask?"

"The king of Tallinad, where we now stand," Korinth replied.

The grin left Ceycil's face as fast as it appeared. He suddenly felt betrayed, let down. A feeling of anger and disappointment welled his whole being. He turned his head sharply towards Kazan and gritted his teeth so loudly that it hurt. "You knew it all this time, didn't you?" he demanded.

It was Kazan's turn to nod. "Of course I did," he said calmly.

"`Of no consequence`!" Ceycil mocked the wizard's words. He could feel his breathing getting faster, his voice rising, but he was too mad care. "That's who my father has been all my life! `No one of importance, son.`!" He stood up and walked over to face the wizard. "Were you ever going to tell me, or was I meant to die a nobody, running from cave to cave like a rat, living a miserable lie?" There were lights flashing before his eyes. He felt like he could smash up a whole army of Iltherians with his bare hands. If he could have brought himself to hit the old wizard, he would have.

Kazan sighed, taking a moment to shoot an angry glance at the elf. "Look here son, the reason I kept your past from you was precisely that, to make sure that you do not die a nobody." He, too, stood up to meet with Ceycil's eyes. "You need to understand, Ceycil. I had to make sure you lived long enough to be ready for your position. You know what kind of a world we have out there, you have seen the Iltherians yourself and what they are capable of doing. What do you think they would do if they heard about you, come over to shake your hand and pledge their loyalty?"

Ceycil fought his anger, trying to keep it together, if only out of respect for his companions that were witnessing the scene. He failed, however. Try as he might, he could not justify Kazan's words. "Ready for my position? And when do you think that would be, when I'm old and grey like you? How much more of my life do I need to throw away?" He could feel his face burning with the heat of his anger. *My identity,* he thought. *My name. My only inheritance. How dare you hide it from me?*

Kazan shook his head. "Your... kingly... reaction here is answer enough."

"I feel betrayed," cried Ceycil, pacing back and forth like a wild cat in a cage. "My whole life, you lied to me! You lulled me into ignorance, like a child. 'Nothing of importance,' you told me, whenever I asked you anything of my past. As if knowing the truth would be too much for me to handle, you lied to me! And I bought into it like a fool, because I trusted you... Because you *have* been my father, whether you like it or not, and I thought you always knew what was best for me. I was mistaken."

"Listen to yourself rant, son," Kazan grumbled back. "You speak of betrayal. Do you not see that I *do* know what is best for you? How long do you think you would survive in our first battle against the Iltherians if you knew the truth? You really would throw your life away then, with the anger brewing inside you for years. You would fight blindly, to the death, as like as not. All I did was to try to save you from yourself, and now you fight me like *I* am your enemy."

As Ceycil and Kazan kept arguing, the giant moved closer to Chalco. "You look upset," he said quietly. "You don't like them fighting."

Chalco bit his lips. "No. And I don't like royalty. They bring nothing but trouble."

The giant shrugged. "Young Ceycil has brought me other things," he said thoughtfully. "If he brings me trouble, too, then I think I shall just have to handle it."

Chalco stared at the giant. "What other things?" he asked, genuinely curious.

The giant held up the iron cuffs on his wrists, with the broken chain dangling on each side. "I was a slave," he said. "My people, we all were slaves. Because we were strong, you see. We could work a long time and not get tired. So the human folks enslaved us for years and years. Then I escaped to the swamp." He frowned, clearly remembering something unpleasant. "When I stood up to fight young Ceycil in battle, he did not strike me. Instead he cut my chains, though I don't know what prompted him to do so." He looked thoughtful. "I sense a good spirit in him, so I respect him, even though he is not my king."

Chalco eyed the giant carefully, seeing in him for the first time a person and not a monster. "Who are your people?" he asked. "Who are you?"

"I am a Neranian, from the western mud and rock Isle of Gurne. My name is Tyrann." He paused. "I only fight for the freedom of my people," he added. "Mine and now his," pointing to the arguing king. "And now yours." Tyrann locked eyes with Chalco who cracked his chapped lips into a slight smile, the first in days.

"I am Chalco," the earthen-skinned man found himself explaining. "I lived across the great western sea in the realms of Thalagrant, but then the Iltherians came and destroyed everything. Some of us managed to sail away, but our ship sank in a storm that the sea spirit sent for us, or that is what my people believed anyway. That is how I got here. No one else survived except me. It must be my punishment for something I have done, being the last..." He ran his fingers over his crossbow, recalling everything. They were bitter memories. He pushed them out of his mind, and stared at Kazan and Ceycil yelling at each other. "I wish they would stop," he muttered. "I do hate to see them fight."

Ceycil was so flushed with anger, he looked like he was about to burst into flames. "You could have at least told me my name!" he shouted. "Is that too much to ask? The empire is out plundering *my* land, and here I am running like a coward, oblivious of *my own name and my birthright.*"

The wizard narrowed his eyes and answered with a cool and composed voice. "Son, you do not know your right from your left. Sure, go ahead, walk into the Iltherian palace and tell the emperor you want your crown back. I will send a broom and a dustpan to collect your remains."

"Look, we can't get anywhere by arguing like this," Sainaa tried to break up the shouting match.

"Well, *I'm* getting somewhere even if I have to get there on my own!" Ceycil clenched his fists. "Because I refuse to crawl up in a wormhole and watch the Iltherians destroy my father's land, when I could be fighting for it! I may have lived like a coward so far, but guess what?" He pointed a finger towards Kazan. "I don't intend to die as one!"

The Khenbish woman sighed and closed her eyes.

Kazan crossed his arms. "What is your plan then, your majesty? How many knights do you think you can kill before they grind you up into fox bait?"

"Father, you're being too harsh on him."

"Quiet, Roessa." The wizard didn't even spare his daughter a glance. "Apparently I have not been nearly harsh enough on him; he is looking for something bigger to kick him in the head." Kazan still hadn't raised his voice. "Ceycil, young fool," he breathed gravely. "I spent twenty years of my life to keep you alive, just so that the land could one day have hoped to have its king back. Now you want to go get yourself killed and let it down for good?"

Ceycil wanted badly to snap back at him, but something inside him made him lower his eyes in quiet shame. *Why are you always right, Kazan?* He thought grimly. *Why do you always have to be right?* The anger inside him drained away like water soaking through fine sand. "I'm sorry," he found himself saying. "I have been a fool, like you said. I did not mean to attack you like I did. I am just so ashamed of running, and I really wish I heard the truth from you instead of a stranger... It would have meant a lot more to me then."

The wizard glared at Ceycil, though the fire in his eyes was replaced with a solemn mist. "I, too, owe you an apology, son," he said softly. "I could not save your father from the Iltherians' wrath. The least I could do for him was to save you."

*　*　*　*

Throughout Kazan and Ceycil's fight, Versai remained silent, sitting slightly outside the circle with his hands around his knees. Without his sword, he felt lacking, and it didn't help that he was in the presence of a strange wizard for even without his sword he could feel the elf's mana floating around the cave like a dust cloud.

A face of two, that is you, a thought crossed his mind. The Iltherian frowned. "What?" he muttered to himself. The thought didn't seem at all like one of his own.

A twice-turned mirror reflecting a sinner, said the thought. *That is what I see in you, no renegade of true, but a harlequin through and through. A secret, a tricky one, to all but the imperial crown.*

Versai felt his blood boiling. He looked up to meet Korinth's almond-shaped eyes staring at him. *What are you doing in my head?* The knight demanded mentally.

Hostility will not bring you much thought, replied the elf. *Try being kind, and answers you will find.*

Fine, said Versai. *So you know. Fine. Go ahead; tell them all who I am while I'm still defenceless.*

111

That is not my place, said Korinth quietly. *Fate shall show its face.*

The Iltherian frowned. *I hate your riddles. Just so you know.*

Korinth smiled, ignoring the Iltherian's mental insult. Something soft was moving up and down the edge of his ear. It was Rooks, studying the elf carefully, with a bold fascination unique to children.

"Pointy," the red-haired child muttered, following the contours of Korinth's elven ear with his finger. "It's an elf." He said the word "elf" slowly, as if savoring its taste. He didn't know quite what it meant, except that it looked something like this curious man who sat in a bubble of glowing light and spoke in strange verses. He ran his fingers over the elf's long hair that flaunted something like a tiny living vine braided into it in several places. He had always thought that only girls wore braids. Roessa kept her hair in one all the time. *Maybe elves are different,* he thought. *Maybe it's okay for elf boys to braid their hair.* Reaching up, he grasped a wisp of his own red hair. It was growing longer since Serje wasn't around to keep it trimmed. Sitting down again, he tangled his fingers in his hair, trying to see if he could braid it.

Once the argument died down into awkward silence, Korinth broke his silence. "I did not intend to cause dismay, I ask you to put aside your troubles today. There is far too much work to be done, and it will not work unless we work as one. The land, you realize, silently dies, as the empire drains its soul of mana till it's unwhole. No more fairies in the woods at night, nor mighty dragons to ignite the air with their blazing fire, nor pegasi to soar higher than the swirling rainstorm cloud, no mermen of the deep so proud..." His voice trailed off as he cast his eyes down thoughtfully at the moving reflections the water-ceiling made on the sand. "Grave times indeed, times of undue power and greed."

The elf sighed deeply, and then went on. "Long-forgotten legends speak, of a ship anchored on the peak of the northern mounts of snow, where its ancient mana glows. It's a ship that sails the skies, away from the empire's eyes, and through this ship lies the final chains that binds the land to what mana remains."

"The Adelphia," Kazan whispered thoughtfully. Long ago, during his apprentice days he remembered the trade unions from the sky realms and the continent of Krymaris, his home. It was said that this mana laced vessel could fly faster than the wind, and go further than the snow geese would travel during their migration. The flying vessels disappeared from the realms when the Iltherians came to rule. No one knows what happened to them. Stories spun around the ship were many, but there was one thing they all agreed on: The Adelphia was a channel of the earth's mana, and when the earth itself was getting ready to die for everything that was born must die someday, the flying ship would be the last standing pillar of mana. "The Last Ley Line of Lunalia… so it is true?" Kazan had never believed the stories, but now he really wanted to. Still, the wizard knew more than he let on.

Korinth shrugged. "Without it, where would we be, mana touched folks like you and me?"

Kazan nodded, a bit of relief seeping into his heart. The elf was right. If the last source of mana didn't exist, he would barely be able to cast spells, if at all. That alone was proof that Korinth was telling the truth. Looking around, he saw that his companions were all looking at him with puzzled expressions. "The Adelphia is an artifact of mana so great," he explained, "that some say it came from the sky realms of our legend. Nobody knows for sure, of course."

"What's a ley line?" Rooks asked, his hair now a fluffy mess.

"Imagine that the world is a giant ball that is filled with mana." The wizard held up his hands, cupped together to form a sphere. "The mana is on the inside, and it can't get out. The ley line is like a crack in that ball, a fountain where the mana can come up to the surface where we can use it."

Rooks looked even more confused, but the others seemed to comprehend. "So if the empire gets it that's the end of mana?" Sainaa squinted until her eyes were no more than sharp little slits. "I don't like the sound of that."

Kazan shook his head. "Neither do I, Princess. Neither do I."

"But…" Ceycil said timidly, "all we need to do is to get there before the empire, right? I mean, if we take the ship… we can just sail away and the Iltherians would never find it."

"Nor would they find us," Chalco muttered thoughtfully.

Kazan rubbed at his eyes with the back of his hand. Young people made everything sound so simple.

Korinth looked at the wizard and smiled. "Judge them not by their fears, nor the number of their years. In their own words they are wise, this fact you must come to realize."

"I agree with Ceycil," said Sainaa. "A flying ship would be a safe haven for all of us, and it would definitely give us an advantage over the Iltherians. If we were to get into another battle with the knights, it's always best to be attacking from above than below. Besides, if the ship truly is the last source of mana, I'd rather have it on our side than the Iltherians'. It's only a handful of us against the entire imperial legion; we need all the resources we can get."

Korinth broke in once again, raising his hand. "This I feel I must bring to light: You are not alone in your fight against the Iltherian knights."

"What do you mean?" Ceycil asked. "There are other runaways fighting the empire?"

"Runaways they are not, but a more dangerous lot. Lovers of shadows, masters of plot. The Order of the Diamond Sage is dark in face and darker in fame, led by a mysterious knight, Valharess by name."

Kazan huffed. "And those are the band of bastards we just fought, are they not?"

The elf nodded.

Now it was Ceycil's turn to huff. "Great. Of all the people on the continent, it had to be those ones that are on our side!" He grumbled to himself for a few seconds, and then frowned at Korinth. "What were they doing in the swamp?"

Korinth blinked. "Valharess, it seems, has also heard my call, and came in to look for the same thing as you all." He took a deep breath before continuing. "And if on lines we must decide, I cannot say he's on our side."

"But you just said he's against the empire," Ceycil interrupted.

"Against the Iltherians he is, but for own causes of his. He cares not for the land, nor for the people will he stand."

"Then what is it that he's after?" *And why did he want my sword so badly?*

"That story you cannot hear from me today, I fear. Now I ask you to rest, for rest you will need, before we lead out of my timeless nest." With those words, the elf opened up the book he was holding, produced a small feather quill from the pocket of his plain tunic and started scribbling, giving his full attention to writing. Ceycil took this as the end of the conversation.

Chalco was already sitting against the crystal-covered wall, polishing his crossbow and chatting with the giant. Ceycil couldn't remember the last time he observed the skinny man so relaxed, if there had been a last time at all. He couldn't hear what they were saying, as the cave oddly muffled sounds instead of echoing them, but he could almost make out a smile on the giant's scarred face, making the huge figure look remarkably less monstrous and almost friendly.

Kazan followed the elf's example and opened up his spell book, which Ceycil also took as a desire to be undisturbed.

Rooks took his earth spirit out of its vial and was busy exploring the rest of the cave, dragging Roessa alongside him and showing her every little thing he discovered. Ceycil had a hunch that the little boy had no intentions of resting, which was a pleasant thought. For the first time since Serje's death, Rooks was finally starting to act like his curious eight-year-old self again as opposed to a small specter.

Versai had been silent since Korinth's initial snap at him. He was sitting in a corner at the back of the cave with his arms around his knees, looking pensive. Ceycil thought he saw the Iltherian throwing angry glances at the elf every now and then, but that was only to be expected. After all, the knight wasn't one to deal very well with a scratched pride, and the elf made quite a verbal stab at him upon their meeting. When Versai finally did get up from his spot, he made an attempt to approach Sainaa. As soon as he moved, the Khenbish woman, on purpose or not, also got up and started walking towards Ceycil. The Iltherian sat back down, looking disgruntled.

Ceycil watched Sainaa walk over, making every excuse to focus his attention on his surroundings instead of having his mind wander back to the argument he had with Kazan. To his surprise, she sat down beside him. Throughout their travels, Ceycil evoked very little interaction with her, mostly small talk over meals and brief discussions of the day's events. Sainaa was a princess, after all, and a foreign one at that. He had no idea what to make of her. Having just heard that his father, whom he had never seen, had been the king of Tallinad had come as a blow. It was a pleasant blow for his ego, but a blow nevertheless. He wasn't even sure where exactly Tallinad lay as far as its borders went. Was it big? Small? Flat? Rough? Did it have a coastline? Ceycil was clueless. Along with nations, the Iltherians had also destroyed the concept of countries in the name of their empire. All Ceycil could remember from Kazan's fireside history lectures was that Tallinad was one of the many kingdoms in the continent of Krymaris that had fallen to the empire some twenty years ago, and it was part of the land they journeyed. *Twenty years ago,* he thought. *I was born twenty years ago.*

"You look worried," said Sainaa.

"I feel out of place," Ceycil muttered. "My father, the King... All this time I've been watching the Iltherians tear apart *my* land. And of course Kazan doesn't tell me a thing all this time." He was breathing harshly, not knowing whether he was still mad or simply and utterly confused. A tiny part of him wanted to disbelieve Korinth's words, just shrug it off and go on with his life. *Go onto what, though?* Still, somehow he knew that the elf wasn't lying. "It's frustrating," he said. "Knowing that my life so far has been meaningless, constantly running and hiding like some prey animal, instead of doing something to save the land that is mine." He took a deep breath. "Then again, now I know. Now I can do something." He lifted his eyes to meet Sainaa's. "I am no longer a nobody, no longer a nameless runaway. I'm the rightful heir to Lynnvander's crown! I know I have the power to face the Iltherians. This land is my birthright, it's my responsibility. I will die for it if that's what is necessary." He shook his head absently, his eyes wandering towards the old wizard bent over his book. "He can't expect me to just sit back and let them destroy it anymore."

Sainaa placed a hand on his shoulder. "Look at me, Ceycil," she said gently. "You are a prince. Do you know what that means?"

Ceycil gave her a blank look.

"It means the land owns you," she said, "and not the other way around. The best thing you can do right now is to stay away from the Iltherians. They are the only ones who can break the bond of your bloodline with your land. If you die in any other way, the land will always bring back another Lynnvander to bear the crown. If you fall to the Iltherian swords, however, all is lost for Tallinad." She bit her lip. "Do you understand, Ceycil? That's why Kazan never told you. How long do you think he could keep you away from charging at the empire if you knew all along that they were responsible for the death of your family and the fall of your country?"

Ceycil stared at her, then averted his gaze. She was right. *Like Kazan. Why do you have to be right?*

"You're young and your blood is boiling with the desire for revenge." Sainaa nodded. "And I understand that." She stared straight into his eyes, and Ceycil remembered that she, too, lost her crown and her people to the empire. "I know how tough that feeling of helplessness can get, Ceycil. I know the remorse that washes over you every night. Feeling like you're a coward, hiding in corners. The burning hatred against the empire. I've been there, I still am there." She shook her head. "Still, you must remember to protect yourself, at least until you find the force and the support to claim your kingdom. Dying for your country won't get you anywhere. You must learn to live for it."

Ceycil felt tears welling up in his eyes, and tried in vain to fight them back. The feeling of being understood, at a time when he failed to understand himself, was both liberating and overwhelming at the same time. *I don't really know you,* he thought, his blurred vision fixed on Sainaa. *But we share a fate, and I feel like I do know you after all. Like that part of myself that I didn't know until Korinth told me who I really am.* "At least we're in this together," he said, not knowing how else to explain his feelings. "I don't know what I would do without you. Without all of you." He smiled weakly, glancing past Sainaa's shoulder towards Roessa and Rooks exploring the cave.

Sainaa smiled back with the hope of a future in her eyes. "You know what you've got to live for," she said. "I know you do. I see you dreaming about it when you gaze into the fire at night. Hold fast onto those thoughts, Ceycil. We can only take you so far in this battle. It is those dreams of your future that will take you the rest of the way."

* * * *

Silence reigned in the cave as the weak light shining through the water-ceiling dimmed into complete darkness. Kazan bothered to light a small magical fire in the sand, only because he couldn't read in the dark. Everyone except the

THOMAS M. GOFTON   -   HANDE BARUTÇUOĞLU

old wizard and the elf was fast asleep, or at least so they appeared. Rooks was curled up beside Roessa, and Chalco had his back against the giant, whose snores could not be muffled even by the crystal walls. Between the battle in the swamp and the tumble down the waterfall, it was a strenuous day. Even Versai and Sainaa slept, each hiding in a separate shadow that the dancing flames cast.

Ceycil lay wide awake next to Roessa, his eyes closed but his mind racing. He wanted to sleep, to go back to the dream he had of the man that he knew now to be his father. *That's why he looked so familiar,* he thought. *I saw bits of myself in him.* He tried to remember the King's face, but all he could recall was snippets: a neatly-clipped brown beard, a pair of green eyes, an expression of intense worry... but the pieces refused to come together. No matter how hard he tried, Ceycil couldn't picture the King as clearly as he remembered him in the dream. The harder he tried, the more frustrated he got, and the more it chased away his sleep.

Sleep you cannot upon that thought, royal blood or not. The voice that penetrated Ceycil's mind was unmistakably Korinth's. Ceycil's eyes snapped open. The elf was still sitting beside Kazan's fire, though his book was now closed, and so were his eyes.

Are you reading my thoughts? Ceycil found himself thinking.

The hint of a smile appeared on Korinth's handsome face, as he promptly ignored Ceycil's question. *A good night's rest is what I suggest, since tomorrow for you awaits a test of broken time and broken heart, one story's end, another's start.*

I don't mean to be disrespectful, thought Ceycil somewhat angrily, *but I have enough on my mind without having your riddles to deal with.*

To deal or not is yours to choose, said Korinth. *But you must be careful whose directions, advice or clues will point you towards the path you use. And sometimes to win one battle, another you may have to lose.*

You're crazy, was the first thing that passed through Ceycil's mind, before taking the split second to remember that the elf could hear his thoughts. *I'm sorry, I didn't mean...* He tried to recover, but it was too late. The elf was already laughing to himself.

Eventually even Ceycil fell asleep, though his thoughts would continue to harangue him in his oblivion. As the ocean-deep color of the water-ceiling started to turn a crimson-blue with the rising sun, Kazan shut his spellbook and shot a very deliberate gaze at Korinth. "Now that it is just you and I, it is time you told me who you really are."

The elf smiled sardonically. *A wizard like you, obvious but true.* The answer rang in Kazan's mind like a bell tolling midnight.

Kazan frowned slightly. *And a psion. That explains Ceycil's dream, but does not explain why you have brought us here. You are no ordinary wizard. No ordinary psion, and definitely no ordinary elf.*

Well said, said the elf. *Though I must add, I can't explain more than I already have before. You, Kazan, have a mission, and I'm in a trap. Here your salvation and mine overlap.*

The old wizard shook his head. *My only true mission is to make sure that the Lynnvander bloodline survives. I do not see how filling Ceycil's young and foolish head with dreams of royalty and heroism can help me achieve that. I was having a hard enough time trying to keep him away from the Iltherians as it is. Now thanks to you, I will not even be able to do that much.*

Korinth lifted his eyes to meet Kazan's. *For that I have my reasons, and you know that it's not treason. I could have*

121

turned in the truth and all that is within, not to you, but one of green and orange hue... is that not true? He paused. *As for that mission of yours, the one you've left behind by force will once again cross your course.*

Kazan blinked, blurry memories rushing into his mind. A cry echoing down a dark tunnel, the distant sound of metal against metal, and the heavy scent of dirty water and blood. *What are you saying?*

The elf closed his eyes again. *Precisely what you recall, that's all.*

* * * *

The morning came around much too soon for Ceycil's liking. He sat up blinking into the dim light that shone through the water-ceiling, his first instinct being trying to remember what he dreamt of.

Slivers of images danced before his mind's eye as he recalled bits of the stories he lived in his sleep. The first one was a rather unpleasant one; fighting against an invisible enemy with his father's sword in his hand, except this time instead of its quick silvery lightness, it was heavy and clumsy to wield.

All that remained of the second one was a single scene, of a small firebird that built its nest among the clusters of rock crystals along the wall of the cave.

The third dream involved a bright summer morning, a waterfall and Roessa. Ceycil closed his eyes. A smile crept onto his lips as he indulged in every little detail he could bring back from the depths of his memory. The waterfall was a small, picturesque one, not monstrous and wild like the one they tumbled through. He could almost smell the fresh morning dew. Roessa had her hair loose around her shoulders. She was splashing in the stream, crystal drops of water trickling down her bare back. Her laughter floated in the air like the spray from the waterfall.

"Ceycil?"

If it had been any other voice that snapped him out of his bliss, Ceycil probably would have bitten someone's head off, but against Roessa all he could do was to retain his smile. "Good morning."

Roessa smiled back. "I almost thought you fell back asleep. What were you thinking about?"

Ceycil shrugged. "Just a dream I had." He couldn't even get mad at himself for not being able to dream of his father again.

Roessa raised her eyebrows. "Tell me you're not planning to take us through any swamps today!"

"No, no more swamps, I promise." Ceycil laughed.

The others, too, were waking up and gathering around Korinth almost by instinct. A breakfast of dried meat from Kazan's pack and some bluish-green grapes provided by the elf were served, all of which was devoured without questions. Everyone was too hungry to worry about the source of their food at this point.

"I thank you for hospitality," Tyrann said solemnly, nodding to Korinth and Kazan in turn. "As it seems, I have stumbled upon your fellowship for a reason. I wish to remain working with you. If you are ever to face the Iltherian soldiers again, I would be honored to fight by your side." The giant showed his companions a half-tusked smile.

Kazan glanced at Tyrann over his breakfast and spoke without a pause. "Of course you can."

Tyrann popped another tiny grape into his huge mouth. "If that is now official, then my first question is, what do we do now?"

"We must leave this place," said Sainaa, tearing into a strip of meat with her teeth. "To go find that flying ship would be my suggestion, and pray we get to it before the Iltherians." She shot a sideways glance at Versai, who flinched uncomfortably and suddenly looked very interested in his fingernails.

"Yes," said Tyrann, picking another grape. "But how do we get out? I don't see no door around here." He huffed in mild frustration and stuffed the whole bunch of grapes in his mouth.

"For now there is no door," Korinth nodded. "Only ceiling and floor."

"Wait, but you said the sword…" Ceycil began, and almost choked on a grape as he heard the elf's voice in his head again.

Search your mind, and the answer you'll find.

Once he stopped coughing, he picked up his father's sword again. It was very well balanced, obviously a work of high artisanship. However, it was still a perfectly ordinary sword, save for the hourglass embedded in its hilt. Its top chamber was almost empty. Ceycil grasped the sword in hand and pointed its tip towards the ceiling, turning the hourglass upside down. Now it was the lower chamber that was almost empty, but the sand kept flowing upwards out of it.

Kazan squinted at it from his corner. "It is a time-trap," he said darkly. "That is a rather advanced magical use of mana…chronomancy, a very dangerous art."

Korinth nodded again.

"A time-trap," Ceycil repeated. "So if I destroy it, time will be released once again, right? The cave will no longer be timeless. That's our way out, isn't it?" He stared at the sword, surprised at his own words. He didn't really know how he knew that. He just did, and somehow it made perfect sense. *What is it that makes me know these things?* He wondered. *The same instinct that made me release Tyrann from his chains, even though I was convinced he was trying to kill me.*

It's the land, said Korinth's voice in his head. *The voice of your blood, your helping hand.*

The land? Of course, all royal bloodlines are connected to the land... Ceycil took a quick glance around himself, at the crystal walls of rock surrounding him. *The earth is thinking for me.* "All right then," he said, more to himself than anyone else. He stood up and brushed the grape stems off his tunic with one hand. "Let's do this, shall we?"

"Hold your horses boy," Kazan shook his head. "Sit down and let people finish their breakfast. There is no rush, time is not going anywhere while we are here."

"But look at the hourglass, the sand is about to run out!" Ceycil tried to protest, but the wizard wouldn't have any of it.

"It did not run out all night, I am sure it can last until the end of breakfast." Kazan picked up some more meat with a hungry expression on his face, but out of the corner of his eye Ceycil saw him scanning the cave carefully. He strutted around nervously with the sword in his hand, wishing people would hurry up.

He couldn't help noticing that Chalco's mood, temporarily improved by Tyrann's announcement to join them, collapsed again at the mention of leaving the cave. The earthen-skinned man reverted to his jittery anxious self once again. Ceycil couldn't blame him. Part of him felt safe here, hidden away from world of Iltherian knights and shadow-fighters. An exit for his friends meant an entrance for his enemies. Together they could hide in this timeless cave forever, away from everything, even death itself. He shook the thought away, angry at himself for even considering it. *Then we would really be miserable rats cowering in a hole,* he told himself. *Then my future, too, would be a lie like my past.*

Once breakfast was over, Ceycil found everyone staring at him expectantly. Kazan packed away his spell book, Rooks had his box of vials tucked into his belt and Tyrann strapped his sword-axe onto his scarred back. There was one last stroll around the cave to make sure nothing was left behind, Rooks brushing the crystal walls with his fingers as he walked.

"We are ready," Sainaa announced, resting her hands on her hips. Versai, standing close behind her, nodded in agreement. Kazan kept staring around the cave, frowning so deeply that his face was nothing but lines. Only Korinth had an air of calmness around him, as if they were getting ready for a morning walk and nothing more.

"Off we go then." Ceycil sighed, and raised his sword.

Kazan had a sudden notion that there was something inherently wrong with the situation. *It should not be this easy to unlock a door out of time, there is a catch somewhere.* "Wait!" He made a move towards Ceycil, but it was too late. The young man swung the sword towards the wall of the cave, the hourglass smashing into bits against the pointy crystals.

The cave shook sharply as part of the wall exploded, shooting large chunks of rock crystals in all directions to reveal an earthen staircase leading up from the cave. As soon as it did, the water-ceiling collapsed and the wild waves of the giant waterfall filled the cave, foaming and roaring like an angry beast.

It was a matter of moments before the wizard grabbed a hold of Ceycil and Roessa and practically threw himself up the stairs out of the cave. He was followed by Tyrann carrying a blanched Chalco under one arm and dragging Korinth by his tunic with his other hand. The elf showed no signs of fear or surprise. Only when Versai and Sainaa appeared at the top of the earthen staircase did they realize that something was wrong.

Very wrong.

Sainaa took one look at the crowd waiting for her, and her face went even paler than it normally was. "Rooks!" she gasped, and before anyone could stop her, she was running back down the stairs towards the madly splashing water.

"Sainaa, stop!" she heard Versai shout over the sound of the waves crashing in the cave, but she ignored his call. She was already at the bottom of the stairs, up to her waist in water, her eyes in search of the red-haired boy. She caught sight of him floating face-down, close to where the waterfall was still rushing in through the gap left by the vanished water-ceiling. *He was too close to the crystal wall,* she frowned, looking around for a less dangerous way to reach Rooks. There didn't seem to be any. There was barely two feet of air between the water and the ceiling of the cave, and it was filling up fast.

Knocked out, she repeated to herself. *Yes, that's all...* She took a deep breath. As she was about to dive in, she felt a hand grab her shoulder. "Sainaa, you can't!" Versai gasped. "You're the last of your people, remember? You've got to think of your nation, you can't just risk your..."

The Iltherian never had a chance to finish his sentence. "You mean the nation you've already destroyed?" Sainaa hissed through her teeth. Without another word, she pushed his hand away and threw herself into the black water.

Versai felt a sudden impulse to jump in after her, but his survival instincts prevailed. Swimming was not part of an Iltherian knight's training. He did not stand a chance against the raging water, let alone having any hopes of getting Sainaa out of it. With sweat dripping down his crooked brows, he held his breath and waited.

The water level was rising by the second, and it was getting impossible to keep neither Sainaa nor the floating body of Rooks in sight. He saw her reach the child, and then they both disappeared among the foam and the chaos. In what seemed like hours later, he felt someone pulling him away from the darkness of the cave.

"Get out of there, you fool!" Kazan's voice was firm but calm as usual. He pushed the knight out of his way, and bent down to see into the cave. "Sainaa?" His shout echoed over the water.

The answer was weak but unmistakably close. "Kazan! I got him!"

Upon hearing Sainaa's voice, Versai almost threw himself back down the stairs, only to be held back by Tyrann. From above he saw a pair of pale arms hand the unconscious body of Rooks to the wizard. "Sainaa!" The Iltherian yelled hysterically. "Get her out! You've got to get her out!"

The only reply he got was a crash as the cave collapsed completely, flooding both Kazan and Rooks up and out of the staircase.

*   *   *   *

"She's gone, Iltherian," Tyrann said patiently as Versai struggled to break away from his grip, kicking and snarling like a wild animal.

"Let me go! We need to find a way to get her out, let me go! It's all your damn fault, I need to get her out of there!" He knew that the giant was right, that Sainaa was gone for good, and he hated Tyrann even more for being

129

right. *She can't be dead,* Versai told himself again and again, knowing very well that it was a lie.

The giant shook his head calmly. "I'm not letting you go anywhere, you'll only share her fate."

Then that's what I will do. Share her fate. Die in that accursed cave, that's what I will do, just let me go... Versai let out a hearty string of curses and struggled even harder.

Kazan sighed audibly, holding Rooks in his arms who was coughing and throwing up a puddle of water onto the wizard's tunic. "Let him go, Tyrann. Maybe that way he will stop his neighing and I will not have to kill him." He sounded unusually tired.

Tyrann shrugged and loosened his grip. Versai stumbled, not expecting the sudden freedom. He ran up to where the cave's exit had been. A small rocky cove on the edge of the river was the only thing that was left of it, now that the cave collapsed. Beside them the waterfall roared and rumbled as before. There was no sign that there was once crystal-covered walls hidden below it. *Nobody will know that it was there,* the Iltherian thought bitterly. *Nobody will know that she is there.*

A feeling of helplessness like he never knew crept into the crevices of his soul. Not knowing what else to do, he ran back up to Tyrann and started flailing at the giant madly, punching and kicking the scarred body and screaming out more frantic curses.

Tyrann remained immobile, watching the frantic Iltherian solemnly. "That won't get you anywhere, you realize."

Versai wished more than ever that he had his sword. *Only pain can kill pain,* the Iltherian knights were taught. *Inflict what you feel. Make them taste your rage, and they will know your power. Then they will fear you.* He stared the giant in the coal-shaped eyes. "Mark my words, beast. Your time has yet to come."

Tyrann stood proud. "That may be," he said calmly. "As will yours, though it is not now. We need you here, Iltherian. Sainaa is gone, and by no fault of yours or mine. Now pull yourself together, you act as if you have never known pain before."

Ceycil and Roessa sat huddled together beside Kazan and Rooks, away from the spray and the noise of the waterfall. "She's gone," said Ceycil echoed grimly. "We lost her," He dropped himself backwards onto the wet soil. "Just like that." He whispered to himself in tears. He covered his face with his hands and let out a desperate sigh. His stomach churned as rapidly as the water before him, and he found it difficult to breathe. "I can't believe it. All her struggle, her escape from the empire, risking her life at the Iltherian camp… All that and she got swallowed by a cave. So much for nothing!" He shook his head, eyes wider than the sky, ignoring the mud that was sticking to his hair. "That's not fair."

Kazan gave him the closest thing he knew as a look of sympathy. "Nobody said life was fair, son. If life were fair, the emperor would have burst into flames long ago for all the atrocity he has brought upon this world."

Ceycil shook his head as he absently plucked the dead grass beside him. "Death is so easy," he muttered to himself, trying to sit up again. "Any minute, it's around any corner, behind any tree. It could have been any of us, or all. We all could have died in that cave." He witnessed Serje's death, too, but that was different or so he thought. Serje was old, and was killed in battle. Ceycil never fully realized before that he, too, was mortal. Being young and having dreams didn't make him invulnerable.

131

Roessa moved closer to him, putting a mud-covered sleeve around his shoulder. "Try to think of it this way," she choked, trying not to sound bitter. "At least the Iltherians can't get her now. Some day… sooner or later, some day she will be back for her nation." The thought gave Ceycil little comfort, but he tried to hold onto it anyway. Anything to float against the dead weight of desperation. He leaned his head against her shoulder. "Maybe… I hope…"

Kazan shook his head. "It was no one's fault," He took a deliberate look at Rooks and shot a meaningful glance at Ceycil, who understood immediately that there would be no mention of Sainaa's sacrifice in the child's presence. "As you said, it could have been any of us. Shame it had to be the princess."

As Versai finally stopped his futile attack on Tyrann, silence settled in. Kazan quietly built a fire to let their clothes dry. Rooks shivered in a corner, still pale and shaken, clutching his box of vials against his chest. Korinth sat by the fire with his hands around his knees, exploring his surroundings with a slightly troubled expression on his face. He hadn't uttered a single word since they left his cave. Chalco sat with his back against the giant's shoulder and cleaned his crossbow with a rag, looking ashen like Rooks and almost as shaken. Every once in a while Tyrann would pat Chalco on the back when he heard a slight sob.

Versai sat by the flooded staircase, feelings of gloom washed him over worse than anything he ever observed, from the victims he laid traps for. In the Iltherian army, he saw people die by hundreds in the battles, his comrades among them. He watched deserters caught and tortured to death, hanging from a tree with their bodies mutilated beyond recognition. He stared at the village raids where the men were enslaved, the women raped and the children slaughtered. The bond that linked him with his anti-magic sword was so strong and so far from human that all the horrors he viewed, not to mention those he had committed, had all seemed perfectly normal. Simple procedures that were part of war and conquest. Then why did his chest feel like caving in now, as if sucked from the inside by a hundred leeches? *It's just a woman,* he tried telling himself. *One like the hundreds of prisoners, slaves and prostitutes we held at the camps.* He bit his lip. He didn't know what it was about Sainaa that made her special, that caused him such grief upon her loss.

She showed you that it is true, that there is a heart even within you.

As soon as the thought entered Versai's mind, his eyes snapped to the elf sitting by the fire, who gave him a brief smile. The Iltherian felt his fury bubbling up in him, ready to erupt like a volcano. *You and your accursed cave,* he thought bitterly. *If you hadn't brought us there, none of this would have happened. You deserved that musty damp prison of yours.*

Believe what you will, Korinth answered his thoughts. *But our destinies we must all fulfill.*

Versai turned his head away sharply. *Enough of your riddles. I'm done with all of you. It's time I finished what I started.*

*   *   *   *

The first flakes of snow were floating down from the clouds as they started marching on again. It was the kind of snow that fell slowly, feathery and soothing. It did not have the biting cold of the late autumn winds; instead it felt gentle on the skin like a lullaby the winter sang for the earth going to sleep.

Chalco wrapped his chest in a cloak he borrowed from Kazan. He had to throw his rabbit skin shirt in the campfire before they left, as it was beginning to rot and would bring him nothing but disease.

Rooks was sitting on Tyrann's shoulders, who seemed no more burdened by the child's weight than he would be by a sparrow perched on his head. The giant was quietly singing a tune whose beat matched his long strides, soft but sturdy:

"Spring is the time to do, summer is the time to see

Autumn is the time to think, and winter is the time to be

The earth is old but I am young, and like the north wind I am free

I sing with my lute unstrung, and like the snowflakes I am free…"

Rooks smiled tiredly. He was still shaken and coughing, but he did enjoy his new lookout post. From the giant's shoulders, the world looked so different. The sky seemed much bigger, but everything else shrunk. He was so used to looking up at people's faces that seeing Ceycil and Roessa several feet below him made him feel grown up. And then there was the snow. He didn't quite understand what became of Sainaa, and he was afraid to ask. From the way everyone looked, he assumed that she was gone for good, like Serje. He frowned slightly, staring at the clouds and wondering where people went when they left like that.

Korinth seemed amused by the giant's singing. For the first time since they left the cave, he broke his silence. "Of your people's songs I know little," he told Tyrann. "But this one sounds like a fine riddle."

Tyrann shook his head gently, taking care not to wobble Rooks too much. "A riddle? Hardly. Just stating the obvious, that's all."

"I see nothing obvious about it," Chalco joined in the conversation. "Spring is the time to do? Time to do what?"

"Everything!" The giant chuckled amiably. "Plant the fields, clean out the home, and take the cows to grass."

"And summer is the time to see?"

Tyrann nodded, and Rooks giggled as he bobbed up and down with the giant's head. "Of course. You see the results of all the hard work you've done in the spring."

"Ah…" Chalco's eyes clouded momentarily. "I think I'm getting the hang of this. In summer you harvest your crops and watch your children grow. And in autumn it's time to think of the winter. Time to pickle the corn, salt the fish and thatch the roof." He seemed to be traveling to a different time, a happier one. "What of the winter then?" He asked, genuinely perplexed. "What happens in winter?"

The giant shook his head again. "Nothing. Winter just is. We just exist through it, that's all."

"Exist or perish…" Chalco muttered to himself, and he drew the cloak tighter around his shoulders.

*   *   *   *

When they finally settled down for camp, it was late. It took them all evening to find a rock large enough to provide them any shelter from the wind. A blurry sunset gave way to a grey, starless sky long ago. The silver halo of the moon shone through the snow clouds, which revealed a thick glowing crescent through wispy gaps as they moved on with the wind. The campfire was little more than a weak flame whipping in the cold breeze, but even a little warmth felt better than none. Chalco shivered and moved closer to the fire at the risk of getting his cloak singed. He escaped from his homeland in the summer, without the slightest hope that he might see another winter. Of what little belongings he gathered, the only object that survived the shipwreck was his crossbow. He loved his weapon, it made him feel at least somewhat protected in this unknown world, but it was no protection against the icy weather. He offered to stand watch with Tyrann, if only because he was too cold to go to sleep. Besides, the giant comforted him the same way his crossbow did.

Tyrann nudged him gently, and pointed across the campfire. "Look at them," he whispered, smiling. Ceycil and Roessa were huddled together, fast asleep. Roessa had her arm around Ceycil, her face buried on his shoulder. "Good kids," said the giant. "Brave. I hope they get to see a better world than this."

Chalco nodded mutely, his eyes fixed upon the darkness around. He had been Ceycil's age once. It seemed like long ago. *Eight years? That's all?* He knew once, that feeling of warmth, not the kind that came from a campfire but the warmth of another soul close to his own. Those days were long gone. *She is long gone.* He felt a weak, forlorn anger against the empire burning inside him like the flimsy flame of the campfire in the snow. His eyes wandered over Versai, sleeping against the rock in what remained of his green and orange armor, his muddy sash wrapped around him like a chain.

The flame of anger inside Chalco burned a little brighter.

First he blamed his imagination when he thought he heard a clanging of metal beyond the sound of the wind wheezing over the frozen earth. *You're being paranoid,* he told himself. His hands were shaking. "It's just the cold," he breathed. *Just stop thinking about the Iltherians, and it will go away.*

It didn't.

He elbowed Tyrann, who was already nodding off. "Do you hear that?" he whispered hoarsely.

"Do I hear what?" The giant blinked sleepily into the greyness of the thickly-falling snow.

"Footsteps. Boots, for sure. And armor."

Tyrann sat up like an owl listening for a mouse running under the snow. After a moment, his eyes popped open. "You're right," he said and jumped to his feet. "We must leave, now."

In a matter of seconds everyone was shaken awake. The panic in the air was so thick, Chalco could almost taste it. The last embers of the fire were doused with snow, Tyrann scooped Rooks up like a kitten and off they ran into the night.

"I can't see a thing," Ceycil squinted, brushing the snow out of his eyes.

"Hold onto someone, all of you," Kazan ordered, his voice muffled by the wind. "No matter what you do, do not get lost by yourself."

Roessa immediately grabbed a hold of her father's clothes with one hand, and Ceycil's arm with the other. Rooks was safe with Tyrann, and Chalco had a hand on the giant's belt. Versai followed them, looking disgusted, with Korinth's slender fingers wrapped around his sash.

They marched on as fast as they could in the knee-deep snow, but they were facing the wind, the going was slow, and the clanging heavy footsteps just got closer and closer.

"They're gaining on us," Versai shouted from the back, trying to catch up with Kazan's strides, Korinth following close behind him. The knight's mood had not improved one bit since the morning came. If anything, it was worse. "Cast a spell, do something!"

"So that they charge at us?" Kazan hissed. "If they are Iltherians, the smallest spark of mana would be the death of us all, so I suggest you shut your teeth and use your energy for running."

Versai opened his mouth to snap back, but he was interrupted by a voice that even the snowstorm couldn't cover up. "Halt!"

They all froze in their tracks. In the distance behind them, they could make out the faint glow of a couple of torches lighting up a blur of green and orange hues.

Kazan shook his head. "This is it folks," he breathed. "Here we fight, or you all become slaves for the empire. I die either way."

He didn't even wait for a response. Raising his hands into the air, the wizard gathered up a huge sphere of mana and let loose a stream of fire that burned through the snowstorm towards the Iltherians in attempt to overwhelm their swords.

A burst of light followed by screams and curses told them that the spell hadn't been wasted. Kazan caught the knights by surprise, not giving them a chance to kill his magical draw of mana with their swords. He knew it wouldn't happen again.

As soon as the Iltherians recovered from the impact of the spell, the voice boomed through the snow again. "CHARGE!"

Tyrann was the first one to react to it. "Slaves," he muttered, handing Rooks over to Roessa. "Not me, not you. Never again!" He drew his sword-axe and ran through the path that Kazan's spell melted towards the Iltherian troops.

*   *   *   *

The clash was quiet like the snowstorm, but equally deadly.

The voice that had ordered them to halt belonged to a young Iltherian soldier who led the troops. He was bearing two short swords instead of the regular long blade, cutting green lines through the snowstorm like flashes of lightning. Tyrann challenged him head on, his sword-axe sending sparks through the air every time it swung against the young knight's blades.

There were about a dozen of them, but many suffered bad burns from Kazan's stream of fire. It wasn't long before several of them fell.

Ceycil found strength in his father's sword, even though it was neither as light nor as swift as it was in his dream. It was the image of the young king with his crown in his hand that gave Ceycil the boost that he needed. Some time, somewhere his father held this sword. The father he dared to imagine had always been a farmer, a blacksmith, a stonemason- someone of physical strength, someone he could wrap his mind around. A frail-looking king that bore neither jewels nor silks that was beyond his reality. Still, something about the King felt very strong, stronger than any farmer or blacksmith Ceycil ever met. He fought on, parrying the knights' blows as fast as he could in the snow and using every drop of his strength to attack. He was hypnotized by the battle, not knowing who he was fighting or when his last opponent fell, his mind safely hidden in a hole in the snow where Roessa and Rooks were huddled without weapons.

Roessa watched the scene from her hiding spot, Rooks wrapped up tightly in her arms. Versai fought like a monster, something out of old story books that unleashed its wrath upon the mortals who dared to disturb its thousand-year sleep. He picked up a green sword off the hands of a charred corpse, and the bad mood the Iltherian built up since Sainaa's death exploded like a magic spell gone astray. His opponents did not just fall, they fell to pieces. More than once Roessa saw him stabbing again and again at a mangled mass in the snow that was long dead.

Once in a while an Iltherian would crumple onto the snow with a blood-curdling scream for no apparent reason. She watched in horror as another knight held his head with his gauntlets and shrieked. The Iltherian fell down on his face, and did not move again. Looking around hurriedly, Roessa caught sight of Korinth standing close to her with his eyes closed, a troubled expression on his ageless face. "Did you...?" She felt her blood freeze. The elf always seemed so gentle to her.

Korinth opened eyes and shook his head sadly. "Desperate times, desperate crimes..." he muttered.

She tried to shake off the shock, and forced herself to concentrate on the battle. She saw Chalco staring at his earthen-colored hands, shaking madly with the cold and the panic. He tried to shoot at the knights several times, but between the shaking and the wind blowing his hair in his face, his aim was off. She wished fervently that there was something she could do to help her companions instead of hiding away, but with her bow broken at the swamp, she had no weapon to fight with. *I feel useless*, she thought bitterly, and she pulled Rooks closer to herself.

Kazan, too, was starting to feel useless. It was a feeling he hated with a passion. His spells were powerless against the Iltherian swords, now that they knew they were facing a mana-user. Besides, he used up most of his energy with his initial fire spell. He couldn't even pick up a sword and fight like Versai, the blade would drain his mana instantly. Gritting his teeth in frustration, he used what little magical energy he had left to put a simple protection spell on Ceycil and to hide its magical residue from the Iltherians' senses. *Well son,* he thought grimly, *twenty years of my life to protect you and all I have for you is a shielding charm I learned in my first week of training.* The wizard sighed deeply. *I hope you have a guardian spirit, your highness.*

Feeling completely exhausted, Kazan backed away from the battle. "Save your bolts son," he told Chalco. "Go sit in the hole with Roessa and the child. If any of the knights come near, do yourself a favor and throw your fear to the wind. You will not need it in another world."

It turned out that Ceycil did have a guardian spirit after all. It was called Tyrann.

The giant already knocked down the young knight with the two swords, and dedicated the rest of his attention to attacking anyone that attempted to sneak up on Ceycil. He smashed through several breastplates with the axe side of his blade as if they were thin sheets of foil. He also slashed down a middle-aged Iltherian whose armor bore decorated markings of a rather high rank. When the last of the knights fell to his blows, the snow under his feet was more green and orange than white, and more red than anything else.

Tyrann wiped his sword-axe on a patch of dirty slush, and pulled a berserk Versai off the body of an Iltherian that bore one too many lethal slashes in it. "Stop it," said the giant, breathing heavily from exertion.

Versai took a blank look at the giant's face, and seemed to snap out of his madness. Dropping his sword, he threw himself down into the bloody snow. Tyrann wasn't sure if it was sweat or tears he saw on the renegade's face.

Wearily everyone gathered around a small sphere of light that glowed in Korinth's palm. In the cold darkness, faces were lined with terror and relief.

"Do you think there are others nearby?" Ceycil asked, oblivious of his blood oozing from several shallow cuts on his arms and freezing on his clothes.

"There will be soon, that was only a scouting unit." Kazan breathed. "The old man that Tyrann killed was a colonel, no less. They will look for him."

"Should we at least hide the bodies then?" Roessa suggested. "It might slow down their search a little bit."

The wizard shook his head. "No time. If we are lucky, the snow will do that for us. We must move on."

They left the battlefield in silence, shivering and full of dread.

8

William hobbled through the snow towards the nearest encampment, muttering curses under his breath. One of his short swords hung at his side, while the other he carried in his hand in case he came up against some hapless creature he could take his anger out of. His other hand was tucked under his green cape, dripping blood from a wound the giant delivered to him with his monstrous weapon.

Every snowflake that fell on his helmet echoed inside the young Iltherian's head like a battle drum. *The emperor wasn't joking when he said these helmets were indestructible,* he thought grimly, running the knuckles of his sword hand against a large dent in the side of the metal. *If it wasn't for the helmet, it would be my skull that with a large dent in it.* He grimaced and spat out a mouthful of blood.

The sheer intensity of the hatred he managed to build up for the giant during their brief battle was frightening. It was rather unlike him, really. William loved his enemies. He loved them, because only by killing each and every one of them, allowed him to rise up to his station in the Iltherian ranks. Nothing frustrated him more than an undefeated foe.

His eyes caught sight of his sash, bloody and torn. His number read 704. Emperor Bravenscu himself had chosen that number, after William had been reported to kill seventy Glarrindall soldiers in four battles, all fought on the same day. *Seventy Glarrindians,* he thought as his fury rose up again, *seventy trained soldiers and I couldn't get rid of one meathead.* No amount of slashing from his two blades had done any more damage than a few scratches on the giant's leathery skin. Trying to stab him was like trying to stick a pin into a dragon's back. Still, William wasn't one to give up so easily. *Everyone has a weak spot,* he thought. *Even a dragon.*

Then there was the so-called renegade. William heard that soldier 451 occasionally fought on the side of runaways, but he had always known better than doing any real damage to the Iltherian troops. Most of the time he was reported to put on a heroic act of standing back to protect the women and the children, and occasionally he would get conveniently knocked out by an Iltherian. *What's come over the emperor's little pet, I wonder?* William thought. *Maybe he's really turned a renegade after all.* Soldier 704 sneered. The fact was that he hated Versai. Enemies could be loved. Comrades that stood between him and his ambitions could not. Becoming the youngest officer in the Iltherian army hadn't been easy, and even raiding a village a day couldn't place William above 451 in the emperor's eyes. Versai was the tack in his boot on his way to glory. *It's time I took him out and crushed him to dust,* thought William. *Let's see what Bravenscu thinks of his favorite spy now.* He snickered to himself and marched on into the night.

*   *   *   *

Ceycil was wrapped tight in his cloak, but it wasn't enough to keep the wind out of his chest. They walked for several days, stopping only for a few hours when they could find shelter from the weather, and sometimes marching right through the night. He could barely keep his eyes open, though he couldn't tell whether it was from lack of sleep or from the specks of ice that kept blowing in his face. He had lost count of time long ago, walking in almost a trance, concentrating on nothing further than moving one foot ahead of the other.

A day or so after their battle with the Iltherian troops, they passed by the outskirts of a village. Kazan snuck his way in with an invisibility spell to procure some food and winter clothing. The village, not surprisingly, turned out to be just a couple of broken families that somehow survived the Iltherian raid, hiding in the ruins of their homes and hoping that the knights would not return. Stealing from runaways was not Kazan's style at all, so he decided to reveal himself, though not much of his story, and ask for help at the risk of leaving a trail for the empire to follow, should they ever come back and question the villagers. The people were willing to help fellow runaways, but offered little to share. All they could spare was a small sack of dried meat, a loaf of hard bread and a couple of ox-hide cloaks that were warm but uncomfortably heavy. It wasn't much, but it was better than nothing.

Next to his own, Ceycil could see Roessa's boots moving on with the same beat. Ignoring his rumbling stomach, he tried to keep his mind on matching her strides. He couldn't remember the last time they ate a full meal. With the winter setting in, game was scarce. If it weren't for Chalco's keen eyes and the hares that still roamed the snowy plains instead of curling up to sleep the winter away, they would have starved.

The first night after the battle, Korinth opened up his bark-bound book and told them another one of his rhyming tales around the campfire. He spoke of the elven cities of the past that were connected by a web of underground tunnels in the underworld of Thar'Nandria, built specifically for the winter when the wind and the cold did not yield passage for travelers. "The Earthen Path", it was called, extending from the southern peninsulas of Ghoremare to all the way up north, well into the lands of winter darkness. The Path, Korinth said, lay unused since the empire wiped out the elves twenty years ago. The Iltherians had not discovered it, since the entrances were carefully hidden. Unfortunately, many of the gates collapsed when the cities were destroyed, but a rare few remained. How Korinth knew all that, being stuck in a cave for what appeared to be years, was beyond anybody's guess. Still, they had no choice but to trust him. If the Earthen Path existed, it would be a faster way to get to the flying ship, and probably a warmer one, too. Ceycil shook his head. *We are riding on one legend,* he thought. *And heading towards another one...*

*   *   *   *

It was several more days before the storm dwindled to a gentle snowfall again, the small white flakes floating lightly in the windless air like dandelion fluff. It was, if anything, colder than before, but without the whipping wind the weather was a lot more bearable.

The landscape, too, changed from barren, white plains to small rocky hills covered with scattered clumps of short evergreen bushes. With the rocks came shelter, and with the bushes, more hares, and even the occasional deer that appeared without warning and disappeared just as fast before Chalco could even lift his crossbow. Still, it was enough to cheer everyone up a little bit. Everything looked a shade brighter after food and sleep, even a harsh, wintery world taken over by the Iltherians.

Versai was the only one that showed no signs of brightening up. He had not spoken a word since they fought the Iltherian troops. He ate and slept little, and when they stopped for rest he would stare into the campfire for hours on end. Ceycil tried to talk to him once or twice, but all the response he got was the crunching of the snow as the knight got up and walked away. Even when they marched, Versai always followed them several yards behind.

"How much longer do you think he'll be like this?" Roessa asked as they sat around the fire, staring at soldier 451 who was pacing back and forth in the distance.

"Who knows?" Ceycil shrugged. "He's certainly in a foul mood lately, though he was never really friendly to begin with." He bit into a piece of roasted rabbit, and almost spat it back out. It was very hot.

"There is something about that man that gives me the creeps," said Chalco, munching on a lump of stone-dry bread. "He's one of *them*, and I don't care if he's a renegade or not. I don't trust him."

Tyrann nodded gravely. "He's dangerous…" he muttered. "That look in his eyes, I've seen it before. It's the look of someone who has nothing to lose. Sometimes the Neranian slaves would look that way before they went into the mines for the day's work. They never came back out."

"What did they do?" Roessa frowned.

147

"You see, it's very easy to collapse a mine chamber if you know which part of the ceiling is holding all the earth above your head."

Roessa's eyes grew wide. "That's horrible!"

"Not if you bear only despair in your heart. If the only future you have is slaving yourself away to exhaustion day after day, with nobody and nowhere to return to even if you were to escape, sleeping in a dark cave for the rest of eternity doesn't seem like a bad alternative."

"But there's always hope," Roessa argued. "As long as there are people fighting, there's hope. You can't just... die like that."

The giant smiled, revealing his entire broken tusk. "You're young," he said gently. "And you have your people here. For you, there'll always be hope. For some, there was never any to begin with." His eyes wandered towards Versai, who was still pacing.

"I wonder who he was before he became an Iltherian?" Ceycil asked, attempting to bite his roasted rabbit for a second time.

"Probably a crook," Chalco replied. "I don't see a grain of humanity in him, with or without that ugly green armor. I don't think he could have loved his own mother if he tried."

"There you are wrong," said Tyrann gently, staring at the Iltherian in the distance. "Love he did. He loved the princess, and it's his love that's killing him now, not his hatred..."

Kazan was already busy packing away the leftover food and getting ready to move on. "Korinth, how far are we from the gates you spoke of?"

The elf was sitting cross-legged by the fire, scribbling something into his bark-bound book again, with

Rooks squinting over his shoulder. The vine that was tangled in his hair was glazed with ice, but the leaves were still surprisingly alive. He briefly looked up to meet the wizard's gaze. "Another day, another night," he said. "We are almost there, but not quite."

"And you are certain that we shall find an entrance to the Path that is still open?"

One side of the elf's lips curled into a half smile. "Have no fear, an Earthen Gate is near. And though it won't be open, nor shall it be broken."

Kazan stood up with mild irritation. "Forget what I said. Let me put it this way: Do you know the way into these bloody passages or not?"

Korinth nodded in response.

"Very well, then. Let us be off."

*   *   *   *

The Emperor Bravenscu, unlike many other monarchs he knew and invariably defeated, did not have a taste for leisure and luxury. He wore neither silks nor jewels, and he preferred to see gold in the purses of his mercenaries rather than on his crown. "With a crown you can rule a kingdom of willing peasants," he often said, "but you need more than a piece of metal to rule an empire." William had always found this statement very ironic, since the power of the Iltherian Empire lay almost entirely in verdium, the green anti-magic alloy that the emperor himself crafted. Without their swords of verdium, the Iltherian knights were nothing more than a well-trained army.

As he walked up the endless spiral of stairs that led to the throne room, William ran his story over and over in his head: The runaways, the wizard, the renegade, the colonel killed. He grinned to himself. *That's the end of you, Versai,* he thought. *No more renegade games for spy 451.* He stopped at the top of the staircase, and knocked on the trapdoor above his head leading to the throne room where his presence was expected.

The emperor took great pleasure in watching his knights at work. His eagle-like eyes scanned the snow-covered landscape from his throne, which was placed on the roof of his palace tower. An invisible ceiling of magical energy domed over the throne room, shielding it from the harsh winter weather. Iltheria was his city, the capital of his empire and the headquarters of the Iltherian army. He watched as his soldiers, visible only as green and orange specks from this height, moved around constantly like ants in a busy nest. Many of them were followed by the brown specks that were his slaves, some small and some much larger than the knights themselves, moving with significantly less energy, but moving nevertheless. Bravenscu smiled, revealing his teeth that were a murky shade of yellow but surprisingly straight. Work meant progress, and with progress came more power.

His smile grew even wider as William entered the throne room. The emperor liked soldier 704, not only because he was a fearless knight in battle but also because he was one of the few people that could stand in the emperor's presence without turning into a fumbling jitterbug.

"I hear you have news for me." Bravenscu ran his pale fingers along the grooves of his metal throne. His voice was raspy and heavy, like sandpaper rubbing on a brick.

"Yes sir." Soldier 704 learned long ago that 'Your Majesty' was not an option to address the emperor. Bravenscu had no more use for flattery than he had for silks and jewels. William tried to meet his monarch's gaze, but even for him it was tough. The emperor's eyes were so small, they could have gotten lost on his pale wide face if they weren't dark like tar pits.

Trying hard not to look away, soldier 704 gave a brief report of his troops' encounter with a group of runaways as the emperor listened with a face devoid of any expression.

"The colonel is dead," Bravenscu muttered to himself. "I hate losing soldiers of high rank. Officer material is hard to come by, and even harder to train."

"Yes sir." William nodded. "451 killed him, I saw it myself." *So easy to lie when there are no other witnesses left alive.*

"Interesting…" The raspy voice betrayed no hint of anger or concern.

"Should I assemble a squad to seek them out, sir?"

The emperor stared at William. "No."

"Sir, the wizard is quite powerful. He might give us trouble again. The Neranian giant is very strong, too." Just thinking about the giant made William's blood boil with fury, but he tried to suppress it in the emperor's presence. "We could use him in the mines here." *Where I'm sure I can find a way of getting him conveniently killed,* he added mentally.

"I don't want you chasing after them," said Emperor Bravenscu. "You are a valuable soldier; I need you for other missions." He paused. "I have thousands of knights in this land; the runaways will be taken care of."

William gritted his teeth. "What about the traitor?"

"451 will take care of himself. Traitors tend to betray more than once, and often they betray themselves at the end."

As the bitter winter sun was setting over the throne room, William was dismissed from the emperor's presence without further orders. *I provide such valuable news, and what do I get in return? Not even the permission for revenge.* He was furious, knowing that Versai and the others were now outside of his reach. Without formal orders from the emperor, he couldn't go after them. He stormed out of the palace tower in a rage and headed towards the barracks, stopping only to punch a jagged dent into a dead tree with his gauntlets.

*   *   *   *

Miles away, the same bitter sun set over rocks glazed with thick ice that formed frozen waterfalls on the edges. There was little if anything left in the landscape that indicated a city may have once stood there not long ago. There were no buildings left standing, no walls or sheds or wells. Even the trees and bushes that always adorned elven towns were gone. There was no sign of life. Only the rocks were a bit too shapely, hinting that they may once have been part of something else.

Korinth gazed at the rocks and let out a sigh. "The town of Shehriyar. Though now it is dead, here we are." Walking up to a seemingly ordinary pile of brick-like rocks, he kicked at the ice that covered one side of it. The snow gave way easily, revealing a hole barely large enough for Rooks to crawl through. The elf crouched down and started digging away at it with his hands.

"It's the entrance!" Ceycil exclaimed. "You found it!"

"That it is not, I'm afraid." Korinth grunted as he kept enlarging the hole, with Rooks and Roessa helping him on both sides. "It's just a place where tonight we rest and wait. In the morning, I'll wake the Earthen Gate."

Ceycil joined them with digging. A few minutes later, the passage was wide enough even for Tyrann to get through on his hands and knees. It led into a shallow cave that was barely enough space to hold them all. The earthen walls were decorated with intricate carvings, depicting a small tree with huge roots that were entangled like a spider's web, with odd symbols scattered among them.

Versai took one look around the place, and walked back out. "I've had enough of caves," he muttered. "I'll sleep outside."

"Suit yourself," Kazan grumbled in response, and proceeded to build a fire.

The meal was eaten in silence. Since it was still relatively early, Chalco offered to go hunting. They would need the extra food if they were to be traveling underground for the next few weeks. Tyrann went with him, finding the cave too cramped for his taste. Rooks busied himself studying the picture on the walls, and Korinth started to scribble into his book again.

At length, Kazan pulled out his blanket and laid down. "I am going to rest for a while," he said looking up to Ceycil and Roessa. "Do not do anything silly."

Roessa shook her head and smiled. "Father, we're not children anymore."

"My point precisely," Kazan grunted and rolled over.

*   *   *   *

Roessa sighed, staring at the dying fire from her makeshift bedroll. Tyrann and Chalco returned from their hunt hours and were asleep next to Rooks. Two fat hares and a large, odd-looking bird were lying in a cooler corner of the cave, ready to be cooked the next day. Korinth was the only one awake, if he could be called that, sitting with his back against the carving on the wall, his eyes closed, in some sort of trance. Roessa sighed again, distinctly aware of Ceycil's arm resting on her shoulder as he slept beside her.

"Let's go for a walk." The voice was Ceycil's; in the same tone he used to have as a child when he got excited about something.

"What?" Roessa turned around to face him.

To her surprise, he was wide awake. "I can't sleep, either. Let's go for a walk."

Roessa frowned. "It's cold out there."

"And it's boring in here. Let's go." Ceycil threw his cloak over his shoulders and sprang to his feet, pulling Roessa up by her hand.

Suppressing a giggle, she shook her head and got up, and followed Ceycil from the cave into the weak light of a winter dawn.

As they left, Korinth smiled in his trance, and his lips began to move.

"Should stars and moon and sun align, in harmony it is a sign.

And all the world should come aright, love is living here tonight.

In errant haste this word I send, to those who threat of break and bend.

A moment's kiss, a soft embrace, love upon a kindred face…"

Though his words were soft, no more than the wind breathing outside the cave, someone had heard him. Rooks blinked into the little red flames and the glowing embers and yawned quietly. In the distance, he thought he heard Roessa laugh.

"I'm still cold," Roessa complained as they sat huddled in the mouth of another cave like theirs, watching the sun rise over the frozen ruins. This cave was obviously been someone's home once. There were remnants of wooden furniture around, and dry branches woven like a giant basket made up the roof.

Ceycil wrapped one flap of his cloak over Roessa and pulled her closer. "Still cold?"

Roessa laughed. Ceycil pulled her even closer, pressing her body against his. "Still cold?"

She laughed again. "Yes," she lied, and wrapped her arms around him as a bright burning warmth spread inside her like the breaking day.

The elf's voice buzzed inside the earthen cave like the beating of a hummingbird's wings.

"Though now you may be far or near, to wish the same 'twixt two, my dear,

Is like the work of only one, and shows such love is rare begun."

Korinth's mind briefly touched something young, warm and glowing in the distance; it was two souls in tune to the same silent music. Then he came upon another mind, like a sad violet hue in the grey winter sky. The image of Versai appeared in the elf's closed eyes, as the Iltherian sat quietly with his eyes upon the horizon.

The elf paused for a moment, and then went on.

"And from it sadness though may spring, a hearty tug on one's heartstring,

Long on this thought sit you dwell, the call to love you know so well."

The elf paused again and frowned. Versai, with a blank expression on his face, walked away towards the rising sun.

"And should such flaming feel return to scorch with passion, let it burn.

Hold it tight, don't let it go, and wish it something all should know."

Rooks smiled, hoping to hear more, but the elf fall back into his silent trance. He made a mental note of asking Korinth about the poem in the morning. As he drifted off to sleep, he thought he saw a bird with wings of flames staring at him from the fire… or was it Serje? He slept soundly, dreaming of his days with the eccentric Birdman. When he woke up again, Korinth was gone.

9

Chalco's day started with Kazan's roaring. He had witnessed the wizard's temper many times over their travels, but this was something else. The old man seemed to be out of his mind. He crawled out of the cave to find Tyrann trying to quiet the raging wizard, who looked like he was about to spontaneously combust.

"Will you please keep calm?" The giant, trying to lay a scarred hand on Kazan's shoulder, felt a slap as the wizard brushed it off brusquely, "I'm sure half the empire can hear you right now!" Tyrann cupped his hands over his ears and shook his head.

"What do I care if the bloody emperor himself hears me?" Kazan raged on, raising his voice even more. "Where are Ceycil and Roessa? Where is the blasted elf? Where is the god-damned bloody son of a dog Iltherian?" He threw his hands in the air and glared at the giant. "Where are they?!"

Tyrann shrugged. "I don't know. They were asleep when we got back last night."

"BLOODY WELL YOU DO NOT KNOW!" The wizard thundered, and turned towards the snow-covered ruins again. "ROESSA!" He called into the vast emptiness. "CEYCIL!"

Rooks' red head appeared at the mouth of the cave. "They went out," he said, trying to rub the sleep out of his eyes. "I heard them early this morning." It was snowing again, with heavy flakes deepening the whiteness by the minute. There were vague depressions in the snow over the ground that resembled footprints, but they were well-covered by now and hard to follow. "I found this inside," Rooks added, handing Kazan something that looked oddly out of place in the grey winter morning. It was a leaf, still green but just starting to turn a bright coppery orange on the edges. "It looks like the vine that grew in Korinth's hair."

The wizard picked up the leaf. One side of it was covered in a fine feathery script:

Autumn's last hues I must trace

We shall meet before Adelphia's grace

"I think Versai has left, and I think Korinth has gone to find him," Rooks commented.

Kazan raised his eyebrows. "You can read this?" His surprise momentarily overridden his fury. Nobody except scholars and wizards bothered to learn script. Even Ceycil, being under Kazan's training for years, couldn't read anything more complicated than a road sign.

The red-haired child shrugged.

The old wizard shook his head remembering Serje's teachings to Rooks. Though he spent years with Serje, he realized he knew very little about the Birdman's little student. "Fine," he said bitterly, to no one in particular. "That is two accounted for, leaving two more. What has become of the young fools, then?"

"Look!" Chalco pointed through the blowing flurry at two spots moving towards them from a distance. It wouldn't take a psion to know that they were Ceycil and Roessa.

Kazan let out an audible sigh. "Thank the ley lines if they ever exist again," he muttered. "I really thought I lost them this time…"

As soon as they were within yelling distance, the old wizard picked up where he left off. "If you two ever wander away like that again, I swear by my fire that I will chain you to myself! Have I taught you nothing over the past twenty years? All that time I have been trying to protect you from…"

As Kazan went on and on, Roessa's face was turning from rosy pink to tomato red, though it was hard to tell whether it was from anger or just sheer embarrassment. Ceycil decided, instead, to study the details of the road wear on the tips of his boots. Compared to Kazan's speech, they were fascinating. At one point he dared to look up briefly and speak, but the wizard would have none of it.

"Dare you not give me that look, your majesty! This was your idea, was it not? Even your father possessed better common sense at your age, and let me tell you, he was a handful!" He paused and stared at Ceycil.

Ceycil stared back with wide eyes. It was the very first time he had heard Kazan mention his father in such a manner.

It was that pause which put out the wizard's fire. "Sometimes I am glad I only have to deal with one Lynnvander at a time…" He sighed and shook his head. "Let us go inside, rabbit for breakfast."

*   *   *   *

Spirits were down despite the hearty breakfast. Korinth's disappearance left them with a fundamental problem: They had no idea where the Earthen Gate was, nor did they know how to open it if they were to find it.

"Why leave now?" Chalco muttered as he licked rabbit grease off his fingers. "The creep can go wherever he likes for all I care, but why leave us here in the middle of nowhere? And I didn't think Korinth would be the type to abandon us." He sounded rather disappointed, and more nervous than he seemed in days.

Kazan stared at the leaf in his hand. "I did not think he would, either," he said gravely. "Alas, I may be proven wrong…"

Rooks was the next to speak up. "What does it say behind the leaf?"

"Behind?" The wizard frowned and turned the frozen leaf over. The back of it was covered in a spidery script, a language alien to many people. His rugged face lightened up visibly at the sight of it. "It seems you were right son," he said to Chalco with the hint of a smile. "Our friend the elf did not abandon us after all."

He threw the leaf into the dying fire and got up. Walking up to the carving on the wall, the old man started running his fingers along the tangled pattern. His hand came to rest upon one of the symbols, a heart-shaped leaf, and he grinned broadly. He gently knocked on the symbol three times. "Wake up, you old fool," he mumbled under his breath. "Wake up in the name of Gaia and all her fair children." The walls of the cave began to buzz softly like a beehive. The wizard went on. "Wake up in the name of your loving kin, the Elven." The spot on the wall where his hand lay started to crack in all directions. "Wake up in the name of peace, and let us be welcome in."

As these last words were spoken, the crack in the wall spread open like a yawning mouth, revealing a narrow stone stairway leading deep into the earth. Kazan nodded in satisfaction. "Elves," he said, "are true artists when it comes to magic. All night I have been lying next to this bloody thing and I never even knew it was there!" Without looking back, he disappeared down the stairs.

"If he didn't know it was there, then the empire certainly won't. Let's go." Tyrann led the rest of them into the tunnel after Kazan.

The stairs didn't go down very far, and soon they found themselves in a large cavern that was lit by two blue spheres of light on each side of the ceiling. The walls were covered with the same kind of carvings as the cave above; depicting what seemed to be the exact same tree with the entangled roots.

As soon as the last person stepped off the staircase, they heard the Earthen Gate close behind them. Chalco shuddered. "We're trapped!" he squeaked.

Kazan shook his head. "Son, if there is one thing to be trusted in this treacherous world, it is elven magic. The elves are born of mana, even more than the bloodlines. If there was a way in, there shall be a way out."

The tunnel continued from the far end of the cavern, its entrance lit by the same cold blue light of a magical sphere suspended from above. "Shall we move on then?" Ceycil suggested, walking towards the Path extending further into the earth.

"Wait," Roessa held his arm. "Do we know where we're going?" She turned towards her father. "Has Korinth left any directions? What do we do if the tunnel comes to a fork?"

Kazan frowned. "Well thought, Roessa. I have no idea. All Korinth's message described was how to open the Earthen Gate. Nothing about how to get to the flying ship." He shook his head in frustration. "There has to be a…" His pale blue eyes settled on Rooks, who was tracing the carvings on the wall with his finger, starting from the heart-shaped leaf symbol that opened the gate as he was moving up the roots. The wizard slapped his forehead. "…a map! Talk about hiding things in plain sight!" He shuffled over to where Rooks was standing, following the child's hand moving up the wall. There was a line leading up from the leaf, which branched into two distinct paths. One path connected to a symbol of three ovals lined up in a row, leading up another short line to a star. The second one, in turn, connected to a wavy spiral, which showed another line going further and further up, stopping at a symbol right underneath the tree itself.

"It looks like a fish on a cloud," Rooks wrinkled his nose and giggled.

The wizard snapped his fingers. "That is the Adelphia!"

Ceycil, behind him, squinted at the wall. "Are you sure? Looks like a fish on a cloud to me, too."

Now it was Kazan's turn to squint. "Well, your majesty, how do you think you could get a fish upon a cloud?"

Ceycil shrugged. "By magic?"

"Precisely. That is where the last ley line, the last source of mana has to be."

"Wait, that doesn't make sense!" Ceycil protested, looking around for some support from his companions, but nobody was in the mood to cross the wizard after his earlier explosion.

To his surprise, Kazan laughed. "No, it truly does not. It is elven logic. If you look for sense in it, we shall be here all winter. Now, for once, stop questioning my decisions and perhaps I will forgive you for courting my daughter."

"Courting? Now I never..." Ceycil protested nervously.

Kazan flung a searing glance at Ceycil, which made the young man's tongue freeze in his mouth like the icy tundra above.

"See this patch over my brow?" The wizard ran brushed his hand across the thinning white hair above his forehead. "That right there is the price of my wisdom, son. Do not try to disguise yourself to me, for it will not work. I cleaned your bottom when you were three. I know more about you than you know yourself."

Rooks laughed at the word 'bottom', which caused everyone to turn and look at the boy, all momentarily distracted from the awkward conversation.

"Does it say how long we will travel below ground?" Tyrann broke in, bringing business back to order.

"No," replied Kazan. "But judging the distance Korinth mentioned in our travels, I would say more than a week."

"Down here?" cried Chalco, staring into the endless darkness.

"Better than the weather and the chance of death," Roessa reasoned.

Chalco ignored her, "I bet this place is crawling with monsters since the elves have been gone."

Tyrann smirked and wrapped his ham-like fists over Chalco to secure him. "Good," he snorted. "I was starting to get sick of eating rabbit."

*   *   *   *

Korinth followed Versai silently through miles and miles of wintery landscape. He didn't even bother to hide himself, for the Iltherian was too lost in thought to pay any attention to anyone or anything. Thus the elf followed the line of thoughts instead of the disappearing footsteps in the snow, keeping close to soldier 451 and the red hot hatred he was trying to mold into something sharp and pointy, like a sword on a blacksmith's anvil.

When Versai walked into the city of Iltheria, the elf put up his first defense. He hid his mind so that even though he was not invisible, his existence seemed too unimportant to acknowledge for any eyes that were cast upon him. He simply became part of the scenery, no more noticeable than a cactus would be in a desert. He knew that it would not be enough protection if he were to run into someone with a particularly strong intuition, but it was good enough to keep the Iltherian knights away, as their connection with the anti-magic swords weakened any mana flow through their souls significantly. Elves knew very well that it was the soul that lived and felt things and called them right or wrong. The mind alone could not perceive such things, it was just a machine that thought and processed.

The frozen streets were full of slaves carrying loads of building stones, coals and iron ore without the slightest trace of vitality in their eyes. Once in a while one of them would look at Korinth and really see him for what he was, but the elf wordlessly silenced them all, and none of them bothered to disobey. Versai himself got plenty of greetings from his fellow knights along the way, some hearty and some obscene, but offered no more than a grunt for a reply. He headed straight for the palace tower, his eyes shifting occasionally towards the only remaining tree in Iltheria. It was a great oak tree on the edge of the city. The Tree of Examples displayed numerous thick branches, and seemed to bear skeletons for fruit. Ravens and vultures circled above it continuously, feeding upon the carcasses of those that had been foolish enough to disappoint the emperor.

Korinth followed 451 up the winding staircase, and doubled his psionic shield, even though it wasn't really necessary. Bravenscu with no more soul than a pile of dry bones, and even though he was an excellent strategist, he would see right through the elf unless Korinth hit him in the face.

A young knight was just finishing reporting to the emperor when Versai was admitted into the throne room. His light brown hair that was ruffled with sweat, and his sash that identified him as soldier 369 was dirty and torn. Korinth sensed that the harried look on the knight's face was not just from being in the emperor's presence; his eyes were much too old for his youthful form.

369 watched as Versai walked towards the throne, completely interrupting his report. Then his eyes settled on Korinth.

"Keep your silence, let me hide. You know you are on my side." The elf nodded at the young knight, whose sole response came as a blink.

"Versai," Bravenscu made a gesture that was perhaps supposed to be welcoming, except everybody knew that the emperor never truly welcomed anyone. He merely tolerated them. "Where have you been for so long? I grew weary of listening to all the rumors spun around you. Every new batch of slaves comes with its own collection of tales of the renegade knight that has helped them in such and such battle." Bravenscu rubbed his wrinkled hands together, each the size of a spade and probably just as sturdy despite the emperor's advanced age. "Getting the tales out of them takes considerable... effort on our part, of course, but you know they always talk in the end. And it never ceases to entertain me how they fail to notice the pattern; whoever encounters the renegade loses the fight in the end. Simple minds, those of peasants." He shook his bald head. "They are so desperate for a hero that anyone who matches the profile becomes pure as an angel in their eyes. They would not disbelieve in you if they saw you slaying a child." He smiled slowly, revealing his yellow teeth. "But enough of my simple amusements, now I want to hear what news you have gathered for me."

Versai hesitated for a moment, but no longer. It was too late for internal battles now. He told the emperor almost everything, the chase and capture of the last of the Khenbish people, the group of runaways with the wizard and the young man who was the king of Tallinad, the battle against the black fighters of the Diamond Sage, the Neranian giant, the elf at the bottom of the waterfall, and the myth of the flying ship buried in Mount Pareth in the north... He didn't talk about the battle in the snow against the Iltherian troops, as he was certain that there were no survivors. The emperor wouldn't need to know about that until later. Nor did he mention Sainaa at any point in his story.

Bravenscu listened to 451 without interruption, his face betraying no sign of surprise or interest.

Once Versai was finished, the tyrant held up his hand. "Soldier 369 here has already reported to me about the end of the Khenbish," he said casually. "Their princess still seems to be missing, though. A rather displeasing detail."

"She's dead." Versai nodded.

"Is she now?" Bravenscu raised an eyebrow.

"Yes." Versai looked directly into the emperor's eyes. "I killed her." He took a deep breath. "I ran into her near the Talian encampment, she must have been trying to save her companions. I finished her off." The lie was a bitter one, even for Versai who was no stranger to turning dark truths into twisted tales. Still, at least the emperor would not be chasing Sainaa if her bloodline ever brought her back to this world again. It was a very small hope, but it was all the Iltherian contained. *Not that I'm likely to be around to meet her again,* he thought ruefully. For a brief moment, Versai wished that he was on the other side of the battle, on the side of the people that fought for their land and the land that fought with them to keep them alive. If he were part of a bloodline, he could be reborn some day, get another chance at this thing called life. Instead he was on the other side. The winning side. *And what exactly have I won?* He kept his gaze fixed on the emperor's pale blue eyes. Then he sighed quietly, it was too late. Far too late.

Bravenscu nodded slowly. "Good," he said. "One less worthless nation to worry about then." He paused for a moment, as if trying to remember something. "A flying ship, you mentioned… and a boy who claims to be the king of Tallinad? Interesting… very interesting." He paused again, watching 451's expression carefully. Then his casual tone took on a hint of menace. "Then tell me, Versai, what of my westward scout troops and the colonel that led them?"

Versai felt his heart sink even deeper as a wave of terror washed over him. *How is this possible? There were no survivors… or were there?* The emperor's expression was impenetrable. *He knows,* thought Versai. *He knows and whatever I say, truth or lie, will be the end of me.* He looked around the throne room that was lit up with the dull winter sun shining on tiles, swords and armor. The emperor's guards were lined up along the edges of the open room, the biggest and strongest men of the Iltherian army. The young knight that had just been reporting when he came in stood against one of the brass columns, the columns that looked like they were built to support an invisible ceiling. 451 shook his head mutely. He didn't stand a chance, neither in denial nor in fighting. Not that he had any will left to do either of those.

He turned his eyes back towards the emperor, and reached for his sword, the one he stole from another knight in that same battle against the westward troops. As soon as his fingers touched the metal, he found himself surrounded by dozens of sword tips, all green and deadly.

"Seize him!" Bravenscu ordered to his guards without even raising his voice.

"Don't bother." Versai drew his sword and threw it on the floor. It landed by the throne in a loud, mocking clank. "I know the way to the Tree, I can go by myself."

*   *   *   *

Kristoff sported a burning desire to rip off his sash and crush it into the icy soil with the heel of his boot. Maybe that way he could tear himself away from the identity that was forced upon him, and soldier 369 would disappear forever, leaving only a human with a heart and a name. He stared blankly at Versai hanging from the morbid oak tree by his wrists, his body mutilated beyond recognition. The Iltherian made no sound when the guards were torturing him. Versai, 451, the renowned spy, the only knight the emperor ever called by his name... he gave up completely.

Somewhere behind him Kristoff could feel the presence of the elf, even though he had not seen him walking to the tree with the palace guards. He found the sensation strangely soothing despite the horror that overwhelmed his very essence.

Korinth reached out with his thoughts to touch what remained of the mind of Versai, who was barely alive and wishing intensely that he wasn't. Mostly, he was numb with pain and stagnant remorse, but the elf sensed a thread of alertness somewhere in the mess that remained of Versai.

Versai remained motionless, his dripping blood melting a pool in the ice below him, and then a single weak line of thought echoed inside Korinth's mind. *You were here the whole time, then. Why didn't you save me?*

Burned by love and froze by hate, Korinth thought, shaking his head. *For your soul, it was too late. You drew your path, and I can't change your fate.*

The elf waited for an answer, a final snappy comment from the ruthless traitor who betrayed the trust of countless innocent people.

It never came.

The single thread of awareness he was holding onto, along with all the murky consciousness that was Versai's mind, broke away from the elf's mental grip and slipped away into oblivion.

THOMAS M. GOFTON   -   HANDE BARUTÇUOĞLU

Kazan led the way through the serpentine passages of the Earthen Path, lighting the way with a small, tame bundle of flames that danced in the palm of his hand. Ceycil had wanted to take one of the blue spheres of light they saw at the entrance of the Path, but the wizard had stopped him. "Elves only put things where they belong, son," he said.

They walked in single file through the tunnels of frozen soil, which were chilly to the body but somehow soothing on the mind. Even Chalco, marching behind Ceycil and Roessa, couldn't see anything scary in the phantom shadows cast on the walls by the wizard's flickering flame. Tyrann brought up the rear, humming a merry tune and chatting with Rooks sitting on his shoulders. Short legs and little steps would only slow down their progression, and both the giant and Chalco were enjoying the child's company. *He makes me feel young,* thought Chalco, letting a brief smile form on his cold-chapped lips. *There's something I haven't felt for a long time.* His mind wandered away to his family across the ocean and the memories came flooding back, of a life that felt like anything but his own now. In this dark maze of slumbering earth, walking alongside this motley crew of strangers that had somehow become his people, Chalco did not at all feel like the man he once was, for better or for worse.

They had lost count of time long ago, as there was no indication of whether it was day or night. Kazan insisted on not stopping, and they ate their meals on foot. Chalco frowned and grumbled as he chewed on his meager ration of nearly-frozen rabbit meat, but agreed with the wizard who pointed out that their resources were limited. "We do not know how long these tunnels are, nor when we shall find another exit to the surface," Kazan told him, not unkindly. "Unless you can live on rocks, I suggest you stop complaining."

"Father, could we at least break for rest?" Roessa asked, dragging her weary feet and throwing an envious glance at Rooks who was snoring gently up on Tyrann's shoulders. "It must have been two days since we last slept." She paused, looking at her father who didn't slow down his pace. "You don't think we are being followed, do you?" she asked hesitantly.

"No," Kazan sighed. "Not followed, that I am sure of. What worries me is that grumpy mule of a renegade. He left without a word and he was not in the best of moods to begin with. I dare not think where he might have gone, or to whom." He turned around to look at Roessa and Ceycil. "He knows where we are heading. It is best to get there as fast as possible."

Chalco shuddered. "You think he betrayed us?" That same dreadful thought harangued him since Versai had disappeared, but hearing it from Kazan made it even worse.

Now betrayal was no longer just a figment of his paranoid imagination, but a very real possibility.

"I can feel it. I know he did." Ceycil piped in wiping his eyes clear of dust. "With Sainaa gone, what else did he have to live for?"

"He was a renegade though, wasn't he?" Roessa broke in, her voice full of hope. "All those tales we heard during our travels, the renegades that helped runaways hide from the Iltherian soldiers... He was one of those, wasn't he? Surely he can't just go back to the empire, I mean, the Iltherians must know by now that he's a renegade. Right?"

Chalco wanted to believe Roessa, but found it difficult. He was depressed that Roessa had a hard time believing in her own words as well.

Tyrann put a giant hand on the girl's shoulder. "I wish I could agree with you, but I'm afraid young Ceycil may be right. I don't think the Iltherian cared much about us; it was the princess that mattered to him. With her gone, I would not be surprised if he decides to put his loyalty elsewhere."

"Maybe Korinth went to stop him?" Chalco asked, trying hard to shake off the bitterness that was gathering around the companions like dark storm clouds.

"Or maybe he tried..." Ceycil met Chalco's eyes with worry.

"Nonsense," Kazan snapped. "Korinth is with Versai, this I am certain of." He paused briefly. "I feel our friend the renegade is about to meet his demise, this I am also certain of. Still, we must move on. Versai knows too much, both about us and our plans. If his words were to reach the wrong ears, it would not be long before we are discovered. The knights have horses and other, quicker methods of travel. Resting is a risk I cannot gamble on."

Roessa nodded in silence, as Ceycil tried to suppress a yawn. In the light of the wizard's magical flame, Chalco could see that they both showed dark circles under their eyes. As for himself, he was practically asleep on his feet, walking only by the same instinct that kept him alive for so long. He noted that Tyrann alone was wide awake, with the red-haired child slumped asleep against his balding scarred head. "Just a little longer," Chalco heard the wizard whisper ahead of him. "The tunnel should soon come to a fork; we will stop and sleep there for a bit. I promise."

*   *   *   *

I need to get away from here, Kristoff thought in the surge of quiet panic that was slowly rising inside him. Soldier 369 was no stranger to the atrocities of the Iltherians that he lived amongst for so long, but until now he thought he knew the rules of the game. Play by them, and you could at least survive. Now he knew that there was no safety in obedience, not even in power.

He felt his fingers curl into a tight fist. Kristoff always believed that only a moment of supreme courage could drive him out and away from this life, but now it was sheer desperation that fueled him. He glanced at the elf briefly, careful not to give away his presence. *The emperor expects me back tomorrow,* he thought. *I delivered him Yakutska's letter. I'm supposed to go back to receive his answer. It'll be suspicious if I don't. After that I want out. Out of this city. Out of this life and this number that I bear. Out of this armor and away from this cursed sword.*

Korinth's answer was gentle, but firm. *If you truly intend to leave all this behind, help you shall need and help you shall find. At the towered palace all you'll receive is death, for in Talia a*

174

man of mana from your grasp has fled. I give you no choice but to trust me on my word, tonight we must flee before the skies are blurred.

Kristoff remained silent, his eyes fixed upon Versai's lifeless body. *We will need horses,* he replied finally. *And there's someone I need to see. I will meet you at moonrise by the slave mine near the northern gate.* Without waiting for an answer, the young knight walked away from the Tree into the city of Iltheria, the heart of the empire that he hated even more than he hated himself.

Korinth waited until Kristoff nearly disappeared into the distance. Then he shook his head grimly and followed the knight into the city. Even the brave needed supervision sometimes.

*   *   *   *

"Lovely." Roessa blinked sleepily. "This is just what we needed." She tried unsuccessfully to suppress a yawn. The fork in the tunnel indeed was close, and marked clearly in elven fashion: one path with a star, and the other with the three ovals. It was perfect. Except half the ceiling caved in long ago, blocking the star-marked path with earth frozen so solid that it was impossible to even make a scratch in it.

"Hmm…" Kazan frowned heartily. "I need to think about this."

Ceycil leaned gently against Roessa's shoulder. "Can we sleep while you think? Please?"

The wizard shook his head. "No, not here. If the ceiling is weak enough to collapse once, it may very well happen again. Let us move on, just a bit longer."

Ceycil opened his mouth to protest, but the only thing that came out was another yawn. "The less you argue, the sooner we get to sleep," he heard Tyrann say. His yawn blending into a sigh, Ceycil slung his backpack onto his shoulder again.

When they stopped again, not much later, it was in a cavern that was so dark that it was impossible to see where the tunnel continued. Kazan made his portable fire brighter, illuminating their surroundings. The cavern was vast and circular, with evenly-sized rocks lined up around the edges.

"Wow!" Ceycil looked up at the ceiling, but saw nothing except darkness. "Are we outside? I don't feel a breeze or anything."

Kazan shook his head. "No. I think we are underneath a hill. The ceiling is just too high to see."

"That means it won't collapse on us." Roessa was already spreading her bedroll on the ground. "That means I'm going to sleep. If anyone has objections, I'm afraid you'll just have to carry me."

Kazan's lips curled into a rare smile. "You are truly your mother's girl sometimes." Without another word, he started setting up camp.

*   *   *   *

Once Kristoff reached the busy streets again, he made a deliberate point of making himself visible to some of the knights he knew, either from the barracks or from previous expeditions. It would look a lot less suspicious if he were seen around the city, a lot less likely to point the clues towards a planned escape once the emperor realized that he was gone. After saluting some ex-comrades with his best army smile that he had learned to wear like a shirt, Kristoff wandered back towards the outskirts of the city, this time towards the ruins. Iltheria was built upon the remains of Tallinad, the main stronghold of the Lynnvander bloodline.

Bravenscu's assault had wiped out all the life, music and mana that dwelled in the central lands, and all that was left of Tallinad was three half-collapsed towers of stone and the Tree of Examples, a monument of morbid irony standing tall and rancid over the slave mines and barren streets of the replacing name Iltheria.

Kristoff paced around the ruined towers, his eyes searching for something that wasn't there. "Renzo!" he whispered almost inaudibly as he glanced around the slabs of stone covered in ice and patches of dead moss. "Renzo, there's no time to play games. I have news. Where are you?"

"Right here," said a crisp voice behind Kristoff, making him jump and turn around.

The young knight let out a sigh of relief at the sight of the familiar figure. "You need to stop doing that," he said to the tall, slender man standing before him. He was dressed in plain black, though his tunic was made from a fine shiny silk and the thin chain that held his monocle was clearly made of gold.

Renzo ran his hands over his sleek black hair and blinked very deliberately, ignoring Kristoff's remark about his sudden appearance. "And the news is..?"

Kristoff took a deep breath. "The emperor's head spy reported today… when I was at the palace to deliver a letter," he explained hesitantly. "He spoke of a flying ship hidden up north in the ice plains. Rumored to be the last major source of mana left in the world."

"Really?" Renzo blinked again, sounding perfectly nonchalant, though his eyes betrayed his interest.

The knight nodded, shooting nervous glances at the shadows among the ruins. "You know the empire will be after it." He bit his lip. "You might want to find it before they do. It may not make you stronger than they are, but it will certainly help. Besides, it will be one less weapon on their side."

Renzo nodded back in approval. "I appreciate the tidings," he said gravely. When Kristoff turned to leave in obvious haste, the black-clad man cocked his head with genuine curiosity. "You're running away, aren't you?"

"That's the simplest way of putting it, yes," Kristoff replied without looking back. "Now if you'll excuse me, I have a life of shame to redeem."

"I'm sure the spirits will be happy to do that for you," said a voice like a box of nails. "If they exist, that is."

Kristoff jumped again as a black knight with armor darker than a tar pit emerged from a seemingly innocuous shadow behind a slab of stone, in a motion so fluid that it seemed like he materialized out of thin air.

The black knight shook his head slowly, his face hidden behind the full helmet adorned with a pair of brass bull's horns glistening in the evening sun. "I'm afraid I have to deny the empire the pleasure of torturing another traitor," he said coldly. "You've played your part well, boy. I'll let you die in peace." It would have been a somewhat soothing statement for Kristoff's troubled soul, were it not followed by an icy, metallic laughter. As the black knight drew his sword, so did the young Iltherian.

"My Lord, I truly don't think it's necessary to kill him." Renzo ran a finger along the rim of his monocle in a mildly concerned manner.

"And I truly don't think it's time to state your opinion, Renzo." Valharess' voice managed to be both casual and menacing. "This wimp here is a threat to my existence as long as he lives." He swung his sword effortlessly, which Kristoff managed to dodge, sweat trickling down his forehead.

"How so, my Lord?" Renzo didn't seem bothered in the least by the swordfight going on by his side, nor did he look interested enough to engage in any way.

"He can be caught. Tortured. You know, the usual. Bravenscu has his ways of getting information out of people. This one is just another footprint I'd be leaving behind, and you know how much I hate leaving a trail."

As Valharess spoke, Kristoff closed his eyes and took a wild blow at him with all his might, certain that he hit the black knight. When he opened his eyes, he saw that he missed by a long shot. The horned figure stood several feet to the side, shaking his head and looking disturbingly unimpressed. The young Iltherian took another swing, again to no avail. The black knight seemed to shift his presence around, giving the illusion of being everywhere and nowhere at the same time. It seemed like mana, but when Kristoff tried to reach out for it with his sword, he found nothing to tap into. The knight's power, like his body, was made of shadows. "Renzo, stop him!" the young knight shouted in sheer panic.

Renzo sighed deeply. "Sorry Kristoff," he muttered, his crisp voice smoothing out in sympathy. "I couldn't, even if I tried. There's no point in killing us both."

"There's a good man." Valharess nodded in approval. Then he lowered his sword and turned to the young Iltherian again. "Sit down, boy," he ordered calmly.

Kristoff shook his head and kept his guard. His face twisted into a mask of terror. His eyes illustrative of the look of a cornered animal, ready to assail tooth and nail if provoked; though he doubted that even teeth and nails would do any good. The black knight was invincible, ethereal like a ghost.

"Drop your sword and sit down," Valharess ordered again.

In one part of Kristoff's mind, the command made perfect sense. *Of course. Drop your sword and sit down.* But there was something inherently wrong about it. Not the order itself, but the part of his brain that accepted it. Too late, he noticed his hands loosening around the sword hilt, moving slowly downwards. *No!* His mind screamed in denial, tightening his grip until his knuckles were bone white. *I WILL NOT SURRENDER TO YOU!* He resisted the black knight's words with all his might, his skull pulsing with the effort as if his thoughts were made of electricity.

The green eyes behind the horned helmet glowed like those of a lynx, piercing and deadly.

Sit down.

The metallic voice echoed, this time directly in Kristoff's head, like the sound of a gong that resonated throughout his body. It wasn't a suggestion. It wasn't an order. It was a solid reality that suddenly became his own reality, cast upon him like a pot of scalding water. Against everything he considered to be part of himself, Kristoff felt his knees buckle underneath him as his sword slipped out of his hands onto the frozen ground.

*   *   *   *

The young Iltherian quietly awaited his end, the black sword of Valharess hovering above him like a child's pin over a hapless fly. He felt his fear breaking apart, melting down his shoulders along with the weight of years of service to the empire's colors. Years that had broken him and built him like a patchwork doll of pain and skill that he would not otherwise have known. He closed his eyes in a final acceptance and tried not to think where the sword would strike, hoping the black knight would be true to his word and grant him a peaceful death.

Kristoff listened for the subtle swish of air that would signal his last breath, but it never came. Instead, he heard the dull crunching of metal hitting ice. When he opened his eyes, both Renzo and the black knight fell to their knees beside him, cursing more profanely than any Iltherian officer he ever heard.

A pair of horns do not make a crown. I suggest that you, too, sit down. The voice tolled inside Valharess' head like a funeral bell, overwhelming his thoughts.

Even without the edge of finality in it, the black knight found it impossible to fight back. While his mind screamed rebellion, his body obeyed the voice like a puppy eager to please its owner. *Who are you?* He demanded. *Show yourself, if you dare.*

Korinth's slender figure appeared from beyond the ruined towers, bearing his usual feline grace and the hint of a smile. "What I dare or dare not, I dare say will not please your lot."

"Who are you?" Valharess asked again, his fury steaming through his voice.

The elf bowed with the exaggerated manner of a bard. "My name is Korinth," he said brightly. "To say the least, I am no one to be trifled with."

Valharess gritted his teeth. "I would hope that you end our lives here and now. For if you do not I will come back to haunt your thoughts until oblivion ceases to exist!" The black knight knew that it was the element of surprise, more than anything else, which presented Korinth an advantage. Given a chance to react, his mind could have resisted the elf's attack. "If you are man enough, fight me with steel!" He hissed.

"I am not here to fight." Korinth shook his head, his eyes fixed upon the black knight's. "Through mind, mana or might. Young Kristoff here must come with me. Once we set off, you shall be free."

Valharess squinted behind his helmet. "And what, o noble elf, keeps you from killing me here?"

"Fate." Korinth shrugged. "That each, their own must create."

The black knight spat down at where he sat. "Of course! Stinking rotten fate!" He stared at the elf. "Look here, clown," he snapped. "If I get a chance to create my own fate, I will make sure it includes getting rid of you, personally. Pray to your pointy-eared mana spirits that we don't meet again."

Korinth smiled sardonically. Helping Kristoff to his feet, he left the ruins without another word.

*   *   *   *

Chalco stared at the dying embers of the campfire, half asleep and half daydreaming. He startled up before everyone else, not knowing whether it was day or night, or how long it had been since they stopped for camp. In the twinkling light the embers cast, he saw shapes that took life, acting out the days he once knew. Happier days, they were, of a different world. He wondered whether there really was another world, another sky where spirits danced when they left this one, like the shamans used to talk about. *I am all that's left. My mind, my memories. And once those are gone...*

"What are you thinking?" Someone whispered, interrupting his thoughts.

Chalco blinked, washing away his sleepiness. The dancing images in the embers disappeared, leaving only the vast cavern full of shadows and the steady sounds breathing. He propped himself up on his elbow, and his tired gaze met Ceycil's. "My people," he said quietly. "I was thinking of my people."

"What became of them?" Ceycil asked, with some reluctance.

"Dust." Chalco sighed. "Dust and ashes, and a few memories." He paused, remembering, and the images in the embers came back. He wasn't sure if he wanted to talk about it, but something inside him urged him on. The story, his story, wanted to get out. "Across the sea in Thalagrant, before the Iltherians came," he began. "I had a home then, a little hut by a river in a country named Ansalebin. My brothers and I built the hut together when I got married. At night I used to go hunting in the forest with the other men in my tribe. It was scary, the forest at night. Eyes watched you everywhere, and you never knew if they belonged to something you could hunt, or something that came to hunt you." He paused again, then went on. "I used to be a decent hunter, believe it or not." He smiled grimly. "We would come home at dawn, and my wife would be sitting on the doorstep, stringing a new bow or sharpening a spear. She always sang the same song, softly but loudly enough that I could hear her before we came out of the forest." He closed his eyes and hummed the eerie melody that he knew by heart. The memory was so real in his mind, he could almost hear his wife's voice. Then he stopped abruptly and stared into the dying fire again, and continued his story. "One morning we returned from the hunt, and instead of the song I heard cries. A green and orange plague took over the village, and the river was running red with blood."

Chalco laid his head down again, one hand resting on his crossbow. "Some of us stayed to fight, but the Iltherians were everywhere. They carried heavy swords against our bare bodies, heavy armor for our simple weapons. Even the mana of our shamans couldn't hold them back." He paused again, and swallowed hard. "I fled." He looked at Ceycil to see his reaction, but found sadness rather than judgment in the young man's face. "I found my younger daughter hiding in the fruit basket," he went on, his voice quivering. "I grabbed her and fled, Ceycil. I don't even know what became of my wife or my other daughter. All I know is that if I stayed to find out, we would be dead, too. Maybe that's what I should have done, I don't know. Maybe that's why I am to suffer now, for leaving them behind and running like the coward that I am."

Chalco sighed again. "There was one ship that my tribe used to sail down the river, out to the sea. A couple of dozen others joined us, mostly children too young to be immediately noticed by the knights. We escaped as the battle went on, knowing that those we left behind would be dead before we reached the sea. We were just as hopeless, none of us sailors, on a ship that was not built to sail wild waters. I'm surprised we came as far as we did before an angry storm took a hold of us." His voice trailed off. "Sometimes I feel like even nature sides with the empire."

Ceycil felt a lump in his throat, not knowing quite why Chalco was telling him all this, and at the same time realizing how little he knew of the earthen-skinned man for all the time they traveled together. "What of your daughter then?"

Chalco shook his head. "I lost her during the shipwreck, along with the last of my people. I'm all that's left of my nation: a miserable coward. Too scared to die, and even more so to live." His fingers ran across the intricate carvings that decorated his crossbow, an almost affectionate gesture. "Next I knew, I was washed up on the shore, with you and Kazan standing beside me."

Ceycil remembered the day they found Chalco half-drowned, with the heat drained out of his body from being in the ice cold sea for who knew how long. It was midsummer then, not long ago at all, though to Ceycil seemed like ages. Perhaps the earthen-skinned man told Kazan his story at some point, but Ceycil never heard it before. Suddenly he felt ashamed for not having asked Chalco earlier and even more so for not having cared. He shook the thought away and blinked, his eyes focused on the exotic-looking weapon. "Your wife made that, didn't she?" he whispered.

Chalco nodded from where he lay, still gazing at what was left of the campfire. His mind seemed to be there and elsewhere at the same time. He let a weary smile escape. "She made it on the day I shot the sacred white stag. It was a ritual gift, a mark of honor."

Ceycil cleared his throat. He wanted to say something to this man who traveled so close to him for months and yet so far from his mind. A stranger beside him. *Yet whose fault is it that he remained a stranger?* "Listen Chalco," he said firmly, but kindly. "You're not a…"

He never got to finish his sentence. Chalco sat up suddenly, putting a finger across his lips. "Did you hear that?"

All Ceycil could hear was a quiet clicking, somewhere towards the further wall of the cavern. "I don't think it's…"

"Shh!" Chalco hushed him again. "Listen."

The clicking again, now slightly louder. Then a voice, no, dozens of voices, all speaking in unison:

"Dark summer. Warm winter. Light. Life."

11

As they rode away from Iltheria with the setting sun on their back, Kristoff couldn't help thinking that his escape out of imperial service had been anything but gallant on his part. After leaving Renzo and the black knight on their knees at the ruins, Korinth took 369 outside the city where two chestnut horses awaited them behind a small rocky hill. Their saddles branded the mark of the Iltherian army, but they bore neither halters nor reins, which made Kristoff wonder why they wouldn't just wander away. Without a word, Korinth helped him onto one of the horses and hopped onto the second one himself. Kristoff considered asking how on earth they would take the horses anywhere without reins, but with a single nod from the elf, the two creatures had broken into a rather purposeful trot, leaving the young knight with even more questions.

Thus they left, unseen and unheard. Iltheria had neither gates nor watchtowers. Nobody in their right mind would willingly walk into it unless they had business. And nobody that walked in with the wrong kind of business, walked out. As for attacks, there were no armies left on Krymaris, perhaps in the world of Imaria, that could even remotely match the power of Iltheria and Bravenscu combined. The city's own name was its defense.

"I owe you my life, Korinth," said Kristoff, the clip-clop of the horses' trot echoing in his aching head. "Probably more than once. I can't believe Renzo betrayed me."

"That he did not," said the elf gently. "It was the black knight's own plot. Valharess is sometimes truly everywhere at once." He seemed to be talking more to himself than anything else.

Kristoff let out a deep sigh. "And what now?" He found himself asking. "Where do we go from here?"

"We must ride forth," said the elf. "To the ship you spoke of, far north. The empire and the Diamond Sage will seek to seize it in their rage. A battle in which we must engage." He blinked at the blurring horizon where a crescent moon was slowly rising and disappearing under the grey clouds of the early winter evening. "There we shall meet others who deserve the flying ship, far more than the empire's troops or a tyrant psion's grip."

Kristoff shook his head. "Fighting against the empire *and* the Diamond Sage? Sounds fairly hopeless to me. Not that I have another choice, mind you. Anywhere where the Iltherian knights walk, I'm as good as dead. And now I know the Sage won't cover my back, either. I might as well make myself useful and do something to annoy them both before they catch up to me."

Korinth chuckled at the young soldier's reply. "Hope in our hearts forever dwells, as long as we can laugh at ourselves." He clucked his horse on, his eyes fixed upon the frozen fields that stretched before them endlessly.

*   *   *   *

"Who goes there?" Kazan demanded. "Reveal yourself!" He was already wide awake and ready to launch a spell into the darkness. Rooks was cowering in the shadows beside Tyrann, his child eyes full of alarm. The giant had his sword-axe drawn, his body a shield for the child.

"I told you there were dangerous creatures down here!" whined Chalco.

"Be quiet!" Roessa hissed.

"Warm." said the voice, again. *"Summer gone? Summer here? Warm. Time to wake."* The clicking sounds came closer, as dark shapes moved against the dim light of the embers.

Kazan waved a palm towards the campfire, and the cinders burst into fresh flames dancing towards the ceiling, illuminating most of the cavern.

Dozens of reddish black creatures surrounded them, each the size of a small pony, with the flames reflecting against their shiny bodies. Their antennae slowly moved back and forth, all pointing towards the roaring campfire.

"Ants," Roessa muttered under her breath, not knowing where to point her drawn arrow. Chalco comprised the same problem. His crossbow moved from one target to another, his hands shaking uncontrollably.

Ceycil took a few bold steps towards the nearest ant, ready to swing his sword. The ants were many, but so were the Iltherians the last time they fought.

"Metal," said the chorus of ants, as if they could smell the steel. *"Weapons. War."* They clicked their jaws tentatively, as Ceycil lifted his sword higher, getting ready to

strike. *"No fight,"* came the answer. *"I feel winter. Early summer. Slow blood. No war."*

Ceycil shot a questioning glance at Kazan, who nodded in reply. Slowly he lowered his sword, but he didn't put it down.

"It is not summer yet," the wizard told the ants coolly. "The warmth you feel is my fire. That is what woke you up from your winter sleep."

"Fire. Warmth in winter. Light in winter."

"Yes. That is fire." Kazan nodded again.

The buzzing of the ants ceased for a moment, as their antennae kept moving. They seemed to be thinking. *"Elves left. Long time, many summers. No people in caves. Why people come to caves?"*

"We only seek safe passage," said the wizard. "The winter is very harsh outside, and there are other dangers afoot. We did not mean to disturb you."

"No disturb. Warm, light. Good."

Ceycil frowned at the menacing figures of the giant ants. "Which one of you is speaking? Do you have a leader we could talk to?"

"I speak," said the ants in unison.

"Who are you?" Ceycil winced, looking around to see if any of the creatures stood out in any way. None of them did.

"I am the Colony," replied the buzzing chorus.

Ceycil shook his head in disbelief.

The ants started to move closer into the camp circle, still clicking their jaws and buzzing even louder. Ceycil lifted his sword again, fearing that the creatures might attack despite their words, but they only seemed interested in the fire.

"Smell people," they buzzed. *"Smell cloth. Metal. Wood."* They paused. *"Little food,"* they added more quietly.

Kazan squinted at the giant ants, his hands still ready for a spell-casting gesture. "Are you trying to make a point?"

The ants started moving their antennae faster. *"I give food. I give passage. Give me fire?"* It was a suggestion, not a demand.

The wizard stared at the closest ant. "Can you get us to the northeastern side of the old Crystalfellen forests? Near the base of Mount Pareth relatively fast?"

The chorus of ants buzzed again, looking at each other and clicking their jaws. Then they turned back to Kazan. *"I can. With warmth."*

The wizard nodded and lowered his hands. "Then we have a deal. I promise you on my honor as a wizard that when we step out onto the northern waste, I will leave my fire with the Colony."

The ants moved their antennae in approval. *"I promise. I trust."*

*   *   *   *

Valharess gritted his teeth as he tapped his fingers against a worm-eaten table. "You should have let me kill him, Renzo. That Iltherian boy is more trouble than he's worth."

"I did, my lord." Renzo looked slightly paler than before, but was otherwise remarkably composed. "It was the elf that hindered you, as I recall. A mind-bender like you, I believe?"

The black knight gritted his teeth even louder. "I wouldn't mind seeing that arrogant bastard roasted in a dragon's fire."

"Shame that there are no more dragons left." Renzo shook his head sympathetically. "Then again, as far as I knew there were no more elves other than Gabriel left, either."

"Elves are survivors," Valharess muttered to himself. "Some always remain, if only to humiliate me to death." Then he turned to Renzo again. "We need to get to that flying ship. I want everyone ready to march before dawn. Everyone! The guards, the pickpockets, that knife-throwing twit survivor elf that keeps my junk together."

"Gabriel is a good fighter," Renzo nodded. "He is quite stealthy, too. He can certainly become valuable in battle."

Valharess waved his hand in a dismissing motion. "Yes, that one. Even the blacksmith and the key keeper. We need everyone we can get, in case we run into imperial troops. We also need fast horses." He waved a hand towards the door. "See if we can steal some from the officers' camp nearby."

Renzo blinked. "My lord, you do realize that all imperial horses are chestnuts. They'll show against the snow, and they'll be hard to hide at night."

"Then paint them or something. We don't have time for excuses."

Renzo sighed and left the room. There was no reasoning with Valharess once he set his mind on something. *Now where would I get white paint?* Renzo pondered as he strode through the dark tunnel that led to his quarters.

*   *   *   *

On the roof of his palace tower, the emperor tapped his fingers against the armrest of his throne that was made of verdium like the swords of his soldiers. If Bravenscu was the yelling type, he would have been screaming furiously. Instead he stared. It was the kind of stare that could pierce stone, that made men tremble before him in fear of not what was happening, but what was about to happen. "What do you mean you can't find him?"

The officer was sweating a small waterfall that trickled down his neck underneath his armor, yet unable to avert his gaze from the emperor's expressionless, varicose face. "We searched everywhere, sir. The barracks, the mines, the ruins, all the nearby caves. 369 is gone."

"And nobody has seen him leave?" Bravenscu's voice had an edge like a razor.

The officer swallowed hard, his mouth dry with terror. "No, sir. People have seen him around the city earlier yesterday, but he hasn't reported to any of the barracks for the night."

The emperor stared at him silently for a few seconds. "You do realize that soldier 369 has witnessed an important exchange of information." He paused. "He was also charged by commander 1001 as a traitor, since his incompetence has caused a wizard to escape from our hands."

The officer nodded, turning even more ashen than he already was.

"If that information falls into unwanted hands, I will charge you as a traitor for similar reasons, and you know how we treat traitors in this place. Until then, your carelessness is forgiven."

The officer realized only then that he was holding his breath. He let out a sigh of relief, feeling as if he had just been reborn. "Thank you, sir," he said, as formally as he could without falling onto his knees.

Bravenscu nodded briefly. "Take tonight to gather up all your men. Send word to other commanders to do the same. I want all troops available for deployment to leave Iltheria by sunrise and head to the north to the mountain Pareth as fast as possible. All commanders are to gather before me to hear their mission before they leave. Understood?"

"Yes, sir."

"Also send word to all encampments in the peripheral territories that soldier 369 is warranted for execution on sight, no questioning necessary. You are dismissed."

Still shaken from the emperor's overwhelming presence, the officer left the throne room, trying hard to keep all his orders straight in his mind finally relieved of terror.

As soon as the man disappeared down the stairs, Bravenscu turned to the head of his guards. "Take him to the Tree in the morning. Incompetence has no place in my army."

*   *   *   *

"There's still something inherently strange about this," Roessa muttered as her six-legged steed advanced nimbly through the tunnels that were lit by Kazan's sphere of fire. The magical torch had to be kept larger than before to provide the ants with the warmth necessary to keep them moving. This took up most of Kazan's energy and made him even more taciturn than before, but it was worth the effort. The ants were not as fast as horses, but they were far more comfortable to ride and certainly faster than walking. At least in the Earthen Path he did not have to spend any energy trying to hide his spells from the Iltherians. The land itself with its earth and stone was shield enough, making it impossible for anyone above ground to track any mana that was used down below.

Rooks enjoyed the ride more than anyone else, constantly asking questions to the Colony and occasionally letting his earth spirit out of its vial to walk alongside them. "Are there any more ants like you? How big is your colony?"

"Many more minds, yes. I am greater than you see."

The red-haired child cocked his head. "Where are the other ants then?"

"Chambers. They sleep. Winter, cold. With fire I wake more minds. Mana master keeps his word. I trust."

"Don't get me wrong," Tyrann joined the conversation. "I appreciate your good will, but how do you decide that you can trust us? It's a dangerous world over ground, especially these days." He was riding two ants that walked side by side like a pair of cart horses tethered together.

"Mana master good, like elves," the Colony replied. The ants clicked their jaws. *"I taste tunnel air. Smell no evil in mana master. No evil in you people."*

The giant raised his eyebrows, which seemed to be made entirely of scars. "Interesting…"

Chalco shrugged. "They say dogs can smell fear. I don't see why ants can't smell evil the same way." He seemed considerably uneasy when the ants first offered them a ride, but had not objected. Now he looked more awkward than scared on his odd steed.

When the Colony called for a break, everyone was hungry, though also wonderfully rested. They marched

THOMAS M. GOFTON   -   HANDE BARUTÇUOĞLU

continuously since they left Korinth's cave underneath the waterfall, and half a day of smooth riding was a nice break for their weary feet.

As Kazan proceeded to distribute what little was left of their road rations, the ants started digging at one of the walls with their strong jaws and front claws, revealing a short and narrow passage that led out of the main tunnel. *"This way,"* the Colony buzzed. *"Food. This way."*

The shiny black bodies disappeared through the passage one by one. Ceycil shrugged and followed readily. Anything the ants could offer was better than stone-dry bread and frozen rabbit.

The first thing that got his attention was something squishy underneath his boots. He blinked into the darkness, feeling Roessa's body right behind him. The blunted footsteps of the others followed, stepping from solid icy earth to softer ground. The cavern was warmer than the main tunnel and a heavy, musty scent hung in the air. Only when Kazan brought up the rear with his fire could Ceycil see what the cavern actually contained. The floor was covered with something like thick rotting moss, which seemed to be the source of the smell. Out of this messy natural rug sprouted dozens of purple spotted mushrooms, each knee-high and rather eerie-looking.

"Food," the Colony repeated. *"Mushrooms good. Tasty."* Before anyone could object, the ants started munching on their strange supper.

Ceycil followed suit and picked the spotty cap off a mushroom. "I suppose it's safe." He broke the mushroom cap in two, and handed one half to a wide-eyed Roessa.

"How does it taste?" she asked curiously as Ceycil chewed on his share of the mushroom.

"Tastes like chicken."

She reluctantly took a bite, then shook her head. "Liar."

Ceycil laughed.

Tyrann picked a particularly large mushroom, and handed a piece to Chalco. "Tastes more like smoked mutton to me," the earthen-skinned man commented.

The giant nodded. "With seaweed sauce."

"Eww..." Rooks made a face, making everyone laugh. They left the cave with both their stomachs and their backpacks stuffed with fresh mushroom.

"I hope the mushrooms don't give us visions," Chalco muttered to himself as he climbed back onto an ant. "I've never wanted to be a shaman."

* * * *

Days and nights seemed all the same on the road: dim, lukewarm and stretching on endlessly like the tunnels they traveled in. The steady, rhythmic footfalls of the ants were only broken by hasty meals on mushrooms and camps made in nondescript corners, cycling like a recurring dream and giving the illusion that time ceased to exist in the Earthen Path as it did in Korinth's cave. On occasion they passed through large caverns with ice-covered rough staircases leading up to the surface. The Colony marched by these without slowing down, only muttering the exotic names of the elven cities that once stood there: *Shehrizaman, Shehrilayl, and Shehrigaib...* These names echoed in Ceycil's mind for hours like some sort of incantation. He tried to remember them, holding onto the names like small children easy to lose in a crowd, attempting to keep at least their memory alive and close. They always faded away in the end, disappearing completely like the ripples that falling leaves

made in water. Still, during their long rides Ceycil dreamed of
elves like Korinth, and what their cities would look like.
Towers, he imagined, made of trees intertwining smoothly
like the fates of people. Summers and springs upon those
towers, of a million shades of green and sky-blue trickling
streams. He dreamed of fair faces, of slanted eyes full of
wisdom and riddles, for having only seen Korinth he could
not imagine an elf being unwise or plain. He thought of
families, of generations past with all the loves and adventures
and misfortunes ever lived among those people, in those
cities that were now even beyond dust and ruins.

The brighter and more detailed Ceycil's fantasies
grew, the more solid his hatred became for the Iltherian
knights for destroying the seeds of reality that gave birth to
his dreams. When they broke for camp, he found himself
staring at the shadows for hours on end, sweating on his
bedroll despite the cold as he fervently thought how or
whether he could face the empire in any way.

*   *   *   *

It was one of these nights when Roessa woke up to
Ceycil's touch upon her shoulder. He was crouched by her
bedroll, and she found it hard to see his expression in the
dark. She was surprised that she hadn't even felt him get up,
his own bedroll was right beside hers. And what had he just
called her? "Roessy!" She hadn't heard that name in at least
fifteen years, possibly more. It was the name he gave her
when they were both too young to pronounce names
properly. "What is it this time, Cess?" She forced herself not
to laugh, but couldn't help the note of amusement in her
voice.

"You've got to see this. I found something." The excitement in Ceycil's voice was a familiar one. It usually meant trouble.

This time Roessa couldn't help herself and let out a small, quiet laughter. "Whatever it is, I have a feeling Father wouldn't like it. Can it wait until people wake up? I have no idea what time of day it is anyway." She shook her head.

Ceycil grinned so wide that Roessa had no problem spotting it despite the dim light. "Of course it can't! Kazan will never let me look at it if he sees it."

She rubbed at her face sleepily. "Then perhaps you shouldn't mess with it? For once?" she suggested hopefully.

Ceycil's grin turned into a fake frown. "Since when did *you* get so boring? Come on!" He gave her a hand and helped her up, ignoring all her quiet protests.

He lit a piece of firewood from the campfire as a torch and led her to a dimmer corner of the cavern they were camping in, walking by Tyrann who was snoring up a storm and Rooks who was curled up between him and Chalco. The ants occasionally clicked their jaws behind them, all settled into a kind of torpor without the warmth of Kazan's magical flames.

Somewhere in the corner, one of the walls made a small pocket, an indentation large enough for someone to sit in. Ceycil crouched beside it and motioned Roessa to do the same. "Look at this." His fingers brushed over something on the ground. It was a dagger, a remarkably small and delicate one, with a familiar shape carved on the hilt.

"That's the tree that was part of that strange map on the wall, where we first entered the Path."

Ceycil nodded. "Same one, yes." He picked it up and brushed the ice off of it. The hilt was not made of metal, but a hard wood covered with silver gild that had surprisingly not peeled off. "Elven made, probably." He handed the blade to Roessa.

"I don't know if I should…" she started to protest.

"Yes, you definitely should. Elves don't come here anymore." He looked directly into her eyes. "There are no more elves left to come," he added softly. "I'm sure they'd rather you have it."

She took the weapon reluctantly. It was small enough to fit into her hand, and still remarkably sharp. She wiped it on her tunic and slipped it into her belt, promising herself that she would put it to good use, and to good use only. Then she looked up and stared back at Ceycil. "This isn't nearly enough to make Father mad." She smiled. "Not mad enough for your taste, anyway. What else have you found?"

Ceycil smiled back. "You know me too well, sometimes you scare me." He crawled into the pocket in the wall and started scratching at the ice.

"We've only been living together for… what, twenty years?" Roessa laughed. Then she interrupted her own laughter and gaped at what Ceycil just revealed. He moved a huge chunk of solid ice from the wall. There was no more wall behind it. Instead the first few steps of a narrow, ice-covered staircase were winding down at a slight incline.

"The dagger was jammed right next to this piece of ice. When I tried to pull it free, the whole thing came loose." He stared thoughtfully into the staircase. "Hold this for a minute?" Ceycil handed the torch over to Roessa. Then he stood up suddenly and started kicking at the edges of the wall, widening the passageway.

"You're not planning to go down there, are you?" Roessa frowned.

"Of course I am. Why did you think I woke you from your sleep?"

Roessa shook her head. "Now *this* will make Father furious, that's for sure."

"Good," she heard Ceycil mutter. "Then at least it's worth doing all this in secret."

Roessa shook her head yet again. "Hold this for a minute." She shoved the torch back into Ceycil's hand and turned to leave.

Ceycil was bewildered. "Where are you going?"

"To get that fancy sword of yours. You weren't planning to go down there unarmed, were you?" Seeing the blank expression on Ceycil's face, she grinned. "I thought so. Hang on while I gather up a few things, will you? Maybe think up an excuse to tell Father when he finds out about this." She smiled again, and walked away towards the camp without another word.

*   *   *   *

The hole in the wall was now large enough for Roessa to stoop through, and the narrow, winding staircase looked impressively uninviting. "Are you sure this is a good idea?"

"I'm not." Ceycil fumbled with his scabbard belt, trying to strap his sword to his side. "But there's only one way to find out, right?" He took the second torch that Roessa brought back, and took the first step down.

Roessa followed close behind. "Father's going to kill us for this one."

"Do you really think we'd survive the curiosity if we just left this and moved on? Come now, we're dead either way. We might as well make it worthwhile."

"How is it that your rationale always overpowers the logical choice?"

"Kazan did say I was like my father now. Perhaps this is a Lynnvander feat." Ceycil replied smugly.

"If such feats ran in families, I should have succeeded in bullying you out of going down there," Roessa tried to reason. Then she took a deep breath and decided to drop the argument. She was too curious herself to do otherwise.

The shallow steps gave them the illusion that they were going nowhere fast. Regardless of the feeling, it didn't take the two explorers more than a few minutes to reach the bottom. The cavern they reached was slightly warmer than the tunnels above, even though the walls were covered with rectangular bricks made of solid, crystalline ice that shimmered under the flames of the two torches. Someone took the trouble of paving this place.

Roessa squinted with suspicion. "If nobody's been in these tunnels for twenty years, then how come these bricks haven't melted through the summer?"

"I'm guessing we are far enough up north that it doesn't get that warm," answered Ceycil. "We've certainly been traveling for long enough. Think of it as an icebox that was built in a cold place to begin with."

The cavern led into several similarly paved galleries, a couple of which collapsed completely. "Which one do we follow?" Roessa asked, just to avoid silence. The place felt haunted, a ghastly look to it and it tiptoed up and down her spine in a constant shudder.

"Put your right hand against the wall," was Ceycil's reply.

"Since when do *you* speak in riddles?" Roessa glared at him, though she was more amused than annoyed.

202

"Just do it." Ceycil moved the torch to his left hand to free up his right. "Keep it against the wall unless we have to fight something."

"Or unless my fingers freeze," Roessa muttered.

"Since when did you start to complain like Chalco?"

Roessa slapped Ceycil's arm and shot a dagger-like gaze at him. "Father's *really* going to kill us for this one."

Ceycil ignored her comment and started explaining. "This way we won't get lost. As long as we stay in contact with one wall, we can always trace the same wall back."

"Ah. Now you're starting to make sense for a change," Roessa nodded in approval. The right-hand wall led them to the right-hand tunnel. "Where did you learn this trick, anyway?" She asked, her fingertips brushing against the bricks of ice.

"It's one of those... gut feelings. Trust me."

All my *gut is saying is that I've never been in a creepier place,* Roessa thought grimly as she walked behind him. *And I can't even explain why.* Really, it wasn't all that different from the tunnels they had been traveling in. It was warmer, for one. Prettier. No rough earthen walls, no funny-smelling mushrooms growing around. *You're just nervous because you feel unsafe,* she told herself. *Nobody knows you're here, and Father would throw a sizzling fit if he did.*

The first tunnel led to a plain wooden door, which much to Roessa's relief was open. It was also disappointingly empty save a single apple that was frozen rock-hard, though still a fresh shade of red. *An icebox,* she couldn't help recalling Ceycil's words. "I wonder why the floor is all scratched up?" She thought out loud.

"A storage room," Ceycil said absent-mindedly. "Emptied out."

"How do you know that?"

"I don't know." Ceycil swallowed. "I just know." All his playfulness disappeared since they descended into the ice-paved galleries. He looked grave, his voice full of an indescribable anxiety.

Roessa remembered her father talking about the royal bloodlines and how they were tied to the land. *Maybe that's what it is,* she thought. *Maybe it's the earth talking to him.*

They backtracked to the staircase, and followed the next intact tunnel. It was shorter than the previous one, and also led to a door. Except this one wasn't so much open as hacked to pieces, with icy splinters covering most of the floor.

As the light from their torches painted the room, Roessa held her breath. She lost her touch on the wall as a flood of dread washed over her.

There were people in this room.

It was exactly what Ceycil feared that he'd see. The figures lying on the floor showed fair, youthful faces, exactly like he pictured in his mind during his long daydreams on the road. Their slanted eyes were shut, with tiny specks of ice crystallized on their lashes. "Elves..." There were several dozen of them in the cavern, which appeared to be larger than Ceycil first thought. They were in armor, holding swords and bows that proved useless against whatever it was that they prepared to face. Unlike Korinth, these elves had silvery blue hair, though Ceycil was certain that their eyes were dark green like his. Their lips too were blue, the same shade of death as their pale faces.

"They almost look asleep," Roessa whispered sadly. "Like they are dreaming."

Ceycil nodded mutely. He felt old, far older than his twenty years.

There was no sign of battle in the room save the shattered door. No blood, no struggle, no dropped weapons. Even all the arrows in the room were still strung on the bows, no longer tight and deadly, but still and dead like their owners.

"I don't understand." Roessa turned her eyes away from the elves. "They don't seem to have died *of* anything. I don't see any wounds, do you?"

The word "icebox" still echoed inside Ceycil's head. These people had died at least twenty years ago, frozen as much in time as in their icy home. He shook his head. "I have no idea what happened to them. Except whatever it was, I'm sure the empire had something to do with it." He gritted his teeth and paced around the room, his anger bubbling as he came across more elven men and women, their ashen faces devoid of expression. He stopped in the corner, and beckoned at Roessa, who followed reluctantly.

There was a small pile of armor and weapons on the floor, laid there haphazardly. The armor was all clean and lined with wood to keep the cold out. The hilts of all the swords and knives were also made of silver-gilded wood, and adorned with the same design of the tree that was on Roessa's dagger.

"Some of this stuff might fit us," Ceycil muttered, more to himself. Then he crouched down and started looking through the armor.

"I... it doesn't feel right. Taking them, I mean," said Roessa. She paused awkwardly. "Ceycil, can we go back now?"

Ceycil wanted to get out of that tomb of ice as much as Roessa did. All the death in the room made him feel like the walls were closing around him. Still, he forced himself to stay. "These are not anybody's," he reassured Roessa.

"Everyone here has their armor and weapons. These are spares." He paused. "Besides, we'll need them if… when we fight the Iltherians again."

Roessa gave him a timid stare, which slowly molded into an expression that was completely unfamiliar to Ceycil. Her face was cold and blank, yet her eyes seemed to be burning from the inside. Without another word, she reached out and picked up a short bow that was beautifully decorated with carvings and frozen white-blue feathers. Then she slung a quiver of arrows onto her back, and started sorting through the armor, looking to carry as much back for the others as they could.

Kazan was waiting quietly by a freshly-stirred fire when Ceycil and Roessa reached the camp. Ceycil thought he could see smoke coming out of the old wizard's ears as they walked towards him. Everyone else was still asleep.

"Maybe I should just kill you two myself and get it over with. At least I would save myself the stress of worrying." The wizard took a deep breath, his fury rising visibly like a wind-up toy. "When will you...?" he gave up halfway through and shook his head. "Never mind. Blood is as blood flows. A Lynnvander and a wizard's daughter, what was I expecting anyway?"

Seeing the oddly decorated armor that Ceycil and Roessa were wearing, Kazan stopped in mid-grumble and frowned heartily. "Can I at least demand an explanation, or would that also be a wasted effort?"

Immensely grateful that the wizard hadn't come out at them in full explosion, Ceycil gave a full recount of what they saw in the galleries below.

Kazan's frown dissipated slowly as he listened. "Ice elves," he muttered thoughtfully. "The blue-haired brethren of sky realm Arial's, flying elves or so I am guessing. Another ill begotten fate then. Seems to be our theme these days."

"Sounds more like another dream dying to me," Roessa commented, her eyes fixed on the flaring fire. "What killed them, do you know? They seemed... just dead. Just like that. No wounds, nothing."

"Elves are not merely users or bearers of mana, like all the other races in the world," her father explained. "They are actually made of mana in essence. Iltherians have no need to shed elven blood, not when their swords can simply drain the life out of them."

Roessa shook her head. "They couldn't even fight back."

Kazan stared at his daughter. "The empire has never claimed to play fair though to perform this feat would not be easy even for verdium steel wielders."

Roessa met his gaze. "It's also cowardly, cruel and shameless. Killing people just because they can, without even giving them the choice to die fighting. Destroying lives, homes, hopes, dreams..."

Kazan broke her off sharply. "And what makes you think the emperor has any use for courage, compassion or shame? He gets what he wants, does he not?"

"We can at least make sure he pays a fair price," said Ceycil, laying a hand on his sword.

The wizard frowned grimly. "There are six of us, son. Even with a giant and your youth on our side, we are nothing against an army of knights. You would be a pile of dust before long, blown to the four winds with your ideals."

"Then we take the choice the elves didn't have," said Roessa solemnly. "We die fighting."

The lines on Kazan's face softened momentarily. "Dying for your dreams may help them last a little longer in this world," he said gently. "But it will not make them come true. You must learn to live for them instead."

Ceycil blinked thoughtfully, staring at the wizard but seeing a different scene in his mind. Sainaa spoke the same words to him, not long ago, about his land. *Coincidence?* He wondered. He would likely never know the answer. "I agree with you," he told the wizard proudly, trying to meet his gaze. "But you must understand that the only way we can live for this dream is by fighting for it."

To his surprise, Kazan looked away at the fire. "Those are words your father would speak," he said solemnly. "Each day I see more and more of him in you. Sometimes it worries me a little, for it was the same courage and will to stand up against the empire that brought your father to his end. But more often than not it makes me proud, Ceycil, for having raised a young man that would be a worthy son for Klavan Lynnvander." He paused and raised his head to look at Ceycil. "Your father was a good man."

Ceycil swallowed hard. "So are you," were the only words he could bring himself to say.

From a corner of the cavern, they could hear the buzzing of the Colony as the ants stirred from the heat of the fresh fire. "It is time to move on," said Kazan, forcing their conversation to an end. "Keep your armor and respect your weapons. And stay out of hidden staircases and such; I am getting too old for all the worry the two of you put me through." He proceeded to wake Tyrann and Chalco. Rooks could sleep a little longer on the road.

*   *   *   *

After a short excursion to resupply from the fallen elves, Chalco was examining the elven armor that stood far too short on his lanky body, as his ant steed moved through the tunnels behind the rest of the Colony. Even with the layer of wood lining it, the thin breastplate felt strange on his chest that was used to being bare for the better part of the year. "It's bad luck to wear a dead man's clothes," he grumbled shaking his head.

"It's still better than wearing no armor," Tyrann commented. The red-haired child was snoring gently in his arms. "Young Ceycil only said he found it in the ice caverns, doesn't mean it belonged to one of the dead elves. Besides, it's always good to have something that has to break before your skin does."

"That's a pleasant thought," Chalco muttered. "Funny you should say that, of all people. Weapons don't tend to break your skin. They tend to break against it, if anything."

"Well, I do have thick skin I suppose." Tyrann chuckled amiably. "It comes with being a Neranian giant. Still, it breaks just fine, thank you very much. I wasn't born with these scars, you know."

The earthen-skinned man smiled grimly. *Scars,* he thought. *One thing you and I have in common.*

Tyrann kept talking, as if he could read Chalco's thoughts like a psion. "Giants don't have very good memories," he said. "Neranians believe that scars are nature's way of making us remember things," he explained. "What we can't keep on our minds, we keep on our bodies." He pointed to a scar on his temple. "That was my very first one. My sister and I were playing by the river. She shoved me; I fell and hit my head against a stone." He smiled, his eyes wandering to a place that no longer existed, to a time that was long gone. Then his expression grew grim, and he touched another scar on his shoulder. "This was the first one given to me by an Iltherian. They raided our village, captured us with thick nets like animals."

Chalco's face froze in a silent question of terror. He wanted to ask, but didn't dare.

The giant must have seen his expression, for he went on to explain. "Giants are too precious to kill," he said. "We are strong, far stronger than the best trained Iltherian. Not made to be victims, and too clumsy to be turned into knights, but alas, perfect for slaves." He sighed. "Hundreds, maybe thousands of knights came that day in boats. By sunset, not one of us was left a free man." He pressed his scarred lips together and stared into the depths of the tunnel ahead.

Chalco remained silent for a while, contemplating the giant's story. "How did you escape?" he asked finally.

"I fought," Tyrann replied. "And I killed." He shook his head. "I don't like fighting. And I certainly don't like killing unless it were a filthy Ogre of course. Even Iltherians are people, if I were born a human I could have been one myself for all I know. Besides, they are slaves in a way, too, at least most of them. Taken from their destroyed homes and forced into a life of war and murder." Then he turned sharply and stared at Chalco. "But I had to be free, you see. I knew that if I spent one more day at that sooty, dreadful mine, I would collapse the ceiling on my own head like some of the others. It was a foggy night. There were maybe a dozen guards. I don't remember how I took them all down. By the time the rest of the knights could figure out what was happening I was gone." His voice was soft, almost sad.

"That was brave of you," Chalco muttered.

"No, it wasn't." The giant looked away. "I was a coward. I ran away. Left my people in that deathly mine." He took a deep breath and glanced back at Chalco. "If I were truly brave, I would have told them I was leaving. We could have escaped together."

"But you can't just sneak a bunch of giants out of an Iltherian city, can you? You'd all be caught then." Chalco tried to protest.

"That's what I keep telling myself, but sometimes I feel like I should have taken my chances. We could all be free together."

Now it was Chalco's turn to stare at the giant. "Or you could all be dead together. And what good would that have done?"

Tyrann blinked, and his facial expression softened up a bit. "Maybe you are right," he whispered. "But either way," he added, "I owe them a chance for freedom. That's why I fight, only for that chance. That's why I kill." He sighed again. "It still makes me a murderer, but I will keep fighting. I owe my people that much."

*   *   *   *

Rooks lost count of time long ago. He was never good about it anyway. Even when he was living out in the open with Serje, days would seem to blend together like the painted colors on the Birdman's face. He let his earth spirit out of his vial the last time they had stopped for camp, and now this massive, stony figure strode beside the Colony without any apparent effort. Rooks ran a hand through his red hair thoughtfully. The ants seemed restless. Further ahead he could hear Kazan talking to the Colony, though his voice was little more than a whisper, barely audible in the tunnel. The only reply that came was a buzzing that got louder or quieter in response. The wizard was more withdrawn than before during the last few days, constantly working on what seemed to be the permanent fire spell that he promised the ants. *That means we are close to the exit,* thought Rooks. *Closer to the sky.* He was weary of the Earthen Path. It was fun for a while, especially when they first started riding the ants, but now the confinement was getting on his nerves. The darkness didn't scare him, but it was suffocating. He longed for daylight, even if it came from a pale winter sun.

Rooks expected their journey to last for at least another couple of days, but to his surprise and delight, the end came much sooner. When they reached a large cavern that seemed no different from dozens of ones they passed through before, the Colony stopped. Somewhere in the corner of the cavern, Rooks spotted an earthen staircase rising up and out of the Path. Beside it, there was a small carving on the wall that resembled a fish on a cloud.

"*Your exit,*" the Colony buzzed loudly. "*Shehrishimal. City of the North. What is left of it. The last home before Pareth, the grand mountain*"

They all dismounted their ant steeds solemnly. Rooks stopped to give his ant an awkward hug around the face, and the Colony hummed contentedly in return. Then Kazan held out the flame in his palm. It now shone a solid core that resembled a red glowing stone. "A wizard must always be true to his word," he said, offering it to the ant that he had been riding. "It will not burn you upon touch, and it should last you a few winters if you keep it off ice and water. Thank you for granting us passage."

"*Thank you for fire,*" said the Colony. "*Wizard honest like elves. I help when I can. Safety and warmth to you.*"

"And to you." The wizard nodded formally. Before he could add another word, Ceycil and Roessa made a wild dash up the stairs. Kazan turned around sharply. "You two be caref…" The end of his sentence was drowned in his own groan, as a blinding wave of light flooded the cavern.

Rooks laughed and ran towards where Ceycil and Roessa stood shielding their eyes. Even after weeks of darkness, the light didn't bother him at all.

"Children are something else," he heard Tyrann say beside him. The giant caught up to, and rested his oversized hand on Rooks' shoulder and blinked into the shimmering whiteness. Together they stepped into the winter world as if walking in a dream, followed by Chalco and Kazan.

*   *   *   *

"I never thought I'd miss this," said Roessa, scanning the snowy landscape laden with small copses of incredibly tall evergreen trees. The trees were a reminder of the thickness that was the great elven forests of Crystalfellen but a ten day away to the west. Her breath was visible in the freezing air, along with tiny flakes of ice that fell sharply against her face. It was the kind of snow that seemed innocuous, but could easily cover the earth with a crisp, solid layer of ice within hours.

"Now, where to go from here?" Ceycil asked. "Did Korinth say where we would find this flying ship?" They emerged from a small hill of some sort, and it was hard to see much of anything beyond a stretch of whiteness so endless that it resembled an eternal nothingness save for the patches of trees. If there were other hills like this one, or even bigger ones, it was impossible to make them out. The whiteness swallowed anything the eye could catch; even the horizon was lost somewhere between the snowy land and the cloudy winter sky.

214

Kazan shaded his eyes with his hand, and squinted at the whiteness. "That he did not." He shook his head absent-mindedly.

"Maybe we should go back to the tunnels?" Chalco suggested. "At least it's warmer there. We could wait for Korinth for a while, see if he shows up."

"No." Kazan's answer was definite, but not harsh. "We have no time to lose by waiting. And yes, the elf will find us, if I know elves well enough." Without further explanation, he picked a direction, seemingly at random, and started walking. Nobody dared to question his decision.

Every now and then pairs of eyes jumped at them from behind invisible dunes of snow, belonging to white hares or foxes. *This is a ghost land,* Roessa couldn't help thinking as she walked. *Its animals are ghosts, pale as death and appearing out of nowhere. Even its light is a ghost light.*

Now that their eyes adjusted to being outside again, they could see that it wasn't normal daylight, but the kind of stagnant twilight that reigned in the northern winters. The sun, they realized, was not obscured by the clouds. It set weeks ago, and would not rise again until the spring.

The eeriness of the place reminded Roessa of the paved caverns of the ice elves. She was so tense that she found herself drawing an arrow at every rabbit that appeared in their path. Every time she let out a deep breath and lowered her bow. Her backpack was still full of mushroom slices, and even if they needed food, she didn't think she could get herself to kill anything that belonged to the whiteness. It was so overwhelming that she did not dare disturb it.

Soon she realized that she wasn't alone in her unease. Every time she reached for her arrows, other hands

215

also grasped weapons. The whole party was like a balloon ready to pop if pressed hard enough.

The appearance of the green and orange figure on horseback was so unexpected that if it wasn't for the whiteness contrasting the metallic colors, they might have hesitated before acting. Instead they gave in to their reflexes. Within a split second, the lone Iltherian found himself in an immensely sticky situation. Blades were drawn, Chalco's crossbow was lined with quarrels, and Kazan's fingers were raised threateningly.

Roessa`s arrow was already in mid flight.

To her surprise, the knight did not react. Not that he had any time to react, anyway, but she had expected at least an angry cry, or an attempt to draw his sword. Instead the knight just shut his eyes and froze. It was a better-aimed shot than Roessa gave credit. Then to her further surprise, it stopped inches away from the Iltherian's neck, and fell onto the snow like a dead bird.

"In fear and rage withhold your haste," called a familiar voice. "Or in enemy's clothes a friend you'll waste." Korinth, on the bare back of yet another chestnut horse, appeared beside the Iltherian who was panting with fright. The elf was unarmed save for his odd-looking book bound in tree bark, and he wore nothing but a light cape over his clothes despite the bone-chilling cold.

Roessa was not intending to attack the knight again, but she drew another arrow regardless. "I hope you'll excuse my excessive prudence, but I think we've all had enough of Iltherians," she said, eyeing the knight menacingly.

Korinth dismounted gracefully and motioned Kristoff to do the same. "Of this story I know you are tired, but young Kristoff here belongs on our side. Strong of heart but frail of mind, in him a true renegade you'll find."

Roessa glanced at her father, who met her gaze and nodded briefly. Reluctantly, she lowered her bow. "So Versai wasn't a renegade after all… And you knew it all along?"

Korinth nodded.

"Why didn't you tell us then?" she pressed, feeling an unfamiliar surge of anger rising in her, difficult though it was to truly get angry at Korinth.

"Certain truths cannot be spoken without having mortal oaths broken."

Roessa turned to her father, "Father, would you mind translating that?"

Instead it was Ceycil who piped up, standing straighter than usual. "I think what he's trying to say is, it's not within his power to say certain things without facing consequences. He can see what lies in our minds, but he can't always reveal what he sees."

Korinth smiled and nodded again.

"Regardless, we are in no position to turn down allies," Kazan said, addressing the knight. "Interesting 369, how we meet again."

"Thank you for not taking my life then," said the Iltherian, still shaken from the close encounter he had experienced with Roessa's arrow.

"You know him?" Roessa interrupted.

"He is the knight that allowed for my escape back in Talia."

"Wow," Roessa exclaimed, shocked. "Thank you," she added, addressing Kristoff. "And I'm sorry I almost shot you a minute ago. It's just that… you *are* an Iltherian. Nothing personal."

Soldier 369 shrugged. "The Empire is no place for me," he explained. "I may have served it for a while, but I never did it willingly." He glanced at his sword with an expression of disgust. "We are bound to our swords, and the foul mana in them sometimes controls what we do, but I have never let it control who I am."

"I'd be happy to take it off your hands if you ever want to get rid of it," Ceycil offered, half jokingly.

"Preliminaries for later," Kazan interrupted him, and then turned to the elf. "What news of the Adelphia? Have you found the ship yet?"

Korinth nodded slowly. "That I have, but so have others. Green and orange, and black of colors." He turned to the horses and whispered something towards them, which sent both animals trotting away calmly.

Roessa frowned. "And what does that mean?"

"Means we are late," Kristoff snapped, with a tinge of regret in his voice. "The empire has brought an entire garrison, camped right by the hollow entry of Mount Pareth to the north that holds the flying ship. The Order of the Diamond Sage is also heading there in full squad I would assume."

"I thought nobody knew about this ship," Ceycil commented.

Kristoff opened his mouth to speak, though he wasn't sure what he would say.

Tyrann saved him the trouble. "We were betrayed," the giant said thoughtfully. "Soldier 451 has done exactly what we feared he would do."

"Where are they right now?" Kazan asked.

Kristoff pointed to the northern part of the whiteness. "The hollow mountain is over that way. Both armies are either on the way or in there right now knowing how fast the empire can move if it wants to."

"Fighting?"

The young knight shook his head. "I doubt it. Not yet, anyway. The Diamond Sage is greatly outnumbered; they will not fight until they can no longer sneak their way in."

"What do you think, Kazan? Do you have a plan?" Ceycil's voice was full of anxiety.

"You are so full of brilliant ideas when it comes to getting yourself in trouble," the wizard grumbled. "But when it comes to strategy, it is always old Kazan that has to work his brain!"

"Father, this is no time to argue," Roessa broke in. "You know if you leave it to Ceycil he'll just barge in. We need your sense of caution, please."

Ceycil stared at Roessa. "Barge in?"

"Well, yes!" Roessa put her hands on her hips. "Look, if I know you well enough, your plan would be to get a battering ram and charge at the front door, if this mountain has one to speak of. Am I wrong?"

Ceycil raised an eyebrow, with a smile twitching on the corner of his mouth. "I figured I was more like a brave knight standing in line to protect his people, actually. But anyway, I *am* asking for advice. Kazan, let's hear your plan of… caution."

Kazan shook his head. "Caution, my tailbone!" he grunted. "I am fresh out of ideas and time is running out. Draw your weapons and tread lightly; we are going into that mountain and you can bet your mana-cowed hides that both Iltherian and Sage are already there."

Ceycil tried to open his mouth again, but Roessa held up a hand cowing him. "Not another word," she said threateningly, ignoring his smug expression. It was bad enough trying to suppress a laugh, and she had no intentions of letting Ceycil see it.

*   *   *   *

The Iltherian camp by the hollow mountain was as empty as the whiteness that surrounded it. "Not a single guard," Tyrann whispered, trying to suppress a shudder as he walked by the green and orange tents. "They all went in then?"

Kristoff shook his head, as they all followed Korinth's lead into the tunnel that entered the mountain. "There is another camp half a mile to the south," he said. "It's a better camping spot, more protected from the weather. About half the troops, the ones that traveled further from the south are waiting there as reinforcements. I bet the northern outposts got here first."

"Only goes to show that the emperor really wants this ship," Kazan commented. "So many precautions for a seemingly easy mission, just in case something goes wrong. They do not want to take any chances."

"What can go wrong, though?" Chalco asked. "It's just a flying ship, isn't it? I don't see anything dangerous about it."

The wizard shook his head. "It is magical, and mana is unpredictable at the best of times. Besides, they cannot know how powerful it is, or how many Iltherian blades it will take to drain it all, if that is what they intend to do. These ships are from a day beyond most of you. They are entirely built of mana."

"Emperor Bravenscu," Korinth broke in, "is as wily as he is evil. Destroying such a source of power would not do."

Kazan shook his head. "Wily as he is, I have a feeling there is more behind his power than good judgment."

Korinth raised his eyebrows at the wizard's words, but offered no reply. Instead he ran his fingers over his bark-bound book and kept walking.

Ceycil walked into the dark tunnel behind them, followed by Roessa. Rooks and his massive earth spirit brought up the rear. Rooks stopped suddenly as Kazan stood pointing at the earth spirit. Kazan mouthed the words "Away, please." Rooks shrugged and drained the earth spirit back into his small glass vial.

Once they were further into the mountain, what little of the ghostly light that seeped in through the entrance died away completely, forcing them to move by feel. They did not dare to use Kazan's fire for fear of attracting attention. The tunnel branched off in many places, resembling a labyrinth, and the walls were uneven with rocks that almost blocked their passage in places and pockets that could very well be side paths. Korinth with elven dark vision seemed to know his way, so they followed him. As they advanced through the tunnels, the elf's voice echoed in their minds. *A helm of silver with gold wings by the pair, to fly the Adelphia her captain must wear. When we reach the center that we must obtain, for without the helm fighting will be in vain.*

At one point they heard a thud, followed by Kazan cursing under his breath.

"What's wrong?" Ceycil almost walked into the wizard.

"Watch your step everyone," Kazan whispered. "I almost tripped over that."

"Over what exactly?"

"A body, an Iltherian by the feel of it. His bloody armor almost broke my toes."

Chalco shivered, running his free hand over his own armor and looking around alarmed, even though all he could see was darkness. "What killed him? What if it's still here?" His voice was starting to crack, along with his nerves.

"One of the Diamond Sage, probably," Kristoff guessed. "They are remarkably well-trained in sneaking about. They will follow the Iltherians and try to reduce the numbers as much as they can, in case they have to engage in open battle at some point." He, too, stepped over the body and kept walking. "I reckon there are many other dead Iltherians lying in the other tunnels, and we will likely see even more along our way before we reach the ship."

Soldier 369 turned out to be right. They did have to step over countless more bodies during their march in the dark. "I don't understand," Roessa whispered. "How can the Iltherian army not notice that people are getting killed left right and center?"

"They probably do notice," said Tyrann. "But they can't do anything about it. Remember how hard it was to fight those bat-faced bastards in broad daylight? In this darkness the knights probably can't even see them, let alone fight them back."

"Tyrann is right," Kazan joined in. "The Iltherians probably think they are being attacked by something that protects the ship. Mana, after all, never comes at an easy price."

For a while they marched in silence, and it was not long before they started hearing noises ahead. The tunnel widened briefly before opening up to a spacious cavern that was as high as it was broad, funneling up towards a rather narrow ceiling. In the center the Adelphia stood on a rock, in the middle of a circular chasm that surrounded it like a moat. Columns emerged from the chasm like stepping stones leading to the ship, all lit up by the same feeble light that seeped in through a few cracks in the ceiling. The helm that

Korinth spoke of was on the other side of the cavern, balanced on a stone pedestal that was too high for even the Neranian Tyrann to reach.

Around the ship, battle ensued.

The empire's forces seemed to be fighting phantoms. In the dim light, the shadow-fighters were just that: shadows, fast and deadly. Despite their advantage in numbers, the Iltherians seemed to be suffering, and everywhere green-and-orange bodies were dropping to the ground lifelessly. A few officers were barking frantic orders, trying to keep their troops in control. Retreat was out of the question, and besides, they still had plenty of men they could afford to lose.

"Of course they are not ghosts, you idiots!" they heard an icy voice shout among the din. "I just killed one; they bleed just like anyone else!"

Kristoff shivered at the sound of it.

"Yakutska," Kazan mumbled to himself. "This is turning into quite the party." Then he turned around to face everyone else. "As much as I hate to put all of you in danger, since we have come this far, we need to move on. I do not intend to walk all the way back to the coast if I can avoid it." He took a deep breath. "Be careful, and try to get to the helm if you can. Fight anyone that gets in your way. Remember, this is not a do-or-die mission." He glared at Ceycil. "If you die for that bloody ship, I will kill you."

* * * *

There was a long pause as everyone watched the battle, trying to catch a moment of opportunity among the chaos to join in. Korinth was the first to step out. Before he left, he handed his book over to Chalco. "In this book lies the future and the past," he said solemnly. "Keep it safe, for through ages it must last. Through darkness and pain you have done your time, but just before a star burns out, its brightest light will shine."

Chalco stared at the crevices of the tree bark that covered the book. "But what do I..." he tried to ask, but when he looked up again, Korinth was already gone.

"Come," said Tyrann, laying a hand on Chalco's shoulder. "I think I can hack my way through that mess over there. If you watch my back for those black assassins, I just might be able to get to that helm." He, too, stepped into the heat of the battle with his sword-axe raised, leaving Chalco with his crossbow.

Kazan did not lose much time with strategizing. He picked a dense group of Iltherians that were fighting a pair of practically invisible shadow-fighters, and let a particularly large sphere of magical fire loose upon them. Among the confusion, he saw Ceycil run into the cavern, wielding King Lynnvander's sword.

"Stay to the edges," the wizard told Roessa. "And shoot anything that comes close to you or Rooks." Then he turned to the red-haired child. "Stay close to her, son. This is no ground for children."

Rooks nodded. "I won't fight, but if he wants to, I can't stop him." He motioned as he unleashed his earth spirit once again, with pure supernatural courage in the creature's eyes.

The wizard nodded back, and without another word, dove into the commotion.

It took both the Iltherians and the Diamond Sage a while to notice the small third party that joined the battle, which gave the companions a brief advantage. While everyone was looking to target either a black cloak or green-

and-orange armor, they managed to edge their way closer to the pedestal that held the helm.

Tyrann was ahead of the others, swinging his sword-axe. Every time his weapon came in contact with the body of an Iltherian, his face took on a disgusted expression, as if he were crushing cockroaches but couldn't bear to hear the crunch. Out of the corner of his eye he saw a ray of magical fire stream towards a group of Iltherians that had just noticed Ceycil. One of them tried to absorb the spell with his sword but failed, being struck in the thigh by one of Roessa's arrows. There was a horrible sizzling sound as the spell hit its target, and four knights fell to the ground in a smoking heap. Tyrann forced himself to concentrate on his own fighting, and lifted his sword-axe once again. Two more swings, two more armored bodies crumpling before him. Just behind them, the giant recognized the tan-skinned shadow-fighter who had tried to kill Kazan at the swamp. The man or elf as belied by the bumps under his hood, produced another dagger at his fingertips, and was ready to launch it at the wizard once again. The tan-skinned shadow-fighter must have caught a glance of Tyrann, for he paused momentarily. He had a split second to gasp before the flat side of the sword-axe caught him full in the back and swept him into the air like a kite, lifting his hood to reveal an oddly tanned elf. Tyrann couldn't help letting out a snort of laughter as the shadow-fighter flew across the battlefield. "Can't kill all them black flies," he smirked. "Not yet. They help pester the bigger pests." He slashed at another Iltherian coming his way, and took another step towards the helm.

Blood trickled from various cuts on the giant's body, but none of them were deep enough to concern him. He shook off the blunt, annoying pain like a dog shaking off fleas. Then he saw yet another knight coming at him with his sword, no, *swords* raised. *This bastard is still kicking, then?* Tyrann thought, recalling the encounter outside Korinth's cave.

William, like most other Iltherians, was not wearing his helmet. Even without one, the light in the cavern was barely bright enough to see. His handsome face was twisted in an expression of cold fury when his eyes met the giant's. Tyrann expected the Iltherian to call out an order of attack, but instead he saw the soldier make a beeline towards him, with the wild look of a jackal that did not intend to share its kill.

Tyrann was not about to waste time with pleasantries. As soon as William was within his reach, he brought his sword-axe down on the Iltherian as heavily as he could. Soldier 704 deflected the giant's blow just slightly to one side by crossing his two short swords and using them as a shield, and managed to step out of the way with surprising agility. Tyrann raised his weapon again, but a group of shadow-fighters picked that moment to swarm around them, and both he and William were stirred away into the swirling sea of battle that surrounded them.

*   *   *   *

Roessa put her back to the wall, and was eyeing the battle scene carefully, like a falcon scanning the ground for prey. She strung an arrow so tight on her bow that her fingers were white with the tension. She didn't want to be spotted as the origin of a shower of arrows, so it paid to be slow and cautious. Besides, her arrows were limited. She couldn't afford to waste any. In the distance she saw another black figure moving in the shadows, getting dangerously close to Kazan. There was a loud twang as her fingers loosened and her arrow flew through the air, only to bury itself halfway into the shadow-fighter's back. The man collapsed instantly. Kazan didn't notice him falling any more than he noticed him approaching, and went on to strike a pair of Iltherians with a spinning disc of fire. The knights were hurled back several yards with the force of the impact, knocking a third one off his feet into the chasm that surrounded the Adelphia. The rest of the knights in the area absorbed the mana residue and blasted auras of essence around them, fending off shadowy figures trying to sneak in for a dagger in their backs.

Kazan was doing surprisingly well, considering he was surrounded by an army of anti-magic knights. Still, he was fully aware that he wouldn't last more than half a minute if it wasn't for the shadow-fighters distracting the Iltherians, along with Roessa and Korinth constantly watching his back. Once in a while he even thought he saw a few of Chalco's crossbow bolts whizzing towards the knights that tried to absorb his mana. Cowardly as it may seem in any other battle, most of Kazan's targets were Iltherians with their backs turned to him. It was the only way to catch them off guard without their swords raised and ready to suck up his spell. Even worse, they could catch the spell and throw it at someone else. *This is no time for gallantry,* the wizard kept telling himself. Besides, it wasn't a fair battle to begin with.

Through all his skirmishing and blasting, Kazan kept an eye on Ceycil, trying to keep as many enemies away from the boy as possible. It wasn't an easy job, since Ceycil was a reckless fighter and the Diamond Sage seemed especially intent on getting rid of him. While he was busy casting a rain of fire onto an area behind Ceycil to keep a couple of shadow-fighters from reaching him, the wizard's eyes met another pair that were a familiar shade of icy blue. With her thick braid tucked into her armor, Yakutska could very well be a man with her sharply-lined face that was frozen in an expression of pure calm hatred. Kazan squinted as he watched her lift her green sword. Then her expression changed, and she lowered it, barking an incomprehensible order at her troops while pointing a finger in the wizard's direction. It was a matter of moments before Kazan was swarmed with Iltherians. Out of the corner of his sight, he thought he caught a smirk on his sister's face.

Ceycil depended mostly on his reflexes to survive the battle, and whatever his reflexes couldn't account for was shielded by his new elven armor. He was not a particularly good fighter, and the only thing that gave him comfort was the knowledge that the sword hilt in his hands once had his father's fingers wrapped around it. He barely dodged a heavy lunge from an Iltherian, who ended up striking a shadow-fighter instead. While the knight was trying to remove his sword from the dead shadow-fighter's body, Ceycil brought his sword down on the knight's neck and tried to suppress an urge to vomit. He didn't even have time to catch his breath before another Iltherian appeared before him; his sword of verdium already raised high above his head. *For all the Realms,* Ceycil thought feverishly, *I think I am about to die.* His mind attacked the morbid thought with the same frantic passion that burned inside him while his body fought the Iltherians. In the split second that he could react, he closed his eyes and swung his sword so hard that he thought his shoulders were going to rip out of their sockets.

He heard a loud clang.

When he opened his eyes again, the knight was flat on the ground, lying in a pool of blood. A wave of intense relief washed over him. *Nice blow, Cess,* he told himself, grinning a little. Then he noticed the arrow sticking out of the Iltherian's chest. His swing merely made a dent in the side of the man's armor. He glanced back and grinned even wider. *Nice shot, Roessy.*

Unfortunately, his moment of victory did not last very long. As soon as he took a few steps towards where the winged helm stood, he found himself face to face with the last person he would ever want to meet again.

*   *   *   *

Valharess shook his head, the horns on his helmet swaying from side to side like a bull getting ready to charge. "Come out and play, Ceycil Lynnvander!" he shouted. Despite the noise, his voice hung in the air like icicles, cold and pointy.

Ceycil felt panic rising inside him for the first time since he joined the battle. The black knight looked like a phantom in the dim cave, and Ceycil wondered for a moment how he could even see with his helmet still on.

Valharess' green eyes glowed like those of a wild animal. "Good," he said with an amused voice. "I like fear. Be afraid. Be very afraid." He let out a hollow laugh.

Ceycil felt his fear growing like a bubble that would soon burst. He saw the tip of his sword start to tremor. His hands were shaking. For a moment, he wanted to let go. *Just drop the sword and run,* he thought. Still, there was something peculiar about that thought, about his fear.

Just drop the sword. It was against everything Ceycil believed in. He shook his head, as if trying to shake the thought away. "This isn't my fear," he said aloud. He glared at Valharess. "Get out of my head," he spat. Then he raised his father's sword and swung it at the black knight without another thought.

In the split second that Ceycil's sword took to reach him, Valharess had already shifted his presence over to the other side. "Fine," said the black knight. "Have it your way then." He reached up with a hand and curled his fingers into a fist. As he did so, chunks of ice broke off from the ceiling and showered down on Ceycil.

Ceycil inadvertently took a few steps back, and tried to cover his head with his arms. It was just as well, because a giant serpent of magical fire had flown its way between the two of them and across the battlefield, clearing a path towards the winged helm and shredding vibrant mana essence away, recharging random verdium swords within the din of the melee.

Valharess let out a roar of rage as he stepped out of the spell's way. "You can't get away so easily, boy!"

Rooks watched the battle from his spot at the entrance of the cavern. His earth spirit smoothly ran off seconds after Kazan left, and was currently taking its frustration out on a shadow-fighter wearing a black silk cape and a monocle. The red-haired child kept his eyes on Tyrann. The giant was remarkably close to the tall pedestal that held the winged helm. Still, when Kazan's fire serpent split through the entire battlefield, he was too busy swinging his sword-axe to notice that his path was now clear.

Rooks had less than a second to figure out what to do. Holding his breath, he ran for the pedestal.

"What the hell are you doing?!" Roessa screamed behind him, but it was too late. Rooks was already in the battlefield.

It took Korinth most of his concentration to make sure that Rooks reached the helm alive. He managed to block his presence out of the minds of the enemy, taking out as many Iltherians and shadow-fighters as he could without revealing himself. He was, after all, a wizard and a psion, and both of those were dangerous titles to claim in this battle. As he walked around calmly and unnoticed, strange accidents seemed to befall those who attempted to reach the child. A patch of icy ground suddenly became too slippery. A dagger that was thrown changed direction ever-so-slightly in mid-flight. A sword that was raised felt momentarily too heavy and fell over backwards. To someone looking from the outside, Rooks would appear miraculously lucky. Korinth watched his work in progress, and allowed himself a brief smile.

He saw that Kristoff, too, was keeping busy. With his green and orange armor, the Iltherians took the young man as one of their own, but members of the Diamond Sage attacked him mercilessly. As Kristoff was trying to dodge the daggers lanced at him by the same tan-skinned shadow-fighter that Tyrann threw across the cavern earlier, Rooks was already climbing the column that the winged helm stood on. From his corner, Korinth watched the child grasp the helm with one hand. That was when the earth started to shake beneath his feet.

*   *   *   *

Ceycil's first impression was that the ceiling was caving in. It was certainly cracking and crumbling in places, with pieces of frozen rocks and debris raining on the battlefield.

It turned out that Ceycil was only partially right. The ceiling *was* coming down on them. Except that what they mistook to be the ceiling all along had just unfolded an alarmingly large pair of leathery wings.

Ceycil had never seen a dragon before, but dragons by nature were easy to recognize, and he held no doubts that with its metallic blue scales and massive reptilian stature, this creature was indeed one. Besides, most people did not get to see more than one dragon within their lifespan, as that would require surviving their first encounter.

If there was chaos on the battlefield until then, with the dragon's arrival, it turned into sheer pandemonium. Between the blinding light and the freezing air that rushed in through the now-open mountaintop and the presence of the creature itself, the fighting all but ceased. The panic in the air was so thick; Ceycil thought he could taste it on his tongue. His own first instinct was to scream for Kazan. Trying to shield his eyes from the light and his head from the falling rocks, he looked around frantically, only to see the wizard take a fist-sized chunk of ice straight to the head and fall over unconscious.

He also caught sight of Rooks on top of the column, who was trying to keep his feet in the cracks in the stone while still trying to hold onto the helm with one hand. With the cavern shaking as it was, it did not take long before the child lost his footing completely and toppled down, taking the winged helm with him.

The strange artifact bounced on the frozen ground once or twice, and as if by magic, lay spinning by Ceycil's feet. There was no time to ponder. He grabbed it as fast as he could and put it on. Around him, people were too overcome by terror to notice or care about either the ship or the helm. The dragon, it seemed, was sucking up any rational thoughts they might have, and replacing them with pure primal fear. Most of the Diamond Sage already disappeared into the shadows, and even among the Iltherians there were those trying to reach the exit despite the two officers that were screaming orders for them to remain in battle.

Yakutska had called for reinforcements some time former, not that they had really needed any at the time, but one never knew. *Definitely a good decision*, she told herself now. With this overgrown lizard showing up, they could definitely use more knights. There was only one thing that troubled her mind. *What's taking them so damn long?* Her eyes peered over the battlefield towards the tunnel that led out of the cavern. The messenger she sent over to the reinforcement camp was returning. *Finally!* She took a deep breath, getting herself ready to snap at the soldier for being late. Then she let it back out. The messenger was walking somewhat strangely, more dragging himself across the ground than limping. A trail of blood marked his path as he walked.

"Where are the reinforcements?" Yakutska demanded briskly, sparing no sympathy for the wounded soldier. "They better come soon, now we have a dragon to deal with."

"Dead," the messenger gasped. "Most of them. Giant ants came out of nowhere. Hundreds of them." He tried to draw his chest up in an attempt to breathe, but failed and fell on his knees.

Officer 1001 pressed her lips together and walked away, ignoring the dying knight completely. Then she ordered her troops to retreat.

William appeared by her side almost immediately. "Are you out of your mind? Just because we have to fight a handful of vagabonds and a dragon, you're going to give up on the mission just like that?!"

Yakutska gave him an icy stare. "The vagabonds have the helm that controls the ship," she said, her voice as icy as her eyes. "Our men are full of dragon-fear and we have no reinforcements. We retreat. It doesn't mean we give up."

William gave her a blank stare.

"We leave the dragon and the others to have their own private party. They scratch up the dragon a bit, and the dragon eats a few of them for supper. Then we come back and clean up whatever is left. Much easier that way, isn't it?" She smiled coldly. "Use your brain, soldier. You'll see that it's better than a fist sometimes."

William's nostrils flared slightly. "And what if they get to the ship, fly out of here and leave us with just the dragon?"

Yakutska's smile widened, revealing a set of pearly white teeth. "They can't, trust me. Dragons guard their treasure to the death."

* * * *

Chalco watched the battle from his corner with Korinth's bark-bound book tucked into his elven armor, firing his crossbow every now and then to protect his companions. It hadn't taken him long to realize that Tyrann only asked him to cover his back to make him feel useful. The giant needed no protection. Nothing seemed to go through his skin anyway.

It was partially this thought and partially seeing hundreds of Iltherians at once that brought his fear back like a creeping monster from within. His hands shook so badly that he was surprised he could still shoot his crossbow and have even one of the bolts hit the target. Even in that state he held his spot, hoping he could at least take out one or two enemies. When he saw Rooks running for the helm, for one brief moment he allowed himself to hope that he might, just maybe, live through this battle.

Then came the dragon.

With it, any trace of valor that Chalco might have found inside him dissipated like smoke. Before the Iltherians could consider retreat, Chalco vanished into the tunnels, away from the new found winged nightmare.

Roessa, too, was overcome by an irrational terror as she watched the dragon descend from its nest above the mountain. She kept trying to tell herself to stay calm, but it was impossible. The creature's presence was overwhelming. Still, she forced herself to put her thoughts into order, perhaps that way she could resist the urge to run away screaming. Her eyes wandered back and forth between Rooks lying motionless beside the pedestal, Ceycil with the winged helm covering his head, and the dragon swooping down towards him. For all she knew, the red-haired child could be dead. And as terrible as the thought was, at least it gave her the chance to focus her attention on helping Ceycil.

The battlefield cleared up almost completely, she realized. That was both good and bad. At least this way they only had the dragon to deal with. Then again, it also meant that they were the only ones left to deal with the dragon. She glanced around the cavern quickly, and saw that there were even fewer people standing than she thought: Ceycil, Tyrann, Korinth, the renegade Iltherian, Rooks' earth spirit and herself. She didn't want to think of what could have become of the others, especially her father, and tried to avoid looking at the numerous bodies on the ground. *Concentrate,* she told herself. *You have four arrows left. Use them wisely.* She had doubts that even at the wisest of moments her arrows would be of any use against this mass of scales and wings, but that was another thought she was trying to suppress. Almost in an attempt to prove herself wrong, she drew an arrow and pulled the bowstring as tight as she could. As the dragon approached Ceycil with its neck stretched out like a solid tree trunk, she let the arrow loose.

The arrow embedded itself between the creature's scales, who flicked its head like a dog trying to shake off a flea. It didn't seem to care any more than Tyrann cared about plucking crossbow bolts out of his shoulders.

Roessa sighed. *Great! Now I only have three useless arrows left.* Still, she strung up another one. Just in case.

Ceycil watched the dragon's crystalline eyes get closer and closer, as if he were hypnotized. *We must get out of here,* he thought desperately. The problem was that he didn't know where half his companions were, and had no intentions of leaving them behind. Trying to get to the ship would be useless at this point. Besides, something needed to be done about the dragon. A silent chorus of *"It's a DRAGON. You're going to die!"* looped around and around in Ceycil's head as the scaly figure came nearer. He told the voice to shut up and clenched his fingers around his sword hilt as tight as he could, expecting to see the dragon's teeth surround him any moment.

To his surprise, the dragon didn't attack immediately. It braced itself and landed right before Ceycil. Then it cocked its spiny head to the side and eyed him with almost a mocking expression. It was at least four times as tall as Ceycil, with glassy teeth that glimmered in the winter light like the icicles that had fallen off the collapsed ceiling. To his horror, Ceycil realized that the dragon was grinning.

It happened even faster than he thought. A claw the size of a millstone swept towards Ceycil. Instinctively, he tried to block it the same way he would block a sword. He couldn't stop the impact of course, but it did give him enough leverage to push himself away from the claw as he was thrown to the ground. The next blow came almost immediately, and it was purely his reflexes that saved Ceycil as he rolled out of the claw's way.

The dragon winced a moment of distraction as it was struck by another one of Roessa's arrows. It shook its claw like a child shaking his hand after trying to touch a candle flame. In those few seconds, Ceycil sprung to his feet again, his sword rose before him. As he was getting ready for the next attack, he saw Tyrann charging at the dragon at full speed.

The giant's sword-axe caught the dragon square between the ribs. The creature roared in pain and flailed its tail, sweeping Tyrann right off his feet. The blow would have broken several ribs in anyone else, but it simply knocked the breath out of the giant, and sent his weapon sliding across the icy ground.

The dragon turned its attention back to Ceycil, ignoring the thick, dark line of blood trickling down its side. "You want this helm." Ceycil whispered, nodding at the gigantic reptile. "I know you do. I'm not just going to hand it over." He was huffing like an overworked horse, dizzy from the blood pounding at his temples. "You'll probably kill me either way, so let's at least see you get some exercise."

Behind them, the earth spirit was quietly at work. With Rooks under one arm and Kazan over its shoulder, it was making its way over the stepping-stone columns, across the chasm and towards the Adelphia`s hull.

* * * *

He's out of his mind, Roessa thought as she watched Ceycil trying to fight the dragon. *And that's why I love him.* She shot her third arrow in an attempt to give Ceycil a moment to recover after being knocked onto the ground by yet another blow from the dragon's claw. He was holding himself up surprisingly well. He had only been hit twice so far. Both times the elven armor he was wearing absorbed most of the impact, so he was probably badly bruised but miraculously not wounded. Roessa even saw him stab the dragon once or twice, but it was like sticking pins into a rhino. It did more to annoy the dragon than actually do any damage. She shook her head in odd scepticism, and strung her last arrow onto her bow.

She saw that the rest of the companions, too, were trying to attack the dragon, or at least to protect Ceycil, but it wasn't an easy job. Kristoff tried to jab at the dragon several times with his sword but he seemed far too nervous. Even Roessa could tell from a distance that the knight's grip on his sword was loose and wobbly; there was no way that he could even break through the dragon's scaly skin. Tyrann tried reaching his sword-axe that slid across the cavern, but by then the dragon was between him and his weapon. *Even a Neranian giant wouldn't dare attack a dragon with his bare hands*, thought Roessa, She watched as Tyrann waited for an opportunity to make a run across, his eyes fixed on his sword-axe.

Korinth alone stood at a distance and watched the battle with interested eyes. Every now and then he would wave a hand towards the dragon in a light but deliberate gesture, and what would have been a fatal blow to Ceycil would miss him by half an inch. The elf held no weapons, and Roessa did not see him make any effort towards fighting.

At one point in the heat of battle, the dragon swung its long neck towards Ceycil, trying to get him with its spines.

238

Ceycil felt the air in front of him suddenly get heavy, as if it was under pressure and was just released. Once again the deadly blow just missed him, as if by miracle, but it did knock the sword out of his hand. He took a feeble glance at the weapon as it went flying.

That glance almost cost him his life. The dragon opened its cavernous mouth and went directly for Ceycil. He saw the razor-sharp teeth come towards him, and for a moment closed his eyes and gave himself up for dead. Whatever was coming after this, he was ready for it.

His heart clenched in a knot as he heard Roessa scream out his name. *Sorry Roessy,* he thought. *This is it. I tried.* In the same split second, he heard another one of her arrows hit the dragon's scaly hide, knowing still that it would not change anything. He braced himself for the dragon's final blow, ready for the end.

What he wasn't ready for was the ground shaking under his feet again. He opened his eyes to see Tyrann, with a strength that could only be brought on by desperation, lift the dragon up by the root of its tail and slam it against the cavern floor.

For a moment, both the giant and the dragon stood still, shaken by what just happened. Tyrann was panting, his muscular arms still wrapped around the massive scaly tail. The dragon was faster to recover from the surprise. After one annoyed look at the giant, the creature lifted its tail and violently slammed him back against the floor.

Tyrann lay motionless underneath the dragon's tail, and did not get up.

*　*　*　*

Chalco hid in the tunnels as the last few knights from the Iltherian army made their way out of the mountain. He was overcome by a terrible, hysterical fear. No longer sure of where he was or what he was doing, he huddled in a corner of frozen rock and shuddered to the point of convulsing. His teeth chattered uncontrollably, and his heart felt like a giant balloon bounding against his ribs, crushing the air out of his lungs. Ghostly images paraded through his mind, hauntingly vivid. For a moment he thought he could hear his wife singing, the same familiar tune. *It's all right,* he told himself in his delirium. *The hunt is over. I'll be out of the forest soon, and Nakai will be at the doorstep, stringing another bow.* He wondered what was he doing in this frozen grave, thousands of miles away from everything he had ever known and loved. Then memories came seeping in, like water through a cracked dam. The blood-red river came before his eyes, and his daughter hiding in the fruit basket, too scared to cry. A mindless run through the tall grass towards the river, and the vast, deadly blueness of the sea. With every image, reality hit him like a hammer. *Everything you have loved is dead and gone. When you get out of this mountain, you will be, too. There's no way you can survive the cold, or the trip back to... where would you go back to, anyway? And when you die, all their memories will be lost forever.*

He took a deep breath, thinking of his companions he had left behind with the dragon, their faces fleeting through his mind's eye one by one. Then one of them, a particular memory, settled his panic the same way rain would settle a dust storm. *You are wrong;* he told the voice of his mind. *There is someone else who holds those memories now. He knows my story, and he can tell it when I am dead and gone. And as long as our memories live, so do our spirits.*

His shuddering calmed down a little bit, and the haze of terror in his eyes gave way to quiet awareness. He knew what to do. *I won't let my people die,* he told himself. *Not again.*

*   *   *   *

In the cavern, Ceycil spared no time to worry about Tyrann. The dragon seemed quite intent on getting the winged helm, with or without Ceycil's head in it. Without his sword, all he could do was duck and dodge and roll to avoid whatever part of the giant reptile was coming towards him, though he knew that he couldn't last much longer. Every inch of his body ached from overexertion, and his lungs felt like he was breathing fire instead of air.

"Just give up the damn helmet Ceycil, it's going to kill you!" he heard Roessa shout desperately.

"No!" Ceycil panted. "I'm not walking back into those tunnels. We're either flying out of here, or going nowhere at all." He wasn't sure if he felt as brave as he sounded, but it didn't matter. If only for the sake of sheer pig-headedness, he was keeping that helm.

The dragon made another lunge towards Ceycil, and Prince Lynnvander barely dodged to one side vaulting over the huge spiny head. This was getting ridiculous. "Korinth!" he yelled. "Can't you do something? I thought you were a mana-user or something?!"

The elf's usual expression of serenity was replaced by one of apprehension since the dragon appeared. "'Tis against my mana-like nature to harm a magical creature," he breathed, his eyes still fixed on the dragon. "And a dragon's mind is truly one of a kind, stronger than a fortress I find," he added thoughtfully.

"That means you can't do anything to destroy it?" Ceycil squeaked as the dragon roared in his face, a clear sign that it disapproved of being turned into a pincushion by Kristoff.

"I'm afraid not. This battle won, by fist or by blade must be fought."

"Great!" Ceycil gasped and threw himself to the ground once again, away from the dragon's teeth. He got back up as quickly as he could, and prepared himself for another leap, but the dragon's next attack didn't come as readily as he expected. He was winded and wheezing like a spent racehorse, his mind clouded from fatigue.

For a moment, he thought the creature had surrendered. It hovered over Ceycil, motionless. Its crystalline eyes had glazed over slightly, as if it was trying hard to concentrate on a thought. Then it opened its mouth slowly, like the beginning of a yawn.

Something clicked in Ceycil's mind. Something about dragons.

The breath, he thought frantically. *It's about to use its breath!* Or had he said it out loud?

Before anyone could react, Korinth hurled himself in front of Ceycil. A white cloud of frost emerged from the dragon's flaring nostrils, precipitating towards the two of them.

The elf held out his palm like an invisible wall, and for a moment Ceycil saw the tiny particles of ice moving through the air. They slowed down, then stopped… and fell to the ground around them with a tinkling sound, barely audible even in the hollowness of the cavern.

It was followed by the dragon's growl of rage, as the creature head-butted the elf square in the chest. Korinth was swerved across the battlefield, unconscious and bleeding from two gashes where the dragon's spines caught him.

Sweat trickled down Kristoff's face as he stood grasping his green sword. His temples were pounding with every heartbeat, and he felt like he was suffocating in his heavy Iltherian armor. Throughout the battle, the elf was his only foothold of hope against the odds. A garrison of Iltherians, the entire Order of the Diamond Sage, and now a dragon. Even a giant like Tyrann could only match maybe a tenth of that at his very best, and that was excluding the dragon... but an elf that could overcome even the mind tricks of the black knight, making him sit down like a trained puppy? If anything could give them the tiniest of chances, it was Korinth's mind and mana, and now he was out of the equation.

Kristoff felt disabled. His sword felt like a pathetic toy in his hands, useless as a blunt kitchen knife against the dragon's overwhelming presence. Korinth's last sentence echoed in his mind again and again. *This battle by fist or by blade must be fought.*

As the dragon tried once more to take a bite out of Ceycil, Kristoff did something very brave and very foolish. Lifting his sword up into the air, he tapped into the mana essence that flowed from the dragon. He didn't care whether his sword could handle such great amounts of mana, and kept draining it until his legs wobbled underneath him. He fell on his knees, but his sword remained upright, loaded with mana and glowing like a beacon. Slowly he felt his consciousness slipping away, overrun by the immense wave of mana that flowed through his sword into his body. As his world blacked out, it took all of Kristoff's willpower to make sure that the last thing that hit the ground was his sword.

When Chalco came running into the cavern, Ceycil and Roessa were the only people standing against the dragon. The creature was briefly distracted by Kristoff's attempt to drain its mana essence, but lost nothing from its strength to matter. Dragons were far more powerful than most Iltherians could fathom. Just as a goblet of water could not put out a forest fire, one sword of verdium could not take down a dragon.

As he scampered across the battlefield, Chalco's mind barely took note of Rooks' earth spirit floating in the background like a lonely ghost; with something quite large slumped across its back. His fear was now something distant, detached from his senses and his being. Courage was far from him, too. He felt nothing at all. Just a solid sense of purpose: *Ceycil must live to tell our story, to tell my story.*

Ceycil and Roessa were backed dangerously close to the chasm, with just a couple of yards between them and the dragon. Behind them, the earth spirit with its awkward load was hopping over the stepping-stone columns that led to the Adelphia.

"Go to the ship," Ceycil ordered Roessa.

"I'm not leaving you!" she protested.

The dragon made another lunge at Ceycil, making him stumble and almost lose his footing. He took half a glance over his shoulder at the chasm behind him. "Please, for once don't argue!" he told Roessa. "Just go to the ship, it's the best thing you can do for me right now."

Reluctantly, she took a step onto the first stepping-stone, without taking her eyes off Ceycil and the dragon.

It was then that Ceycil saw Chalco barge into the cavern, running towards the dragon like a man with nothing to lose. That was the last thing he expected. For a moment, he wondered if this man was indeed the Chalco he knew or perhaps the spirit of him, so ethereal and different than the earthen-skinned man had seemed during their travels. The corner of Korinth's book stuck out from the collar of his elven armor too short for his lanky body, and there was a wild look in his eyes.

The dragon attacked yet again. Ceycil managed to dodge the sharp teeth one more time, but was unable to get away from the edge of the chasm.

When the dragon raised its head again, Chalco already reached Ceycil. The huge creature hovered over them like a giant vulture. Ceycil wanted to step away from the icy monstrous figure, but his heels were already an inch away from the chasm. Then he saw the earthen-skinned man raise his crossbow.

"Chalco, what are you doing?"

"The eyes," the man answered hazily, even though he looked more lucid than he ever had. "If I could only aim for…" For once, his hand was steady as a rock. He squinted in concentration.

Unfortunately, he took a moment too long.

The dragon, suddenly perceiving him as a threat, gave Chalco a whack with the flat side of its head, knocking him back. The earthen-skinned man was forced to take a step back, into the deep chasm that separated them from the Adelphia.

Ceycil let out a shriek, then a sigh of relief. Chalco managed to stop his fall. He leaned on an elbow, his crossbow in his free hand and his legs dangling into the chasm.

Clambering over to the man instinctively, Ceycil held out a hand. "Give me your hand!"

Chalco did not seem to hear him. His eyes were fixed on a point over Ceycil's shoulder. His face was blank and calm. He lifted his hand that held the crossbow. Ceycil reached out to grasp it, but the hand moved on quickly.

Ceycil heard a grunt over his shoulder, followed by a click, a twang and a sickly crunch, all within the same split second. Over his shoulder, he saw the dragon's head up close, far too close. Between the deadly jaws, he could see two crossbow bolts embedded halfway into the roof of the dragon's mouth. He felt a rush of intense relief as the creature swaggered back and forth… and fell forwards.

It was pure reflex that made Ceycil throw himself sideways. Rolling over, he saw the dragon topple over into the chasm, taking Chalco with it.

Hours later, Tyrann woke up with such a headache that even a catapult`s boulder could not elicit so. His brain felt like it was being beaten by several mallets, and he felt slightly dizzy, as if the ground was swaying gently under his feet. Then he realized that it really was swaying up and down, very very slowly. There was a soft but icy wind whistling by his ears. As his mind raced back to the battle and the dragon, his eyes popped open and he sat up.

Around him, the whole world seemed to be made up of endless white fields, puffed up like the cotton flowers that grew on riverbanks, or clouds in the sky.

Clouds in the sky! His eyes wandered back from the horizon onto the surface he was sitting on. He was on a ship that much he could recognize. *The Adelphia,* he thought with a smile. *So we made it after all.* He tried to recall how he had arrived on the ship, but he only got as far as banging the dragon against the floor. The rest was oblivion.

The flying ship looked much bigger than in the cavern. It was built like any other ship that sailed the seas, except its two masts were not adorned by sails. Instead they contained rows of wings covered in what seemed to be feathers made of cloth. Some were as large as the dragon's, and some were barely the size of a songbird's. The wings were all white like the clouds, and moved with the grace of swans over a lake. Between the two masts, there was a short pole that held a large blue crystal on its end. The crystal glowed with an inner light that reflected off the fluttering wings. Tyrann considered the sudden feeling that the Adelphia was the most beautiful thing he cast his eyes on.

Toward the bow of the ship, he could see Ceycil and Roessa sitting side by side, having a heated conversation with Kazan and Korinth. Ceycil seemed to do most of the talking while Kazan was clearly asking a stream of questions. Korinth simply nodded sullenly at Ceycil's words, and Roessa looked grim and forlorn. *Something is not right,* he thought. Looking around, he took a quick head count. Kristoff was passed out beside him, while Rooks lay quietly in the earth spirit's arms. "We are missing one," Tyrann muttered to himself. His heart sank. *We left Chalco,* he thought bitterly. *He fled from the battle and we left him behind.*

He tried to stand up, and found that it wasn't only his head that ached. His ribs, his back, his arms and legs were all sore, too. Slowly, he made his way towards where the others were sitting. As soon as they noticed him, they fell quiet. "We are going back for Chalco, right?" he said, even though he knew very well that it was out of the question. It would not do to take the flying ship right to where the Iltherian army could be waiting. Still, it was a hope, and maybe if he said it out loud his words would work some sort of miracle.

Ceycil stared at him, and swallowed hard. "Chalco is dead, Tyrann," he said softly. "He and the dragon went over the edge saving my life, saving all of us."

The giant's eyes glimmered against the light blue sky. His lips slowly formed a slight, sad smile. "I knew he had it in him," he whispered with grieving pride. "He had it in him all this time."

"I still… I still don't understand why he did it." Roessa shook her head, her eyes cast on the horizon. "He was a survivor. Why sacrifice yourself after working so hard to get through so many dangers?

"You said it yourself," said her father. "Chalco was a survivor. Except this time it was his spirit, not his body that was striving to survive. If we died, his memory would have died with us, and nobody would be left to remember him."

"Or his people across the sea," Ceycil added thoughtfully.

"Then remember him we shall," Tyrann said solemnly. "We'll keep his memory alive."

Roessa suddenly seemed to remember something. Reaching into her backpack, she pulled something out and handed it to Tyrann. It was a crossbow bolt. "This one missed the dragon," she said quietly. "You have it."

The giant ran his fingers over the bolt and nodded, lost for words.

*   *   *   *

As the Adelphia was picking up speed over the fields of clouds, the companions gathered near the crystal between the masts of the ship. Ceycil was getting better at controlling the Adelphia. The winged helm seemed to form a connection between his mind and the ship, which took some getting used to. Even though all he had to do was to will the ship to move a certain way, the Adelphia seemed to have a mind of her own that he had to work to override. "I can't just order the ship around," he tried to explain it to Kazan. "I have to *convince* her!"

The wizard chuckled in response. "I knew there was a reason that ships are always female," he muttered.

Kristoff finally lurched awake, though he was still weak and somewhat incoherent. "That was a foolish thing to do, son," Kazan reprimanded him. "It is a miracle the dragon's mana has not killed you."

"Courage is not always bright," Korinth broke in. "But sometimes the foolish way is right, in hindsight." The elf was surprisingly energetic, and the deep gashes the dragon's spines left across his chest were already healing. Ceycil couldn't help noticing that for another man, the wounds would have been deadly. *What are you made of?* He found himself wondering about the elf. *Are you immortal?* Then he recalled the elf's habit of answering his thoughts and his mind went silent, expecting a reply. It did not come. Korinth reminded him of Kazan in many ways, cryptic and full of secrets, with every revelation bringing another mystery. *Maybe it's a mana thing,* he thought. Then he noticed how solid the ageless elf and the old man both seemed. *Solid like ancient mountains, as if they have been here forever, and will endure ever more.* Was that a mana thing, too?

His thoughts were scattered by Rooks grumbling as he woke up. The child did not look particularly happy to be awake, muttering about his leg hurting. Ceycil wasn't surprised. The boy received quite a fall, and was lucky to be just sore and not badly injured. He watched Kazan fuss over Rooks' bruised leg, more an act of affection than actual worry. "Do not go back to bed now," he heard the old wizard say. "There are things we need to talk about." This, too, was no surprise to Ceycil. Serje never left Rooks out of whatever news was brought, and always involved him in every important interaction of the mutate birdman. The red-haired boy was no stranger to grown-up talk and business.

Kazan's words caught the attention of everyone else sitting in the circle, and once again Ceycil felt their gaze wandering towards him. He found the sense of responsibility odd, both satisfying and intimidating. He cleared his thought and broke the expectant silence. "It's time to decide our next course of action," he said to his companions. "We have the Adelphia. We can't keep on running like we used to. This ship is a powerful weapon against the empire. Not using it would be a waste of a good hope."

"Ceycil is right," Roessa backed him up heatedly. "This ship keeps us safe, but how far is safety going to get us if the earth beneath us is destroyed?"

Tyrann nodded in agreement. "With the Adelphia on our side, running would be selfish and shameful. I will not sit here and watch the Iltherians slaughter my people. I would much rather be dead with my friends than alive without them."

"I have no past to go back to," said Kristoff weakly. "If we decide to fight the empire, I might have a future, I might not. If we decide not to fight, then I am left with nothing at all. I am with you, whatever you choose to do."

Ceycil turned to Kazan, expecting a protest, but the old wizard shook his head. "I will not stop you son," he whispered. "I cannot stop you, not any more than I could stop your father if he were here. May your will be your fate."

Korinth and Rooks remained silent.

At Kazan's words, a strange feeling washed over Ceycil. Was it relief for the wizard's lack of resistance? He recognized it as pride, and allowed himself a faded smile. *That,* he realized, *is the closest thing to support that I will get from him.*

"It is decided then," Ceycil declared slowly but firmly.

"We will need plans, though," said Roessa. "We can't just go and storm Iltheria. We may have the Adelphia, but it's still the seven of us against the entire Iltherian army. Have you thought of where we should start?"

Ceycil smiled again and shook his head. "I haven't gotten that far yet. Give me some time; I'm sure I'll come up with something. I've been getting the craziest ideas out of nowhere lately, I almost feel like the realm is talking to me."

Now it was Kazan's turn to smile.

*   *   *   *

As the journey upon the Adelphia stretched on over the endless whiteness of clouds and the snowy continent beneath, the graven silence on the winged ship gave way to buzzing activity. The companions quickly learned that life under sail, or wing, was a lot more bearable if one found something to do to pass the days that blended into each other like the blueness of the sky and the sea on a low horizon.

Kazan was buried into his spellbook more often than not, refreshing his memory of old spells, and trying to learn new ones he copied from fellow wizards long ago. His focus was unbreakable, brutally aware that worry for his children must be put aside—no distractions, however important, could be allowed.

Once recovered, Kristoff spent most of his time giving sword fighting lessons to Ceycil. "That way you can rely more on your weapon than your reflexes," he said. "You defend yourself well. Now let's teach you how to attack." The clashing of the green sword against Ceycil's blade with the broken hourglass in its hilt went on ceaselessly. Even Kazan, despite the headache he had to nurse every day because of the noise, did not object to the training.

Roessa, for lack of arrows, took up a new sport. She marked a target spot on one of the masts, and was practicing throwing the elven-made dagger Ceycil gave her in the Earthen Path. Initially there was grumbling and avoidance on the part of the companions as the dagger bounced off the mast in all directions, or missed it completely and went who knew where, but after the first few days of clumsiness Roessa learned to control her throws. First she learned to hit the target, then to flick her wrist just the right way so that she could choose whether to hit the mast with the blade or the hilt of her weapon. Every day she stood another step away from the mast, and it was not long before her dagger could find its target as well as her arrows used to.

Rooks kept his spirits out of their vials so often that there was almost always one translucent figure sitting by his side. He spoke to them in a whispered undertone, and sometimes it seemed like the spirits whispered back.

Korinth and Tyrann alone did not seem to have a solid pastime. The elf, having lost his bark-bound book with Chalco, stood at the ship's bow and stared over the clouds for hours on end. As for the giant, he sharpened his sword-axe with a flint stone, and quietly sang songs that spoke of eternal freedom.

At mealtimes, ideas were discussed over dried meat and mushrooms left over from their underground march, with water derived from the moisture of the clouds that crystallized into sheets of ice on the windward side of the ship.

"Maybe we should try gathering up all the runaways," Roessa suggested. "I bet there's enough of them to make a substantial army. Then we'd have a greater force to stand up against the empire."

Ceycil shook his head. "We're talking about a bunch of scattered, scared people here. Even if we could convince them all to fight, it would take us years. The Iltherians would also be much stronger by then and we'd be back where we started."

Roessa frowned. "You're probably right." She sighed.

"We need allies," said Kazan, picking the ice crystals off his beard. "People who are already organized and ready to fight the empire."

His daughter raised her eyebrows doubtfully. "And you think such groups exist?"

The wizard nodded. "Wherever there is oppression, there are always those that resist. They may be silent and still, but they are always there, awaiting their chance to fight back."

Upon Kazan's words, Tyrann looked up from his meal for the first time. "The giants at the slave mines would join us," he said. "However many we can free. They await their chance."

"I'm sure the Colony would be on our side, too," Ceycil added. "I saw some of the ants around the Iltherian encampment when we first flew out of the cavern; they seemed to have ripped the whole place to shreds, knights and all."

A slow smile spread on the Roessa's cold-chapped lips. "That adds up to more than seven," she said. "It's not much, but it's a start."

*   *   *   *

It wasn't long before they needed to take a break from their journey, as food was running dangerously low and everyone was longing for the warmth of a fire. Between their winter cloaks and the crew bunks underneath the deck, they managed to stay reasonably warm on the Adelphia regardless of the icy wind of high altitudes. Kazan considered building a magical fire to keep them warm, but keeping it alive in such wind and cold would have drained his energy so quickly that he dismissed the thought. Roessa was already dreaming of stretching her feet out towards the flames and warming her toes that were numb since they first boarded the flying ship, and Rooks wanted to free his fire spirit of its forced confinement in the red glass vial. As for Ceycil, he could use a nice greasy pheasant for supper instead of stale mushrooms.

It took Ceycil half a day of stubborn concentration before he could get the Adelphia to land in a small clearing within a snow-covered pine forest. When the ghostly light of the north gave way to true nights and days, they knew that they were finally leaving the northern wastelands behind, and getting closer to inhabited grounds. It also meant that they were in higher danger of encountering Iltherians, but it was a risk they had to take sooner or later. At least here the trees hid them from anyone outside the forest. In the northern wastes, they could have been seen from two days away.

As soon as they landed, Kazan conjured up a blazing fire. One advantage of the overcast winter sky was the smoke from the campfire vanished into it quite nicely, making it impossible for anyone to spot the camp from a distance. Kristoff and Ceycil left for hunting almost immediately.

Roessa gathered up some wood, then leaning her back against the hull of the Adelphia, set to making some new arrows while enjoying the warm blood flowing into her feet. Rooks' fire spirit hovered between the two of them, a figure of swirling red flames that danced in tune with the campfire, melting the snow around it into a muddy puddle.

Tyrann refused Ceycil and Kristoff's offer to go hunting. His small, dark eyes stared into the campfire. Since Chalco's death, he didn't seem interested in much of anything. He spoke less and less by the day, and ate only when food was handed to him. He seemed like he was breathing a different air, walking a different earth.

Korinth alone seemed to know what was going on in the giant's head. He came over and sat beside him, his elven figure dwarfed by Tyrann's massive body. "The past is past," he said softly. "Alas, it does not last."

Tyrann shook his head. "No, it doesn't… Nothing lasts. Nobody lasts." He breathed deeply, and sat quietly for a while. "Korinth," he said finally. "Is it wrong to want revenge, for the future that was taken from me? I know that nothing will bring back the days I will never have with the friends that I have lost. Nothing will bring back the laughter we never got to share, and the songs we never got to sing together. "He paused. "I have promised myself that I would only fight for freedom, but now I find myself wanting to fight for revenge. I feel angry, empty… and I know that even revenge won't fill that emptiness, but I still want to do something, strike back pain for pain. Tell me; is it wrong to feel this way?"

Korinth closed his eyes and bowed his head. "To feelings there is no right or wrong," he said. "When our hearts are on fire, to us they still belong, and to quench those flames is for what we long." Then he looked up at the giant again. "If by wanting revenge a promise you broke apart, 'tis not revenge but that promise that will poison your heart."

Tyrann remained silent, though his eyes were not cast as low now, and his shoulders sagged a little less.

"Serje used to say that it's wrong to want revenge if someone has done you harm," Rooks added thoughtfully. "And equally wrong to not want revenge if someone has harmed your friends."

Kazan stared at him. It was the first time the red-haired child had mentioned Serje since the birdman's death during their first encounter with Iltherian troops. It seemed like centuries ago, their simple nomadic life before they witnessed with their own eyes what the empire was capable of. Before the Khenbish woman and the renegade knights, even before Korinth's riddles and Tyrann's friendship with Chalco. So much happened in one autumn and one winter. The wizard couldn't help but think of Ceycil and Roessa, and how much they changed in the last few months. *They are no longer the children that I am used to shepherding around,* he told himself. *They have grown up. And I have grown old…*

* * * *

When Ceycil and Kristoff returned from their hunt with two large birds, the sun was resting behind a thick layer of clouds.

"Where did you catch these things?" Roessa asked, watching the birds roast on a spit over the campfire. "I've never seen birds like this before."

257

"Nor have I," Kristoff replied. "But birds are birds; you can eat them no matter what kind."

Ceycil nodded. "I'm fine with anything that's not mushrooms at this point." He poked at the fire with a stick as he tried to ignore the loud rumbling coming from his stomach.

The forest around them faded entirely into a nondescript darkness, with the occasional shadow of a tree branch that came alive in the light of the campfire. Every now and then a pair of eyes glowed in the distance, only to disappear again.

The companions ate their supper over a lively conversation, chewing on more ideas and planning. Still, even after they were comfortably full and sleepy, Roessa couldn't help feeling like the forest was watching them. She kept stealing furtive glances into the darkness, hoping she would see nothing of the horrors her mind was busy fabricating. *Darkness is emptiness,* she tried telling herself. *It's a lack of things. There is nothing in it, nothing at all to be scared of.*

Still, in this place the nothingness was not at all reassuring, mostly because it was the kind of nothing that made a lot of rather disconcerting noises. Owls hooted unseen in the treetops, and once in a while a howl would echo through the air, though she could not tell whether it was a jackal or a wolf, or an altogether different creature. Leaves rustled in the darkness as something made its way through the trees, and over the wheezing of the wind, she thought she could hear…

Roessa straightened up so suddenly that all conversation around the fire ceased immediately. Her heart was thumping against her throat, and her hand instinctively reached for her bow. "Hoof beats," she whispered.

More hands reached for weapons. If there were horses around, then most likely there were Iltherians, too.

The hoof beats came closer, accompanied by the cracking of branches and the crunching of snow, though without the clanging of armor. Ceycil listened as the sound of galloping turned into the calm clip-clop of a trot, then slowed down even more. "It's a single horse," he whispered. "A single rider." Still, he kept his guard.

The companions tensed up visibly as the branches of the tree closest to them rustled. It was, as Roessa had rightly heard, a single horse, such a silky shade of white that it almost disappeared against the snow. It had no rider. A single golden horn shimmered on its forehead like a star fallen from the heavens.

Roessa felt her bow slip out of her hand. A warm peace like she had never known in her life on the run settled inside her, both strange and familiar. She felt like she found something she never knew she lost. It made her want to sing and weep at the same time.

As the unicorn walked towards them, the companions froze still like statues; for fear that the beautiful creature might disappear like an illusion if they dared breathe too loudly. It walked slowly around the fire, its white mane unstirred by the blowing wind, stopping only when it reached Rooks sitting with his back against the Adelphia. There the unicorn did something that nobody expected: Bending one front leg, the creature bowed down gracefully, almost as if it was saluting the flying ship.

Rooks held his breath. The unicorn was so close to him that he could see the spiraling groove on its golden horn. Before anyone could object, he found himself reaching out and stroking the creature's muzzle.

The unicorn nickered and rubbed back against the child's fingers.

"It's real," Rooks whispered.

The creature stood up calmly, turned around and trotted away from the camp, its breathtaking whiteness disappearing back into the dark of the forest.

Silence and stillness reigned around the campfire for a few minutes, only to be broken by Ceycil's sigh. "Wow!" he breathed. "Wow... that's all I can say."

Roessa blinked and shook her head in latent disbelief, her voice reflecting her amazement. "Was that a dream?"

Kristoff nodded. "If it was, then you and I share a dream. That was incredible."

Ceycil sat down again. "I thought you said unicorns were extinct." He addressed Kazan.

The wizard looked equally surprised as everyone else. "So I had believed, son, but you know how these things are. For all we know, wizards and elves are extinct, too." He looked at Korinth and one of his rare smiles spread across his face. "I must say I do enjoy being wrong sometimes."

"What was it doing here?" Rooks asked. "Why did it come to me?"

Kazan shrugged. "All I can think of is the Adelphia. The ship is supposed to be a ley line, the last major source of mana, and unicorns are mana-laden creatures. The presence of the ship must have drawn it to us."

"Mana to mana always connects," said Korinth. "And power to greater always respects. Eyes of a unicorn can see through fire, know the fruit of ashes that can take to wing higher."

Rooks shrugged, and his eyes caught sight of Tyrann, smiling for the first time in days. "If such beauty still exists hidden in the shadows, maybe there's hope for this world after all," said the giant. Rooks smiled back at him and closed his eyes, listening to the sounds of the night.

Even to Roessa, they sounded less sinister now. If the forest could hide a unicorn, perhaps it wasn't as full of horrors as she imagined. There might even be sprites in there somewhere, who knew?

She was so lost in those thoughts that it took her a few seconds before her brain could register what her eyes spotted ahead.

Not far ahead.

She jumped up in panic for the second time, disrupting yet another conversation. This time, her bow was strung and ready to fire. It was aimed at a black figure, bearing a pair of bull's horns on his head and a cloak whose purple hues flickered in its folds like fireflies. His green eyes glowed through his visor like a nocturnal animals.

"I'd put that thing down if I were you, girl," Valharess told Roessa. "You might take someone's eye out if you're not careful."

"If I *am* careful, it'll be your eye." Roessa hissed.

Korinth motioned her to sit down. "No need for alarm, he means us no harm."

"The psion has read me right," Valharess nodded without any sign of surprise. "I'm not here to ask for trouble. I have come alone, and unarmed." He held out his empty hands.

"Like that makes a difference," Roessa muttered without lowering her bow. "Last I checked you didn't need a sword to fry people with lightning bolts."

"Settle down Roessa," Kazan said gently. "Let us hear what he has to say." Then he turned towards the black knight. "We accept your peaceful arrival. You better keep to your word, or else your stay here may be briefer than you think."

The green eyes flashed with irritation inside the horned helmet, but Valharess kept his voice level. "I am here to talk business," he said. "I understand that you," he was looking directly at Ceycil, "and I have some things in common."

Ceycil nodded. "A common enemy. You fight against the empire, like we do."

"Correct." Valharess averted his gaze and turned back to Kazan. "Bravenscu and his minions need to go," he declared. "The Order of the Diamond Sage is strong, but the Iltherians are stronger in numbers. You have the mana of the Adelphia. And you have a giant, a wizard and a psion on your side. Those, I would say, are valuable assets." He paused, trying to arrange his words. "I'm willing to shake the hand I can't break," he said finally. "My shadow-fighters, your magic and anything or anyone else we can convince, against the empire. All our power, assembled together for one final attempt. Win or die. What do you say?"

"You are mad, is what I say." Kazan shook his head in disbelief.

"You refuse then?" Valharess' voice was cold and expressionless.

"That is not my call. We are in this together." The wizard looked around at his companions.

Ceycil stared at Valharess. "I'm with you," he said firmly. "If we plan it well and time it right, one attack is all we need. We have to take the empire in one blow, at the heart."

For the first time since he arrived, the black knight looked surprised. "You're smarter than you led me to believe, boy."

"I'm with you as well," said Tyrann. "Win or die. No point in dragging this on. Young Ceycil is right, the slower we act, the faster we'll get murdered. We should attack before the empire becomes aware of us."

Kristoff nodded tiredly. "I can offer my sword and my knowledge. I know my way around Iltheria well enough, and I have been inside the imperial tower."

Korinth shrugged, and Rooks remained silent in his corner, moving closer to his fire spirit.

Valharess' eyes settled on Roessa, who shook her head. "Fine," she said. "I'm in, but only because I trust the judgment of these people. I still think you're a sleazy creep."

The black knight let out a short, hollow laugh. "Coming from you, I'll take that as a compliment," he said. Then he stared at Kazan expectantly.

"The decision is made then, is it not?" the wizard muttered.

Valharess took off a black glove and held out his hand. It was splattered with pink and purple scars.

Kazan glared back at the black knight. "The hand you need to shake is Ceycil Lynnvander's," he said. "I am just an old man trying to serve his king."

Ceycil's heart leapt at the words. Without daring to meet Kazan's stare, he reached out and shook Valharess' hand. When his eyes met the black knight's piercing gaze, something about him looked oddly familiar to Ceycil. *I've seen those green eyes before, in a different face.* But no matter how hard he pushed his memory, he couldn't remember when or where.

The knight nodded solemnly. "I, Valharess, give you my word on my honor that the Order of the Diamond Sage will be loyal to you and your people against the Iltherian armies until this matter is settled. Let me know when you are ready."

Ceycil nodded back. "I, Ceycil Lynnvander, give you my word on my honor that my companions and I will fight by your side against the Iltherian armies." He paused. "How will we send you word, though?" He asked, genuinely curious.

"And how did you find us here, anyway?" Roessa barged in.

"The elf will know how to reach me," the black knight replied. "I will keep my mind open to his thoughts." He turned to Roessa. "As for finding you, let's just say I have many eyes. Eyes that can see things others cannot."

"You're a creep." Roessa repeated through her teeth.

Valharess shrugged. "Being a creep has its uses." He turned back to Ceycil. "I'll be expecting news from you," he said firmly.

Ceycil nodded. "You will know as soon as we are ready."

"Good. Don't take all year. The sooner we strike, the better our chances." With that being said, Valharess turned on his heels and disappeared among the trees and the shadows.

That night Ceycil went to bed with the hope of dreaming of the unicorn, but the silken white horse did not visit his sleeping thoughts. Instead the only dream was of darkness.

It was not the kind of darkness that comforts a soul in sleep, but a darkness that would only mask the dangers that were brooding in it. Ceycil saw nothing, felt nothing. He could taste a wet musty tinge in the air, and in the distance he heard a commotion. Heavy footfalls merged into the clanging of metal against metal. Gruff noises of swearing and fighting came echoing through, and blended into the desperate gasps that always ended in a final note of a muffled choke. Ceycil realized that he was moving through the solid darkness, though he could feel no legs running for him, nor the lightness of flying that often came in dreams. Instead it was a gliding motion, staggered by a constant shaking like a light earthquake. He did not know where he was or what was happening, except he was certain that somewhere in the distance death was taking its toll. Among the noise, he thought he heard a voice that did not fit into the battle cries and curses. It sounded like the cry of a child, lonely and scared. Perhaps even in pain. Ceycil was surprised to see that the cry awoke no emotions in him, no fear or pity arose in his soul, and a calm stillness in his chest replaced the mad beat of his heart. He was unable to feel anything at all, filled by a blankness that let him take everything in but process none of it. He was plainly there. Things were plainly happening. As he moved further away from the source of the noise, the child's cry, now vaguely familiar in its shrillness, faded into the darkness with the other sounds of despair.

Ceycil woke up as the dream ended. It was still dark, though the embers from the fire glowed reassuringly, and the clouds swept past the sky to reveal the stars. He stared at them for a while, and found comfort in their presence. *It's good to know that some things remain the same even as they change,* he thought. *Like the stars, like the spring. Always there, but a little different every time you see them.* It made him feel good to think about the spring, to see something in the sky other than the dull greyness of winter. He half considered waking Roessa to show her the stars, but he was still unsettled by his dream. She could always tell when he was preoccupied, she would ask what was wrong and he didn't feel like talking about it. Instead he lay quietly with his hands behind his head, gazing at the glittering skies.

It was maybe minutes, maybe hours later when he heard Kazan's voice beside him. "You need to sleep."

"So do you," Ceycil replied promptly.

"You are the one that will need the energy to get the Adelphia off the ground tomorrow," the wizard snapped back. "I can sleep aboard if I wish."

"But you won't."

"Of course I will not." Kazan chuckled. "I hate sleeping in broad daylight."

Ceycil liked the tone of amusement in the wizard's voice. It was that rare tone that made the old man seem like the father Ceycil never knew, not the voice of authority that ordered and counseled him so often.

"I had a disturbing dream," he found himself saying, and he moved on to tell Kazan about it in detail. When he was done, he thought he could hear the frown on the wizard's face.

"I had a dream just like that once," the old man whispered. "A long time ago."

"Really?" Ceycil's interest grew. "Do you think it means anything?"

"Maybe it does," said Kazan. "And maybe not."

Ceycil rolled his eyes, knowing the wizard couldn't see. "You're starting to sound like Korinth."

Kazan chuckled again. "Maybe I do, and maybe not. Go to sleep, it probably means nothing. Just a bad dream." He wrapped his blanket around his shoulders and rolled over.

Ceycil let out a deep sigh. *Last time I had a dream this clear, it became my future.* He thought about it a bit more. *Well, I was the one who dragged everyone to the swamp. I made the dream become my future.* He closed his eyes. He had no intentions of trying to find that dark tunnel, wherever it was. Still, as he fell asleep again, he could hear the child's cry echoing in his mind.

* * * *

They left the camp early in the morning. As the Adelphia rose above the clouds once more, Roessa gazed over the bowsprit with sleepy eyes, thinking of the unicorn hidden among the trees below. She didn't even hear Ceycil approach through the wind sweeping by her ears until she could feel the warmth of his breath brushing against her cheek.

He grinned and ran his fingers over her straw-colored braid. "Good morning, winter sunshine."

Roessa laughed. "Aren't you supposed to be sweet-talking this ship into moving higher or something?"

Ceycil's hand moved onto her shoulder and rested there, holding her close. "She seems to know what she's doing." He shrugged, taking a brief glance at the wings of the Adelphia fluttering above their heads. "I might as well enjoy the ride for a while." Then his eyes settled on the horizon, a line where the grey blanket of clouds met the pale blue sky, and he fell silent.

"What's on your mind?" Roessa asked.

He just blinked and shook his head, trying to chase the memory of the previous night's dream out of his mind. The sounds, the taste of mold in the air, the darkness… it all seemed too real, even after a full night's sleep.

Roessa didn't wait for his answer. "It's that black knight, isn't it? You're thinking about that deal we made."

"Yes," Ceycil lied, forcing himself to really think about his promise to Valharess. "Kazan probably thinks I rushed into that decision too fast," he thought out loud.

Roessa sighed. "So do I, to be honest. We've seen what that bastard can do; he's sly as a snake in an oil barrel." She paused and took a deep breath. "And if I were to trust either one, I'd take the snake in the oil barrel."

Ceycil shook his head again. "It's a chance we have to take," he said. "We've killed at least one Iltherian officer of high rank, back when we left Korinth's cave, so the emperor knows that we exist. We've been betrayed, so he also knows about the Adelphia. And on top of all that, we've faced Iltherian troops inside that mountain. It's virtually

268

impossible that the leading officers didn't notice us among that crowd, we don't exactly look like the shadow-fighters of the Diamond Sage. By now the emperor knows who we are, and probably has a good idea as to where we stand in the grand scheme of things. He will want to get rid of us. And now that we have the Adelphia, he'll want to get rid of us *really fast*. We have no time to go turning down alliance offers." He sighed, and then added quietly. "We are dead whether we decide to fight back or not. It's only a matter of time before the Iltherian army tracks us down. We might as well give it a shot; at the worst case we'll be dead a few weeks sooner."

"And at the best?"

"Well let's wait and see?"

They stared ahead quietly for a while, taking in the brisk morning breeze that hinted spring was coming. It was still freezing cold, but it carried a faint scent of moist earth, the same kind that would linger in the air after the rain. Somewhere, out of their sight, perhaps the snow was melting…

A polite cough behind him brought Ceycil back to the reality he was trying to escape. "Forgive me for interrupting your precious moment, but if you two lovebirds are done twittering, we have a few things we need to discuss." Kazan's voice was kind in the face of his mocking words. He beckoned them towards the circle between the ship's two masts where the rest of the companions sat thoughtfully around the remnants of breakfast.

Kristoff was the first to speak. "We've been thinking," he said. "At this speed we should reach Iltherian territory in less than a week. If we are aiming to act as soon as possible, then we should get a plan together before we are close enough to be spotted by the empire."

Ceycil blinked. Kristoff's words had hit him like a hammering blow to the chest, knocking the breath out of him. *Less than a week.* He hadn't expected the battle to come up that soon. Less than a week after the decision of war and the final battle, less than a week for all preparations to take on hundreds, maybe thousands of trained Iltherian knights... The previous night, when he was talking with Valharess, he felt like a hero. Now the whole thing sounded like madness. *Beyond madness,* he realized. *This is suicide.* "You mean we attack as soon as we get into their range?" he asked with a choked voice.

The young knight shrugged. "We could linger on the outskirts of the cities and hide for a bit longer, but that would not do us any good. We could maybe get a handful of runaways to join our ranks here and there, but I doubt they would be strong or numerous enough to give us any advantage over the empire. What we really need on our side is the Neranian giants, and to free them we have to break into the slave mines. And we must not give Bravenscu any time to get suspicious about something greater being on the move, so it is best to free the slaves after the battle has commenced. That way the defenses around the slave mines are likely to be weaker, too, since the Iltherian army will mostly be busy fighting us off."

Ceycil sighed. "Well, that's a start for a plan." He tried to gather his scattered thoughts together, but they eluded him like smoke slipping through the fingers of a hand. He was surprised and terrified that he had suddenly become the head of this expedition. When had he grown up so much? He was neither a soldier nor a commander. He knew nothing of strategy. *Still, I'm a king no?* He questioned. *I'm the king of Tallinad. It's my land. It's my home, my responsibility.* His mind wandered back to his first dream. He recalled the face of king Lynnvander, his father, and how thoughtful and determined he seemed. *This is not an easy fight,* he told himself. *It wasn't meant to be easy. My father fought it and lost. I must at least match his effort in battle, if not surpass it in victory.* He felt pride swell inside him like a cat puffing up its fur in the face of an enemy. He felt duty's call, a marching tune breaking the silence of dawn. What he didn't realize was that he was actually hearing the call of the land, to which his blood was linked with mana more ancient than the dragon he had fought.

"Now," he said, rubbing some heat back into his hands, "broadly there are two things we need to figure out: where and how do we attack? And how do we free the slaves?"

Ceycil looked at Kristoff expectantly, but it was Tyrann who answered. "For that last one, I think I have a plan." The giant turned to Kazan. "Do you think you could get us in touch with the Colony?"

The wizard thought about it, then nodded solemnly. "I can trace my own work of magic, yes. As long as they have the fire rock I gave them, with some effort I should be able to find a ley line of mana and contact them."

"Then I think we may be able to work something out together, especially if those tunnels… the Earthen Path goes anywhere close to Iltheria. I've heard it was a connection from Crystalfellen all the way to Tallinad before the empire destroyed it." The giant's eyes wandered over to Korinth.

The elf bowed his head sadly. "Tallinad, once it was. And yes, a branch of the Path yonder lies."

Tyrann nodded back. "That is settled then. I'll deal with my people while you hold up the Iltherians."

"That still leaves us with the battle itself." Ceycil stared into the horizon. "And as much as I hate to say this, I think we need to see that Valharess guy again quite soon. If he is to join forces with us, we have to know what he has for assets, and what we can work out together."

The rest of day was spent in heavy discussion, as plans and ideas were stretched, flipped around and stitched together like the pieces of an ancient map. By the time the night fell on the wings of the Adelphia, there were still parts missing. Unpainted gaps in the picture that was to be their grand scheme, their only chance at a war strategy.

"Perhaps Korinth should go ahead and contact the Diamond Sage this very night," Kristoff suggested. "It will likely take us a while to find them anyway, best not to waste time waiting."

"Probably a good idea." Ceycil stood up, and to everyone's surprise, drew his sword. "In the meantime, you and I have some business to take care of." He frowned. "Like that fancy parry you promised you'd teach me." His frown dissolved into a grin.

Kristoff groaned and pulled himself up. "Don't you ever get tired?"

"Not from talking, I don't. Besides, if we're going to be facing the Iltherians soon, I'd rather be tired and tough instead of rested, but without proper training."

"Fair enough." The young knight drew his sword as well. "If you wish to be tired, that can be arranged."

*   *   *   *

As the dawn was breaking, Ceycil found himself trying to land the Adelphia on the edge of a barren hillside. It should have been easy, except the ground was covered with jagged rocks that were barely visible through the snow that covered them, and a deafening wind rocked the winged ship. "Are you sure this is where he said he'd meet us?" he asked Korinth doubtfully. There was no sign of life within sight. Even the snow underneath them was swept clean with the wind, clear of any tracks.

The elf nodded. "His mind to mine he has bound, the message is sound. This is where Valharess is found."

"Looks like his type of place," Roessa muttered, trying to rub the sleep out of her eyes. "Pain in the neck, like himself."

"Tell me about it." Ceycil frowned, concentrating harder on the controls of the ship.

It was another hour before the Adelphia's wings could slow down their flutter and settle the ship's shiny hull safely into the snow. Ceycil sighed and loosened his mind's grip on the ship. As soon as he did, he heard a knock.

Much to Ceycil's surprise and confusion, Korinth smiled, glided over towards the gangway and calmly lowered it to the ground.

The dark-clad figure of Valharess appeared seemingly out of nowhere, and made his way on board. "I admit I'm impressed," he addressed Ceycil. "You got your act together faster than I thought. Now it better be a good act."

Ceycil took a deep breath. "Well, we have some plans, and we need to make some more. With you, that is. Work out a strategy."

The black knight nodded. "Yes, let's do that, but let's do it in our place. It will be warmer there." He shook his head, reminding Ceycil of a bull shaking off the flies around its ears. "Follow me." Without expecting an answer,

Valharess turned around and headed back down the gangway.

Ceycil took a quick glance of suspicion towards Kazan, who shrugged his shoulders slightly. *Yes, it could be a trap,* the wizard seemed to say. *But we do not really have another choice, do we?* As if to confirm Ceycil's answer, the old man stood up from his spot by the mast and followed the black knight into the snow.

Tyrann picked up Rooks onto his shoulders and followed Kristoff and Korinth into the strange procession.

Roessa brought up the rear, one hand resting on Ceycil's arm. "Why do you trust him?" she whispered, her voice all but disappearing in the whistling wind.

"I don't," Ceycil whispered back. "Nor does Kazan, but what he said before is right. We don't have the luxury of turning down allies." He took a breath. "Besides, what's the worst that can happen? If it's a trap, we all die. If it isn't a trap, we'll probably die in the battle against the empire anyway."

Roessa raised her eyebrows. "We are fighting for victory, Ceycil," she said seriously. "You might want to start by believing in it. You are our king."

Ceycil gritted his teeth. "I am the king…" he whispered to himself. "I am the king." Somehow hearing those words from Roessa was even more comforting than hearing them from Kazan. "Thanks Roessa, I needed that."

Valharess led them to a spot between two rocks, one curved overhead towards the other like an awning. He walked over to the curved rock and knocked on it with the back of his gauntlet. To Ceycil's surprise, it made the hollow sound of metal on wood, instead of the solid silence of stone. The curved rock had a door cut into it, only it was painted the same color as the rock, complete with cracks and frozen moss, and was practically impossible to see unless one knew precisely where it was.

The door opened without a sound, revealing nothing but a couple of inches of darkness. "Be welcome, or be ready to die," said a ghostly whisper from the inside.

"Shut up and get out of my way Gabriel, save your drama for children." Valharess swung the door wide open, almost knocking the tan-skinned young elf off his feet. The door led to a steep but surprisingly spacious staircase lit up by a single lantern that hung by the door, burning smokeless under its metal hood.

The companions followed the black knight down the stairs, as a rather confused-looking Gabriel stumbled behind them, carrying the lantern and shooting a sly wink at Roessa. She in turn tapped her bow in her hands reminding the tanned elf of the scar somewhere on his head he gained at the swamp.

Rooks wandered near Korinth. "Is this part of the Earthen Path, too?" he asked keeping a hand on his wooden box of vials. The elf shrugged, looking at the walls of the tunnel devoid of bricks or carvings. "Does not look elven to me, but it could be."

Roessa did her best to walk as quickly as possible without slipping on the ice that covered the stairs, all the while staying close to Ceycil and throwing razor-sharp glances at Gabriel. This was the man she had noticed trying to kill her father with his daggers after all, the same one she slapped and broke her bow over. She had no desire to be any closer to him than she absolutely had to, as she sported a burning urge to slap him again and possibly punch him in the nose while she was at it, then break her bow again. *That would not go over so well,* she told herself, shaking her head at the thought. *We're supposed to be here as allies. Shame, it would be so satisfying.*

The tunnel twisted and turned, going far deeper than the Earthen Path, eventually merging into a cavern almost as huge as the mountain that had held the Adelphia. The first thing that struck them as odd was the warmth. Despite there being no fires or torches in sight, the air in the cavern was warm enough to be comfortable without a thick winter cloak. It was also humid and stuffy, smelling strongly of mold and people. Roessa wrinkled her nose in distaste. A single large sphere of light hung at the center overhead, illuminating the strangest community she had ever seen during her twenty years of travelling. Hundreds of black-clad shadow-fighters were scattered across the cavern, mostly sitting in small circles and whispering. Initially she thought they were all men, but looking closely, she realized that there were quite a few women under the black cloaks, though their faces exhibited sharp, fierce features and they were completely devoid of any ornaments. Then she noticed the scrawny little figures like black little spiders scurrying around the place, tough and unsmiling. There were also a few dogs curled up here and there, their shaggy coats thick with the winter, the only creatures in the place with a touch of color.

Valharess' metallic voice almost with the hint of pride in it. "Orphans," he said, not particularly to Rooks. "Children whose parents were killed or taken captive by the empire. Children who were not given another chance by anyone else." His green eyes met Kazan's, and the wizard shivered despite himself.

Valharess motioned them to keep walking, and led them halfway across the cave to a circle of shadow-fighters that seemed to be in deep discussion. One of them, with a surprisingly neat appearance and a monocle over his left eye, stared at the party with a hint of recognition. The shadow-fighters fell silent as they saw the companions. "Who are these miserable bundles of rags?" one of them demanded. "*These* are the allies that you spoke of?"

Valharess folded his arms and nodded slowly, a gesture that was both simple and dominating at the same time.

"I thought you of more sense than bringing lesser scum into our den, Valharess." One of them spat. "I wouldn't have…"

The black knight cut him off. "Last I checked I was in command here, not you." His voice had the edge of an axe. "Among them is a psion, a giant and the same wizard that burnt the hair off the back of your head at the swamp. You better show him some hospitality, or if he wishes to exchange your animosity, I assure you I will not hold him back."

The shadow-fighter opened his mouth to speak, but immediately clenched it shut when his eyes settled on Kazan's stern face.

"We are here to discuss plans, not to bicker," Valharess declared to the circle of shadow-fighters. "These are our allies for the upcoming battle against the empire." He looked around at his officers. "Anyone who has a problem with that is free to… talk it out with me." He brushed his cloak aside and laid a hand on his sword. Roessa caught sight of something glittering among the black-and-purple hues of the black knight's cloak. It looked like a small branch of sage pinned into the lining of the cloak, though it was a crystalline white instead of the typical grey-green of the plant. *It's not called the Order of the Diamond Sage for nothing then,* she mused.

Silence reigned at the circle for a few more seconds. "Good." Valharess nodded. "Since that's settled, let's get down to business."

* * * *

As the adults settled into strategizing, Rooks kept eyeing the strange crowd around him, receiving curious stares in return. He met less than a handful of other children in his life; he by no means thought that there could be so many in the world. "So many people like me," he found himself whispering, as his mind went back and forth between the desire to run up and meet them all, and the shyness of not even knowing quite how.

My parents weren't killed by the empire, Rooks thought. *So I'm not a…*What was that word the black knight used? *An orphan. I wonder if they will still talk to me?* He stared at a nearby child, who stared back unblinking, the way children do without feeling awkward or turning their eyes away. *Serje was taken by the Iltherians,* Rooks kept thinking. *So maybe I do count as an orphan, like them.* He didn't spare a thought to what *had* happened to his parents. As far as he knew, he never had any to begin with. He had not yet learned the nature of human life to know that that was not possible.

The first one to approach him was a black-haired girl a bit smaller than himself. There were no greetings. "You are one of them," she observed calmly, looking over at the companions talking to the Diamond Sage officers. Rooks nodded. She pointed at Kazan. "Is that your father?"

"No," he replied. "That's Kazan. He's Roessa's father, over there." He pointed at the blonde girl sitting next to Ceycil with a troubled expression on her face. "I don't have a father," Rooks added, and then paused. "I had Serje, but he's dead now." Then a thought crossed his mind, and he frowned. "What makes someone my father?"

The black-haired girl stared at him, but she didn't have an answer. "Come with me," she changed the subject, holding Rooks by the wrist. "I'll show you my dog. He's the best rat-catcher we have."

Rooks followed her eagerly, all questions banished from his mind for the moment.

*　*　*　*

"You're saying you can get the Neranian giants to join us? With the help of an army of giant ants?" Valharess tried not to sound doubtful, if only to ensure the support of his officers.

Tyrann nodded. "Kazan has already been in touch with the Colony, they have agreed to lend their help digging into the slave mines. They don't like the empire any more than the rest of us; the imperial mines are taking over some of their best nesting grounds."

The green, cat-like eyes of Valharess blinked inside the horned helmet. "A small group of my shadow-fighters will join you," he said. "The only way you can get past the mine guards without raising alarm is by stealth," he stated as Tyrann tried to object. "And no offense, but you are not exactly built to sneak around. Hamza and his men will accompany you."

The officer that called the companions a bundle of rags shifted uneasily, as his fingers brushed through his thick mustache. "I've seen them ants before," he muttered. "They roam the tunnels in the summer, feed upon human flesh. I'm not going anywhere with…"

Before he could finish his sentence, Valharess' sword was unsheathed in a flash and pointing against the man's throat. "Perhaps you'd prefer to go where this blade would send you?" He hissed icily.

Hamza swallowed and shook his head, sweat immediately appearing and trickling down his scruffy face.

Valharess lowered his sword. "Good. You are in charge of the mining team. You will take your orders only from Tyrann during the battle."

The officer's eyes grew wider, but he did not dare object.

"Now, we will need someone to lead the troops that will be holding the main castle in siege," Ceycil went on, trying to break up the animosity in the air. "They will be there more for distraction than anything else, keeping the Iltherians busy until Tyrann and Hamza can free the giants. We need people who can fight off a lot of knights, without getting crushed right away."

The black knight's eyes immediately wandered over to Renzo, who was cleaning his monocle with a fold of his black tunic. "Renzo will do that," he declared with a note of finality.

Renzo looked up sharply, with an expression of immense distaste. "You're looking for victims," he objected, staring right back at Valharess. "Bodies to be massacred! I have the best team of shadow-fighters in the entire Order, why do we have to be the fish bait?"

"Because you *are* the best." Valharess nodded solemnly, his voice devoid of anger or irritation. "You said it yourself. If you can't hold up the Iltherians long enough for the rest of us to take care of things, then nobody else can."

Renzo did not object any further, though he looked no less disgruntled by the decision.

"That leaves us with the Adelphia." Ceycil stated. "And our main target, the emperor."

The Diamond Sage officers looked aghast. "The emperor? Are you out of your minds??" It was the same burly man who called them lesser scum and was subsequently told off by Valharess.

"We have no other choice," Kazan explained patiently. "No matter how many Neranian giants we manage to free, our numbers will still not match the Iltherian army. We will not even come close. This serpent is too long and too strong for us to wrap our hands around, son. We cannot wrestle it, but we can try and crush its head."

"Kazan is right," Kristoff broke in. "Many of the knights are under the imperial flag not because they want to, but because they have to. It's a sort of… spell maybe, something about these cursed swords." He glanced at his own green blade in disgust. "It suppresses our will in a way. It's very difficult to break away even for those that really hate fighting for the empire."

"Is that right Iltherian?" hissed the Diamond Sage officer. "Then how do you have control?"

"I don't know," replied 369, "What I do know is that if Bravenscu falls, many more minds will break free to join us."

"So you are saying that if we kill the emperor, some of the knights will turn against their own kind?" The question came from one of the officers that up until now, remained silent, and it was only the voice that gave away that it was a woman. With her hair cut short and her figure hidden beneath her cloak, she could easily pass for a man.

Kristoff nodded. "Probably more of them than we expect, yes."

Valharess squinted at Kristoff, his emerald orbs no more than mere slits. "Now, there's an insane idea if I've ever heard one." He took a breath that sounded like the hissing of a snake. "Though it might just work."

"The question is, how exactly do you plan to take out the emperor?" It was Gabriel, the young knife-thrower that was sitting at the outer edge of the circle. "I heard that he's an extremely powerful manipulator of mana. They say he can kill people with a flick of his finger, that he's almost sort of… a perfect power."

Valharess sighed and shook his horned helmet with an air of irritation. "You hear too many things, Gabriel, and you make up just as many. Bravenscu is no perfect power, nor is he a manipulator of mana of any kind other than his verdium steel." He glanced over at Kristoff in his green and orange armor. Then he turned over to Ceycil. "So we have the Adelphia. There's you and me, your lady friend, the wizard and the psion, and our Iltherian over here. I can only think of one thing to do."

Ceycil nodded. "We fly the Adelphia to the castle tower, find a way to get in, and go for the emperor."

Roessa raised her eyebrows. "If only it were as simple as you make it sound…"

Valharess shrugged. "If it were as simple as it sounded, I wouldn't bother to do it."

"Who will be flying the ship?" Roessa asked, secretly hoping that Ceycil would step up to the position and not risk the dangers that lurked in the castle tower.

Ceycil ran his fingers over the wings of the helm that was still on his head. "I think Korinth should do it," he said thoughtfully. "I need to be in the battle. It is *my* battle after all, to an extent. I have to fight for my own land." He didn't notice that Valharess winced at his words. "Korinth can fly the Adelphia, that way he can look over the battle field as well and help anyone that might need an extra hand."

The elf nodded silently, accepting his position.

"Our plan is mostly…" Valharess started to speak, but Gabriel interrupted him.

"There is one thing you're forgetting."

The black knight looked annoyed, but urged him on with a gesture.

"The other cities," said the elven shadow-fighter in a breath. "There are too many Iltherian cities close to the capital. As soon as we attack, troops from neighboring camps will be on their way to join the battle. They must be delayed, or else Renzo's men will be wiped, and the slaves with them."

Valharess folded his arms. "Gabriel, you may just have said the first intelligent thing in your life. I give you command of half the troops that will do precisely that, keep the imperial reinforcements from arriving at the capital." He motioned at the shorthaired woman. "Smerai, you will lead the second half. Divide up the roads among each other and find out what the best spots are for traps and ambushes. I don't care what exactly you do, but the more of a nuisance you create, the better."

Smerai looked worried by her new mission, but Gabriel was absolutely radiant.

"What about Rooks?" Roessa asked abruptly, breaking the pensive silence.

The black knight shrugged. "The child is free to remain here. There are other children, and a couple of the less experienced fighters will be staying to keep an eye on them."

Roessa absent-mindedly wrapped a finger around her blond braid. "Do you think he'll accept that?" she asked

Kazan. "Being left behind? We've never left him out of anything before."

"He shall have to," said Kazan sternly. "I am not taking him into the battle. Serje would kill me just for thinking about it."

Korinth shook his head. "Try as you may, you'll find that child will not stay."

"He shall have to," the wizard repeated, more to himself. "Children do not belong in battles. He shall have to stay here."

*   *   *   *

Night at the den of the Diamond Sage was uneventful. The large sphere of light in the middle of the cavern was dimmed to make it more comfortable to sleep, the light itself being a work of Valharess' psionic powers. After all, the cavern was deep enough to keep the empire from following the threads of psionic energy. And even if it were followed, Iltherians were easier to keep out of the narrow twisted tunnels than torch smoke.

Despite the usual silence that governed in the den, there was a tension in the air, as if the whole place was infested with poisonous vermin that could crawl out of any crack, any moment. Rooks was curled up in a corner, next to the black-haired little girl and her dog, an almost pure-white collie, with a long, flowing tail that wagged occasionally even as it slept. Any other child might have felt estranged by the orphans of the Diamond Sage, but Rooks, not knowing what children are supposed to be like, warmed up to them quickly. He was as quiet and reserved as the orphans, and he didn't know how to play any more than they did. If it weren't for his brown tunic, nobody would notice that he was an outsider.

He lay awake for a while, enjoying the quiet sounds of breathing around him and the soft warmth of the dog against his back. The tension didn't seem to affect him for some reason. He kept thinking about the heated discussion that Ceycil and the others were engaged in, along with the shadow-fighters, and he knew that something terrible was about to happen. The battle was approaching, and he knew that it would be greatest spectacle of life so far. Worse, than the battle inside the mountain. Still, there was a light, fluffy feeling inside him, and he smiled as he lay. As he drifted off to a peaceful sleep, he had visions passing before his eyes, vivid dreams as his mind shut itself off to the world. He dreamt of sitting around a campfire, warm and welcoming. Across from him was Serje, his feathered costume flaring red and orange with the dancing flames. He smiled at the old man, and felt the warmth of the fire embrace his body, except he couldn't be sure if it was the flames or the Birdman's arms wrapping around him.

Unlike Rooks, Roessa's heart was so heavy that she was afraid it would sink into the ground beneath her. Try as she might, she couldn't sleep, and with every passing minute she felt like the cavern was closing in on her. "Ceycil?" she whispered, almost desperately, and let out a sigh of relief as Ceycil stirred.

"Yes?" His voice came tired, but not particularly sleepy.

"The silence is driving me crazy," she said, trying not to sound whiny. "I don't know what to make of all this, what with the battle coming up so soon and everything... Maybe I'm just not ready for it, I don't know. Or maybe I'm scared..."

Ceycil propped himself up on his elbow. "I know what you're talking about."

"Do you?" Roessa rolled over to face him.

"This isn't what you had in mind, is it? I mean, when you dream yourself up a future, where does all this fit in? It can't just end here, there are just too many things I still want to do." He paused, his eyes fixed on a spot in the darkness. "Since I got my father's sword, I've been picturing how things would be like years from now. I keep thinking about rebuilding Tallinad's capital city. Rebuilding my father's castle, the one I saw in that dream, simple but beautiful... We could even have a little royal garden. Nothing fancy, but maybe a few rose bushes you and I could sit by, and a couple of fruit trees for our children to climb."

Roessa blinked at him, looking astonished. "*We* could have a garden? And children? You mean you want me to be…"

"Not unless you don't want to, of course," Ceycil replied hastily.

"I'd love to, more than you can imagine!" She laughed. "I mean, I don't care much for being a queen, but being *your* queen…" She smiled broadly.

"Do you think Kazan would approve?" Ceycil asked, genuinely curious.

Roessa shrugged. "I don't see why not. You're not some handsome stranger galloping into my life out of nowhere to whisk me away. He knows you. He's raised you, for realms sake. He knows you wouldn't do me any wrong."

"That's true, I know better." Ceycil chuckled. "Though I don't know if I would fear his wrath more, or yours."

Roessa laughed again and punched Ceycil playfully on the shoulder. Then she snuggled herself closer to him and closed her eyes. When sleep finally found her, she dreamt of rose bushes.

Ceycil lay awake beside her, afraid that all his worst nightmares would catch up with him if he fell asleep.

* * * *

In the morning, the den of the Diamond Sage resembled an ant's nest, buzzing with quiet activity. Everywhere there were circles of shadow-fighters talking through the battle plans one more time, as swords were being sharpened and arrows feathered. The speed at which the Diamond Sage was preparing for full-blown battle was making Ceycil's head spin. Once again, things were moving faster than he expected. There was talk of marching to Iltheria the very next day. Just the thought of him made him nauseous with anxiety. The only things that gave him any comfort were Roessa's constant stream of pep talks and Kazan's unshakable calmness. He was amazed that the wizard showed no signs of being at all disturbed by the turn of events. *He's probably seen worse,* he thought gloomily. *I can't even imagine worse.*

In fact, Kazan was as restless as everyone else, though it wasn't the upcoming battle that bothered him. He sat in a corner, seemingly buried in his spellbook, though anyone looking closely could have seen that he never turned the pages. With the edge of his eye, he constantly watched for the horned helmet of Valharess. The black knight seemed to be always busy talking to his officers, whispering orders at the shadow-fighters getting ready for battle, stopping only momentarily to greet one of the orphans or pat a dog on the head. The wizard entertained a vague notion that the man might, just maybe, have a care for something other than himself. Just maybe.

Kazan approached Valharess when he finally sat down over a shabby old map with his cloak folded under him, and shooed all his officers away. When the wizard sat down across from him, the black knight barely looked up from the map, and offered no words of greeting. After almost a full hour of mutual silence, he lifted his head and shot a tired glance at Kazan. *What do you want?*

The question penetrating his mind took Kazan by surprise. He completely forgotten that Valharess was a psion. He stared at the green catlike eyes glowing through the helmet. *You have your father's eyes,* he thought inadvertently.

"I have no father," Valharess said out loud, spitting the words out like snake venom.

Kazan hung his head, his whole being overcome with a deep sadness. "We need to stop pretending," he whispered. "Both you and I, Rhyley."

Upon hearing the name, Valharess sprung to his feet, and briskly made his way towards the tunnel that led to the cavern's exit.

Kazan got up and followed him calmly, keeping up with his pace with some effort. *You cannot run away from your name,* the wizard thought.

The mental reply came almost instantly. *Either I run away, or I kill you here and now. Which would you prefer, old man?* He kicked the camouflaged door open in a rage, and stormed out.

The wizard smiled in spite of himself as he followed Valharess into the bright frosty morning. "You have inherited the Lynnvander temper, too, I see."

Valharess turned around sharply and glared at him, his eyes flashing like the bolts of lightning he drew from the sky. "You left me to die," he hissed. "Allow me to be angry."

Kazan's smile faded into a mask of grief again. "I know that no amount of apologizing I can offer you will make you forgive me," he said. "And I cannot expect you to understand why I had to do what I did." He took a deep breath. "But please at least listen to what I have to say."

"I don't want you to explain anything," Valharess interrupted him, his metallic voice echoing against the frost-covered rocks.

The wizard shook his head. "Not explain, no. Just let me tell you the story, my side of the story."

The black knight looked like he was about to object again, but he remained silent. "I watched your father get killed by the Iltherians," Kazan began. "I do not know if that means anything to you, but he was a good king for his people and an even better friend for me."

Valharess smirked bitterly. "You've had twenty years to mourn him, get over it."

Kazan looked up at him and shook his head. "And you have had twenty years to brew your anger against me, I see…"

"You left me alone in an irrigation tunnel, with an army of murderers running after me," he snapped back, his voice raising just enough to be menacing. "If you loved my father so much, you could have at least bothered to save the heir to his throne." He was breathing heavily. "But no, you picked Ceycil. Must save the baby!" He paused mockingly. "How heroic!" Then he turned his head sharply and stared at Kazan. "I was eight years old," he hissed. "And you just ran like the coward that you are. You didn't even look back."

"You said it yourself," said the wizard. "You were eight years old. If I were to try and carry you, I could not run fast enough nor far enough to get us away from the knights. We would all die. You and me, Ceycil and my daughter. Running away with Ceycil and Roessa was the only way I could save the Lynnvander bloodline. It was the least I could do for your father, Rhyley. And for my wife Annika." Kazan felt old as he spoke the words, even older than he already was.

Valharess squinted behind his helmet. "I remember your wife," he said, more to himself. "She used to make me those magical popping toys for my birthday every year, the ones that changed colors every time I picked them up." He seemed to be travelling back in time. "I remember seeing her swarmed by Iltherians, down in those tunnels. Right before you left me."

Kazan nodded. "Roessa was with her when the knights came. She died to save our daughter, the way mothers tend to fight to the death for their children." He stared at Valharess meaningfully, who dismissed the comment.

"Sacrifices come with a price, old man. That's why they are called sacrifices."

The wizard raised his eyebrows. "What would you know about sacrifices?" he muttered. "You have the Diamond Sage; I have seen you wear it inside your cloak. With that brooch comes power, easy and absolute. You have your shadow-fighters that will help you obtain whatever you want, and it is them that pay the price of the crime. You are still the same spoiled prince, Rhyley. Tell me not of sacrifices."

Valharess gritted his teeth. Then he reached up, grasped the two sides of his helmet and slowly took it off.

"For all that you have said, this is the price I paid," he whispered. "And though I may have the Sage, I still have not obtained the name that was my birthright, nor my land. *My land*." He put his helmet back on. "Now tell me wizard, if that little redhead boy were to fall behind in a chase, would you leave him to be slaughtered like you left me?"

Kazan blinked, his face devoid of expression, though his heart was beating faster than he had ever recalled it to be. "The circumstances are entirely different." He swallowed hard, but something hard and burning hot stuck in his throat and would not budge.

As he opened his mouth to explain, Valharess silenced him with a wave of his hand. "I didn't think so…" Then he turned around and disappeared through the door camouflaged in the rocks, the purple hues of his cloak flapping behind him like a closed curtain.

Kazan followed him into the cavern. He walked slowly down the winding tunnel, as if he was in a trance, with Valharess' face etched in his mind. Desperately he searched for a reflection of his old comrade somewhere behind the deep, twisted scars covering the black knight's face. Maybe if he thought hard enough, he could find a familiar line, a subtle angle, anything at all that reminded him of Klavan Lynnvander beyond those burning green eyes… But try as he might, he could not.

*   *   *   *

Why do I feel like a sacrificial sheep? Ceycil thought grimly, as he was finishing up his preparations for the morning's march.

Into Iltheria.

One of the Diamond Sage children handed him a cloth sack full of stone-dry bread and jerk meat, for one last breakfast on the road. Ceycil tossed it into his backpack, doubting he would have the appetite for it. His stomach felt like it was in his throat. His eyes searched for Kazan, hoping he could get a few words of comfort, but the old wizard was seated in a corner with Korinth, exchanging what seemed to be wizard talk. Ceycil didn't feel like interrupting them. He wasn't sure if he could handle any riddling remarks Korinth might make, as he was frustrated enough without puzzles to solve. Not that the elf spoke much these days, but it was best not to take any chances. A pain in his shoulders made him realize that he was hunching them tensely. He let his muscles relax, and then shuffled over to Roessa.

"I just want this to be over with," he whispered over her shoulder.

She turned around and set her quiver down. "I know what you mean." She sat down with a sigh, and looked around, motioning Ceycil to sit beside her. "I keep thinking that I may not see some of these people again," she muttered. "You know, some of the shadow-fighters aren't that bad. The young one over there helped me feather my arrows; he's upset he has to stay with the children. And that girl lent me her spare pair of gloves, so my fingers won't freeze by the time I need to shoot some arrows." She sounded oddly thoughtful. "I didn't even ask them, they just offered…" She paused, and went on, "The more people I meet, the more I realize that I have met so few of them to know what to expect from anyone. We've seen so much of the world, Ceycil." She sighed. "But we haven't really seen so much of life. And we won't, unless we get rid of the empire. The only problem is, we might die doing so, and that really doesn't help."

"No, doesn't help at all." Ceycil tried to piece together what she said. Somewhere deep inside it all made sense, even though his half-panicked mind did not register it fully on the surface. Nor did he notice Tyrann standing over the two of them, somber and silent.

"Tyrann, you look terrible… is something wrong?" Roessa asked with genuine concern.

The giant shrugged. "I'm leaving."

Ceycil and Roessa stared at him blankly.

"We need the whole night to dig our way into the slave mines," he explained. "The Colony is already waiting for us. One of Valharess' officers, a few shadow-fighters and I, we are heading out now."

Roessa stood up, trying to object, but Tyrann stopped her. "I heard what you were telling young Ceycil," he said. "After I'm… if I don't come back… remember what you said. There is much of life to see. There are people to meet, cities to build, fields to plant, children to raise. There are dreams to dream and songs to sing. You two do all that for me. I can't do any of it while my people are in chains under the ground. And to set them free, I may have to…" His voice started to crack, and he cast his eyes down. "Doesn't help at all," he whispered. "You know what I mean."

"We know what you mean." Roessa whispered back, wrapping her arms around the giant's waist.

Tyrann turned to Ceycil afterwards. "You will make a great king," he said. "You have it in your blood, I can see it. Even Kazan will be proud of you."

The way he said it made Ceycil smile, but as he hugged the giant, his few words of thanks remained stuck in his throat. *This is not how it ends,* he kept telling himself, like a child trying to believe that the monster was not real. *This can't be how it ends...*

15

The morning did little to improve Ceycil's mood. No matter how hard he had tried, he had barely slept. It was still dark when they had left, and a sharp drizzle of rain was falling on the snow, turning it into packed ice instead of melting it. *Some glory,* he thought bitterly. *That's all the stories ever speak of. Nobody mentions all this weariness or this feeling of dread.* He tried to wipe the rain out of his stinging eyes. *And somehow we never hear about the losing side.* As they boarded the Adelphia, he wished he could quit thinking altogether. Failing that, he turned his thoughts towards the dream he had of his father.

For a moment, the scene before him shifted from the cold twilit morning to that of the empty castle courtyard. The young monarch sat in front of Ceycil with his simple silver crown in hand, his expression one of worry. Then, to Ceycil's further surprise, the king's face lit up into a subtle smile. Then as quickly as it appeared, the vision of the dream faded into the shiny woodwork of the Adelphia, leaving Ceycil himself with the hint of a smile on his face.

He watched Rooks tuck himself under an empty crate near the bow, still marveling at how Kazan let the child on board. The wizard had a long and serious conversation with Rooks that morning, and announced to the party that the boy was to come with them on the Adelphia, but to remain on the ship during the battle. When Ceycil tried to object, Kazan given him a grave reply. "Serje trusted the child to my care, son. I cannot leave him to strangers, especially ones like the Diamond Sage. If we were to perish in battle, I cannot bear the thought of Rooks being raised as a shadow-fighter." Ceycil could not help but agree.

Dead silence reigned aboard the flying ship. Beside where Rooks was huddled, Korinth and Kazan sat together, both looking grim, yet surprisingly serene. Roessa stood with her back against the mainmast, thoughtfully sharpening the wooden-hilted dagger she picked up at the ice elves' cavern. Her hair was pulled back in a tight braid, and she looked more determined than worried.

Kristoff looked like he was about to be sick. His face was ashen, his movements jittery. He couldn't seem to settle down, pacing back and forth on the deck like a restless animal. Every now and then he glanced at his Iltherian sword, and his expression changed from distress to disgust.

Flying above the clouds, the rain no longer bothered them, but the wind was unbearable, beating into their faces like a whip. Valharess was the only one that didn't seem bothered by it, his face hidden behind his helmet. He stood at the bow of the Adelphia like a strange figurehead, with his green eyes fixed on the grey horizon. Ceycil had a vague notion that the black knight was avoiding him, but he brushed it off without further thought. There were more important issues to think about. Even though they couldn't see the ground from that high, he thought he could hear the silent footsteps of the shadow-fighters marching under the falling rain far below. Somewhere down there, Tyrann was digging his way towards the slave mines along with the Colony. Gabriel, the dark-skinned shadow-fighter, was stirring mischief to deter the Iltherian troops at the neighboring camps. *And here we are,* he thought. *Six of us against the man that rules half of Imaria, the known world.*

You think we are insane, Korinth's thoughts broke into Ceycil's mind. *But sometimes a lion comes without the mane. No life, no fight, no sacrifice is in vain.*

Ceycil shook his head, staring into where the rising sun was hiding behind the clouds. *I know you are right Korinth, I really do.* He closed his eyes, taking in the dull morning light, and let out a deep, longing sigh.

Ceycil found himself wishing he could stop time. Stay on the Adelphia forever and never make it to Iltheria. But the more he counted the moments, the faster the sun seemed to rise, looming over them like a giant bird of prey. He almost jumped when something light brushed against his arm. It was Roessa, pointing at something over his shoulder. Ceycil squinted at the horizon, his eyes watering with the wind.

Then his heart gave a lurch. Stabbing its way through a thin sheet of fog was a tower, looking as sharp and deadly as a dragon's fang.

They had arrived.

*   *   *   *

Earthen Path ends, the Colony buzzed quietly, as the ants spread aside to reveal a hole in the tunnel wall, where a dim red light shone through. *Mines begin. Now you lead, I help.*

Tyrann nodded wordlessly, put out his torch and proceeded to enlarge the hole with his spade-sized hands. Once it was wide enough to let him through, he stepped back and motioned towards the handful of shadow-fighters accompanying him. "Kill anyone in green and orange," he whispered. "Don't harm the slaves. They won't give you away." He turned to the beefy Diamond Sage officer that Valharess sent with him. "Hamza, see if you can clear the path towards the main exit. We can't lose time backtracking through the tunnels."

Hamza twisted his moustache with his fingers, frowning. "And what are you going to do?"

"Spread the word. The slaves need to know what is happening, else they will scatter away."

Hamza shrugged, grunted an unintelligible reply and disappeared through the hole in the wall, his shadow-fighters following behind him.

Tyrann wiped his face with his dirty sleeve, wondering why on earth he was trusting this man.

Worried? The Colony buzzed, moving beside him into the mines.

Tyrann couldn't help noticing how the ants blended into the tunnel walls in the dim light, becoming all but invisible even as they moved. "Yes," he whispered. "I'm worried. We have much to do."

I help, the ants clicked their mandibles. *How?*

The giant thought about it for a moment.

Click click click…

"How strong are your mandibles?" He asked abruptly. He knew it was a silly question. He had seen the

298

ants pick up boulders the size of their own bodies, and dig their way through granite as if it was no more than soft limestone. "Can you cut through iron?"

The Colony buzzed softly, as if thinking. *Metal hard,* it said. *Metal strong. Not easy. Maybe. I try.*

Tyrann nodded. "That's good; try is all I can ask for right now. Follow me."

In the distance he could hear the sound of metal clanging, though he could not tell whether it was armor, chains or a pick against stone.

Somewhere down below the Adelphia, Renzo was blinking into the same dull light as Ceycil and his companions, and heartily cursing the rain that speckled his monocle and blurred his vision. His men were anxious, and he couldn't even blame them. In less than half a day, they would be among the ruins that surrounded the city of Iltheria. *At least we will have some cover as we initiate the attack,* he thought. *That will maybe give us a couple of hours before we are hunted like a herd of deer,* he added mentally. He had a burning desire to punch a dent into Valharess' helmet for putting him in the position of a sheepdog against a pack of wolves, or at least give him a piece of his mind, but it was too late now. He bit his lip and marched on, doubly upset by the mud that was soaking its way up the hem of his velvet cloak. Being an exceptionally skilled fighter, Renzo hated battles. It was impossible to stay clean through them.

Between the whistling wind and the ringing in his ears, Renzo couldn't hear himself think. The weather was driving him crazy, though he was aware that it gave them the briefest of an advantage. With the wind and the rain whipping through the city, his shadow-fighters had managed to infiltrate the ruins of old Tallinad without being seen or heard. *The element of surprise,* he thought with bitter sarcasm.

Meaning we might just take a few more of them with us before we meet our maker. Fabulous. To his surprise, he realized he was looking forward to the battle. At least he could take his anger out on someone.

In the distance he could see groups of Iltherians patrolling the streets. They were more numerous than he had expected. He imagined one of his arrows going through the visor of a green and orange helmet, and the thought of it gave him an immense satisfaction. A menacing grin spread over his face, and he motioned his troops to ready their weapons. He strung an arrow onto his bow, and drew it back until his knuckles were white.

"This one is for your awful taste in colors," he hissed through his teeth, and fired.

His men fired right after him, letting loose a shower of arrows towards the unsuspecting Iltherians.

Only a fraction of the arrows met their targets. The rest bounced off shields that were drawn up quickly in defense.

Too quickly.

Rotten flaming dragon tails, Renzo thought, panic rising up his throat. *They knew we were coming.*

*   *   *   *

As the line of cavalry came tumbling down in a landslide of man over horse over man, Gabriel couldn't help laughing from where he hid among the trees with his troops. It was surprising how a simple trick like a hemp cord strung tight across a path could be so deadly. The Iltherians had been moving in a hurry, careless and unforeseen. They had not spotted the greyish white rope against the dirty snow. It had almost been too easy. As the horses stumbled and fell over, the riders crashing down with their heavy armor, many more behind them toppled over the first fallen line. Only the last handful managed to halt their horses before it was too late.

That left the foot soldiers, and a few unhorsed riders that were not crushed by their fallen steeds. *Next time they'll look down where they're stepping,* Gabriel thought. *So we'll attack from above.* A smug grin spread over his face. Smerai had taken another path with her troops, blocking the way from yet another Iltherian camp towards the capital. He had no doubt she was doing a good job, she was one of the best trappers the Diamond Sage had ever trained. *This is good,* Gabriel thought, listening to the frantic shouts and neighs echoing in the forest. In his eyes, every fallen Iltherian was a step up the ranks of the Diamond Sage, and he felt like he was running like the wind.

*   *   *   *

High over the city of Iltheria, Kristoff shivered and shook like a dry leaf in the wind. Looking over the rail of the Adelphia through the clouds that floated below, he could see the battle breaking out down on the ground: the toy-soldier figures of the Iltherians and shadow-fighters alike, with arrows flying in all directions like wasps. To anyone else looking from such distance it might have seemed like a small and harmless image, like a minstrel story told with puppets or children playing war, but for Kristoff it was only too real. He could smell the fear and the sweat, the mind's hunger for fame and valor, and the soul's desperation to stay alive. He could hear the heartbeats pulsing in the temples of every soldier; feel the biting dryness in the back of every throat. It made him nauseous with a feeling he knew well, but could not name. He kept shivering, and tried hard to keep his thoughts focused. *Nothing matters,* Kristoff kept telling himself. *Nothing matters. At worst we will die here in Iltheria and this feeling will disappear with everything else. Then at least there will be no future for me to worry about. No, doesn't matter at all now if I die in Iltheria... for I will not die an Iltherian.* His fingers clasped around his sash, now tattered and covered in mud and dried blood and who knew what else, his number 369 all but invisible among the stains. Without another thought, he tore it off and cast it to the wind, watching it drift down through the air and fade away like pain.

*   *   *   *

Tyrann tried to hide his huge figure among the shadows as well as he could. He couldn't help being impressed by how efficiently the shadow-fighters were working. *Efficiently murderous,* he thought bitterly, as he stepped over another dead Iltherian lying in a pool of his own blood. Around every corner he turned, he found more bodies in green and orange armor, though the tunnels were strangely quiet save the same metallic sounds he had heard when he first entered the mines. *No panic,* he thought. *No alarm calls. At least not yet.* He could see the Colony moving around him, barely visible against the earthen walls in the dimly lit passages. Kazan's fire rock glowed in the jaws of one ant, keeping them just warm enough to remain awake in the bitter cold.

He found the first group of slaves in an unlit cavern, shivering with cold and terror. Two Iltherians lay dead beside them, and Tyrann could tell that it was partly the shock of being free and partly the fear of the unseen killers that was keeping the slaves quiet. He picked up a torch from the ground beside one of the Iltherians, and lit it from the fire rock, spreading a ghostly red light over dozens of thin faces staring at him in silent apprehension.

The mismatch of sizes was the first thing that threw him off. At Tyrann's eye level were a handful of Neranian giants, his people. But among them stood frail-looking humans and shaggy-bearded dwarves. They were all chained together, to each other and to the heavy picks that some carried over their shoulders and some rested on like canes. The only thing this motley crew had in common was the faces all pale and dirty, with eyes open wide with fear, and red with weariness.

The giant swallowed. "You are free to go," he whispered, for fear that his voice might break if he spoke any louder. "Or to join us in war. Against the empire."

The slaves stared at him, some blinking as if trying to wake from a dream. A few of them looked around at each other, expecting some sort of reaction. Anything to reassure themselves that someone else was sharing the same illusion, for it had to be an illusion...

One of the giants, slowly, raised his pick. Then the other giants, followed by the rest of the slaves.

Tyrann let out a sigh, and managed a weak smile. Then he grew serious again. "There is something you should know," he said. "Our numbers together are strong, but the empire is even stronger. Likely we will not make it through alive. Should you choose to run out of here and not fight, I will not hold it against you. You are free men now. You make your own decisions."

One of the dwarves shook his head. "No man is free while the empire lives. In these mines we have died every day, what's another death for the hope of freedom?"

A giant with a bundle of dark curly hair shrugged, "We have nothing left to go back to, where would we run to anyway? I'd rather take the shortcut to the other side than starve alone in the bush." He ran his fingers over the steel of his pick. "At least that way I can give a knight or two a taste of this." His eyes met Tyrann's gaze. "Show us the way, brother," he said. "Lunalia to Thar'Nandria, it's all the same to us."

A hint of a smile appeared on Tyrann's face again. He motioned to the Colony to move closer. As the giant ants appeared from out of the shadows, a few of the slaves stepped back inadvertently. "The ants are with us," the giant reassured them. "Hold out your chains, let's see what we can do."

He was still smiling as they moved on silently into other caverns, where more slaves awaited in fear around their slain captors. He knew it would be a matter of minutes before the Iltherians noticed the infiltration, but it did not matter now. Even if a battle were to break out, he doubted the Iltherians could stand for very long against the growing mob of slaves that were all too eager to take over the shadow-fighters' duty of knight-hunting. If anything, he had to hold them back, to save their energy for the battle in the city.

When the alarm calls finally echoed in the tunnels, Tyrann was marching shoulder to shoulder with hundreds of slaves through the wider caverns that were leading to the exit. At every intersection, more and more pale faces joined them, released from their chains by other freed slaves and the ants that accompanied them into the smaller chambers. The flood moved on, taking down any hapless knights that got in their way, led by Tyrann and the shadow-fighters that had by now discovered the path towards the surface.

Only when they came into a vast cavern did the avalanche of slaves falter for a moment. From a staircase up ahead, the dim winter daylight seeped in. Between the staircase and the slaves was several dozen Iltherians, armed and ready.

"Surrender, you miserable rats!" One of the knights cried in his arrogant confidence, holding up two short swords of verdium above his head. Tyrann recognized him as the young officer he had fought what seemed like centuries ago, during the battle outside of Korinth's cave. "I thought I had killed you," he muttered to himself. "I suppose I'll just have to do it again." Tyrann's gaze met William's, and the giant thought he could feel the cold rage radiating from the young knight's eyes. *Shame,* he thought inadvertently. *To see such passion wasted on hate.*

"Surrender!" William screamed again, through clenched teeth, his stare locked on Tyrann.

For a moment, silence reigned over the slaves, as they blinked into the daylight they had not seen in years, and the wall of knights that stood between. Then a cheer erupted from the crowd, and turned into a battle cry as the slaves charged with their picks above their heads, swinging metal against metal upon the green and orange armor that barred their way to the light of day.

Tyrann was not surprised to find William standing against him almost immediately, his handsome face twisted into something so evil that it made the giant flinch. Out of the corner of his eye, he saw Hamza and his men sneak out of the cavern, avoiding the fight. *Treacherous dogs,* he thought bitterly, and raised his sword-axe.

A dirty grin spread over William's face as he quickly ran both his swords against his belt that wrapped around the middle of his armor. Tyrann could hear the crunch of blade against blade against leather, a sharp sound like breaking glass. Without wasting another second, he swung his sword-axe towards the young Iltherian.

William jumped out of the way nimbly, and slashed Tyrann's side with one blade. "You'll have to do better than that, meathead." He smirked as a thin line of blood appeared on the giant's dirty tunic.

Tyrann shook his head calmly and swung again. This time the edge of his axe caught William's shoulder, splitting the armor just deeply enough to cut through his flesh. The knight howled a hearty curse, and stabbed at him with both blades furiously like a wounded animal gone berserk. Tyrann paid no attention to the trickles of blood running down his arm and his chest. He could feel the biting pain, but in the end it was just another scar or two added to the hundreds of blades and arrows that had pierced his skin in the past.

He swung again and again, but William was fast, and he found the low ceiling of the cavern getting in the way every time he tried to wield his weapon. *I'm getting old,* he thought as he fought. *Even my Spathaxine, my trusted weapon, feels heavier than before.* Still, he wasn't about to let it get to him. He shrugged off another couple of slashes that William's blades burnt into his body, and tried a sideways swing this time.

Only when William leapt over his blade like a child over a jump rope did Tyrann realize that he was moving slower than he had thought. He barely even noticed the short swords stabbing into his skin, drawing more and more blood. He glanced around him, and saw that a small pool had formed at his feet, red and sticky. *I'm losing blood,* he thought grimly. *Far too much of it.* His head felt light, and even William's figure looked a bit fuzzy. "You can't win, sir knight," he spat through his teeth.

William laughed a hollow laughter that echoed through the din of battle. "No, *you* can't win!" He roared and stabbed Tyrann again and again.

The giant could scarcely feel the pain of his wounds. His head was spinning, beads of sweat rolling down his face. His feet kept slipping on the pool of blood congealing on the stony ground.

There was something unnatural about this, all this dizziness and feverish daze. Then in a fleeting moment of clarity, his mind finally grasped it. *A sharp sound like breaking glass,* he thought, cursing himself for not realizing it earlier. "Poison," he muttered. "You poisoned me."

William laughed again. "Took you that long to comprehend, you daft boulder?"

His laughter ended in a choked grunt. With a rush of anger and desperation running through his muscles like lightning, Tyrann found the will once more to swing his Neranian sword-axe, known in Neranian as the Spathaxine, this time with the flat side to avoid missing. It swept the Iltherian off his feet, sending him flying towards the wall. His armor clanged loudly against a rock in the wall.

Tyrann squinted at the Iltherian, who rose up again, one of his short swords still in his hand. Then the young officer's face froze in an expression of terror, as the giant flung himself against the knight with what strength he had left.

Tyrann fell against the wall with a sickening thud, his sword-axe embedded fully through the break in William's shoulder pads, all the way down to his stomach. The Iltherian made a last gurgling sound, and fell silent.

The world swimming before him, Tyrann stumbled his way up the stairs, along with the rest of the slaves that had taken down the remaining knights. The light hurt his eyes, beyond his eyes and into his head. Once outside, he slumped down with his back against a rock.

"Are you all right?" One of the giants asked, running past him.

"I'm fine," he said. "Just a bit beat up, nothing to worry about. Keep moving, I'll catch up with you shortly."

He watched the slaves running by, hundreds of feet making their way towards Iltheria. He watched until they were mere blurs moving against the melting snow, against the dying winter, until he could see them no more.

*   *   *   *

Renzo watched his arrow fly towards the swarm of Iltherians gathered around the palace. He didn't know whether it was the rain or his own sweat that was trickling into his eyes, but he did know that his blurred vision was at least as annoying as his carefully slicked hair turning into a wet bundle of frizzles.

Some of his men had sneaked their way into the battlefield, quietly taking down as many Iltherians as they could while the knights were still distracted by the arrows, but the act of stealth had not lasted for long. Already the Iltherians were more wary of their surroundings, and the shadow-fighters were getting spotted and attacked before they could strike. *We can't hold up these ruins for much longer,* Renzo thought. *We're not doing much damage from here, and we're running out of arrows. Soon we'll have to charge.* He wrinkled his nose in distaste, staring at the green-and-orange sea of soldiers stirring in the distance. *And then we* really *won't hold up for long.* He sighed and raised his eyes skeptically towards the sky. "You know, I could do with a miracle right now," he whispered. Renzo had never been much of a believer in any of the myriad of deities that were rumored to watch over the land, but he realized that he was running out of resources pretty fast, so there was no harm in trying. As far as he was concerned, if there was a hell, he was going there anyway.

He strung up another arrow and let it loose towards the Iltherians. Much to his satisfaction, this one caught a knight square in the back of his neck. As the soldier toppled to the ground, a slow grin spread over Renzo's face. *This one is for being stupid enough to stand with your back…* His thought stopped in its track. His grin broadened as he heard, before he could see, precisely what had made the Iltherian turn around.

A black flood was spreading over the battlefield, as the battle cries of the knights were replaced with shouts of surprise mingled with panic. The giant ants of the Earthen Path had set upon the Iltherians like a plague out of legends, attacking without any fear or pity for the people beneath the green and orange suits of armor. *Life for land,* the Colony buzzed loud and clear, through its many voices. *Life for land. Death for empire.*

"Now or never," Renzo spat. Dropping his bow, he drew his sword and ordered his troops to charge.

As they ran through the icy mud into Iltheria, Renzo raised his eyes towards the sky again, this time in search of the Adelphia. "Now or never," he whispered again, hoping that someone up there could pick up his thoughts.

*   *   *   *

Ceycil watched the angry throng of ants streaming out of the mines collide with the Iltherian troops. He thought he could almost hear the Colony's cry of fury on the

309

shrieking wind. As if reading his mind, Korinth gave him a nod. "This distraction we need, onward we must lead."

Holding his breath, Ceycil removed his winged helm and handed it over like a crown. "It's your show from now on, Korinth," he said, his nervousness ringing in every word like alarm bells. "I have no idea how you'll get us into that tower, but I have no doubt that you will."

The elf picked up the helm almost ceremonially, and placed it on his own head. "Your trust, King Lynnvander, does me great honor," he said solemnly. "The day we face ahead grows denser and darker." He stared at the towers ahead, and then shifted his gaze towards Kazan. "For our fates will prevail, a different dawn we'll hail." He paused. "And when all our wisdom shall fail, this old world will be another."

Ceycil shrugged off his puzzling words in familiar frustration, but Kazan nodded at the elf slowly, seeming to comprehend something in Korinth's riddle that the others couldn't.

As the Adelphia approached the palace tower, the tension on board grew so great that Ceycil thought the air around them was about to snap like a wire. Kristoff kept pacing like a caged tiger, and Roessa fumbled with her bowstring, avoiding Ceycil's glances in her direction. Kazan rubbed his hands together and stood up, getting ready for whatever awaited them ahead, while Rooks watched them with frightened eyes from his spot under the crate. Valharess alone stood motionless at the bow like a black statue save for his cloak flapping in the wind. He had not spoken a word since they left the den of the Diamond Sage.

"What's wrong with that one?" Ceycil asked Kazan quietly, as Korinth steered the Adelphia into a slow descent. It was more for the sake of conversation than anything else, for if he didn't focus on something other than the horde of knights below them, Ceycil thought he was going to lose his mind.

The old man appeared to be busy tightening the belt around his tunic. "The usual, I presume. We beat the stinking mud out of his men at the swamp, excuse my pun, and claimed the sword he had come to find. Not to mention we fried him first, and then froze him into a river. He hates us son; that is what is wrong with him."

"But he's chosen to work with us!" Ceycil tried to protest, his eyes continuously veering over the edge of the ship towards the pointy tower ahead.

The wizard shook his head. "Only as long as he has to. After that, I would watch out, if I were you." He looked up at Ceycil, and then focused his attention back onto his belt. "What I have done to him is a sharp stone to swallow, just because we are fighting by his side now does not mean we are forgiven."

Ceycil stared at the man who had raised him, knowing that behind Kazan's answer was something he could not reach; just like the words "no one of importance" had hidden his father's name from him for twenty years.

His pondering was interrupted suddenly, and he was slammed against the windward rail as the Adelphia rocked violently, followed by a thundering noise.

We are struck by lightning, was Ceycil's first immediate thought, though he realized just as quickly that it was unlikely. Despite the high winds and the rain, they weren't in a thunderstorm. "What's going on?" He braced himself with both hands, leaning over the rail to look down. Towards the aft of the ship, Rooks caught his eye momentarily. He had curled up into a tight ball under his crate, his arms wrapped around his knees, looking terrified.

"Look not below, son, but ahead!" Kazan growled beside him, pointing towards Bravenscu's palace tower.

On the open roof of the tower, a rather large group of Iltherians were streaming out of what seemed to be a stairwell, crowding around the emperor's throne with their swords lifted up towards the Adelphia. Ceycil could see a silvery ray of light traveling down into the green blades. "They're tapping the mana of the Adelphia!" He shrieked. "Korinth, do something!"

Ceycil's words were unnecessary, as the elf had already closed his eyes, and was raising the flying ship back to an altitude above cloud level.

Once they were safe behind the thick rain clouds again, the silence that had settled onto the ship turned into a worried buzz of muttered comments. "We'll never make it down onto the throne room." Kristoff shook his head, wiping the sweat off his brow with his sleeve. "We have to find another way in."

"Could we land somewhere else, then climb our way up the tower?" Ceycil asked, half wishing they could just turn around and go back to the Diamond Sage's den, back to being runaways in forests and caves, anywhere but into this cursed city. Then the image of King Lynnvander sitting thoughtfully on his throne appeared in Ceycil's mind, and he pushed all his fears back into the crevices of his soul. There was a battle to be won.

Kristoff looked thoughtful. "We can try doing that... I can lead you upstairs to the roof. I've been in the palace tower before." He took a deep breath. "The problem is, there are far too many knights in the city; we'll probably die before we even make it to the tower." He ran a hand through his rain-soaked hair. "You can hack and slash at an eel all you like, but the only way to kill it is to bite its head off. Our only chance to take down the empire is to go directly for the emperor. And for that, we have to reach the throne room alive."

As the discussion went on, Ceycil noticed that Valharess had his green eyes fixed on Korinth. The elf looked uncomfortable, his usual air of serenity disturbed for the first time. His hands moved restlessly, as if in search of the notebook he had lost into the abyss in the dragon's cave, along with Chalco.

The black knight folded his arms, and spoke for the first time since they had left the den. "You know the way in," he told the elf solemnly, almost with a hint of respect in his voice. "You can get us into the tower."

Korinth nodded slowly, with visible reluctance. "One way I do know... Not onto the roof, but to a floor or two below." He paused, trying to steady his jittery voice. "Whenever you are ready, the path to you I'll show."

Kazan shot a quick look around, receiving curt nods from everyone in the group. "We have no time to lose," he told Korinth. Then he turned around sharply to look at Rooks, who had just crawled out of his spot under the crate, with his box of vials tucked into his belt. "Stay close to Korinth, son," he told the child calmly, with a touch of affection in his voice. "He will watch out for you."

"But I..." Rooks stood up, trying to protest, but the old wizard cut him short.

"This is a war, Rooks," he snapped. "A war is no place for children." He sighed. "Besides," he added, gently this time. "Serje would kill me. You should stay here, it is safer."

The red-haired child looked disappointed, but did not argue.

The wizard then turned towards Korinth. "We are ready to go. No better time than now."

The elf nodded solemnly, and then closed his eyes. Before him, the air started to shimmer and wave, like a translucent curtain of light and smoke. Beyond the curtain, Ceycil thought he could see phantom figures of green and orange moving, with the distant sound of armor clanging, reminding him of wind chimes.

"Go now," said Korinth in a flat, tired voice. "And go with hope. That's all we have left, further than that I can't help you."

Ceycil froze in his spot, thrown off by the plainness of the elf's words that held neither riddles nor rhyme. He wanted to say something, but before he knew it he was dragged through the curtain by Kazan and Valharess, Roessa and Kristoff following close behind.

Korinth remained perfectly still, with his eyes closed. In his mind, he saw a short, red-haired figure scrambling towards the smoky veil between the Adelphia and the palace. As Rooks disappeared through the portal behind everyone else, the elf did nothing to stop him.

*   *   *   *

Gabriel frowned and hid himself deeper in the shadow of the boulder he was crouched behind. As more and more Iltherian troops had arrived from nearby encampments to join the march along the main road towards the capital, his men had slunk away into the background, less eager to attack. True, their traps and sneak attacks had reduced the first couple of armies into harmless packs of paranoid soldiers, but with the new reinforcements the Iltherians were still a power to be reckoned with.

Gabriel's main problem was, as the knights grew in numbers again with the joining factions, their paranoia, too, had grown into aggressive caution. The Diamond Sage's last assault had failed so miserably that Gabriel was still steaming with the fury of their defeat. His archers had managed to distract the Iltherians momentarily, but one of the knights that led the march had spotted the tips of the sharpened stakes his men had hidden underneath a loose layer of snow. Let alone impaling a single knight, Gabriel had lost almost half of his shadow-fighters to an immediate counter-attack. The remaining half were hidden somewhere among the boulders, though he wasn't sure how willing they would be to follow his next set of orders. "Let's find out," he whispered to himself, and signaled for the next attack.

Even before his men crawled their way out of their hiding spots, Gabriel saw the Iltherians reach for their weapons. *Or maybe not,* he thought darkly. After a brief moment of contemplation, his decision was made. *Rising to an officer rank would have been nice, but it won't do me any good if I'm drained dead.* He stepped back and quietly disappeared back into the rocky terrain, leaving his shadow-fighters to deal with the rising battle.

* * * *

Sitting silently on the deck of the Adelphia, Korinth felt like he had been blinded. His mind still gave him a clear picture of the battle below, of his companions inside the palace tower, and the windows he had to the minds of others were still open. The door to the future, however, was now closed. *Like every mortal I can only look into the past,* he thought bitterly. *Like every mortal.*

315

He had seen the future, he had known the end all along.

And he had not liked it.

His mind searched for someone, something, to ask for forgiveness, but he could not even figure out who he had committed a crime against except for himself. *I have broken the chain of fate,* he thought over and over again. *I have broken the chain of fate, and the oath of my existence.* The future, as he had foreseen it, was now altered. Lost into oblivion, cast aside like his rhythm and rhyme that prophets are bound into all their lives lest they should reveal too much of their knowledge. With that, Korinth had lost his vision of fate, of knowing where stories would begin and where they would end. Now the only fate he could foresee was his own. "You are your own destiny now, Ceycil Lynnvander," he whispered into the wind. "I hope you write it well."

Once inside the tower, Ceycil tried to contain his worry, but it was like trying to shove a porcupine into a sack. Whichever way he pushed it, it pricked him back. Still, he didn't have the luxury to give in, not when battle was imminent. Already green and orange figures were crowding his sight and his mind.

The level they had landed in held about a dozen Iltherians, looking at the strangers that had arrived out of thin air with stunned expressions on their faces. It was more their surprise than anything else that gave Ceycil the touch of initiative he needed. He didn't bother to gather his thoughts or to try and shake off his sense of shock. He knew he would never feel ready for what was about to come. Raising his sword, he charged at the nearest knight.

Commotion erupted like a volcano, flowing out of the room in barked orders and battle cries. Heavy footsteps traveled through the staircases that led up and down from the room, echoing through the stone floor they were standing on. Within seconds, they knew, hordes of Iltherians would be pouring into the room.

Roessa took her stand against the wall at a spot where she could see the only entrances to the room, shooting her arrows as fast as she could until her fingers were cramping. Kazan stood before her with an old metal staff he had borrowed from a shadow-fighter back in the den, guarding her as best as he could. It was useless wasting his mana here, there were just too many Iltherians around and drawing all their attention would not be wise this early in battle. Wishing he had paid more attention to fighting lessons during his training days, the wizard heaved a sigh and swung his staff as hard as he could against the side of an ugly green helmet.

Kristoff felt unusually composed as his sword of verdium went slashing through flesh and metal alike. He was trained for this. He hated it with every fragment of his soul, but it was still his element, what he did best in life. With every knight he took down, Kristoff felt like he was killing a piece of the Iltherian that he himself had been forced to become. So he continued his massacre sturdily and purposefully, stabbing soldier 369 again and again with every strike and blow, his attack on his own identity no longer a frantic charge but a well-planned murder.

*   *   *   *

Despite his afternoons of training with Kristoff, Ceycil felt like he was fighting worse than ever. His father's sword with the broken hourglass in its hilt felt clumsy as a log in his hands. Still, he had no choice but to keep hacking and slashing as best as he could. Thankfully the sheer tightness of space was enough to give him an advantage. The room being full of Iltherians by that point, even if he missed his primary target, chances are he would hit another knight. He dodged yet another green blade that missed his shoulder by an inch, rolling sideways onto the floor, and pushed the knight's legs as hard as he could with both his feet. The man toppled over with a satisfying clang. The choked scream that followed immediately was good enough for Ceycil; he didn't bother to check where exactly the knight's sword had landed.

Out of the corner of his eye, he could see Valharess exploding like a wizard's fireworks, his sword swinging in all directions like a deadly whirlwind of steel. Around the black knight, Iltherians fell like reeds against a scythe, some with their bodies slashed open and others clutching their heads as Valharess invaded their minds mercilessly.

Instinctively Ceycil turned to the nearest patch of green and orange within his sight to direct his momentum towards. There was certainly no shortage of Iltherians to attack, so he hefted his sword yet again, and let its weight down. He missed the knight by an inch, but thankfully Kristoff was close by to take over the attack before the Iltherian had a chance to turn on Ceycil.

He stepped aside, letting Kristoff take his spot, and just then his eyes caught a glimpse of a small figure hiding under a cracked wooden table among the turmoil of battle.

Ceycil's heart sank like a lead block in his chest.

"Rooks!" he shouted, but his voice was lost among the din. Dodging a blow from an Iltherian, he ran towards the table, though he had no idea what he would do once he got there. Korinth's portal into the room had closed behind them a few seconds after the battle had begun, and Ceycil couldn't possibly guard Rooks and fight at the same time.

Rooks had noticed Ceycil running towards him. He had also noticed the knight that had just missed Ceycil with his sword, but that was not the problem. The problem was, the knight had noticed Rooks as well.

The Iltherian, not having to fight his way across the room, was about to overtake Ceycil when Rooks dashed out of his hiding spot towards the only exit: the staircase. He climbed the stone steps as fast as he could with his short legs, his box of spirit vials clutched tightly under his arm, neither stopping to look back, nor to catch his breath. His fear was past the point of caring where he would end up, it just urged him to move onward, away from the immediate danger that he could feel on his neck like a dragon's hot breath.

As the Iltherian disappeared behind Rooks into the stairwell, there was only one thought ringing in Ceycil's mind, like a bell tolling for midnight in a winter village. *Not upstairs,* he thought desperately. *Please Rooks, not upstairs!* But Rooks could not hear his thoughts like Korinth, and as Ceycil ran up the stairs behind the child and the knight as fast as his beating heart, a thorny feeling of dread rose up inside him with every step.

The staircase spiraled upwards, first through another floor like the one below, which was empty now that all the knights were downstairs for the battle. Rooks kept running up without stopping, but the Iltherian stalled for a moment, reluctant to follow the frantic child any further.

Ceycil took advantage of the knight's moment of hesitation, and jabbed the tip of his sword as hard as he could into the crack between the Iltherian's shoulder plate and helmet. Ignoring the agonized scream of the knight, he scrambled up the stairs behind Rooks, who was already forcing the doorknob at the top of the staircase.

"Rooks, it's me, Ceycil, stop!" he yelled, his lungs hurting with the effort, but it was too late. The red-haired child had already burst through the door, into what seemed to be a sphere of blinding light.

Ceycil bounded up the last few steps, practically throwing himself into the light. It took him a moment to realize that he was in open air again, with the cold white winter sky above his head.

Then he froze. His stomach clenched into a tight fist, and he felt dismay wash over him like cold water.

Equally terror-stricken, ahead of him stood Rooks, paralyzed in his spot.

And before them both was a man that Ceycil recognized immediately, even though never having seen him. The baldhead and the white-blue expressionless eyes could have been part of any old face in any run-down village, but this man seemed to glow with darkness the same way fireflies radiate light. He was the source, Ceycil knew, of the poison that had caused the world to decay, setting his Iltherians to feed upon it like flies on a carcass.

It all happened very quickly, before Ceycil could raise his weapon, or even gasp for breath.

A thin, sharp smile like the edge of a blade spread on Emperor Bravenscu's pale lips, as he swung his sword sideways towards the red-haired child. A light gesture, almost casual.

Instantly Rooks' headless body slumped onto the floor, the red of his hair melting into the red of his blood.

*   *   *   *

Renzo dodged another blow from an Iltherian, wondering how much longer he could keep this up. With the arrival of the Colony, the battle had evened out to an extent, but there seemed to be an infinite supply of Iltherian knights in this mana-forsaken city, and it frustrated him more than anything. For probably the first time, he felt proud of his shadow-fighters. They were using the terrain well and taking good advantage of the ants' actions, and he had not lost more than a handful of them. Still, he knew they were getting tired. *And so am I,* he admitted to himself bitterly. His rapier was light and fast against the clumsy swords of the knights, but even so, Renzo was at the point where he would welcome a rest. *I could do with a goblet of Daleborunian wine,* he thought, gracefully stepping out of the way of an Iltherian that was charging towards him at full speed. He gave the knight a rather satisfying kick in the rear to add to his momentum, letting a pair of ants finish him off. He took a quick glance at the sky above, his eyes searching for the Adelphia, which was nowhere to be seen. *I hope you folks up there are just about done,* he thought impatiently, stabbing through the visor of another knight that had the misfortune to pick him as a target. *'Cause this is starting to get old.*

The more he fought, the more Renzo had the impression that the Iltherians were multiplying. *Either they have nine lives, or they are dividing like starfish,* the shadow-fighter thought fervently. He forced himself to slash and parry faster and faster despite his aching muscles. Still, every knight he dropped seemed to be replaced by two others. Without daring to slow down his blade, he danced around the battlefield with the grace and ferocity of a cornered wildcat, until he found himself fighting back-to-back with one of his men. By that point, he felt like he was swimming in a green and orange sea. "Where did all these *things* come from?" he asked the shadow-fighter, trying to keep two Iltherians off of himself.

"Reinforcements," the man in black gasped, sweat dripping into his eyes. "That's what we get for trusting Gabriel to stop them."

Renzo spat out a string of curses and jammed his sword into a knight's armpit as hard as he could. It gave him some fulfillment, but did nothing to ease his frustration. In the extra second he took to free his sword, a third knight came charging at him, giving him no choice but to roll out of the green blade's way. "Disgusting," Renzo muttered as he threw himself into the mud. "Absolutely disgusting…"

*   *   *   *

Ceycil fought his body's urge to be sick, as Rooks' fall flashed before his eyes again and again like a recurring nightmare. His brain pulsed inside his skull, though his heart seemed to have stopped. His fingers, wrapped tightly around his sword hilt, began to shake first slightly, then violently. He felt cold, even colder than he had felt in the death-laden halls of the ice elves.

Bravenscu let out a brief, heartless laughter, taking a step towards Ceycil.

Ceycil thought his world was imploding. Seeing nothing but the pale varicose face of the emperor and feeling nothing but pure streaming hatred, he threw himself forward, swinging his sword wildly with all the strength he had left. He was vaguely aware of the Iltherians around him, lined up by the columns that held up nothing, but they did not appear to be moving and he didn't care. He barely felt the impact of metal against metal when his sword clashed against Bravenscu's; it seemed as if his body had evaporated.

Bravenscu's smile only broadened as he parried Ceycil's blows with ease, moving his wrist no more than a few inches to block every attack. While Ceycil was leaping around the room like a shaman in a dancing trance, the emperor barely seemed to move, his motions precise and controlled. Then, unexpectedly, he swung his sword with a sharp sideways motion, cutting into Ceycil's side and sending his weapon flying towards where the lifeless body of Rooks lay.

Ceycil had no time to recover. Raising his massive hand, the emperor hit him across the face with the back of his gauntlet. He fell onto the stone floor, his blurred vision catching a glimpse of a metallic shine moving towards him. Clenching his teeth, he shut his eyes, unsure whether the coming end was a relief or a shame.

*　　*　　*　　*

There was a steady stream of knights pouring into the room downstairs where Kazan, Roessa and Kristoff were fighting. The small space limited the number of Iltherians it could hold at one time, which was a relief, seeing as they stood no chance against the entire imperial guard if they were in an open field. *Besides, nothing like a good wall against your back,* Kazan thought, bashing his staff into the neck of an Iltherian. Roessa seemed to be taking care of most of the knights coming in through the staircase, though there seemed to be no end to them.

It took Kazan a few minutes to realize that Ceycil had disappeared. *Where the hell is the boy?* He thought, trying not to let his worry affect his fighting. *And that bloody Valharess?* The battle was not getting any easier without them, and the wizard noticed that instead of showing any signs of dwindling down, the flow of soldiers into the room seemed to get stronger. Trying to push his thoughts back

323

inside his head, he clashed his staff against yet another green sword with yet another Iltherian attached on the end.

"Fancy seeing you here, old fool," said the knight holding the sword, staring Kazan in the eyes.

The wizard did not have to read the sash number to know that he was fighting officer 1001. There was no mistaking the icy voice and the deadly blue stare behind the helmet. A smile formed on Kazan's lips. "Well met, Yakutska. Playing knights and wizards again, are you? Such a boring game, the end is always the same."

"Humor your sister and play along," Yakutska replied in an even icier tone. "I promise you won't get bored this time." She swung at Kazan, missing his shoulder by a mere inch as the wizard stepped aside with surprising agility for his age.

"Tsk tsk…" Kazan shook his head. "That is no way for a lady to behave, attacking your own blood. People will think our mother has taught you no manners."

"The only blood I care about is the kind I spill," soldier 1001 spat. "And I'll be glad to see yours adorning the floor!" She raised her sword again, shouting "WIZARD! KILL THE WIZARD!"

It was a matter of seconds before all the Iltherians in the room swarmed around Kazan like bees around syrup. The wizard threw caution to the wind, and cast a ring of fire that expanded around him like ripples in a pond. The knights tried to absorb his spell with their swords, but a good number of them still fell to the floor, their armor scorching hot. Yakutska managed to tear a piece of the mana essence into her sword, and immediately threw it across the room.

Roessa caught it in the shoulder and yelped, almost dropping her bow.

As more Iltherians coming up the stairs filled the room, Kazan was fuming as much as the smoking heap of knights on the floor. Raising his staff, he hit the knights before him as hard as he could, without bothering to aim or control his blows. From the way some of them were falling before he could even touch them, he assumed that Kristoff and Roessa were doing their part in the battle, too. His eyes kept searching for Yakutska, who had slunk back to let her soldiers take care of the situation. Once or twice he spotted her by the wall, casually leaning on her sword, and he didn't have to see through her helmet to know that she was grinning.

The wizard tried to make his way towards Yakutska, but the steady flow of knights slowed him down considerably. When he finally reached the wall she had been standing by, officer 1001 was no longer there.

She was halfway across the room, moving towards Roessa. With her sword raised high.

Kazan felt his brain go numb with the thought of what might happen. Shoving a couple of Iltherians away with his staff, he gathered up all the mana he could muster through his body, and threw it towards Yakutska.

The spell did not even take form. It left the wizard's fingertips as a ray of raw mana, sparking and fizzing in the air. Quickly it weaved its way through all the other knights in the room, towards Yakutska.

Officer 1001 had a split second before the spell hit her, but it was enough. Instinctively she turned and held up her sword in a parry. The sword soaked up the spell like a sponge, until the green blade was glowing with the mana loaded onto it.

Then without wasting another moment, she flung it back.

The spell hit Kazan square in the chest. As he fell onto the stone floor, so did Yakutska, with Roessa's elven dagger running through her throat.

*   *   *   *

The final blow that Ceycil awaited never came. Instead his blurred vision caught a glimpse of a black shadow springing out of the staircase, onto the open throne room. Propping himself up on his elbow, he saw the hazy figure of Valharess intertwined with that of the emperor in an intense battle. Without taking his eyes off the blades clashing at lightning speed, Ceycil pushed his body towards where his sword had fallen. His fingers slowly wrapped around the familiar hilt, sticky with Rooks' blood that had pooled on the floor. He could not find the heart to glance at the boy's body, but he did note something else... the wooden box of vials that Rooks had carried through their travels. With a trembling hand, Ceycil reached out and pulled the box to him. Tucking it under his arm, he forced himself to his feet, trying hard not to stagger.

Valharess was moving at a dizzying speed, giving the impression that he was made of darkness alone. Every time he swung his sword towards the emperor, the horns on his helmet swayed like an angry bull's. Ceycil attempted a side swing towards Bravenscu and winced behind his helmet as the emperor deflected his blow as if it was little more than a slap. They danced around the small fountain in the middle of the throne room, until Valharess started to feel his arms getting heavier. *This is not working,* thought the black-knight desperately. *I need something else. Something more.* Instinctively his mind reached out to call for the lightning, the little particles of energy in the air that he so enjoyed to manipulate.

But even as the silvery bolt formed above him, the emperor started to laugh. The lightning that was aimed for him ricocheted off the tip of his sword and hit the fountain, shattering it into rubble and splashing water everywhere. "Mind magic?" he asked with an amused tone. "Not bad, boy, not bad! Unfortunately for you, I can deal with that." Moving surprisingly fast for a man of his age and size, he struck Valharess across the arm.

The black knight made no sound, but a trickle of blood appeared at his shoulder, quickly turning into a stream. He felt a small bubble of fear forming in the small of his stomach, a disturbingly unfamiliar feeling.

That moment of surprise could have cost Valharess his life, but before Bravenscu could strike again, Ceycil flung himself at the man with a clumsy but determined motion. The emperor sidestepped, and as Ceycil lost his balance, hit him full in the chest with the hilt of his massive sword and flung him away.

Something more, something more, Valharess thought as he clashed blades with the emperor again and again, in vain. He had already acquired several more cuts, some of them quite deep, and he could feel himself slowing down. He could not keep this up for much longer. He looked around desperately, trying to find something he could use to his advantage, but the only thing that caught his eye was the motionless knights standing around the columns. *They are mind-locked,* he observed with some satisfaction. *Now, what are the chances I can break into their heads?* As he fought, he let his thoughts slip into the mind of the Iltherian closest to him.

Much to Valharess' annoyance, Bravenscu only showed the slightest sign of surprise when one of his own soldiers broke out of his trance and charged at him. The Iltherian lasted barely a few seconds before the emperor slashed through his throat. The next knight's fate was no different.

"I designed this armor, remember?" the emperor smirked, showing his yellowed teeth through one side of his twisted mouth. "And these knights, for that matter. I know all their weak points."

"Maybe, but you don't know mine, do you?" Valharess growled, and attacked again before the Bravenscu could reply, afraid that the emperor might actually have an answer to that.

In his desperation Valharess let loose every single Iltherian on the throne room that he could hook his mind onto, but even with them on his side the emperor was still too strong. *What is he?* He thought bitterly. His strength was starting to fail as he lost more and more blood, and he was starting to feel light-headed, detached from his surroundings. Bravenscu pushed him closer and closer to the edge of the throne room, dangerously near a drop that was higher than he wanted to think about. There was little comfort in that thought.

Once or twice Ceycil tried to help him, only to get another cut in his side and a kick in his knee that sent him crashing onto the floor, unable to get up. *Nice try boy,* Valharess thought. *You're useless...*

Valharess tried to step away from the edge of the throne room, but it was impossible with the emperor's sword swinging so close to his neck. For a moment he almost blacked out, but then caught himself. He saw Bravenscu's sword coming down onto him. The blade sliced through one of the horns on his helmet, and with the last of his strength, Valharess blocked it before it hit his body.

What he did not see coming was the emperor's fist. The punch caught him full in the face and he felt the floor slip from underneath him, the air embracing his body as he fell down the palace tower onto the battlefield far below.

*   *   *   *

Korinth sat on the bow of the flying ship with the winged helm on his head, his mind buzzing like a hive of hornets. Dipping just below the cloud line again, Korinth kept the top of the tower in sight. Keeping the palace guards on the throne room out of the battle had drained him of most of his energy, and still it hadn't been enough to turn the battle around. With closed eyes he had watched Ceycil and Valharess fight the emperor, letting Valharess take over one by one the Iltherians he kept mind-locked. He had never really expected them to win, but there was always hope. *There always is,* he thought. *There is always another riddle to solve before the final call, always another turn of destiny no matter how the story ends, always-another leap of faith into the unknown... And maybe the next one is mine.*

It was with that thought that Korinth opened his eyes and gave the Adelphia its last silent command.

It seemed like a lifetime before Roessa could fight her way across the room to where her father lay. She barely noticed the knights ducking out of her arrows' way and disappearing into the staircase. The world had stopped turning. Nothing mattered. Not the battle, not the empire, not the freedom.

Kazan did not appear wounded, but all color had drained from his face and he could barely breathe. "Your mother always used to say mana was the bane of our existence," he whispered hoarsely through chapped lips as

Roessa knelt down beside him. "Twenty years later I must say I have to give her credit." He gasped for breath, failing miserably.

"Father... you're all right. You'll be all right!" Roessa didn't bother to fight back her tears. "We'll get you out of here."

The wizard put on a mock expression of severity. "You shall do no such thing, young lady," he murmured. "You shall leave this place this moment. There is nothing to be done for me."

"No!" Roessa protested, her tears dripping over the old wizard's tunic. "We can get you out of here, find a healer..."

Kazan cut her short. "Do you know how much raw mana I put into that spell?" he coughed. "Enough to knock down a dozen herds of oxen." He sighed. "I am just an old man. My time is done Roessa, just go. There is nothing anyone can do."

"I'm not going anywhere without you!" Roessa sobbed. "Do you hear me? I'm not going anywhere."

"Do *you* hear that?" Kazan asked her quizzically.

She shook her head hysterically. "Hear what? I don't..." Then she stopped, and became aware of the silence for the first time. Save the distant din of the battle outside the tower, it was quiet. They were alone in the room. "Where...what..?" she looked around, confused.

"The knights all left," said Kristoff, who was standing behind her with his bloodied sword still in his hand. "When they saw that coming." He pointed out one of the windows.

Roessa didn't even turn to look at what he was pointing towards. "I don't care if it's a whole flight of dragons coming," she shrieked. "I'm not leaving without Father!"

Kazan closed his eyes briefly, and then turned them towards Kristoff. "Take her and go," he said, his voice breaking. "Carry her if you have to. Just get her out of here."

Kristoff grabbed Roessa's arm and firmly pulled her up to her feet despite her protests.

"Roessa," said the old wizard softly, as if tasting the sweetness in her name. "Roessa, my girl… Go and raise some grandchildren for me. And tell Ceycil I'm proud of you both, he deserves to hear that."

Roessa wanted to scream, but it choked down her throat. She would not have left that desolate room for anything in the world if Kristoff hadn't picked her up and scrambled down the stairs, leaving the palace tower, leaving her father behind forever.

* * * *

Valharess landed on the ground as softly as a falling leaf, his mind holding tightly onto the air around him. He muttered a silent word of thanks to the old shadow-fighter that had trained him as a psion, and then he stood up and shook the dust out of his bloodstained cloak. Without sparing so much as a glance at the battle around him, he hobbled away from the tower, out of the city of Iltheria and back into the frozen woods that he had come from.

Ceycil was barely conscious when the emperor stood over him like a creature of nightmares that was only too real. "Look at you!" Bravenscu growled with amusement. "The son of some king or another, they told me, one of those pathetic worms I crushed years ago. Whatever made you think you'd be any better than your father, may I ask?"

Ceycil clutched Rooks' box of vials closer to his body, and the only reply he could offer was a groan of pain.

"Answer me!" the emperor roared. Then he kicked Ceycil in the chest, shattering the wooden box.

Ceycil felt the last bit of breath knocked out of him, and he knew no more.

As soon as the box was smashed, two wisps of smoke emerged out of it and began to swirl around the throne room.

One of them immediately took the shape of dancing flames, setting the emperor's skin on fire. The man let out a yelp of surprise and tried to break away from it, in vain. It was like flaming oil covering his body, impossible to shake off.

The other cloud of smoke, a light blue in color, settled onto the stone floor that was washed by the water splashed from the broken fountain. Quickly it covered Ceycil's unconscious body, drawing the water towards it and pooling it around him.

Even in his moment of panic, Bravenscu could sense the magical nature of the fire surrounding him. Concentrating on his arms, he grasped his sword hilt and tapped into the mana of the fire spirit. The burning feeling died away as the spirit helplessly fizzled into the green metal. The emperor took a breath, and then pointed the glowing sword towards Ceycil, ready to scorch him into a pile of ashes.

It was then he saw the Adelphia, dangerously close and murderously fast. His eyes met the slanted eyes of Korinth momentarily, and for the first time in his life the emperor was afraid.

They were the last thing Bravenscu saw before the flying ship crashed into the palace tower at full speed, its mana released with the impact into a thunderous explosion.

The palace tower crumpled down like a house of cards, reduced to nothing but rubble and smoke.

16

Renzo realized that he was running out of curses and blasphemy as he tried to focus on his sword that seemed to dance on its own, held by a pair of hands that no longer felt like they belonged to him. Most of his men were dead or dying, and he knew that he would take his ranks among them shortly. *What a way to go,* he thought resentfully. *With blood in my hair and mud up my nose. If hell has a dress code, I don't think they'll let me in.*

He wasn't even paying attention to his fighting any more, but going on by pure instinct and reflexes, slashing and parrying in a sort of trance. His elegant cloak was torn to ribbons, and his face was dirty beyond recognition. Stabs of pain were coming through several spots in his body as if from a distant dimension, making him vaguely aware that he was wounded. He was ready to give up, holding on only out of habit. *If I kill a couple more of these less than orc-kin, maybe it'll make me feel a bit better.* Only when his knees started shaking under his weight was he forced to admit that the end of the road was unpleasantly and unavoidably near.

Except it wasn't just his knees that was shaking. The whole ground was trembling, buzzing like a light earthquake. A growling noise was moving onto the battlefield, growing louder and harsher like a hurricane coming closer. There were shouts, too, battle cries from the sound of it. And the ones he could make out among the din were not in the name of the empire.

They were in the name of freedom.

Renzo sobered up instantly when he saw the wave of slaves flood over the battlegrounds, taking it over in a matter of seconds like locusts invading a field. Pale faces dirtier than his own surrounded him, charging at the Iltherians more violently than anything the shadow-fighter had ever seen. The knights still outnumbered them greatly, but the unexpected attack gave Renzo time to breathe. *At least it'll buy Valharess and the others a little more time,* he thought. *What's taking them so long, anyway?* He squinted up towards the palace in the distance, his eyes searching for a familiar figure on the open roof.

He caught a glimpse of a large man in green and orange armor with two puffs of smoke around him, one red and one blue. Then he saw the Adelphia, entirely too close to the palace.

As the tower came down, Renzo threw himself to the ground. He tried to guard himself from the pieces of stone that hailed down onto the battlefield, his mind suddenly discovering brand new colorful curses to shout out.

He wasn't sure how long he lay on the ground, motionless, half expecting to be dead. When he could finally pick himself up again, he didn't know what to do. Fighting seemed like a good idea, but there was something fundamentally wrong with the battle now. Some of the Iltherians, he noticed, were fighting other Iltherians. "What the...?" he whispered to himself, looking around. Then his eyes caught sight of Roessa's blonde hair near the ruins of the tower. The figure standing next to her looked familiar, too.

Weaving his way through the battle, Renzo ran towards them. Roessa looked like a mess if he had ever seen one. Her face had pale lines on it where her tears had washed away the dirt. Her eyes were red, her clothes singed badly, and she was sobbing uncontrollably.

"Where's Ceycil?" she shrieked hysterically. "He was in the tower! Where is he?" Kristoff was trying to comfort her, but she wouldn't have any of it.

Renzo didn't even know what to say. "What's going on?" he asked Kristoff. "The knights are fighting among each other. I don't get it." He shook his head, not knowing what to make of the situation. A straightforward battle he could deal with, but crying women and enemies that turned upon each other were beyond his area of expertise.

"The emperor must be dead," Kristoff explained, following Roessa as she searched frantically through the debris. "The knights are no longer bound to their swords. They have free will. I can feel it." He turned to stare Renzo in the eye. "Some of us never wanted to be part of this." He sighed. "I hope Ceycil is alive," he whispered.

*   *   *   *

Roessa found Ceycil lying in the midst of a large puddle, soaked to the skin with water and blood. He was motionless, his eyes closed.

"Ceycil!" she wailed, kneeling down beside him. "You can't die... that's not allowed! What about the rose bushes you promised me? The castle gardens for our children to play in... I don't care about being a queen and all, but being *your* queen... " She sobbed, her body shaking with every choppy breath. She seemed to have run out of words.

Renzo put a hand on her shoulder. "Hold it girl," he whispered. "He's breathing!"

The semblance of a smile appeared on Roessa's face, but turned into a frown immediately. "Ceycil," she wailed again. "Talk to me, please!"

Ceycil's face, covered with blood and dust, twitched ever so slightly. He groaned, and then opened his eyes slowly, as if it hurt too much to do so. "Roessa..?"

Roessa tried to wipe away her tears, but only managed to smudge them even further into the caked dirt on her face. "I don't know how you made it out of that tower alive," she whispered. "And I don't really care. You're still with me, and that's all that matters."

Ceycil glanced at the smashed wooden box that was still resting against his chest. He could see pieces of two glass vials sticking out of it. Then he looked around at the water surrounding him. "It must have been Rooks' spirits," he muttered. "If not, your guess is as good as mine... I must have blacked out." He sighed, more in pain than relief. He wanted to tell her what had happened to Rooks, if only with the hope of lightening the dead weight that had settled into his soul, but he didn't have the heart. "Where is Kazan?" he asked, trying to change the subject.

It was a mistake.

Roessa shook her head, her loud sobbing her only reply. Her voice cracked as she covered her face with her hands. "This is horrible, Ceycil. Is this all there is to the emperor's demise, and our victory? Dead people and a world broken up with hate…"

"The empire, too, is dead," ," Ceycil replied weakly. "Nobody else has to die. And nobody else has to hate anymore." He tried to find comfort in his own words, but it wasn't working.

"Father is gone, everyone is gone…" Roessa gasped for breath between sobs, wiping her face with the back of her wrist. "What do we do now?"

Ceycil blinked into the sun setting over the body-strewn battlefield. Then he took a deep breath, and spat out a mouthful of blood. "The world is ours once again. A clean slate, where evil and hate have lost their hold," he said softly, mostly to himself. "And with that, I can only think of one thing to do. We build it up again."

He turned, the force of his stare riveting, "We start over, Roessa."

December 20th, 2008

Toronto Pearson Airport

ABOUT THE CREATOR

The Legacy of Mana Chronicles and it`s story has been Thomas` passion and ultimate dream since he was in elementary school. In class, while working or during any time he could, Thomas would daydream the story, develop characters and flesh out the world of Imaria itself. Thomas attributes his fervor for Legacy of Mana as the source of all inspiration for his career.

Born in Guelph Ontario, Thomas initiated as an actor and is the founder of Lynnvander Productions Inc. which is a Southern Ontario based company with a vision for storytelling. Founded in July of 2005 and after obtaining a degree in psychology and classical linguistics at the University of Guelph, Thomas became responsible for the inception of several media initiatives including projects of film, literature, design and company leadership.

In 2007, Thomas co-founded Synn Studios Inc., a media production facility that Lynnvander operates out of. Thomas also founded SharpCuts: Genre Film Festival, GenreCon Media Inc., Instant FX Company and the recent children`s fantasy-action television series Mind`s Eye.

Lynnvander is a company that takes pride in the creation of entertaining and imaginative intellectual content and choosing to work with many talented and inspirational people/companies.

ABOUT THE AUTHOR

Hande Barutçuoğlu was born in the city that is no longer Constantinople, and found her way into the New World as a student over a decade ago. Since then, she has two children's novels and a short story published in her home country of Turkey.

She currently works as a veterinarian by day, and most nights she can be found in various coffee shops, fervently spinning tales and dreaming up new universes. She was last seen living on the coast of British Columbia with a small zoo for a family, and if she hasn't run away to join the circus yet, she is probably still there.

THOMAS M. GOFTON   -   HANDE BARUTÇUOĞLU

The Full Series

Hope's Ordeal

Loyalty's Race

Love's Mercy

Wrath's Conviction

Rivalry's Vie

Join our role-playing game's living world! Compatible for Dungeons & Dragons, Savage Worlds and Pathfinder Systems. For information on further products from the Legacy of Mana series please visit our website at

www.legacyofmana.com

If you're a role-playing gamer, a dreamer or just creatively gifted then note this world and story was created through many years of rolling dice, not paying attention in school and day dreaming during family socials... Cheers to the mind's eye!